Table of Contents

Inheritance

Cover design by Alysabeth Vale
Interior design by Alysabeth Vale
ISBN: 979-8-9945284-7-1

The Veilmarked Saga: Book 2

Inheritance

Every inheritance comes with a price.
Hers could burn the world.

By Alysabeth Vale

Dedication:

For the siblings of the soul.
For those who remind me that family is not always given; it is chosen, shaped, and fiercely protected.
You are proof that love does not need to inherit wounds to be real.
Thank you for being my mirrors, my roots, and my shield.
This book carries your names in every thread I kept, and every curse I let die.

Ritual gate

� ☽ ϟ ☾ �

The Second Gate
This is Inheritance.
The choice between curse and continuity.
What lives on through us—and what ends with us.
Here we sift the ash for seeds.
Here we name the line and break it clean.
Take only what you need.
Leave the rest behind.
The past does not own you.

Prologue

There was no time in the Veil—only before and after.

He stood upon a field of fractured glass, the sky above torn open like a wound. Light did not exist here, only echoes of it—refracted and wrong, bending around shadows that moved without form. Beneath his feet, the ground pulsed. A heartbeat, slow and ancient.

Kaelith did not blink. He had no need to. His gaze fixed on the horizon, where the Gate slumbered—massive and black-veined, a circle of stone that once held back gods.

It was beginning to hum.

"You hear it too," he said to no one and everything. His voice was smooth, quiet, and hollow as a blade drawn too long ago.

Around him, the Veil breathed.

Tattered spirits seeped from the cracks in the sky. Creatures born of sorrow and silence slithered at the edges, whispering truths never meant to be heard. The boundary weakened with every breath the world above took.

And the girl—the girl—was tearing it faster than the ancients ever feared.

He saw her in his mind: a flicker of fire and light, a name etched into prophecy like rot beneath gold—

Camomile Layton.

Chosen. Cursed. Catalyst.

Kaelith stepped forward and the glass cracked beneath him, splintering like ice. His bare feet did not bleed. He was never meant to feel. Once, perhaps, he had—but the light was stripped away, leaving only the echo.

"The Gate is waking."

He lifted his hand. Where fingers should have been, there was smoke; where his palm opened, a thin thread of light slipped out—a wound in reality.

He gripped it.

Pulled.

And the Gate shuddered.

From far away—on the other side of the worlds—someone dreamed of him, screamed his name in silence.

Not yet, he thought. *But soon.*

The Gate is opening. The girl is awakening. And the world that cast him out will remember what it means to fear its own shadow.

"Let her come," he murmured. "Let her walk into my city with her dragons and her hope. She will light the fire that unravels everything."

Kaelith smiled—

and the sky screamed.

Part 1

The threads hold

"So long as we hold the thread, we are not lost."

Chapter 1: The Weight of Waiting

The dreams had been worse since the ruins—since the night they almost died drawing the Veilborn away from Haldrin's Keep.

They were always the same—Cam in chains, screaming through smoke, her hand reaching for him while his legs refused to move. And sometimes Kaden was there too, shackled at her side, his eyes burning with shadows he couldn't fight. Other nights, the chains were empty where his brother should have been, as if the dream itself hadn't decided what to make of him. Both of them slipping farther away, no matter how he clawed toward them.

He woke with a gasp, her name caught in his throat, sweat chilling his skin. The echo of fire still burned behind his eyes.

He never told Kaden. Some visions were glimpses of what could be. Others were just nightmares twisted by fear. He didn't know which this was. Only that every time he saw her now, awake and real, he wanted to reach out—to make sure she was still there.

Dawn crept pale against the frost-rimmed window. Wyatt sat in silence until the first light touched the floorboards, jaw tight, heart still hammering. And in that silence, one thought rooted deep and unshakable:

If the dream was a warning, he would burn the world before letting it come true.

He'd spent his whole life trusting what he saw in visions, but belief was harder when it came to himself. When the light faltered, what would be left?

Steel clashed.

Wyatt pivoted, blocking Kaden's swing with a grunt. The impact jarred his arms, but he channeled it—feet shifting, magic surging to the surface. A burst of golden light ignited in his palm, forming a radiant flare that he hurled toward Kaden's flank.

Kaden twisted away, impossibly fast. Air whipped around him like a shield. Shadows gathered under his boots, spiking up through the ground—black and sharp, teeth of living night.

Wyatt leapt back, chest heaving, heart racing. They had sparred a hundred times before, but today the rhythm was off.

Kaden was faster than him—always had been—but he was sloppy now. Not in his movement, but in his mind.

He was somewhere else.

Wyatt had seen that look before, usually when Kaden caught sight of the ridge or the watchtower, gaze lingering longer than it should. Didn't press the next blow. He just stepped back and lowered his blade.

"Time," he said, voice cutting through the wind.

Kaden froze mid-step. Then sighed, dropping his stance, hands on his knees. Steam rose from his skin, sweat warming the cold air.

For a moment, neither of them spoke.

The wind whistled through the trees beyond the fence. Somewhere in the distance, a dragon cried—low and mournful. The sound tightened something in Wyatt's chest.

"They're strong," he said, voice gentler now. "They'll hold on."

Kaden straightened, wiping his mouth with the back of his glove. His laugh was short and dry. "You don't know that."

Wyatt met his eyes, steady. "No. I don't. But I believe it."

Kaden looked away. His jaw tightened. The frost at his feet began to melt from the heat of the shadow leaking off his fingertips. Wyatt's stomach knotted—Kaden didn't even seem to notice when it happened anymore. The darkness responded faster each time, like it wanted out.

"You always believe," he muttered. Not accusing—just tired. "Even when you shouldn't."

Kaden's gaze flickered, the shadows at his boots dimming as if they listened too closely.

"I don't know how not to," Wyatt said. "Especially now."

A moment passed.

Then Kaden exhaled sharply and shook his head. "When do I ever *not* trust you?"

Wyatt's lips quirked. "Exactly. Still older by four minutes. You should listen to me more."

He reached out and ruffled Kaden's hair, grinning.

Kaden groaned and swatted his hand away. "Gods, stop. I'm taller than you now."

"Barely."

"You're all radiant light and glowing destiny. Let me have the height."

Wyatt chuckled, the warmth between them settling like a fragile truce over grief. For a moment, it felt almost normal.

Kaden arched a brow, casual.

"So... you and Cam?"

Wyatt's breath caught—just a fraction—before he masked it with a shrug.

"She's still figuring things out."

He smirked. "You've been seeing her in visions since we were kids. Pretty sure you've already made up your mind. Don't pretend this is new."

Kaden gave him a sidelong look, his mouth quirking like he meant to tease—but when he spoke, his voice softened, threaded with something steadier.

"You've never looked at anyone else, Wy. Not once. All these years—it's always been her, even before you knew her name."

The words hit differently than a jab. There was no mockery in them, only understanding, quiet and sure. Wyatt felt it—the rare kind of empathy only Kaden ever gave him without asking for anything back.

Wyatt exhaled, gaze drifting to the frost-glittered grass. "Those visions... they were always pieces. Never enough to make sense of. But I knew she was real. I knew I'd find her."

Kaden gave him a sidelong glance. "And now you have."

Wyatt's lips curved faintly, but his voice softened.

"One of the first visions I had of her... she was sitting under a tree, reading. Sunlight kept catching in her hair, and she looked up—like she knew I was there. Like she'd been waiting. But she didn't see me."

He shook his head slightly. "I didn't even know her name, but... it felt like home."

Kaden's expression flickered, something unspoken passing between them. "Then don't lose her."

"Wasn't planning on it," Wyatt said, quiet and certain.

Kaden bumped his shoulder as they started walking back toward the barracks. "Good. Because if you hurt her, I'm telling her every embarrassing thing you've ever done."

Wyatt huffed a laugh, the warmth between them settling like a fragile truce over grief.

They did not need to say more. Not about Cam. Not about the rescue.

Not about the fear crawling just beneath their skin.

They sheathed their swords, boots crunching frost as they walked back toward the barracks. The sun was rising—just barely—and it threw long shadows behind them.

But they walked forward anyway.

Together.

◈ ☽ ⚡ ☾ ◈

Corin's fingers drifted across the vellum. Another report. Another knot of bad news.

Caerthalen patrols had tripled.

Three messengers had never returned.

Signs of a leak in the southern supply line.

He read each line twice, then again. His brow furrowed with the weight of it all. He had learned to move in silence, to carry the burden without flinching—but tonight, it pressed deeper than usual.

The next parchment he picked up was thin and weather-worn. He almost didn't see it at first, until a circled date near the top pulled him still.

Solstice. Two weeks.

He leaned back in the creaking chair. The candlelight wavered as if stirred by breathless memory.

Lira's voice returned to him, vivid and uninvited.

"Keep them safe, Corin."

Six-year-old twins, blinking up at him with too-big eyes. Kaden had clung to Wyatt's hand, silent and defiant. Wyatt had already started asking questions. Lira had kissed their foreheads once, and then she was gone.

And Daren... gods. Daren had always been steady. The quiet anchor to Lira's storm. He had stood at Corin's side when they smuggled relics past the Academy, when they hid truth beneath coded sigils, when they dared to defy the bloodline mandates.

Corin had felt it like a blade when word arrived:

Both dead. Mission failed. Boys orphaned.

He had never wanted to be a father. Still didn't think he was meant to be. But what choice had he really had?

He had trained them. He had taught them restraint and runes, taught them to see past the propaganda and sharpen their minds.

He had loved them—imperfectly, quietly, relentlessly.

"I was never meant to be a father," he murmured aloud.

The candle sputtered.

His hand found a piece of parchment and scratched a reminder into the margin:

Wish them a happy birthday.

They would turn twenty-one on the solstice. Legal age for conscription in the old system. Symbolic age of inheritance in the older, truer ways.

His gaze lingered on another report—the list of names confirmed inside Caerthalen. Valerie. Sharp, disciplined, clever beyond her years. She was not blood, but Corin had begun to wonder if inheritance might choose her too, if only she survived long enough to claim it.

Corin closed his eyes. The air stilled. Then—

A flicker. Not of flame, but something colder.

A shadow passed across the far wall. It was nothing he could see directly—more of a pressure behind the eyes, a hum in the spine.

The Veil was stirring. Already.

He opened his eyes, sharp and steady once more. Whatever was coming wasn't waiting for the solstice. It was moving now.

He set the reports aside and reached for his warding stones, placing them precisely. One for light. One for binding. One to anchor memory.

It was going to be a long two weeks.

⟐ ☽ ⚡ ☾ ⟐

Ben stood just beyond the perimeter ward, one boot on stone, the other on wet grass. Behind him, the rebel fortress rose—old bones and watchful eyes. In front of him, the sky stretched wide, bruised with the coming storm.

Above the distant ridge, a flash of gold sliced the clouds.

Cam.

Sylithra's wings beat the wind into submission as they flew, wide and high—too high for anyone else to follow. The dragon's body coiled through the air with terrifying grace. Cam was a narrow silhouette on her back, barely visible but unmistakable. Controlled. Fluid.

Distant lightning flickered behind her.

She had been flying more often since they returned from the ruins. Sometimes at dawn, sometimes when the wind howled loud enough to drown out thought. Always with that same fierce silence.

Ben watched her arc toward the mountains and disappear behind a jagged peak.

She's pulling away, he thought. *From all of us. From me.*

There had been a time when she would have landed just to talk. Asked questions. Laughed too loud. Argued about tactics until he gave in just to hear her stop talking.

Now... she spoke only when spoken to.

Wyatt was the only one who could get a full sentence out of her, sometimes Kaden. The rest of them got glances. A nod. A yes or no. And those eyes of hers—

They weren't cold. Not exactly.

Just... quiet. Like she was holding something back. Like she had seen something she couldn't unsee.

Ben pressed a hand to the short sword at his hip. The metal hummed faintly under his fingers, etched with runes he still hadn't taught her.

Gods, he was proud of her. Everything she had survived. Everything she was becoming. Her elemental control was sharper, cleaner—fire and water and earth moving at her command like breath and heartbeat.

But it terrified him, too. Because something had shifted inside her. And he didn't know what it had cost.

He heard footsteps behind him and didn't turn. Corin's voice was low.

"She's flying again?"

Ben nodded.

Corin stepped up beside him, arms folded, eyes fixed on the distant sky. "We'll need her grounded. Soon."

Ben's jaw tightened. "That's not going to be easy."

"Nothing worthwhile is."

A beat passed. Then Corin added, quieter, "There's been movement in Caerthalen. Three captives confirmed. We have a location. But word's spreading. Someone here's leaking information."

Ben finally turned. "Who?"

"We don't know. Yet."

Ben didn't curse, but it was close. "Then the rescue stays between us. No council. No strategists."

Corin nodded. "Just us."

Ben glanced back at the sky. Cam reappeared for a moment, silhouetted in lightning. She dove hard, cut through a thick cloud, then rose again—untouchable.

"She can't go," Ben muttered. "Caerthalen is poison."

"I know," Corin said.

But they both stood there, saying nothing more.

Because they both knew Cam would insist. She would go, no matter what they decided. It was in her blood. In her fire. In whatever strange inheritance she had only just begun to understand.

Ben's gaze narrowed.

The solstice was two weeks away. The Veil would thin. He could feel it already in his bones—in the subtle flicker of magic beneath his skin, in the way shadows moved just a second too slow.

And beneath Caerthalen... something ancient waited. Watching. Breathing.

He didn't say it aloud. But he thought it, steady and sharp.

If it takes me to keep her alive... I'll burn the city myself.

Cam sat with her knees drawn up, elbows resting on them, chin tucked low. The last warmth of the sun clung to her skin like an afterthought. Below, the world stretched wide and waiting—the forests, the ravine, the outpost tucked into its jagged spine. Above, the sky began to change.

She'd built walls out of motion—if she kept flying, no one could see how close she was to breaking. It was easier to burn through the wind than admit how much she needed the people waiting below.

Six dragons surrounded her. Silent sentinels.

Sylithra slept nearby, curled like a living eclipse—obsidian black and night blue scales catching the last of the sunset, gold veins pulsing faintly beneath the surface like molten light beneath stone. Her breath was steady, coiling warm smoke through the cooling air. The other dragons lingered at a respectful distance, giving Cam space. But none of them left. Not tonight.

Brontheus paced along the edge of the cliff. His green-black wings flared now and then, agitated. Sparks flickered at his feet—lightning itching beneath his scales. He growled softly, tail twitching.

Cam didn't need to ask why.

She rose slowly and crossed to him, laying a hand on Brontheus's side. The dragon stilled but didn't relax.

"I know," Cam said, voice rough. "She's hurting."

Brontheus lowered his head, nuzzling Cam's shoulder with a low, vibrating thrum.

"We'll get them back," Cam whispered. "I swear it. I won't leave her there."

The air shifted. One by one, the dragons echoed a rumble—deep, low, resonant—vibrating through the stone beneath her feet. It wasn't clear if it was warning or agreement.

Maybe it was both.

Cam swallowed hard, throat tight. Her hand lingered on Brontheus's scales, then fell back to her side.

She turned back to the edge of the roost and sat again. The sun was gone now, only embers clinging to the edges of the sky.

She thought of Tessa's laugh—bold, unapologetic, loud in the quietest rooms. Of Valerie's calm, the way her words carried weight even when her voice barely rose. Of Alex's grin, clever and crooked and full of rebellion. Even with them, she measured her words. The closer they tried to stand, the quieter she became—like distance was the only way to keep them safe.

She pictured Caerthalen burning. Brick and iron and fear melting beneath her fury.

She clenched her fists, nails digging half-moons into her palms. Her voice was barely audible.

"I won't lose anyone else."

Not like her mother. Not like the ones who had vanished into the Veil. Not like the pieces of herself she had already buried. It was easier to promise vengeance than admit the truth—that what terrified her most wasn't losing them. It was being the reason they were lost.

The dragons did not speak. But they didn't have to.

They felt it too—something shifting beneath the surface. Something waking.

Above her, the first stars pierced the veil of dusk—cold, watchful.

And far in the distance, past mountain and ruin and city, something stirred.

Not seen. Not heard.

But felt.

And it was waiting for her.

◈ ☽ ϟ ☾ ◈

The night pressed heavy, but Sylithra felt the tremor beneath it—the fear her rider swallowed down and buried in silence. Cam wrapped herself in steel and fire, but the dragon knew. She always knew.

Humans forgot the First Flame, but dragons never did. They had carried it in bone and breath since the sky first opened. Cam would need to remember, though she had no memory to draw from. What was lost lived only in echoes, and in her.

Sylithra lowered her head, wings folding close, and let the silence stretch. The world was shifting, and the girl she guarded was walking blind into it.

Chapter 2: The Quiet Blade

No moon. Just darkness layered thick between the trees.

He crouched low on the slope, cloak drawn tight, breath shallow. Every twig beneath him had been cleared before the sun set—he hadn't been careless. Not anymore. Not with a place like Haldrin's Keep in sight.

It rose from the mountains like a secret carved in stone—ancient, armored by cliffs, hidden by cloud and ward. And quiet.

Too quiet.

He adjusted his scope, the enchanted lens flickering as it caught the faint glimmer of sigils along the walls. The outer wards pulsed gently—wards of concealment, protection, containment. Old magic. The kind of magic he had been trained to dismantle since childhood.

But he hadn't come to bring down the Keep. Not yet.

He had come to watch.

And then, without warning—light.

No warning burst, no chant, no build.

Just detonation.

The night ruptured in fire and flame—not from the Keep, but within it.

A sharp, concussive pulse of magic cracked the air. Something exploded, and not from this world alone.

Then the screams began.

Not human. Not quite. Twisting, choral, wrong.

They reverberated through the trees and across his bones. The sound of Veilborn surfacing. Of the boundary between worlds thinning. He knew it well. Too well.

He didn't flinch.

He focused.

From his vantage point, he saw the protective wards ripple—then stutter.

Flicker. Collapse.

Only for a moment. But it was enough.

He unspooled through the breach, silent as smoke.

Inside the Keep, no one noticed him. Not through smoke and screams. Not when half the outpost surged toward the breach and the rest scrambled to protect what remained.

He left no mark. No footprint. No sound.

And just as he passed through the outer ring, something else moved behind him.

A blinding flare of white-gold light lit the edge of the forest.

It hadn't been part of the detonation.

It wasn't a weapon. It wasn't Veilborn. It had been something else.

It had called to something deep in his marrow—something buried so long he couldn't remember when it started to rot.

He didn't look back. The feeling was enough.

Like a question left hanging in a cold room.

I don't know what you are, he thought, slipping into shadow, *but even the shadows hesitated.*

He moved like water through stone.

A name. A uniform. A map tucked under one arm. That was all it took. Scouts came and went often now—runners from the outposts, messengers between fractured alliances, couriers delivering false hope in parchment and wax.

No one questioned a man with a list in his hand and a purpose in his step.

Not here. Not now.

He had been inside Haldrin's Keep for seven days.

Long enough to learn its pulse.

The fortress was alive, but fraying. He could feel it in the stone—a kind of tension beneath the surface, like a blade held just behind the eye. Soldiers trained harder. Commanders barked softer. Plans were whispered instead of written. Wardlines redrawn. Schedules shifted daily.

They had been preparing for something.

A mission, maybe. Or war.

The Keep bore its wounds well, but they were still fresh. There were scorch marks that hadn't been cleaned. Places where the stone still smelled like blood and ozone. Where magic had burned through something permanent.

He had watched. Listened. Learned the names.

Corin Veyr, Ben Miles, and the twins. Valehart blood. One of them with too much light, the other with too much shadow.

But none of them mattered.

Not like her.

He stepped out into the midday sun, blinking against its warmth. The courtyard was half-full—trainees running drills, dragons circling like watchful gods high above the cliffs.

Then movement caught his eye.

And time slowed.

She crossed the courtyard alone.

Dark clothes. Wind-tossed hair. A short sword at her side. Her gait carried a strange kind of stillness—like she moved through a world that didn't quite touch her anymore.

Above her, two dragons banked low across the sun. One a storm-colored beast with crackling wings. The other obsidian and night-blue, gold-veined and silent.

She didn't look up. She didn't need to.

The dragons followed her.

There she is. The one they fear. The one they called chosen.

He hadn't known what to expect—someone louder, maybe. Brighter. Or broken. But she had been none of those things.

She had been... still.

And that was worse.

Because the ones who were still were the ones who saw.

He stood in the sunlight, just another shadow among many.

But for the first time in years, he felt the faintest prickle of something beneath his ribs.

Not doubt. Not yet.

But the ghost of a name that he hadn't heard since childhood. A warning wrapped in prophecy.

Camomile Layton.

He watched her pass through the courtyard without speaking to anyone. Without looking back.

And somehow, that silence had said everything.

He watched her for four days.

From rooftops, corridors, shadows that didn't move. He had always been good at going unnoticed—his entire life built around silence and precision. He made notes without ink. Catalogued every pattern, every flaw.

Only there hadn't been many.

Camomile Layton had been disciplined. She rose before sunrise most days, though never at the same time twice. Unpredictable. Smart. She trained in solitude and with others—always with intensity, never for show.

Her elemental control had been...

Wrong.

Too fluid. Too much. Fire one moment, water the next. Then stone. Wind. Lightning. It hadn't been layered magic or split casting—it had been a kind of instinct, like her body already knew what the world needed before she did.

No one should have held that much magic.

Not naturally. Not safely. And yet...

She laughed. Not often, but when she did, it was real. Mostly with Kaden Valehart—sharp-tongued and observant. She listened when Wyatt spoke, her silence not passive but attentive. She practiced until her hands shook and didn't try to hide it. She bled and didn't flinch. She failed and learned.

She was never still unless she meant to be.

Then there had been Sylithra.

He had seen bonded pairs before—many. But nothing like this.

They had moved as one. Not just in flight or battle, but in presence. Like twin echoes of the same pulse. When Sylithra growled, Cam tensed. When Cam narrowed her gaze, the dragon adjusted her stance.

It had been seamless. And it had been ancient. Too ancient.

He watched her more closely.

She stayed late in the kitchens, helping scrub vegetables with worn-out fighters and exhausted staff. She carried extra water to the healers. She stopped in the corridors to check on a young boy whose mother was still missing. She listened. Always listening.

And once—

Once she had turned a corner too quickly and nearly collided with him.

He had mumbled something about a delivery. Eyes down. Not too fast, not too slow.

She had paused. Smiled.

And offered him a canteen of water.

"You look like you've been running all day," she had said. "Need anything?"

That moment—

It lingered longer than it should have.

Later, back in the quiet of the upper loft of the abandoned barracks wing he had sat in the dark and stared at his gloved hands. Remembering.

She asked if I needed anything. The end of the world offered me water.

He told himself it had been a trick. Magic users often used charm as camouflage. Illusion as kindness. Light to hide the rot.

But the words had sunk deeper than they should have, as if brushing against a place in him that remembered kindness and didn't know what to do with it.

He had seen it before. He had killed it before.

But this time, the thought hadn't settled right.

A fracture formed.

Doubt. He hadn't chased it out.

Not yet. But it had begun to grow roots.

He sat alone in the upper loft—a place no one visited, too unstable for storage, too quiet for comfort. Which made it perfect.

Candlelight flickered low, casting shadows that danced across the cracked walls. His cloak was folded beside him. Weapons hidden. Mask off.

In his lap, a thin leather-bound book rested open, its pages filled with looping glyphs—delicate, precise, unreadable to anyone but him.

He dipped the tip of a bone-carved stylus into ink and wrote:

Day 7. Subject remains unmarked.

Elemental composition unstable but controlled.

Primary behaviors: observant, restrained, merciful.

No Veil activity observed in proximity. No sky tearing. No collapse.

He paused, stylus hovering above the page. A drop of ink trembled, then fell.

Another line, this one slower: *She gave me water.*

He shut the book carefully. Let the ink dry before slipping it into the inner lining of his pouch—shielded with sigils that erased presence, blurred memory.

It wouldn't have mattered if someone found it. They'd have forgotten what it was the moment they looked away.

Still, he kept it close.

He leaned back against the stone, closed his eyes, and recited the mission under his breath:

Observe. Locate. Mark the subject.

Await orders.

Orders were easier than names. Missions didn't lie, didn't leave, didn't look at you with mercy you didn't deserve.

Observe. Locate. Mark.

Only... he hadn't. Not quite.

The tool sat untouched in his satchel—the one for marking. A delicate rune, a sigil of anchoring. Just a scratch on her coat, or skin, or the clasp of her blade. She'd never have felt it.

He could have done it days ago. When she had brushed past him in the corridor. When she had helped that wounded soldier rewrap his bandages.

But something in his hand—or maybe deeper—had refused.

His thoughts drifted, unbidden, to the words of the High Scholars:

She will bring the Veil crashing down. She is the breach reborn. The sky will split at her scream. The sun will bow to her shadow.

He had believed them. Had to. They had shown him fragments of vision, old testimonies drenched in blood and prophecy.

But now—

All he saw was a young woman carrying a weight no one else could touch.

She didn't seek worship. Didn't chase control. Didn't wield her power like a banner.

She knelt beside injured soldiers. She shared her meals. She laughed when someone made her laugh, and her grief lived just beneath the surface—raw and real.

He breathed deep.

Then thought: *Is that why they fear her? Because she won't become what they want her to?*

The candle flickered once, then died.

He didn't light another.

◈ ☽⚡☾ ◈

They moved like a constellation—orbiting one another in an invisible pattern he had yet to fully map.

Always her at the center. Always.

And yet... the pattern felt incomplete. As if a star had been hidden from his chart, waiting for its place.

From his vantage near the east wall, half-hidden behind crates of dulled weapons and stripped armor, he watched.

Wyatt walked beside her, a half-step behind, eyes on everything but her—and yet he saw her more than anyone else. The way his hand drifted toward his blade whenever she flinched. The way his posture shifted, subtle but instinctual, when anyone raised their voice near her.

A protector. Loyal. Predictable. Dangerous, if cornered.

Then there had been Kaden—the restless one. Always pacing, always thinking. His sharp gaze missed nothing. He argued often, laughed rarely, and carried shadows in his eyes that no one seemed to ask about. The man had blood on his boots and strategy in his bones.

If Wyatt was her shield, Kaden was the knife she kept hidden in her boot.

Ben Miles lingered on the periphery. Watchful. But his silence hadn't been emptiness—it had been weight. The kind that meant something. Every glance he gave her had been measured, too careful. He wore duty like a second skin, but there was more beneath it. Devotion, maybe. Or something worse.

And then Corin Veyr.

He stood apart from them all—not in distance, but in presence. The rebel general. The scholar. The ghost of something broken and still burning.

There had been something wrong about him. Not in his posture or behavior, but in the way the world seemed to bend slightly when he moved through it. The mage hunter could feel it in his bones—a pressure behind the eyes, like the moment before a sigil detonated.

Corin knew things.

That made him the most dangerous of them all.

The mage hunter kept his head low. Eyes sharp. Hands steady.

He wouldn't act yet. The order hadn't come. And even if it had...

He had watched her smile at something Wyatt said. Saw Kaden roll his eyes and mutter back. Sylithra's shadow had passed overhead—massive, ancient, unbothered.

Camomile Layton was powerful, yes. More than powerful.

But she had also been something else. Something his training hadn't prepared him for.

He couldn't mark her until he understood her.

And you didn't kill what you didn't understand.

Still, the Veil had been shifting. He could feel it in his marrow—like cold fingers brushing the inside of his ribs.

The solstice was coming.

And when it came...

He might no longer have a choice.

Chapter 3: The Breaking Line

The wind hadn't stopped whispering since Haldrin burned.

Kaden stood at the edge of the war-room threshold, hands braced on the cold frame, watching the others gather inside. Maps. Ink. Strategy. Corin's domain.

But before plans came silence—and in that silence, Kaden heard what no one else said: exhaustion disguised as purpose, grief wearing command like armor.

He could still taste ash. Every time he blinked, the world went gold again—veins of light racing beneath skin that should've split open. Cam on her knees, fire spilling from her chest. Wyatt beside her, cracked with the same glow. Himself, dragging breath through shattered air, forcing wind through a body that had already failed him. The memory lived behind his ribs like a brand.

They'd called it victory. Kaden remembered the cost.

The smell of scorched wards. The sound of Cam's scream when the light took her.

Wyatt's hand reaching for hers—and falling short. Three lives burning just long enough to save everyone else.

The healers had mended what they could, but not the fracture underneath. It ran through all of them—the pulse that hadn't faded when the battle ended. Some nights, he felt it flicker inside his own chest, answering something he didn't understand. A rhythm that wasn't his alone.

He told himself it was memory. Or guilt. Anything but what it felt like: a tether—alive, restless, dangerous.

And in the quiet, it hummed with the same sound as his shadow magic when it stirred too close to the surface—like something patient was waiting in the dark, listening for its name.

He tried to bury it under motion, under plans, under reason. But stillness always left too much room for thought, and thought always brought the storm back—

Worry for Cam, who kept pretending she wasn't breaking.

Fear for Wyatt, who kept pretending he was fine.

Guilt that he hadn't stopped any of it—that he'd been one step too slow, one spell too weak, one twin heartbeat behind.

The mix of it pressed beneath his sternum, restless and unspent—the kind of feeling that made you want to run just to prove you were still moving.

Inside, Corin and Ben bent over the map, voices low. Cam stood at the center again, shoulders squared, light shuttered behind her eyes. Wyatt, close enough to catch her if she broke, pretending he didn't want to.

Kaden drew a slow breath. The line between survival and collapse was thinner than anyone admitted.

Someone had to see it.

Someone had to hold it together before the cracks widened.

He pushed off the wall and stepped forward.

Time to move before they shattered standing still.

◈ ☽ ⚡ ☾ ◈

The room smelled like old paper and dusted stone.

Cam stood at the edge of the table, her fingers curled tight around the worn wood as she stared down at the sprawling map of Caerthalen. Ink-stained streets bled into alleys, twisting like veins around the hollow heart of the capital. At its center: the Iron Hold. Deep beneath that, older than the city itself—the mage containment vault.

The place they would have to break into.

A pale beam of early light filtered through the narrow window behind Corin, casting long shadows over the map. No one spoke for a long moment. Even the air felt like it was listening.

Finally, Corin's voice broke the silence. Low. Certain.

"There's a shift change at midday. For six minutes, the lower wards falter as the elite guard rotates. That's our window. Small, but not impossible."

Ben exhaled, arms crossed, eyes locked on the northern gate. "You're assuming the inner wall won't be fortified further by then. If they suspect even a whisper of movement—"

"They don't," Corin cut in, calm but edged. "They've grown overconfident. The city is theirs, and they think we wouldn't dare strike the Iron Hold. Let them think it."

Cam dragged her gaze over the highlighted marks and notes Corin had scrawled in his sharp hand. The Iron Hold sat like a tumor beneath the city, unreachable from above, and nearly impossible to breach from below.

She looked up, her voice steady.

"Then we move quickly and quietly."

Corin met her eyes. "You'd be walking into the eye of the storm."

"Then let the storm know," she said, "I'm not afraid of it."

Kaden gave a quiet snort, but it wasn't mocking. It sounded like approval. Ben said nothing, only tilted his head, considering her with that unreadable look he always wore before things turned dangerous.

"We'll go in through the lower merchant ward," Kaden offered, stepping closer to the map. "I left sigils there during my last recon. Hidden in mirrored glass behind a spice vendor's stall. I'll need six seconds to anchor the portal without triggering nearby glyph traps."

Cam nodded. "Six seconds you'll get."

"Illusion magic will keep us from being seen," she added. "But not from being sensed. If any of the High Wardens are nearby— "

"We won't be able to hide," Ben finished. "If they catch even a flicker of your magic, they'll recognize the signature."

Kaden frowned. "Then we don't give them time to."

Corin's fingers traced a small spiral etched near the southern district. "Valerie and Tessa are being held here. Deeper than the others. They are not just a prisoner—they are bait."

That made Cam's stomach twist. Of course they were.

Beside her, something in Kaden's posture altered—a single, measured breath that didn't quite make it out. His thumb dragged once over the edge of the map where Corin had written VALERIE in tight script, then stilled.

The silence thickened.

Cam looked to her left. Wyatt hadn't said a word since the meeting began. He stood still, shoulder to shoulder with her, eyes locked on the map like he could burn a hole through it. His jaw was tight. His posture taut, coiled like a bowstring.

She reached out, brushing his arm with the edge of her fingers.

"You with me?" she asked softly.

He didn't look at her.

"I always am."

But his voice... it sounded farther away than usual.

◈ ☽⚡☾ ◈

The dragons had dreamt. Not of stone, nor sky, but of threads moving in the dark. Three pulses, unsteady, brushing together where no touch should yet be. Sparks trembling at the edges of a weave not meant to be drawn.

Too soon, their hearts rumbled as one. Too soon, and yet unstoppable. The pattern stirred, old as the First Flame, restless as stormfire beneath the skin of the world.

They woke restless, eyes turning toward the training yard.

◈ ☽⚡☾ ◈

The morning sun hadn't yet warmed the training yard. Cold steel whispered through air as Wyatt spun, ducked, and struck—a motion repeated so many times it had become muscle memory. Across from him, Kaden matched his pace with surgical precision, every strike sharp and efficient, as if he could see Wyatt's movements a beat ahead. Both of them working through the infiltration drills they'd designed just days before.

Step. Pivot. Low strike. Retreat. Again.

Wyatt moved like a man possessed—not with passion, but with pressure. Sharper. Quieter. Fractured.

"You're off-tempo," Kaden said, catching Wyatt's wrist mid-strike.

"I'm fine," Wyatt muttered, pulling back. But his breath was ragged, jaw clenched.

Kaden didn't press. Not yet. Instead, he tossed Wyatt a second dagger. It flipped once in the air before landing handle-first in Wyatt's palm. Wyatt caught it without looking, eyes already scanning the edges of the yard as if expecting something to emerge from the fog.

He'd been like this for days.

"You were the one keeping me steady," Kaden said after a moment, sheathing his blade. "Now I'm wondering if I need to do the same for you."

Wyatt's mouth twisted—half a smirk, half a grimace. He didn't respond. Not at first.

Then, low: "I can't lose her, Kade."

The weight in his voice stopped Kaden cold.

"Cam. And the others, yeah. But her... it's different."

He shook his head like the words weren't enough. "She's here now, but it feels like something's closing in on her. Like the moment we step into that city... we're not all coming back."

Kaden frowned. "The city?"

"No," Wyatt said. "Something else."

He didn't explain the dreams. The figure wrapped in steel and smoke. The way his visions had turned to ash the moment they'd set the plan in motion. He didn't say how the Veil, once a quiet hum at the edge of his magic, now throbbed like a pulse behind his ribs.

But he felt it, waking and dreaming—the shift. The silence before the collapse.

"She's been in my dreams," he said instead, softer now. "Behind bars. Screaming. And I can't get to her. I can never get to her in time."

Kaden exhaled slowly. His gaze turned toward the mountains barely visible beyond the far wall of the yard. "It's a mission, Wy. We move when the signal's clear, we follow the path, we get them out."

"And what if there's no clear path?" Wyatt asked, his voice barely above a whisper.

Kaden didn't answer. Couldn't. Because he'd felt it too—the tightening around their odds, like the world itself was bracing for something they hadn't named yet.

They fell into silence again, blades whispering through the mist, their sparring rhythm relentless. Wyatt forced precision into every strike, but Kaden adapted like water around stone—reading, adjusting, shifting the pressure back on him each time. But there was no ease in it.

No humor. No spark.

Only the storm building between them.

"We have to be perfect," Wyatt said, eyes skyward. "Because we won't get another chance."

Kaden turned to him, quiet for a beat.

"We will be."

But even as he said it, neither of them were sure.

When they finally paused, Wyatt stood still for a long moment, head tilted to the sky. The mist had lifted just enough to reveal the faint shape of dragon wings above, cutting silent lines through the light.

Sylithra.

Her vast form descended through the thinning clouds, obsidian and night-blue scales veined with molten gold. The ground seemed to tremble with her approach, the beat of her wings scattering the mist that clung to the yard.

Wyatt's chest eased just a fraction. Cam was with her.

"Looks like we're not done," he murmured, sheathing his blade as Sylithra swept low over the training ring.

The dragon landed in a swirl of wind and ash, her talons carving into frost-hard soil.

Cam slid down from her back, boots crunching against the stone. Her braid was loose, strands of hair stuck to her temple with sweat, but her gaze was steady—unyielding.

Wyatt's heart thudded once, sharp and certain.

◈ ☽ ⚡ ☾ ◈

The training yard air was heavy with frost and sweat when Cam hit the ground beside Sylithra. Kaden's voice carried across the circle, dry but edged with something tighter.

"You're late."

Cam smirked faintly, brushing her palms against her trousers. "Or you're just impatient."

Wyatt exhaled, relief flickering in his eyes though his voice came wry. "Both can be true."

For a heartbeat, the tension between them all stretched taut, unspoken but undeniable. The rescue mission loomed in every silence. The absence of Val, Tessa and Alex clung like ghosts to the edges of the yard.

Cam flexed her hands, feeling the hum of elements stir beneath her skin. "So," she said, meeting both their gazes in turn. "Are we sparring, or standing around pretending to be philosophers?"

Kaden rolled his shoulders, smirk tugging sharp. "Don't start something you can't finish."

"Wouldn't dream of it," Cam shot back.

Steel rasped as three blades came free almost in unison, the sound sharp in the stillness. For a breath, none of them moved—just eyes locked, shoulders angled, each testing the air the way fighters test the tide before diving in.

They moved almost without thought—circling, testing, blades and magic weaving in tandem. Kaden's air cracked sharp around him, shadows sliding at his heels. Wyatt's strikes were steady and relentless, light flaring golden at his palms and stone rising to meet his steps. Cam countered with fire and water in quick succession, steam hissing between them as the three collided in rhythm.

Steel clashed. Sparks hissed. The yard lit with flashes of power.

Then, all at once, their strikes converged.

Cam's violet-black fire crashed into Wyatt's light while Kaden's wind whipped through both. Instead of breaking apart, the forces bound together—flame, air, and light spiraling in a single current. For a heartbeat it hovered between them, alive and whole. Not hers. Not his. Not Kaden's—something new.

Something alive.

Something inside Cam whispered—woven.

The blaze arced high into the mist. Cam froze, chest heaving, eyes wide. Wyatt staggered back a step, his jaw clenched but gaze fixed on the glow. Kaden's composure cracked, breath catching as if he'd seen something he couldn't quite name.

Then it broke apart, bursting outward in harmless heat and dust. The three of them stumbled back, blades half-lowered.

Wyatt was the first to find words. "What in the hells was that?" His voice was raw, disbelieving.

Kaden didn't answer right away. His gaze lingered on the scorch mark, the faint shimmer that still clung to the air like threads refusing to fade. "Something we're not ready for."

Cam's hand trembled, but her voice was steady. "Maybe not ready... but not an accident."

No one spoke after that. The mist closed in again, but the air still hummed faintly, as if it remembered what they had done.

Twilight pooled along the edges of Haldrin's Keep like ink spilled across the stone. The roost sat high on the plateau's northern crest, wind-chiseled and open to the sky. A hush lingered there—thicker than silence, reverent. The kind of quiet that belonged to old places.

Cam walked slowly across the gravel-strewn path, boots stirring dust and frost. Her fingers ached from the cold, but she didn't notice. Her eyes were on the dragons—six titans of scale and breath, stretched across the uneven stone like slumbering gods.

Sylithra lay furthest from the others, her massive body curled into the shadow of a cliff, obsidian-black scales catching hints of deep blue and gold where the light touched them. She looked like night given form, the gold veins in her hide pulsing faintly as if remembering some deeper fire.

Cam approached her in silence. No one else dared come this close without invitation.

She rested a hand against the dragon's flank. Heat radiated from beneath the scales—dry and steady, like the heart of a forge long banked but never extinguished.

The dragon did not move.

"You know where we're going," Cam whispered

Sylithra's golden eye opened, slitting toward her with something unreadable. She didn't blink. She didn't speak. She simply watched.

Cam exhaled slowly, hand still pressed to the warmth. In Sylithra's silence was no cruelty—only weight. The weight of knowing more than she could say. Of watching mortals rush toward war again, fragile as they were.

Cam dropped her hand, stepped back. The wind picked up, threading through her braid, carrying the sharp scent of pine and the faint metallic tang of dragon-hide.

She turned to go—and stopped.

A figure stood at the far edge of the roost, just beyond the wardstones. Cloaked in ash-brown and shadow, hands visible at his sides. He hadn't made a sound.

Cam narrowed her eyes, instinct prickling. "You're a long way from the training yard."

The man lifted his hands slightly in peace. "Didn't mean to startle you."

He stepped forward enough for his face to catch the fading light. Young—mid-twenties, maybe. Dark-haired. Pale eyes. The hollows under them spoke of travel or sleep rarely earned.

"I didn't think anyone would be up here," he added. "Didn't mean to intrude."

"You didn't," she replied, but her tone was neutral. Measuring.

"I'm Orren Hail," he offered, with a nod. "Transferred in a week ago. From the Rendvale post."

Cam's gaze sharpened. "Border village. Scorched when the Knighthood passed through last winter."

His expression didn't change. "What's left of it."

She let the silence stretch, waiting to see what kind of man he was under grief.

Orren's eyes drifted to the dragons. "I've never seen one up close. Always thought the stories exaggerated them. They didn't."

Cam's posture eased just slightly. "They rarely do."

His eyes landed on Brontheus—Tessa's bonded dragon—resting near the ledge. His scales were dark moss-green, veined with black, his wings folded so tightly to his sides he almost seemed carved from stone.

"He hasn't flown," Orren said.

"No," Cam said softly. "Not since Tessa was taken."

"May I?"

Cam studied him. The way he stood. The way he waited. He didn't approach blindly.

"It's not up to me," she said. "Ask him."

Brontheus turned his head slowly. His emerald eyes locked onto Orren's—deep, ageless. And after a long, still moment... he lowered his head, shoulder tilting toward him in quiet allowance.

Orren stepped forward, one careful footfall at a time. When his palm touched the dragons scales, he froze—breath drawn in like it startled him.

"He's warm," he said quietly, more to himself. "Alive in a way nothing else is."

He swallowed. "I didn't think you could hear them," he added, turning to Cam. "But you do, don't you?"

"I always have," she replied.

The wind curled between them, lifting strands of her hair, stirring dust around his boots.

Orren backed away slowly. "Thank you... for letting me see him."

He turned and walked down the path, disappearing into the lavender mist that clung to the hillside.

Cam stood still.

Brontheus rumbled, low and gravel-deep, a sound that thrummed through the earth beneath their feet.

He smells of smoke... and forest, the dragon said. *But beneath it, iron. That one carries chains... and wings not yet claimed. He walks with old things.*

Cam's hand pressed gently to Brontheus's shoulder, warm and still beneath her touch.

The dragon exhaled slow and long. Then, without a word, he stretched his wings toward the sky, as if remembering how it would feel to soar.

◈ ☽ ⚡ ☾ ◈

The gravel crunched beneath Cam's boots as she walked, and the wind sweeping along the wall was colder now, touched by the hush of approaching night. Twilight draped the sky in deep indigos and coppered rose, casting long shadows over the Keep. The horizon felt stretched too thin—like the world itself was holding its breath.

She descended from the roost in silence, boots quiet against the stone. Her thoughts were heavy, full of unsaid things and the steady weight of what was coming. She didn't notice Kaden until he was already there beside her, falling into step with a soft exhale.

"You always walk like the ground might give out," he said, tone light but edged.

She glanced at him. "And you always show up when I need someone to catch me."

He smiled crookedly. "Bad habit."

They moved in a quiet rhythm for a while, the wind brushing past them, carrying the distant clang of steel on steel from the training yard. Birds wheeled overhead in lazy arcs.

"Your new friend's interesting," Kaden said after a pause.

Cam raised a brow. They walked the cliff path down from the roost, twilight deepening with each step.

"Orren," he clarified. "Didn't peg him as the type to hang around dragon roosts."

"He said he just wanted to see them. Never got the chance before."

Kaden made a noncommittal sound, eyes squinting toward the tree line. "Still. He watches too much and speaks too little for a harmless new recruit."

Cam didn't answer at first. Her thoughts were still tangled in Brontheus's voice, in what the silence of dragons might mean.

But the ease faded quickly, like breath on glass.

"I keep thinking about the ruin," Kaden said after a pause. "About Val... and Tessa."

Cam's chest tightened. "I know."

He didn't need to finish. She saw it on him—behind the calm, behind the sharp plans and well-measured words. Guilt didn't always scream. Sometimes it just sat with you, quiet and patient, like a second shadow.

"I told myself we made the only choice," Cam said. "And I know that's true. But I still see the moment I turned away. Every night."

Kaden nodded once. "Val made me promise not to be reckless. And I left her anyway."

"She'd understand," Cam murmured.

"That doesn't make it easier," he replied. He rolled his knuckles once, like he was feeling for the weight of a promise he refused to set down. "I keep my word, Cam."

They walked a while in silence. The wind caught her braid, tugged at the edge of his cloak. Distantly, a dragon shifted its wings—metal scraping against sky.

Cam's gaze followed the sound, then drifted toward the dying light bleeding across the mountains. The silence between them wasn't empty—it was full of everything they hadn't said.

She felt it pressing in around her ribs. The questions. The fear. The knowledge still buried beneath her skin like a blade not yet drawn.

What if telling the truth meant unraveling everything they were holding together by thread?

What if silence was safer... but cowardice?

She swallowed, pulse a steady thrum behind her teeth.

"If you knew something that could change everything," she asked quietly, "would you say it?"

She didn't meet his eyes. The words she hadn't spoken yet lived in her mouth like a storm waiting to break.

"I'm not afraid of Caerthalen," she whispered. "Not really."

"What then?"

"I'm afraid of what it might pull out of me," she admitted. "Of what it might prove right."

Kaden's gaze didn't falter. "Then let me remind you who you are when it tries to make you forget."

Cam finally looked up. And for a moment, it didn't matter that the sun was gone, or that war loomed. In that thin space between night and nothing, they weren't alone in the weight they carried. And that was something.

He reached out and placed a hand gently on her shoulder—grounding, not gripping. She didn't flinch. Instead, her fingers came up, resting lightly against his forearm. Not needing more than that.

Just a touch. Just enough to say: *I see you too.*

Kaden's steadiness had always been her truth—quiet, relentless, impossible to shake.

And for the first time that day, something in her chest eased.

◈ ☽ ⚡ ☾ ◈

The chamber was narrow and cold, carved into the outer wall like a forgotten vein. Torchlight flickered low in its sconce, casting long shadows across the stone. Outside, the last violet threads of twilight unraveled into night.

He sat at a small desk with a worn leather journal open before him. The ink in his pen bled just slightly into the parchment, but his handwriting remained meticulous—measured lines, clean strokes. He paused only once to flex the fingers of his left hand before writing again.

She speaks with dragons. All of them. Not like a commander—but like a friend.

He dipped the pen again, frowning slightly as it scraped across the page.

She doesn't use her power to rule. She listens. She laughs. She stays until the wounded fall asleep.

The words slowed.

He leaned back, eyes tracing the dancing shadow of the flame. The sound of distant boots echoed faintly down the corridor, then faded. No one knew he was here.

Observe. Confirm. Report. Capture.

That was the order. No interpretation. No emotion. He had followed variations of it since he was fifteen. Never questioned it. Never had reason to.

And yet...

His pen stilled. The line of ink ran longer than it should have.

The girl they fear doesn't exist. But the young woman they've made her into... might.

He set the pen down, eyes narrowing at the blank margin where his mental chart should have resolved. The pattern around her still felt incomplete—like a star missing from a sky he'd sworn he'd already mapped.

The thought sat heavy in the quiet.

He remembered the way she had looked at him earlier—not with suspicion, not with fear. Just... curiosity. Recognition, perhaps. A flicker of something that said I see you—and didn't recoil.

That was the problem. She didn't flinch. She felt. Even toward the dragons. Even toward him.

He closed the journal but didn't stand.

He hadn't marked her location. Not yet.

Not because he couldn't.

But because—for the first time—he wasn't sure if he should.

◈ ☽ ⚡ ☾ ◈

The stone beneath Wyatt's boots still held the warmth of the day, but the air had turned sharp—tinged with pine, wind, and the kind of stillness that came before everything changed.

Cam was already there, leaning against the edge of the watchtower, her silhouette framed in the bruised sky. The forest of Karethwyn sprawled out beneath them, shadows layered over shadows. The last of the light was slipping below the trees, dragging the day with it.

She didn't turn when he approached. She didn't need to.

Wyatt stood beside her, close but not crowding. The silence anchored them both. Like the air had agreed to hold still just for them.

Cam's eyes were fixed on the horizon. Her hands rested on the stone; knuckles pale from tension she hadn't noticed.

Without thinking, she leaned into him—just enough for her shoulder to meet his. He didn't move, didn't speak. Just let her rest there. A steady presence in a world that felt anything but.

The silence cracked softly when Cam whispered, "I'm scared."

Wyatt didn't flinch. "Good," he said. "Means you still care."

Cam closed her eyes. Her voice was smaller this time, rawer. "If I lose myself in there..."

Wyatt didn't hesitate. "I'll bring you back."

A breath caught in her throat. She didn't answer, but he felt the tension in her start to shift—unwinding, even just a little.

Above them, wings beat against the darkening sky. The dragons circled high, silent sentinels in motion. Their shadows passed over the tower like omens—vast, watchful, loyal.

Wyatt watched them, then turned his gaze back to the forest.

The last light vanished beyond the trees.

"We leave in two days," he murmured.

He reached out and gently took Cam's hand, his fingers curling over hers.

She didn't pull away.

Two days. That's all the world would give them.

Chapter 4: Time Is Running Out

Virellan stirred in the shadow of the roost, lightning crawling faintly across her scales. A whisper had brushed her mind—not from her rider's voice, but through her. Thin, fragile, reaching.

The girl of water had touched minds as their kind once had, before the Veil thinned and bonds were shackled. She remembered without knowing she remembered. Echoes of the old ways lived in her veins.

Virellan exhaled, wings shifting. It would tear her open to use such power from chains, but she would do it. And when she did, someone would hear.

◈ ☽ ⚡ ☾ ◈

The cold had teeth down in the dark cell.

Tessa pressed her back to the wall, her knees drawn in close, one trembling hand pressed to the side of her ribs. The wound still wept beneath the filthy bandage—hot and angry like it had a will of its own. The stone beneath her spine felt like ice, but she stayed there anyway. If she moved too much, she might not stop.

She didn't know how long they'd been trapped. Maybe a week. Maybe longer. Time bent strangely in the dark. But she remembered when they took Alex—three days ago.

Three days of silence from the cell across the hall. Three days of not knowing if he was alive.

She breathed through her nose, slow and shallow, trying to keep from coughing. The air tasted of rot and iron and wet stone. Every breath scraped. Every heartbeat throbbed in her ribs.

But she held on.

Cam. Wyatt. Kaden.

She whispered their names in her mind like a spell, like if she could string them together often enough, they'd hear her through the walls. Through the world.

They would come. She knew it in her bones—deeper than pain, deeper than fear.

The guards had brought water earlier, sloshed in a dented tin bowl. She dipped a corner of her sleeve into it, biting down on a cry as she pressed the wet fabric to her side. The fever had already taken root; she could feel it climbing her spine, wrapping its claws around her lungs.

She tried to focus—on the drip of water from the ceiling, on the cold, on the steady rhythm of breath in, breath out. But her mind drifted.

Flickers of lightning flashed behind her eyes. Brontheus's roar echoed faintly in her skull, all storm and defiance. She remembered wind in her hair, laughter that made her stomach ache, Cam yelling something over the wind with that wild look in her eyes.

Then it was gone.

The darkness stretched wider. Her limbs felt too heavy, her thoughts slowing.

Still, she clung to a single word, a whispered tether from a place far above the stone and filth:

"Hurry."

And then, the dark took her.

◈ ☽⚡☾ ◈

The walls whispered louder than the guards.

Valerie sat cross-legged on the cold floor, spine straight despite the chill gnawing at her bones. She wasn't huddled like they expected her to be. She didn't pace. She didn't beg. She listened.

Not with her ears. Not entirely.

They passed often—those armored men and women who thought cruelty was strength. Some joked. Some muttered. Some held thoughts like blades, serrated with fear or worse, delight.

They think we're broken.

They think we're weak.

She let the stillness wrap around her like armor, even as something inside her clawed to the surface. The hum had started two nights ago—a pressure behind her eyes, between her ribs. Familiar and foreign. It hurt sometimes, but it was clear now: something was changing.

Her breath slowed. She focused.

Not on the damp stone. Not on the groan of footsteps echoing past. But on the thrum beneath all things. The pulse of connection.

And then—stretch.

She flinched as the world slipped sideways. A sharp pain lanced behind her eyes, but she didn't stop. She reached—find someone.

The first thread she brushed sparked like lightning. Familiar. Frustrated.

Kaden.

He was dreaming—half-conscious—standing in a crumbling hallway of memory. His thoughts were tangled with plans, pain, and someone's name.

Val?

Yes, she pushed gently, *it's me. But I don't have long.*

He frowned, unsure. *This isn't real.*

Then let it be a useful dream.

She didn't linger. There wasn't time.

She stretched farther.

And found Cam.

The girl stood alone in a twilight forest of mist and ash; trees bare and twisted. A dream, yes. But not a peaceful one.

Cam turned when she heard the sound of leaves rustling behind her—though there was no wind.

Hello? she said, cautious.

It's me, Val thought, shaping her voice inside the dream.

Cam blinked. *Val? Am I dreaming?*

Yes. And no. Val's voice trembled now—not from fear, but strain. *I'm walking through your mind. I don't know how I'm doing it—but you need to listen.*

Cam took a step forward, shadows clinging to her boots. *Tell me.*

Tessa is alive. But she's sick. Fever. Infection. It's getting worse.

Cam's dream-face paled.

Alex was taken days ago. They haven't brought him back. I don't know what they're doing to him.

Cam's fists clenched at her sides. *Where are you?*

Beneath Caerthalen. Heavy guards. The worst ones carry sigils—wards that mess with power. There's... something else too. Her voice thinned, cracking. *I heard whispers. They're planning a trial. A test. To see if one of us is the chosen one.*

Cam's expression turned to ice. *What kind of test?*

I don't know. But it's coming soon.

The world around Val started to flicker. Like firelight snuffed by wind. Her focus slipped.

Cam—you need to hurry. Time is—

The connection shattered.

Val was yanked back into her body so hard she gasped aloud.

Stone. Cold. Metal. Footsteps echoed outside.

◈ ☽ ⚡ ☾ ◈

Cam woke with a violent gasp, as if dragged from drowning.

Her fingers clutched at the blankets tangled around her legs. Her chest rose and fell in rapid, shallow bursts. Moonlight spilled across the stone floor like a trail, and the room felt too quiet—eerily still after the echo of Valerie's voice.

Not a dream. Not a dream.

She sat up, her hand pressed to her heart.

"I saw her," she whispered to the dark. "She was there."

The details clung to her: the way the trees bled into fog in the dreamscape, how Val's eyes didn't blink, her voice like a thread barely holding. Tessa, burning with fever. Alex—gone. Chains. A trial.

They were running out of time.

Cam threw off the blankets and stood too quickly, swaying as a chill slapped her damp skin. Her breath came in steadying exhales as she moved fast—boots, tunic, cloak. No time for armor. No time for questions.

Only movement.

The Keep was hushed at night, save for the creak of old stone and the flutter of torchlight along the walls. She passed a few guards on quiet patrol, but none stopped her. Something in her gait, or maybe the fire in her eyes, warned them off.

Far above, in the shadow of the watchtower, unseen eyes tracked her passage, cataloguing every breathless step.

Cam didn't knock.

She slammed open the door to Kaden and Wyatt's quarters, breathless and fierce.

Kaden jolted upright, reaching for something under his bed. Wyatt blinked into the low light, shirtless and tense, already halfway out of bed with one hand on the hilt of his blade.

Cam didn't wait for them to speak.

"Val reached me," she said, her voice low but edged like a blade. "It wasn't a dream. She mind-walked. I don't know how long she was holding on, but she found me."

Wyatt was already out of bed, crossing to her. For a split second, Cam's gaze snagged on him—on the sharp lines of muscle, the lamplight brushing across his chest. Heat stirred unbidden, and she shoved it down as if it were dangerous. She couldn't afford distraction.

Her breath caught—dangerous. Not now.

"What did she say?"

"Ah... Tessa's alive but barely—burning up. Fevered. She sounded scared. Alex... they took him days ago. She hasn't seen him since."

Kaden was awake now, sharp-eyed and deadly calm. "And they're in Caerthalen?"

"Below it. Deep. Guarded."

"The Iron Hold," Kaden said.

Cam's voice dropped, rough with something deeper than fear—certainty.

"She said there's going to be a trial. A test. To see if one of them is the chosen one."

That landed like a dropped weapon. The silence after was thick, weighted with too many possibilities.

Kaden rose slowly, the expression on his face unreadable. "Then they're running experiments again."

Wyatt's jaw clenched. He had seen enough of the Capital's cruelty to know exactly what "experiments" meant. But what held him wasn't the dread—it was the fire in Cam's eyes, the steadiness in her voice even as it cracked at the edges. She looked like a storm barely contained, and gods help him, it made his pulse stumble.

"We leave now," he said, before Kaden could temper it. The words came out iron-sharp, but beneath them was something else—an ache to take the weight off her shoulders.

She nodded. "I'll wake Corin. And tell Ben. We'll move before dawn."

Cam turned, but he reached out before she could go—his hand finding her shoulder. Warmth leapt between them, steady, grounding. She froze, just for a heartbeat. She didn't let her gaze linger—he saw the flicker, the way she pulled herself back with iron will.

Her hand brushed his forearm in return. Anchor to anchor. For a moment, she felt the world steady, as if the storm inside her had recognized its equal. Then she slipped into the corridor, cloak catching the wind like a shadow at her heels.

Wyatt stood in the silence she left behind, the echo of her presence still humming in his chest. That unspoken pull tugged again—quiet, relentless. But he shoved it down. There would be time for nothing else. Not until their friends were safe.

Dawn would come, and none of them would be ready—but they would go anyway.

Chapter 5: The Edge of the Flame

The stars were fading.

Not all at once—but slowly, as if even the sky hesitated before surrendering to what was coming.

Wyatt stood near the top of the watchtower steps, wind cutting through the gaps in the stone, the night around him hushed but not still. The air tasted like snow that hadn't yet fallen. Like a warning on the wind.

Below, the valley stretched wide and unknowable—black hills, skeletal trees, the faint shimmer of the river coiled like a sleeping thing in the dark.

He'd strapped on his armor piece by piece, methodically, each buckle like a prayer he didn't have the words for. Not because he wanted to feel brave.

Because fear was already there, coiled in his gut.

Cam's voice still rang in his ears—raw, breathless, fire-bright. Not the voice of the girl he'd first met in the storm, or even the girl who'd faced down Veilborn beside him. No—this voice had cracked open with something deeper.

Fear. Determination. Grief that hadn't happened yet.

He closed his eyes for a moment.

He'd seen Caerthalen. Once. A mission with Corin when he was just barely sixteen. The city had carved itself into the land like a wound—cold stone, colder laws. The kind of place that turned people into shadows of themselves.

This is a trap, he thought. *A test we don't understand. And yet—there was no other choice.*

And somewhere beneath it, the people they loved were trapped.

Tessa, sharp-tongued and stubbornly loyal. Valerie, all flame and control and hidden kindness. Alex—Wyatt hadn't said it aloud, but the boy had grown on him. Too young to be there. Too brave.

He feared for them.

But that wasn't what made his breath catch.

It was Cam.

Not just because she was powerful. Not just because she was the fulcrum of prophecy and war. But because he saw the toll it was already taking. How fast she moved now. How quiet she grew when she thought no one was looking.

How easily she'd thrown herself into this mission—no hesitation. No self-preservation.

And Kaden. His twin. His mirror and his reckoning. If this went wrong... if either of them—

He gritted his teeth, swallowed the thought like ash.

We're walking into a trap, he thought. *And we're doing it anyway.*

Because they had to. Because this was their family. Because he would go first, shield them all, if it came to that.

He adjusted the final strap on his gauntlet. Exhaled once. Let the wind rake through his hair.

Behind him, footsteps—Cam again, or maybe Kaden this time. But Wyatt didn't turn right away.

He kept his eyes on the dark.

The edge of the flame was coming.

And he would be ready to burn.

◈ ☽⚡☾ ◈

The armory was quiet at this hour—rows of weapons cast in moon-pale steel, shelves of warding stones and sigil-bound leather gleaming faintly in the torchlight. Kaden moved like a shadow through it all, methodical, practiced.

He knew what they would need. More than swords and armor.

Sigil chalk. Binding thread. Null-inked ward tags. Most mages fought with raw power or finesse—but Kaden fought like every battle was a puzzle waiting to be dismantled. And Caerthalen was the cruelest puzzle yet.

And this wasn't a normal rescue.

He grabbed two spare blades, smaller and lighter than his main set, and slid them into hidden sheaths along his boots, and one more slipped into the small of his back. His hands didn't shake. But his jaw locked tight.

Valerie.

Her name had echoed in his skull since Cam burst into their room. Not just because she was in danger—but because for a single, fragile moment, before Cam even spoke—

He'd thought it was her.

Her mind. Her voice. Brushing the edges of his dream.

He'd told himself it wasn't real.

Didn't let himself hope.

But Cam had seen her. Heard her. And if Val was strong enough to force a dream-walk, then it meant she was still fighting.

Still alive.

His grip tightened on the hilt of the last blade.

And it meant she was terrified.

Because Valerie never reached out unless she was out of options. Because she hated asking for help.

And Cam's mention of a test—whatever the hells that meant—sent a cold sliver of dread through his chest.

He looped the last ward-bag over his shoulder, tucked a blade into the small of his back, and checked the position of the moon through the narrow window slits. It was just past midnight.

Not enough time. There would never be enough time.

Kaden exhaled once—slow and controlled—then pushed open the heavy door and slipped into the hall, his boots barely making a sound.

Every step toward the tower, every turn through the Keep's winding passages, his thoughts spiraled tighter.

Tessa was hurt. Alex was gone. Val was being hunted by something unseen. And still, he worried most about Wyatt and Cam—because he knew how much both of them would be willing to give.

Too much.

He reached the final stone stairwell, where the chill bled in through the cracks. Up ahead, he spotted Wyatt's silhouette near the top—still and tall against the stars.

Kaden paused at the threshold, just for a moment. The torchlight caught the sharp line of his cheekbone, the quiet resolve in his eyes.

He whispered it under his breath, not for anyone else to hear—just for her, just in case she could:

"Hold on, Valerie. *We're coming.*"

And then he climbed the steps.

◈ ☽⚡☾ ◈

Cam stood frozen outside Ben's door, light breeze blow through the corridor cool against her face. The torches lining the hall hissed and crackled, their shadows dancing across the wood grain. Her hand hovered just inches from the handle, but she didn't move.

She could leave now—slip into the dark with Wyatt and Kaden, no words, no goodbyes. Ben would understand. Corin would tell him.

She'd woken Corin already, a brief touch at his door, his tired eyes meeting hers with that silent weight of understanding. No words had been needed—only a nod.

Now all that was left was Ben.

But something deeper—older—held her there. A pulse in her chest. A tug in her stomach. A knowing. He deserved to hear it from her.

She knocked twice, softly. The door opened a breath later.

Ben's eyes were heavy with sleep, his hair unkempt, but he was already alert. His gaze swept over her in one quick, assessing glance—bare boots, travel cloak, fire in her eyes.

"I need to go," she said. "Tonight. Tessa's in danger. So is Val. Alex might already be—" She stopped herself. "We're going."

Ben didn't interrupt. He just listened, jaw tight, shoulders tense. Then, after a long pause, he stepped closer.

"I'll be waiting when you get back," he said quietly. "Go now."

Cam blinked, throat tightening more than she expected. When he pulled her into a hug, she sank into it for just a moment longer than she meant to—steady warmth, solid breath, the smell of ash and steel clinging to his shirt. Old instincts told her to pull away first. It was easier to face shadow creatures in the dead of night than this—than letting someone care long enough to notice she was afraid.

Just as she pulled back, he spoke low against her hair.

"Thank you for saying something. I would've worried."

She nodded once. "I'll be back. I promise."

Then she was gone—racing down the quiet halls, her cloak snapping behind her. Past the war room. Past the kitchens. Through the open archway leading to the stairs that curled up toward the watchtower.

The sky outside had begun to shift—ink-black softening to the faintest gray.

Time was already moving.

So was she.

The old wood steps creaked beneath Cam's boots as she climbed the tower, the cold air pressing tighter with each step. The chamber at the top was dim, the only light a low-glowing lantern swinging near the center. Shadows stretched long across the walls. Wyatt and Kaden were already there—silent, still—each standing like the calm before something irreversible.

Neither looked up at first.

Cam stepped in, the door clicking shut behind her. Her heart drummed too loudly in the quiet.

Then, Sylithra's voice coiled gently through her mind—steady, low, and ancient.

Be cautious. The dragons of the Knighthood may not be enemies—but not all of them remember the time before the First Flame.

A pause. Then distant echoes followed—Brontheus and Virellan.

Trust only what you know. Brontheus, pulsing like thunder in the bones.

Move like light in the dark—seen, then gone. Virellan clear and sharp like wind over steel.

Cam took a breath and crossed to the weapons bench. The hum of magic and memory didn't fade; it just folded itself into the edge of her focus.

She began strapping on her daggers one by one, tightening the small sheaths around her thighs and waist. The long sword, however, resisted—its scabbard pulling awkwardly against the strap across her shoulder. She cursed under her breath and tried again.

A quiet voice came from behind her.

"Let me help you."

Wyatt stepped forward, his expression unreadable, his voice steady in that way it always was when she most needed it to be.

Cam stilled.

He reached past her, fingers brushing the leather near her collarbone. Adjusted the angle. Shifted the balance with practiced ease. His closeness was quiet and sure—not intrusive, just... there.

She looked up at him.

His brow furrowed in concentration, mouth slightly parted as he checked the strap's tension. It should've been routine. Just part of the mission.

Warmth rose, quick and unfamiliar, before she could shut it away.

Wyatt noticed her watching. His eyes met hers. The lantern's glow caught a flicker of something soft, vulnerable, unspoken.

Neither of them moved.

The silence curled around them like smoke—until he cleared his throat and stepped back.

"You're ready," he said.

Cam blinked, then nodded. "Thanks."

She glanced toward Kaden. He hadn't said a word—but his jaw was tense, and his gaze was fixed on the far wall. He'd seen.

He turned now, slowly, and looked between the two of them.

"Ready?" he asked, voice low.

Cam nodded. Wyatt did the same.

Kaden raised his hand and drew a swift, glowing sigil into the space before them. It shimmered, then split—tearing open into a wide, jagged oval of light and shadow. On the other side, the faint sounds of Caerthalen rose—metal, wheels, and distant voices. A city that never slept.

Cam stepped forward. Wyatt's hand brushed her shoulder—light, grounding. She paused, turned slightly, and let her fingers curl around his arm where it rested.

A silent exchange.

Then, one by one, they stepped through—into the edge of the flame.

Chapter 6: Through the Veins of the City

The portal snapped shut behind them, leaving only the murmur of the city and the press of foreign air.

Cam stumbled a step forward into darkness—then stopped, blinking hard.

The streets of Caerthalen stretched out before her like veins cut open, lit with hanging lamps that buzzed and hissed. Smoke curled from iron vents in the walls. Lanterns cast yellow light that seemed to flicker wrong, too fast, too sharp. The buildings loomed tall, crowded close, their spines stitched with crooked ladders and bridges. Metal, stone, glass—everything was dense and layered and breathing.

There was no stillness here.

A distant horn blared. Somewhere behind them, a dog barked. A shadow moved across a balcony and vanished.

The city wasn't asleep. It was alive and watching.

Cam's breath hitched before she could stop it.

She tried to exhale quietly, but her chest stayed tight. The taste of copper and smoke lingered on the back of her tongue. Haldrin's Keep had been cold, quiet, ordered. Even the dragons knew how to hush their power.

But here...

Chaos pulsed through every brick.

She took a half step back without thinking—and bumped straight into someone behind her.

Wyatt.

His hand steadied her at the elbow.

"You okay?" he asked softly.

She hated how easily he could read her. Fear always found its way through the cracks, and Wyatt had learned to see light through broken things.

Cam's spine went stiff. "I'm fine."

Too fast. Too clipped.

Wyatt didn't say anything. But he was still looking at her, not with suspicion—just knowing. Like he saw through the cracks before she'd even noticed them forming.

Cam couldn't meet his eyes. Instead, she looked out over the city and said nothing.

They need me, she thought.

Not because she was the strongest. Not because of the prophecy. Just because they couldn't do this alone—and neither could she.

That truth steadied her more than anything else.

Wyatt's fingers found hers. Not forcefully, just gently, like he was asking. She didn't pull away. His hand was warm—firm, real. The contact quieted something jagged inside her. Just for a heartbeat. Then the walls came back up.

Ahead, Kaden gave a small nod. Time to move.

Cam nodded back and stepped forward. She closed her eyes, raised her hand, and summoned the spell Val had taught her—an illusion that shifted the edges of their appearance just enough to blur their shapes. Nothing dramatic. But in the flicker-light of the city, they would pass unseen.

A quiet act of magic. A quiet tribute to the girl who wasn't here.

The spell settled over them like mist. Not just her own magic, but Val's hand still guiding hers—even from chains.

Cam drew in one last breath. *I can't fall apart. Not here. Not now.*

She opened her eyes and followed her friends into the dark.

◈ ☽ ⚡ ☾ ◈

The streets of Caerthalen murmured around them—sharp with smoke, iron, and old oil. Under Cam's illusion, they moved like shadows through the arteries of the city, blurred at the edges, unseen.

It worked.

People glanced their way, then looked past, as if their eyes caught on something that never quite came into focus.

Kaden kept his steps light and even, eyes scanning rooftops, alleys, windows. The illusion was smart—Val had taught Cam well—but Kaden trusted preparation more than magic. People underestimated how quickly control could vanish. A turn too early. A slip in tone. A name said too loud.

Overprepared was how he survived.

Even at night, the city had its rhythm. Beneath the chaos, there was structure. The same cart circled twice, bearing crates of damp cloth. Patrols moved in time with the clock towers. Kaden tracked their patterns, catalogued exits, pressure points. The pulse of Caerthalen was mechanical—efficient in a way that made his teeth itch.

They turned a corner and passed a tavern spilling over with noise—clattering mugs, drunken laughter, the occasional shout. It reeked of sweat and spice.

He barely glanced at it—until a voice cut through the din.

"The Pale Fang's in the city."

A moment of silence followed.

Then someone muttered, low and reverent, "The Capital's Hound. First sanctioned kill at fifteen."

The words stopped Kaden cold. *If the Pale Fang was truly here, then Caerthalen wasn't just a city of chains—it was a trap with teeth already bared.*

His feet kept moving—muscle memory, survival instinct—but something inside him stilled.

That name. That title.

The Pale Fang. The words hung in the smoke like a blade just drawn.

It stirred something. Not recognition—something deeper. A ghost of a memory, submerged in shadow. A door half-opened, long ago, and slammed shut before he could see what lay inside.

He blinked hard and shook it off. Not now. Not here.

Beside him, Wyatt's hand drifted toward his own blade, just slightly—subtle, but enough to show he'd heard it too. Kaden didn't meet his eyes.

He couldn't afford to linger in fear.

Not with Val and Tessa trapped beneath stone and steel, gods knew how many stories underground. Every minute wasted was one more they spent in chains.

He drew in a breath through his nose, exhaled slow. Let the weight settle where it belonged.

Stay sharp. Stay ahead. Survive.

They slipped down the next alley, silent as breath, into the beating heart of the city.

◈ ☽⚡☾ ◈

The streets narrowed the closer they drew to the Iron Hold.

The glow of Caerthalen's upper tiers faded behind them, replaced by grim silence and steel. Even the air felt colder here—sharp, thin, like the city itself was holding its breath.

Wyatt walked just behind Cam, gaze flicking between her shoulders and the looming shapes of guards posted farther down the lane. Their footfalls were soft, muffled by the illusion Cam still held over them. It had held up through the entire descent—longer than most mages twice her experience could manage.

He noticed the subtle strain in her shoulders, how her hands twitched slightly before stilling again. But the magic hadn't cracked.

He remembered how her breath had hitched when they first stepped through the portal. How she'd bumped into him, wide-eyed, barely hiding her panic.

He hadn't known what to say then—no speech would've helped. It wouldn't save them from what waited ahead. The Hold wasn't a prison—it was a stage. And someone meant to see what would break them first. So he'd just taken her hand. Simple. Solid. Quiet.

It was what she'd needed. Maybe what he needed, too.

Now, watching her cloak them in near-invisibility with the weight of the city pressing in, something stirred in him that had nothing to do with survival or strategy.

Pride.

Not the kind that bloats the ego—but the kind that tightens the chest, quiet and full. She was holding it together. Not because she wasn't scared. But because she chose not to break.

They rounded the final corner.

Ahead stood a door—if it could be called that. A slab of blackened iron set into stone, unmarked. No signage. No guards. But power radiated from behind it like heat from a furnace. Ancient, oppressive. It pressed against his ribs. The air pressed tighter, humming faintly in their bones—like the Veil itself had thinned here, waiting.

Wyatt stopped beside Cam. Kaden came up beside them. None of them spoke.

There wasn't anything left to say.

He looked at each of them. Cam's jaw was set, her eyes shadowed but steady. Kaden stood with that calm calculation in his eyes, his hand already near the hilt of his blade.

Wyatt gave a nod.

Cam nodded back. Kaden, too.

They stepped forward together—through the city's final vein, toward its blackened heart.

Into the dark. Into the Iron Hold.

Chapter 7: The One They Fear

Val woke with a sharp inhale, breath catching in her throat. The connection to Cam had vanished like a flame snuffed out—no fading, no warning. Just gone. The silence that followed wasn't empty. It was *hers*.

Her heart pounded as she blinked into the dim cell. Stone walls, iron bars, silence. The stink of rot and something chemical hung in the air, too heavy to ignore.

Across the narrow aisle, Tessa lay curled in the corner, barely more than a silhouette in the gloom. Still breathing. But shallow. Too still.

Val pressed her hand to the cold floor and pushed herself upright, every muscle tight, coiled. Something was wrong. More wrong.

She didn't have time to think before the heavy clang of the cell door echoed through the corridor.

A Caerthalen guard stepped inside—armor dull, face hidden beneath a visor etched with runes. Wordless. Mechanical.

Val rose to her feet, chest tightening.

He grabbed her by the arm.

She resisted on instinct—jerking back, twisting, slamming her heel into his shin. It was enough to stagger an ordinary man.

But this one was laced with enhancement sigils. Magic hummed faintly from beneath his armor, pulsing like a second heartbeat.

He barely flinched. Just drove her back against the wall with a brutal shove, then hauled her forward again.

"Where are you taking me?" she snapped, breath ragged.

The guard didn't slow. "To test you."

Val's stomach knotted. She dug in her heels as he dragged her toward the open corridor. "What about my friend?"

A pause. Then a voice like scraped metal: "She's dying. They don't want her."

The words struck harder than the wall had.

Val twisted her neck to look back.

Tessa hadn't moved. Pale in the shadows. Too pale.

Her throat tightened. Fury surged up fast and hot—but she didn't let it break the surface. She couldn't afford to.

Not yet.

She turned forward again, jaw clenched.

She'll survive. She has to.

Val let the guard shove her down the corridor.

I just need to buy time.

◈ ☽ ⚡ ☾ ◈

The Iron Hold was colder than Cam expected—not just in temperature, but in feeling. The kind of cold that settled in the bones, humming beneath the stone.

She walked silently beside Kaden and Wyatt, illusion magic woven tightly around them. Her focus was razor-sharp, every step calculated, every breath measured. The enchantment held steady—light-bending, sound-muffling—letting them slip past guards like whispers on the edge of hearing.

And yet... no sign of Val. No sign of Tessa.

They passed room after room. Empty cells. Abandoned chambers. Corridors that seemed to stretch too long and lead nowhere. Cam felt the pressure building beneath her ribs—like something in the stone itself was watching, waiting.

Kaden gave a quiet shake of his head. Nothing. Wyatt scanned the doorways like they might open just by will.

They didn't have time for dead ends.

Cam stopped. Just ahead, a lone guard sat behind a warped wooden desk, his posture slouched, face lit by the glow of a flickering crystal lamp. He was bored, barely skimming a stack of parchment.

A risk. But one she had to take.

She stepped forward, dropping the illusion just enough to be seen. Not recognized. Just... seen.

Calm. Controlled.

Kaden hissed under his breath, sharp and urgent. "Cam—what are you doing?"

Wyatt leaned in behind her. "No—Cam, wait—"

But it was too late. She was already walking toward the desk.

"The prisoners from the ruins," she said, voice steady. "Where are they being held?"

The guard didn't even glance up. "Bottom of the Hold." His voice was flat. "Don't know why they left redhead."

Cam froze. Just for a second. The redhead?

Before she could ask more, the guard shoved a rusted key ring across the desk. "You'll need that. Stairs are west wing, past the wards."

Cam nodded once. "Thanks."

She turned and walked back into the hallway, illusion magic sliding back into place like armor locking shut.

Both Kaden and Wyatt let out the same breath at the same time—a short, barely-audible sigh of relief.

"You're insane," Kaden muttered, keeping pace.

"That was reckless," Wyatt added, his voice tight but low.

Cam didn't disagree. She just kept walking, the keys cold in her hand and her pulse louder than footsteps.

"They're below," she murmured.

And without another word, they descended into the Hold's depths—toward the dark, damp air, where silence had weight, and something far worse than steel waited in the dark.

The stairs spiraled down like a wound, stone slick with moisture, the air growing heavier with each step. Cam's breath tightened. She could feel it—the closeness of pain, of loss. The kind of silence that meant something had gone wrong.

None of them spoke.

The torches here burned lower, barely more than embers behind soot-stained glass. Shadows clung to the walls. Every footstep felt too loud. Even Wyatt's breathing had gone tight with unease.

Cam's magic pulsed faintly in her chest, like it was warning her. Or bracing her.

The lowest level smelled of rot and rust. The air was wet, metallic. No guards. No voices. Just the steady drip of water and the whisper of chains shifting with some far-off draft.

They reached the last bend in the stairwell, the air damp and metallic. Cam's skin prickled.

Sylithra's voice slid sharp and low into her thoughts, heavy as stone. *This place is older than your wars. The Hold remembers more than prisoners. Beware what sleeps beneath.*

The warning pressed cold into her ribs, gone as quickly as it came.

Cam swallowed hard, tightening her grip on the wall. She didn't answer. She couldn't.

She moved ahead, hand brushing the wall for balance as they passed one barred cell, then another. Empty. Always empty.

Then—

She saw her.

Tessa.

Curled into herself on the cold stone floor, pale and still and too small in the shadows. Her braid was half undone, the side of her face bruised. She looked like a memory worn thin.

Cam didn't breathe. Just ran.

She knelt, hands shaking as she forced the key into the lock and flung the door wide. Tessa looked like she'd been carved out of wax—pale, feverish, her breath shallow, one hand twitching near her chest.

"Tessa," Cam whispered, dropping beside her, voice breaking. "I'm here. We're here."

Kaden pushed in beside her, already reaching to check her pulse. "She's alive," he said, barely above a whisper. "But the wound—gods, it's bad. Infected. They just left her down here."

Tessa stirred. Her eyelids fluttered. She blinked once, then again, slow and unfocused.

"I knew you'd come," she rasped, voice almost too soft to hear.

Cam reached for her instinctively. Her fingers brushed Tessa's cheek.

And then it happened.

A glow—faint, gold, and warm—spread from her hands into Tessa's body. Cam froze. It wasn't healing magic she'd studied. Wasn't anything she understood. But it came anyway. Flowed through her like sunlight breaking through cloud.

Kaden stilled beside her. She didn't have to look to know he'd seen it; the sudden quiet in him was louder than words.

Tessa gasped, her back arching slightly, chest rising with a fuller breath. Color bled back into her cheeks, the fever-shine dulling, the tremors easing.

Cam snatched her hand back as though burned, heart pounding. The glow faded.

Silence pressed in, broken only by Tessa's steadier breathing.

When Cam finally dared to glance at Kaden, his eyes were locked on her hands, wide with something sharp—shock, disbelief, maybe even fear.

Tessa blinked again, more alert now. "What took you guys so long?"

Cam let out a choked laugh, half-sob. "You're okay. You're really—"

"She's stable," Kaden said, checking her over again. "But we need to get out of here. Fast."

Wyatt stood near the doorway, eyes scanning the hall behind them, jaw tight. "Val's not here," he said quietly. "I searched the other cells."

Tessa's smile slipped. "They took her," she whispered. "About an hour ago. I don't know where, but... they went up."

Up.

Cam stood so fast she nearly stumbled. "No."

If she stopped to feel, she'd fall apart. So she ran instead.

Kaden looked up at her, eyes narrowing. "Cam—"

But she was already moving. Running.

Up the stairs. Up into the dark. Her promise burning in her chest like fire.

Cam burst up the stairwell two at a time, her pulse thrumming in her ears louder than the clang of her boots against stone. The moment she hit the corridor, she didn't hesitate—her feet carried her straight back to the entry hall where the guard still sat behind the rusted desk, surrounded by quiet and ledgers.

Same slouched posture. Same glazed eyes.

He didn't even flinch when she approached.

Cam forced her voice to stay level, though the panic was bubbling up again, thick and hot in her chest. "Where did they take the other girl?"

The guard didn't glance at her. He flipped a page lazily, ink-stained fingers smudging the margins. "The arena," he muttered. "Protocol testing."

Her stomach dropped.

"The arena?" Her voice sharpened.

He shrugged. "Two blocks north. Big iron doors. Can't miss it. You'll hear it before you see it."

Cam stared at him for a breath too long, willing him to care. He didn't.

She turned and ran.

The night air slammed into her like a wave as she pushed out into the open streets. The illusion dropped without thought—she didn't have the focus for it anymore. Cold wind needled her skin, the city's sharp smells and distant noise crashing in all at once. Behind her, she heard the sudden scuffle of boots on stone as the others caught up.

"Cam—wait!" Wyatt's voice cut through. Urgent, but winded.

She didn't stop.

Kaden's voice was lower, tighter. "What are you doing?"

No response. Just the sound of her breath ragged in her throat.

Cam didn't see the iron doors yet, but she could feel it now—a growing weight in the air, like thunder before a storm. The magic in her veins thrummed like it was already reacting to what lay ahead. Her heartbeat pounded, not from exhaustion, but from dread.

They were close.

And Val was in there—alone.

◈ ☽ ⚡ ☾ ◈

The cold of the stone seeped into Val's bones.

She stood shackled at the center of a wide, circular platform—raised and exposed like a lamb for slaughter. Above and around her, an enormous underground coliseum curved into darkness. Tiered balconies encircled the space, layered in shadow, veiled by shimmering wardlight. She couldn't see the spectators—only the vague silhouettes of cloaked figures and the occasional glint of enchanted eyes behind protective glass.

But she could feel them.

Dozens. Maybe hundreds. Watching. Waiting.

She swallowed hard. The air was too still.

Her arms were bound in heavy iron chains that ran from her wrists to carved rings in the stone beneath her. They looked ordinary—but they weren't. Every time she twisted her wrist or pulled too hard, the links flared with red-hot sigils, searing magic into her skin. Suppressing, punishing.

Her magic—which had always been an anchor, a quiet rhythm beneath her heartbeat—was silent.

And that silence was terrifying.

Val clenched her jaw, forcing herself to breathe. In. Out. In. Out.

She glanced upward. There were no windows, no moonlight, no stars. Just the weight of rock and the invisible gaze of a hundred voyeurs.

Then a sound broke the silence: a voice.

Female. Cold. Warped slightly, stretched thin and metallic through some kind of amplification magic.

"Are you the chosen one?"

The question echoed, bouncing off the walls like a curse. Val's chest tightened.

She knew this game. Answer, and they learn what they need.

Deny, and they'll test her anyway.

Her lips pressed into a thin line. She stared up into the dark with the stillness of stone.

"Are you the chosen one?"

Slower this time. Sharper. Like the voice was trying to carve the words into her.

Val said nothing.

They weren't asking her. Not really.

Because she already knew the answer that terrified them most was waiting above, in the hands of a girl with fire in her veins.

Her silence was armor. It was loyalty. It was defiance wrapped in quiet. Because Cam will always be the answer they fear most.

Then, final and unfeeling, the voice declared:

"Whether you answer or not, the test will begin."

A rumble answered her words. Low, deep, and wrong. The floor vibrated beneath her feet—heartbeat, breath, or beast, she couldn't tell.

Somewhere to her right, a rusted gate groaned open.

The scent hit her first—damp rot and sulfur, like something left to fester beneath the world.

Shadows spilled out onto the arena floor.

Not beasts. Not illusions.

Shapes emerged from the dark, crawling, slinking, upright. Wrong.

Their bodies moved like men, but their limbs twisted too far. Eyes too crimson. Smiles too wide.

One stepped forward—a figure cloaked in shadows; its body draped in mist that never touched the ground.

Val knew what it was. Her knees nearly buckled from the sight of them.

She wasn't ready. Not like this. Not chained. Not alone.

But she met those eyes—those void-filled sockets—and squared her stance the best she could, arms straining against the chains, breath caught between fear and fury.

They wanted to test her? Let them.

Even if she burned for it.

◈ ☽ ⚡ ☾ ◈

Cam ran like something inside her was breaking open.

The city blurred around her—lamplight streaked like fireflies, shadowed figures turning to look as she tore past them. Her boots hammered the cobblestones. Breath rushed in and out like wind through a cracked window. Kaden and Wyatt followed behind, and Tessa, weak but determined, clung to their pace. But Cam didn't slow.

She couldn't.

Valerie.

She rounded a sharp corner and there it was.

The arena.

It rose from the center of the northern district like a wound—ancient and brutal, carved from dark stone, its columns lined with flickering braziers. Light spilled from its massive open archways, gold and violet and unnatural. The sound—subtle, eerie—was like a thousand held breaths.

Cam didn't hesitate. She slammed into the entryway, brushing off startled guards with a flash of illusion and sheer force of presence. The stone halls inside echoed with tension and the scent of damp smoke.

She broke into the main coliseum—and stopped.

The world stopped.

Her stomach dropped like it had been ripped from her body.

There, alone at the center of a massive stone platform, stood Val.

Chained.

Wrists bound in cruel, glowing iron. Her knees bent, her body bruised but upright—defiant even in stillness. Blood marked the side of her face. Her chest rose and fell with shallow, fast breaths. Around her, silence reigned.

Until the gate opened. Cam saw the shadows slither forth.

They were worse than what she remembered in the forest. Their shapes were almost human, but stretched, twisted, soaked in veiled corruption. Mist poured from the archway behind them like smoke from a dying fire.

Veilborn.

Tall. Cloaked in a darkness that shimmered like oil. Eyes like pits. It moved with purpose, head tilted as though sniffing for something.

Cam's body went ice-cold.

"They're using her," she whispered. "For sport."

They'd known. They'd known someone would come for Val—and they'd set the stage. A trap. A test. A show.

Her hand curled around the hilt of her sword. But it was her magic that answered first.

It surged through her—not the calm channeling she'd grown used to, but wild, crackling, hot. Every element she carried flared within her, tangled and riotous. Fire, air, light, shadow. All rising. All ready.

It wasn't harmony. It was collision—forces thrashing together, refusing to separate. For a heartbeat, it felt like the world itself might tear if she let it go.

Cam stepped forward, past the last row of guards.

Toward the edge of the arena. Toward Val.

The Veilborn turned—sensing her.

Cam's eyes burned gold.

The woman they feared had arrived.

Chapter 8: Reckless

Tessa stumbled as they rounded a corner, her vision briefly swimming. Kaden caught her with a steady hand under her arm, his grip firm and grounding.

"I'm fine," she muttered, breath catching in her chest. "Keep going."

Her legs ached. Her ribs still throbbed from whatever gods-forsaken thing the Capital's mages had done to her—and Cam's magic had healed enough to get her upright. Adrenaline did the rest. But worse than pain was the hollow pull deep in her chest, sharp and thin as wire.

The bond.

It was always there when Brontheus was too far—an ache under the ribs, a thread pulled near to breaking. She couldn't hear him, not at this distance, but she knew he felt it too. Dragons were never meant to be left behind.

They were running again before she could blink. Stone walls blurred past, torches casting jagged shadows as the three of them charged through the winding underhalls. Cam was ahead—far ahead—her steps swift, silent, decisive. Like she knew something. Like she was chasing more than just a location.

Tessa couldn't understand how Cam was still moving. Not after what they'd seen. Not after what they'd done.

But even without understanding, Tessa trusted her.

Her heart pounded louder than their footsteps. Just behind her, Wyatt cursed under his breath as they barreled up another flight of stairs. Kaden kept pace beside her, eyes sharp, his movements precise—even as sweat glistened at his temple.

Then Cam was gone.

She vanished through the final set of doors at the end of the corridor like a shadow slipping out of reach.

"Cam—!" Wyatt called, but the door slammed shut behind her.

A guard was stationed just outside it—his head snapping up far too late.

Recognition flickered across his face.

His mouth opened. "Wait, you're—!"

Too slow.

Kaden surged forward, shadows snapping to life around his arms like living smoke. A blast of dark energy cracked into the guard's chest. He crumpled against the wall, unconscious—or worse.

Tessa didn't stop to check.

Kaden cursed softly, eyes still on the fallen man. "Gods, Cam. Reckless again..."

But Cam was already gone.

Tessa's feet slowed as she passed the downed guard, and something cold coiled in her stomach.

She turned to Kaden, panic rising. "Where's Alex?"

They all froze for a beat. The question hung in the air like thunder.

Kaden's mouth tightened. Wyatt swore, scanning the hall behind them like Alex might appear around a corner.

"I didn't see him," Tessa said, her voice rising.

"We'll find him," Wyatt said quickly, stepping closer. "We'll go back if we have to. I promise."

Kaden nodded. "Not a chance we leave without him."

Tessa nodded once, sharply, swallowing down the panic. She couldn't afford it. Not now. Not when every second might mean life or death for Val.

But memory clawed at her anyway—her mother swallowed by a storm; her father dragged away in chains. Two goodbyes she never got to undo. Two people she couldn't save.

Not again.

Then Wyatt said, "Two blocks north. That's what the guard said. The arena."

They took off.

Pain lanced through Tessa's side with every stride, but she gritted her teeth and kept going. Her breath came short, vision flickering at the edges—but she didn't slow.

She couldn't lose anyone else.

Somewhere above them, thunder cracked. Not in the sky—inside the stone. Then the world lurched forward.

◈ ☽⚡☾ ◈

Wyatt tore through the crowd, shoulders slamming against strangers, curses flung at his back. He didn't care. His pulse pounded too loud to hear them anyway, his breath ragged as he ducked beneath hanging banners and vaulted over a broken cart someone had abandoned in the chaos.

Cam was gone again—but he knew where she was going.

The arena.

And he was going to find her.

He would not let anyone get left behind. Not this time. Not Cam. Not Val. Not Alex.

But the visions still haunted him—Cam slipping from his grasp in dream after dream, always just beyond reach. A vision he couldn't outrun, no matter how fast he moved.

He burst through the tall iron doors of the arena. The shift hit him immediately—light dimmed, sound warped, like the walls drank every footstep. Cold stone stretched out before him, narrow halls twisting off like veins from the heart of the place. The air stank of blood, smoke, and old magic.

Wyatt didn't hesitate.

Room after room. Door after door. He flung them open with frantic hands, calling softly for Alex, hoping—praying—for any sign.

And then—

There.

Curled in a corner of a storage chamber, chained to a rusted iron post, face swollen and lip split—Alex.

He hadn't realized he'd been holding his breath until Alex opened his eyes.

"Gods," Wyatt breathed, dropping to his knees.

Alex blinked up at him, eyes glazed but conscious. "Took you long enough," he rasped, forcing a crooked smile.

Wyatt didn't laugh.

He broke the chains with the hilt of his blade and caught Alex before he fell.

"You alright?"

"Peachy," Alex muttered, staggering as Wyatt slung one of his arms around his shoulders.

"Come on," Wyatt said, voice low. "We're not done yet."

They limped through the halls, Wyatt half-carrying him, shadows twisting across the walls with every flickering torch. The silence of the place was wrong. Too quiet.

Then they reached the edge.

Wyatt froze.

The arena opened before them like a gaping mouth. A pit of cracked stone and scorched dust, surrounded by looming stands and iron balconies cloaked in shadow.

There, at the center of the arena floor—Val.

Chained. Alone. Light from above catching on her black hair. Her shoulders were tense; her chin lifted in defiance even as her limbs shook.

And near her... something shifted in the dark. A figure—slender, wrong, cloaked in trailing shadows. Veilborn.

Wyatt's heart slammed against his ribs.

And then—

A shape burst from the upper rafters. A body. Light glinting off a blade. Hair catching the glow like fire.

Cam.

She landed hard, knees cracking against the stone floor, blade already drawn. No fear. No hesitation.

Just fury and fire and wild, reckless love.

"Gods damn it, Cam," Wyatt muttered, jaw clenched.

But even as the words left him, he knew the truth.

Reckless wasn't weakness—it was love that refused to wait.

He would've done the same.

Chapter 9: The Arena

The arena towered ahead, jagged and ancient against the night sky. Kaden's heart slammed against his ribs as they neared it—he could feel something wrong curling beneath his skin, like a storm pressing in.

Val was in there.

Every part of him screamed to run faster, to charge ahead and burn the world down if he had to—but he didn't. He matched his pace to Tessa's, his hand never leaving her arm.

She was limping, her face tight with pain, but she didn't complain. Of course she didn't.

"We're almost there," he muttered, not sure if it was for her or for himself.

Tessa nodded once, jaw set.

Kaden pushed open the massive iron doors of the arena, and the cold swallowed him. The inside was cavernous, too still, the air heavy with heat and fear. The echoes of their footsteps bounced like warnings off the walls.

"Wyatt?" he called, voice low but sharp.

A figure moved in the corridor ahead.

Wyatt. Kaden exhaled a shaky breath of relief.

And next to him—Alex. Bruised, bloodied, but standing. Kaden's heart stuttered.

Tessa didn't wait. She stumbled forward, nearly falling into Alex's arms. He caught her clumsily, and for a heartbeat, neither of them spoke.

Then Alex buried his face in her hair. Tessa clung to him like she was afraid to let go.

Kaden looked away.

Not out of discomfort, but to give them a moment—and to focus on what really mattered next.

His gaze lifted.

Beyond the arched hallway, past the last balcony rail, the arena pit stretched into a wide circle of stone. A pit made for blood, for sport.

And there, at its center—

Val.

Chained. Head high, but trembling. Black hair tangled around her face. Alone.

Kaden's breath caught in his throat.

And Cam—Cam—was moving across the pit toward her. No hesitation. No backup. Just raw magic stirring like the wind around her feet.

Kaden's jaw clenched.

Reckless as ever. Brave as hell. But gods... she shouldn't have to be.

His hands curled into fists, shadow magic sparking faintly at his fingertips.

You're not alone, Cam. Not anymore.

◈ ☽ ⚡ ☾ ◈

The memory of leaping from the balcony was already fractured—stone flashing beneath her, wind tearing past, the impact of landing rattling through her bones.

None of it mattered.

Only Val.

Cam hit the arena floor and rolled hard, the shock ricocheting through her shoulder. Pain flared, but she didn't falter. She rose in a single breath and ran.

Val was chained to a stone pillar, her face bloodied, eyes dull. At first she didn't recognize her. Then her lips parted.

"Cam—?"

"I've got you," Cam whispered. Fire bloomed at her fingertips. The locks hissed, melted, fell.

She pressed a dagger into Val's trembling hand. "Run. Don't ask. Find the others."

Val hesitated, heart visibly racing—then vanished into the maze of columns and smoke.

Cam turned.

The air was wrong.

And then—they emerged out of their shadows.

Three Veilborn, ink-drenched corpses dragged from the Veil itself. Skin fissured with shadowlight. Eyes hollow.

Silent. Intent.

They circled.

Cam exhaled once. Centered herself.

And attacked.

Her sword moved like lightning, cleaving through the first before it could react. A shriek split the air—but the sound was already behind her. She spun, fire and wind swirling with her blade. One staggered, burning.

The third leapt.

She ducked low and drove her blade up through its jaw. It fell away into ash.

Two down. One left.

The last Veilborn stalked her, obsidian armor cracked, smoke bleeding from the seams of its body. It lunged, faster than the others, blade flashing like shadow-forged glass.

Steel rang. Sparks flew. Sand kicked high.

She parried once, twice, forcing it back—until a jagged strike slipped through her guard. The knife sliced across her cheek, hot and sharp.

Cam recoiled with a short gasp—but didn't falter. Pain burned bright for a heartbeat, then vanished into the storm of her focus.

Her blade answered with fury. Fire bloomed from her palm. Earth split beneath her feet. Wind surged behind her strike. The Veilborn reeled, burning, unraveling.

For a heartbeat, the magic didn't feel separate at all, but one current—wild, whole, alive. It surged through her veins like something ancient remembering its shape.

With a final scream, it turned to ash. Silence fell like a stone.

Cam stood alone in the ring, blood slick on her cheek, shoulders heaving—but unbroken.

Slowly, she lifted her head. To the stands. Guards. Officials. Spectators. All watching. All silent.

Let them stare.

She raised her chin, magic still humming in her bones, blade still warm in her hand.

"I am Camomile Miles-Layton," she said, loud and clear. "I am the one you've been hunting. You wanted the 'chosen one'?"

Her voice cut like steel.

"You're looking at her."

Silence broke—not with cheers or jeers, but a ripple of whispers, sharp and unsettled. A hundred unseen eyes shifted, as if the word itself had weight now that it had a name.

Then—

A shimmer carved the air behind her. Not summoned by her hand. Not quite of this world. A rift, flickering with golden threads and deep shadow.

She glanced once toward it. And stepped back. Into the unknown.

Chapter 10: The Way Back

The moment Cam pressed her dagger into Val's hand and pointed to the far wall, Kaden understood.

She wasn't planning on making it out with them. Not yet.

She was buying time—with her own blood, if it came to it.

His chest tightened, but his mind locked into place.

"Follow me," he said sharply to Wyatt.

There was no room for argument. No time for fear.

Tessa helped Alex up, her movements still slightly uneven, her breath coming shallow. Wyatt hesitated, eyes scanning the pit as if willing Cam to be done, to be safe.

Kaden grabbed his arm.

"She knew exactly what she was doing," he said. "And I swear on my life—I won't let them take her."

Wyatt held his gaze for one long second, torn between rage and faith. Then he gave a single, sharp nod.

Kaden turned and sliced the air open with his hand. A shimmer tore through the shadows, swirling into a dark, violet-lit portal.

"Go," he ordered.

Tessa vanished through first with Alex leaning heavily on her. Wyatt paused once more—then stepped through.

They were gone.

The portal collapsed with a snap of air.

But Kaden wasn't finished.

He closed his eyes, grounding himself in the shifting rhythm of the arena. Focus. Not with logic, not with sight—but with connection.

Val.

Her presence sparked like static at the back of his mind—a flicker of gold and storm-light just a level below. Hurt, shaken, but alive.

Kaden reached for her across the distance like pulling toward gravity itself—and vanished.

The hallway stank of blood and fear.

Cracked stone and flickering torches framed the narrow corridor beneath the arena. Somewhere above, the crowd's cheers had turned uncertain—murmuring, shifting like a tide unsure whether it had just witnessed glory or betrayal.

"Val," Kaden called, quiet but clear.

A breath caught. A gasp behind a broken column. And then—

"Kaden?"

She ran toward him, barely able to hide the shake in her voice. Dirt streaked her cheek, and her wrists bore the red lines of chains. There was bruise along her jaw caught the torch light, and a tear in her sleeve across her forearm.

Without thinking, he pulled her into his arms.

She didn't hesitate.

Their lips met—hungry and aching. The kiss was rough, desperate, nothing like the steady stillness on the ridge. This wasn't a promise not to rush. This was proof that they were alive, here, now. It was fire and fear tangled together, the kind of kiss that bruised because it had to.

When they broke apart, she clung to him, her fingers still tangled in his jacket. "Cam?" she whispered, like a prayer she already knew the answer to.

"She's holding the line," Kaden said. "But she won't be for long."

A ripple of shadow tore open beside them. The portal glowed softly, pulsing like a heartbeat.

"I'll be right behind you," he said, brushing her hair from her face.

She gave a watery laugh, but her eyes didn't waver.

He kissed her again—slower this time.

"Keep Wyatt calm," he added with a smirk.

Val huffed, rolled her eyes, and stepped through the portal without another word.

The light swallowed her.

Kaden exhaled once—and when he breathed in again, he was high in the stands, hidden in shadow beneath the crumbling balcony.

Below, the battlefield was chaos turned still. The air pulsed with heat and magic. Scorch marks smeared across the sand. Two Veilborn corpses lay motionless—bodies warped and twisted in their final moments.

Only one remained.

He circled Cam like a starving wolf—his obsidian armor cracked, jaw slack with unspoken hate. Veil-smoke bled from the seams of his body.

Cam stood tall, though her stance swayed with exhaustion. Blood matted her hairline, and her breathing came in ragged bursts. Still—she didn't back down.

Kaden's fists clenched. The moment stretched tight as wire.

The Veilborn lunged.

Cam parried—once, twice. Sparks flew. Sand kicked up. Her blade sliced low, catching the creature across the leg—but not fast enough.

A jagged obsidian knife slashed her cheek.

She recoiled with a gasp.

Kaden surged forward—

But stopped himself.

Trust her.

He swallowed hard, forcing himself to stay hidden, his heart roaring louder than the crowd. It wasn't just fear. It wasn't just pride. It was something sharper, unnamed, threading tight in his chest as he watched her fight alone.

Cam turned with fury. Fire bloomed from her palm. Earth split under her feet. Wind surged behind her strike as she unleashed every element she had left.

The Veilborn staggered—burning, unraveling—and with a final scream, turned to ash.

Silence fell like a stone.

Cam stood alone, blood on her face, shoulders heaving—but unbroken.

Then, she looked up—toward the highest row of the stands. Her eyes didn't meet his, but he knew she felt him there. For a breath, it was as if the entire arena vanished and there was only the two of them, tethered by something he couldn't name.

She raised her voice.

"My name is Camomile Miles-Layton," she said, clear and proud, her voice echoed of the stone and metal walls.

And with that, Kaden vanished.

The world shifted, pulled sideways, and a heartbeat later he stood in the center of Haldrin's Keep infirmary. Cold stone beneath his boots. Firelight flickering against the high arching walls. The others were here. Good.

He heard voices—Tessa's sharp, relieved laugh, Val saying something breathless, Wyatt's deeper tone, low and tight with worry. A few healers rustled past, murmuring instructions, gathering salves.

But Kaden didn't hear them. Not really.

He didn't hesitate.

Kaden raised a hand and carved a portal into the air—his magic precise, focused, sharp. Through it, he glimpsed the arena once more—Cam standing, framed in blood and smoke and starlight.

His eyes were locked on the air before him—on the portal still flickering faint and gold in front of him.

One more heartbeat. Two.

She flinched as the light opened behind her, then turned her head slightly, just enough to recognize what it was.

Her shoulders dropped—not in fear, but relief.

Cam didn't run. She didn't rush.

She stepped backward—head high, gaze still locked on the stunned crowd—as if to say you don't own me.

Cam backed into the room like a warrior stepping away from the edge of a battlefield—bloodied, breathless, but alive. Her foot caught slightly, and she stumbled.

She made it. They all made it.

But gods... they were not done yet.

The portal sealed behind her, leaving only the echo of her name in the air—eyes still on the space where she'd stood.

Even here, safe among her friends, she could still feel it: her words hanging in the silence like an open wound. The whole arena had heard her claim the title they feared most. And there would be no taking it back.

◈ ☽ ϟ ☾ ◈

She stumbled backward into the infirmary, her boots skidding on stone. Her knees nearly buckled, every heartbeat echoing the roar of the arena still lodged in her bones, and was immediately tackled by a blur of limbs and tears.

The portal sealed behind her, leaving only the echo of her name in the air, heavy as a brand. Even here, safe among her friends, she could still feel it: her words hanging in the silence like an open wound. The whole arena had heard her claim the title they feared most. And there would be no taking it back.

Val and Tessa collided into her, nearly knocking her off her feet. The force of their embrace stole the air from Cam's lungs—but she didn't care. She clung to them just as tightly.

Laughter, relief, the tremble of adrenaline still leaving their bodies.

"We knew you'd come for us," Tessa said, voice thick.

"I'm so sorry," Cam breathed. "We left you—"

"We knew the risks," Tessa interrupted, pulling back just enough to meet her gaze. "And we'd do it again."

Val nodded against her shoulder; arms still wrapped around Cam like she didn't dare let go.

The healer arrived, coaxing the three of them gently apart. Cam and Tessa were guided toward clean bandages, while Val sank onto a nearby cot. Kaden hovered close—not so near that he crowded her, but not far enough that anyone could mistake where his attention was. His eyes never left her, steady as a shadow at her side.

The room buzzed with quiet motion—Tessa talking to the healer, Alex in the corner being patched up, a few others moving in and out—but Cam's eyes found Wyatt.

He stood just a few steps away, watching her. Something unreadable flickered behind his eyes.

Before he could speak, she blurted, "Look I know, I was reckless. But in my defense—"

He didn't let her finish. He stepped forward and wrapped her in a tight hug, burying his face in her shoulder.

Cam froze for half a second—then melted into him, her arms slipping around his waist, holding him just as tightly. She didn't realize how badly she needed this until now.

"Don't scare me like that again," he whispered, voice rough with emotion.

"I promise," she whispered back, her cheek pressed against his collarbone.

A minute passed—and then:

"Gods, just kiss already," Tessa said with a grin.

Cam and Wyatt broke apart, cheeks flushed. Cam shook her head but didn't step far.

Val, still standing nest to Kaden, reached into her torn tunic and pulled out two rolled parchments—hidden so cleverly they looked like part of the seams.

"They never found these on me," she said with a triumphant grin.

Laughter erupted—bright, unfiltered, full of life.

For now, at least, they were safe.

She barely noticed the healers swarming around them, or the bandages being pressed into her hands. The world narrowed to laughter, warmth, and the sound of Wyatt's voice cutting through it all—steady, real, alive.

Chapter 11: The Ones Who Can Read It

The Keep was silent but for the wind. Dawn had yet to touch the mountains, and the corridors of Haldrin's Keep breathed with the soft creak of stone settling against the night's chill.

Corin stood alone at the war table. Maps lay scattered beneath his hands, corners weighted by spare daggers and empty mugs. Caerthalen's jagged streets were etched into the parchment, black ink lines twisting through memory and blood. His eyes traced the path of their retreat again and again, though he knew it by heart. He'd slept, perhaps, for an hour—long enough for the ghosts of the Iron Hold to drift into his dreams and leave him awake once more.

The latch clicked.

He turned as the door opened, light spilling across the threshold. Valerie entered with the soft steps of someone who had learned to move silently in captivity. Her hair was unbound, a curtain hiding the bruise along her jaw. Her coat was torn at one sleeve, but she carried herself straight, chin lifted.

Without a word, she approached the table. The faint scent of damp leather and travel clung to her. She set two wrapped scrolls down with care, the soft thud against the wood breaking the stillness.

"These came from the Knighthood ruins," she said at last, voice low but steady. "I kept them hidden... even when they took me."

Corin's hand hovered above the scrolls for a breath before he touched them. The bindings were worn, frayed at the edges, yet humming faintly with the residue of old wards. "You protected them," he said.

Val's mouth set in a firm line. "Cam said to give them to you. Said you'd know what to do with them."

Slowly, Corin unwrapped the first scroll, treating it with the reverence of a relic. Age had turned the parchment a deep, weathered gold. Veil sigils lined the edges, nearly invisible until the lamplight caught them. The scroll seemed to thrum in his hands, as if aware it had survived chains and fire to reach this room.

Corin drew a slow breath. Whatever is written here... it waited for us.

The scroll's weight was more than physical—it pressed on him, on the quiet room, as though the words within already knew their importance.

Corin brushed the dirt from the worn cloth, then glanced toward Valerie. She stood at attention; shoulders squared despite the bruise along her jaw and the faint tremor in her fingers.

"You've done well," he said quietly. "Cam trusted you, and you did not falter."

Valerie dipped her chin, a soldier acknowledging a commander's praise.

"Go," Corin added, softer but firm. "See the healers. Rest. There's nothing more I require of you tonight."

For the first time, a flicker of relief crossed her face. She nodded and slipped out, boots whispering against the stone floor. The door closed with a muted thud, leaving Corin alone with the war table and its waiting secrets.

He set the scroll down carefully and crossed to the tall cabinet beside the table. A single lock held the Book of Unbinding; its black leather cover etched with curling silver veins that pulsed faintly as he touched it. Cam had carried it back from the Academy vault months ago, and he had barely dared to open it since.

Tonight, though, there could be no hesitation.

He placed the book beside the scrolls, fingers brushing the sigils on the cover. Cold hummed through his palm, like river water in midwinter. He flipped to the first page and began the careful ritual of alignment: scroll atop the markings, his hand over both, voice low in the old tongue.

For a moment, nothing happened. Then—

A shimmer of Veil-magic rippled across the table, as if the air itself were water. The book's cover quivered under his touch. The scrolls vibrated once, softly, and then the page beneath his hand glowed.

Words began to bloom in light, curling in ancient script across the first page:

"Only the chosen may read: Flame, Mercy, and Truth. Balance must speak for the Hollow to fall."

Corin drew his hand back, heart thudding once, hard. The glow reflected in his green eyes before fading to an ember-like pulse, leaving the room dim again.

He let the silence stretch, thoughts moving as precisely as a blade in his mind.

Not me.

Foresight tugged at him—a flicker, not of vision, but of recognition. These words were not warning him. They were reminding him of what he'd already set in motion years ago.

The wards weren't rejecting the scrolls—they were rejecting him. He had studied the Veil for decades, commanded armies, broken seals that should have held for centuries... and still, the book denied him.

He exhaled slowly, considering the words. Flame. Mercy. Truth.

His mind turned to the only three who could possibly match those names:

Cam – the Flame, though hers burned not as destruction but as raw, unshaped power.

Valerie – the Mercy, who had carried the scrolls through capture and suffering without faltering.

Wyatt – the Truth, untested but emerging, a man who saw through shadows even when he didn't wish to.

The realization was a cold settling in his chest: I can bring them here, guide them—but the Veil will speak to them, not

Corin let the silence settle again, the only sound the faint ticking of the lantern's cooling glass. His gaze lingered on the scrolls, their parchment edges catching the soft light. They seemed almost alive, patient in their waiting, as if they had chosen their readers long before they were ever found.

He drew a fresh sheet of parchment toward him and dipped a quill in ink. His hand, usually steady, paused a fraction before he began to write. The words were brief, to the point:

Camomile, Valerie, Wyatt

Meet me in the war room at dusk.

– Corin

The letters dried in an instant, sharp against the pale parchment. He folded the note and set it aside for a courier, then leaned back in his chair, allowing the weight of the night to press against his shoulders.

His thoughts drifted over the faces of the young ones he had sworn to guide.

Cam, with her strange bond to the Veil, a current of raw power she feared as much as she carried.

Valerie, unwavering even in chains, who had protected these fragile scrolls when no one else could.

Wyatt, quiet but changing, a man whose emotions were sharpening into something clearer—an instinct for truth that could no longer be ignored.

If the scrolls are to be read, he thought, it will not be by me. My role is no longer as the interpreter. I am simply the one who listens.

Rising from the chair, Corin crossed to the tall, arched window. Outside, the mountains slept under the first pale wash of morning. Stormlight rolled along their peaks, turning the snow to silver. For a moment, he allowed himself to breathe, to feel the turning of the world.

Behind him, the scrolls remained on the war table, their faint hum of power thrumming in the quiet room. They waited—not for the strategist, not for the commander—but for the ones the Veil itself had named.

Outside, the wind shifted, carrying with it a low, distant hum from the mountains.

Corin rested his hand against the cold glass of the window and whispered to the empty room,

"Then speak to them... before the Hollow learns they are listening."

◈ ☽ ⚡ ☾ ◈

Val closed the war room door behind her, the echo of Corin's voice still heavy in her ears. The lamplight from the hall caught the scrolls in her memory—their weight, their hum—and for a moment she pressed her palm against the cool stone, steadying herself.

Then she saw him.

Kaden stood exactly where she'd left him, leaning against the far wall, arms crossed. Waiting. His shadow stretched long under the torchlight;

sharp edges softened only by the way his gaze caught on her and didn't move.

"You stayed," she said. Not a question.

His mouth curved—just barely. "Of course."

The bruise on her jaw pulsed as she straightened her shoulders. It shouldn't have mattered, him being there. She'd carried herself through worse. Through chains. Through loss. She didn't need someone waiting at the door.

But gods, it mattered anyway.

She crossed the corridor, her steps quiet but unhurried. When she stopped before him, the air between them felt thinner.

The kiss in the arena still lived in her bones—wild, desperate, the kind born of fire and fear. This wasn't that. This was quieter. Heavier. The kind that asked a question without speaking it.

Her throat worked. "I thought... maybe you'd gone after her."

Kaden's jaw tightened. "Cam has Wyatt. And she has herself. She didn't need me in that moment." His eyes stayed on her, unwavering. "You did."

Something inside her flinched, not from the words but from the truth in them. She hated needing. Hated relying. But he'd seen through her anyway, and it didn't feel like weakness when he said it.

Silence stretched—sharp, pulsing, alive.

Finally, she asked, softer than she meant to: "And now?"

His eyes flicked down—her split lip, the dirt on her sleeve, the scroll-shaped bulge she no longer carried. Then back to hers.

"Now," he said, "I'm still here."

Her heart kicked hard against her ribs. The tension between them wasn't the wild fire of the arena—it was steadier, hotter, a flame banked but refusing to go out. She didn't step closer. Neither did he. But the space between them thrummed like it might collapse at any second.

Val exhaled, forcing herself to turn toward the stairwell. "Then don't stop."

She felt him fall into step beside her, as natural as breath.

Tessa sat on the edge of the cot; fingers tangled with Alex's. He'd drifted in and out of shallow sleep all night, but each time his eyes cracked open, he smiled like she was the only thing anchoring him there.

"You're supposed to be resting," she whispered.

"So are you," he rasped, lips twitching into that crooked grin that made him look far less battered than he was.

She didn't answer—just tightened her grip. After what they'd almost lost, words felt too fragile.

Somewhere far above, thunder murmured against the mountain peaks. Even here, her magic answered her moods—air restless, sound drawn tight, lightning sleeping just beneath her skin.

Silence stretched between them, the murmur of healers and distant footsteps filling the edges. Tessa traced the fresh bandage across his temple with her eyes, remembering the moment in the Iron Hold when she hadn't known if she'd ever see him alive again.

"You disappeared," Tessa said quietly. The words had been burning her tongue since the forest. "At the ruins. I saw you—your sword was raised; you looked right at me—and then you turned away."

Alex's jaw tightened for the barest second before smoothing. His gaze flicked toward the wall instead of her. "I wasn't turning away from you. There was a break in the line—mages coming through the smoke. If I'd stayed, they would'd've cut straight across to you and Val."

His voice was steady, practiced. Almost too measured. "So I drew them off. Got them chasing me deeper into the trees. By the time I shook them, the wards were already closing. If I'd tried to come back, I'd have led them straight to you."

It made sense. Gods, it made too much sense. She wanted to believe it.

Something about the way he said it—measured, neat, like he'd already rehearsed it—made her chest ache.

Her instincts whispered of shadows. Of a choice made in the smoke.

For a breath she thought she saw it again—the flicker behind his eyes, like he was listening for something far away—but exhaustion swallowed it before she could name it.

Tessa blinked hard and shoved the thought aside. She was exhausted, raw, still half-shaking from the fever that had nearly killed her. Doubting Alex now, after all they'd survived, felt like betrayal of her own.

So she only pressed her forehead lightly to his shoulder and whispered, "Next time, don't vanish."

His answering smile was soft, almost boyish. "I won't."

She wanted to believe him. She let herself.

◈ ☽ ⚡ ☾ ◈

Night pressed heavy over Haldrin's Keep, but the roost did not sleep.

Brontheus shifted first, a low rumble rolling from deep in his chest as sparks flickered faint across his scales. *The storm still lingers in her bones. She hides the pain, but I feel it. My rider bears lightning—and the silence after.*

Virellan's wings stretched against the stone, their edges glinting faint silver in the moonlight. *Chains cannot bind her mind. She touched the old ways without knowing, walking dreams as we once did. That thread is awake now, and it will not sleep again.*

Tenebrin's voice slipped like smoke through their link, cool and sharp. *Shadows pressed close around them in the pit. I tasted it even from here. It was not only the Hollow's spawn—they were being weighed, measured. Watched.*

Sael stirred, pale hide catching the faintest light, eyes half-lidded but awake. *The measure was not theirs to take. He is mine—bright one—and I will not let the dark unmake him. The Hollow stretches, but his reach is not yet whole.*

Sylithra opened one great golden eye, the veins in her scales pulsing faintly as she turned her gaze south. *The flame has named herself. The Veil trembled when she spoke. The Hollow heard it. He listens now more than ever.*

Skylith's growl rumbled from the far side of the roost, firelight spilling between her teeth. *Then let him listen. Let him remember that dragons do not bow. Not to kings, not to Hollow things.*

For a long moment, silence stretched between them, broken only by the sigh of wind over stone.

Then Sylithra spoke again, softer, but with weight that pressed against them all.

The circle stands... scarred but unbroken. Yet every scar is a door. And the Hollow waits for doors.

The others stilled, each feeling the truth of it coil through their bonds. Their riders had returned, alive. But the air itself carried warning—threads tightening, pulling them all toward something vast and dangerous.

The dragons turned their eyes to the horizon, to the south where the Veil shivered faintly.

And in the silence, they waited. Sylithra's golden veins glowed once, faint but steady.

Sael's mind brushed hers, the bond between them resonant and unbroken despite distance.

The Hollow heard her, she whispered through the bond. *But so did the First Flame.*

The words lingered, heavy as prophecy, carrying both dread and a fragile, burning hope.

Chapter 12: Between the Lines

The air was sharp with morning cold when Wyatt pushed open the door to the courtyard. Frost clung to the flagstones, thin and glassy, and the mountains beyond the Keep glowed with the first blush of dawn. The storm from the rescue had passed, leaving the sky clear and brittle, but the pressure in his chest hadn't lifted.

He drew a slow breath of the crisp air, hoping it would ease the knot in his ribs. It didn't.

A laugh broke across the yard—bright, warm—and his head turned.

Cam and Tessa moved across the courtyard in a rough circle, wooden practice swords in hand. Tessa's cheeks were flushed, hair flying, her movements uneven but determined. Cam ducked a swing and countered with a playful tap to Tessa's shoulder, grinning.

It stopped Wyatt where he stood.

I haven't seen her laugh like that in weeks.

A flicker of last night's dream tried to press through—the chains, the smoke, Cam's hand reaching as his legs refused to move. He shoved it down. Daylight didn't leave room for that kind of fear. Not here. Not when she was laughing.

For a heartbeat, he just watched. Tessa lunged clumsily, Cam sidestepped, and both of them burst into another fit of laughter that carried over the cold air.

A movement to the side caught his eye. Orren leaned against a timber post at the edge of the yard, arms folded, gaze locked on the sparring pair. His expression was unreadable, all edges and stillness, but he didn't look away.

When Tessa finally lowered her sword, panting and smiling, Cam crossed to Orren. He straightened a little but didn't unfold his arms. They exchanged quiet words Wyatt couldn't hear—and then Cam laughed again, soft and genuine. Something in Wyatt's chest tightened.

He barely speaks, Wyatt thought. *But she hears every word.*

He shifted his weight, suddenly aware of the empty space around him. He could feel the warmth of their little circle from across the yard, but it didn't reach him.

"Don't be stupid," he told himself—too late to stop the ache. "She listens to everyone who talks to her."

By thc time he glanced back, Orren had joined Cam, Val, Tessa, and Kaden near the far wall of the courtyard. Their heads bent together in quiet conversation, voices low. Val's hair caught the sunlight, Kaden gestured once, Cam nodded.

No one looked his way. He forced his shoulders loose, the way Sael taught him—breathe, then look again.

Wyatt's hand curled against the stone railing beside him, the cold biting into his palm. He told himself it didn't matter—he'd been on the outside before. He was used to it.

But some part of him whispered anyway: *You're not part of that conversation for a reason.*

◈ ☽ ⚡ ☾ ◈

Kaden caught Wyatt lingering near the railing, his expression shadowed, but he didn't call him on it. Not now. The air was already tight enough with everything pressing in. Instead, he stepped into the training circle as Cam turned toward him, her wooden blade already set aside in favor of bare hands and open magic.

"Your turn," she said. Her voice was steady, but the challenge in her eyes was sharper than steel.

He gave a short nod, rolling his shoulders. Around the ring's edge, Val, Tessa, and Orren stood together, their murmured conversation fading as the two of them faced off. Val's calm gaze missed nothing. Tessa leaned forward, fists on her knees. Orren's arms stayed folded, unreadable as ever.

The cold air stung Kaden's lungs as he drew it in and let his magic answer. Shadows stirred first, curling like smoke at his heels. Then he pushed air through them, sharp and cutting, until the dust in the courtyard swirled with restless current.

Cam's fire bloomed in answer—violet laced with black, strange and searing against the pale morning. It shimmered across her hands, curling up her arms like living ink. She didn't hesitate. She never did.

Their first clash was elemental, not physical. A burst of wind slammed against her fire, scattering violet sparks across the ring. She countered with earth, stone rippling under his boots to break his stance, but he twisted away, shadows yanking him back into balance.

They moved faster. Harder. Cam struck with fire, Kaden with air. She layered water over stone; he cut it apart with shadow. Sparks and dust flew between them in a rhythm as old as survival, neither giving the other room to breathe.

And then—something shifted.

Kaden thrust a wave of air forward at the same moment Cam hurled fire. Instead of snuffing one another out, the two forces bent together—wind latching onto violet-black flame, carrying it higher, sharper, until the blaze roared like a living storm.

Gold shimmered through its core. Not hers, not his—something that only existed when they collided. The fusion streak arced across the courtyard, violet firestorm shot through with gold, slamming into the far wall and leaving the stone smoking, cracked.

Silence.

For a heartbeat, only Kaden and Cam seemed to feel it—the hum of something alive in the air between them, neither hers nor his but both.

Cam's chest rose and fell; eyes fixed on the scorch mark. Kaden's pulse thundered, his breath caught halfway to words he couldn't voice. It wasn't attraction—not exactly—but the weight of recognition, like standing too close to a mirror and seeing something more than yourself reflected back. He knew she felt it too—the strange weight of it, the way their magic had tangled like threads refusing to pull apart.

Far above, in the roost, the bond stirred. Tenebrin's voice cut sharp through Kaden's chest, cold and certain. *It is woven.*

The words echoed long after the firestorm faded, heavier than any victory.

Very cryptic of you, Tenebrin, Kaden sent back, but the dragon did not reply. Only silence pressed back, a weight that made his pulse stutter.

Across the ring, Cam shifted, her eyes flicking toward nothing—like she was listening to someone who wasn't there. Her shoulders tightened, unease written in the small set of her jaw.

Kaden swallowed hard. She'd heard Sylithra, same as he'd heard Tenebrin.

And neither of them had answers.

At the ring's edge, Val frowned faintly at the scorch but said nothing. Tessa gave a low whistle. Orren's gaze lingered on the wall, unreadable as ever, before he looked away.

Kaden forced his stance back into readiness, masking the unease rattling in his bones. "Again?" he asked.

Cam met his gaze, something steady and knowing flickering behind her blue-gray eyes. She nodded once.

They reset. But the echo of that shimmer still burned between them, quiet and unspoken.

◈ ☽ ⚡ ☾ ◈

By midafternoon, the cold bite of morning had softened, and a weak sun glimmered through the high windows of Haldrin's Keep. Wyatt was halfway through a mug of bitter tea in the mess hall when a courier found them.

The young runner held out a folded parchment, sealed in dark wax. "For Camomile, Valerie, and Wyatt," he recited.

Kaden leaned over, squinting. "What about me?"

The boy just shrugged and ran off.

Wyatt felt the faint pulse of unease in his chest as Cam broke the seal. Her brow furrowed in concentration, lips moving as she read silently. Then she looked up, meeting both their eyes.

"Corin wants us in the war room," she said. "At dusk."

Val nodded once, calm as ever. Wyatt set his mug aside, anticipation tightening his chest.

Cam folded the message and tucked it into her belt. "We've got a few hours before dusk," she said. "Corin doesn't want us until then."

Val gave a short nod, already glancing out the Keep's window toward the roost. "Flight training?"

Wyatt sighed into the last of his tea, the taste bitter on his tongue. "Flight training," he echoed, though his chest was tight with unease.

By the time they reached the roost, the chill had lifted from the stone, and dragons shifted restlessly in their alcoves. Tessa was already there,

Brontheus coiled close behind her, scales catching the light in green-black sparks. She looked steadier than she had in days—her color returning, her shoulders no longer sagging with the exhaustion she'd carried since the rescue. Wyatt remembered how hollow her eyes had been when they'd pulled her from the Capital's grip; today, at least, there was a spark back in them. It eased something in his chest.

Kaden wasn't with them. Second-in-command duties had pulled him elsewhere—reviewing patrol reports, settling disputes among the younger riders, his mind already bent toward the kind of order the Keep needed to stay standing. Wyatt had grown used to his brother's steady presence in the air, and its absence felt sharper than he wanted to admit.

The sky was pale and open when they launched. Sael moved beneath him with glass-cut precision, every wingbeat steady as stone. Beside him, Sylithra surged upward with Cam astride, violet fire curling faintly across her arms like an extension of the dragon herself. Brontheus wheeled wide with a crackle of storm-light along his scales, Tessa's laughter carrying faintly over the wind. Val kept Virellan close, silver arcs of lightning threading through her wings as they climbed.

Other riders joined them over the valley—Miraen Veyth on dusk-dark Cindralis, always quick to show her sharp dives; Jorrel Dane with hulking Harrowfen, his wingbeats shaking the air like drums; Erynd Kael on Thalora, emerald-bright and swift as thought. Wyatt had known them most of his life, trained beside them since he was barely more than a boy. But even familiar faces carried strain now. Their formations were too tight, their movements too sharp, as if every rider felt the world's edge pressing in.

The drills carried them until the sun bled toward the peaks. Frost shook loose from the cliffs under their wings, dissolving into white plumes that caught the dying light. One by one the others peeled away, dragons banking back toward the Keep until only the circle remained. Together, they cut a final arc through the clouds and dropped toward Haldrin's stone courtyard, landing in a chorus of wingbeats that echoed off the walls.

Wyatt dismounted, boots crunching against frost, and brushed a hand along Sael's shoulder before turning toward the Keep. Cam and Val fell in beside him. Tessa caught sight of Alex entering the courtyard from patrol; she smiled, lifted a hand in a brief wave of goodbye to them, then went to meet him. Her steps quickened, the heaviness she'd carried since the rescue easing a little at the sight of him. Brontheus rumbled low, his storm-scent lingering in the air, before taking off back toward the roost.

The war room was dim when they arrived. Heavy tapestries had been drawn across the tall windows, muting the dusk light to a dull glow. Candles burned in careful lines across the war table, their light glinting on the steel pins of the map spread across its surface.

At the center lay the two Veilbind scrolls, unrolled but untouched, their faintly etched sigils catching the candlelight. Beside them, the Book of Unbinding rested like a sleeping beast, its black leather cover webbed with silver veins.

Corin waited at the far end of the table, hands clasped behind his back. He didn't sit, didn't greet them—just regarded the three of them with that measured, weathered gaze.

"You all know why you're here," he said finally, voice low but carrying in the still room.

Wyatt shifted under the weight of that look, but Cam's chin lifted slightly, and Val stood as steady as the stone walls around them.

Corin moved closer, gesturing toward the table.

"These are the scrolls you took from the Knighthood ruins," he said. His tone softened, almost reverent. "Valerie carried them through capture, kept them hidden when no one would have blamed her for giving them up. Because of that, they survived to reach this room."

Val's face remained calm, though her fingers twitched briefly at her side.

"And this," he continued, resting his palm lightly atop the black leather cover, "Cam recovered from the Academy vault, just before the fall. The Book of Unbinding. It is the key to translating what's on these scrolls—or so I believed."

He let the silence stretch, and Wyatt felt it bite.

"I have tried everything I know," Corin said finally, his voice tightening on the edge of frustration. "Every incantation. Every alignment. And still the text will not reveal itself to me."

Wyatt frowned. "So... it's locked?"

"No." Corin's gaze swept over them. "It's not locked. It's waiting. For the right hands."

A faint shiver ran up Wyatt's arms, though the room was warm with candlelight.

Cam's eyes were fixed on the scrolls. She took a small step forward, almost unconsciously. "I think... we should try," she said softly. Her voice carried a certainty that wasn't entirely hers. "I don't know why, but... it feels like this book knows us."

Cam approached the table first, her hand hovering over the Book of Unbinding. The black leather seemed to drink the candlelight, its silver veins pulsing faintly like something alive.

"Go on," Corin said quietly. "Follow your instinct."

Cam's fingers brushed the cover.

A golden sigil flared to life beneath her hand, spiral-like and pulsing, a warm light crawling along the edges of the book. Wyatt inhaled sharply as the first line of a page revealed itself, letters blooming in soft gold fire across the vellum.

"...Bound not by death, but by Balance..."

The words shivered in the air before settling into stillness.

Valerie stepped forward next, her movements precise and calm. She pressed her palm to the book's opposite corner.

A silver-blue emblem flared beneath her touch, cooler than Cam's, flowing like water over the leather. Another section of the text revealed itself, glowing with pale light.

Wyatt swallowed. He felt every beat of his heart in his throat as both girls looked toward him.

"Your turn," Cam said gently.

He hesitated. His fingers hovered just above the black leather, a tremor in his hand he couldn't quite still. The book was alive beneath him—waiting, watching.

When he finally pressed his palm down, a red-gold sigil burst to life, jagged and burning like sunfire. Heat licked at his fingertips, and a third section of the page revealed itself in bold, bright letters.

Light filled the war room, painting their faces in gold, silver, and scarlet. And then—

Nothing.

The remaining text stayed black, inert, as if turned to stone. The three sigils pulsed once, twice, then dimmed to a waiting glow.

"It's not enough," Cam murmured, voice low with frustration and certainty. Her gaze never left the page. "It's waiting."

Corin's jaw tightened. "Four readers. Four keys."

Wyatt looked up sharply. "Four?"

"The spell isn't broken," Corin said. "Not fully. The book has accepted your hands, your intent—but the Veil is asking for more. It wants completion."

Silence fell again, heavy and humming with the magic still thrumming across the table.

Cam glanced toward the door as if she already knew the answer. Her voice was quiet but firm. "We need Kaden."

Corin studied her for a long moment before nodding. "The text responds to blood. Purpose. Balance. If the Book chose you three—it will choose him."

Wyatt exhaled slowly, feeling the weight of the moment coil in his chest. The Book hadn't just chosen them.

It was testing them.

Corin's voice broke the silence. "That will do for today."

The glow of the sigils had long since faded, leaving only the flicker of candlelight across the war table. The Book of Unbinding sat dark and still, its silver veins no longer pulsing.

"We'll try again tomorrow at noon," Corin said, his tone final. "With Kaden."

Cam and Val nodded. Wyatt hesitated a moment longer, glancing at the scrolls like they might start glowing again if he stared hard enough. But nothing stirred.

Corin gestured toward the door in dismissal. "Get some rest. You'll need your strength."

◈ ☽ ⚡ ☾ ◈

Twilight pooled in the courtyards by the time Tessa slipped away, the last warmth of day giving up to mountain chill. She left the lamps and voices behind and took the gravel path that climbed the spine of rock behind the Keep—the one her boots knew even when her mind was tired.

The roost opened above her like a held breath.

Wings shifted in deep alcoves, scales catching the fading light. The air smelled of stone and storm and the clean bite of height. Before she even stepped past the arch, a familiar awareness unfurled warm through her ribs, like a cord easing slack.

Stormsinger.

Brontheus' head lifted from his coil, green-black scales pricking with a faint shimmer as he turned toward her. The word wasn't sound so much as certainty, rolling through her chest.

Tessa's throat tightened. "Bron," she whispered, and the ache that had lived under her sternum since the Capital finally loosened. She crossed the stone without hurry and set both palms against the strong curve of his jaw.

You were too long away, he rumbled, thunder soft and close. A flicker of light chased along his wing-edges, restrained. *The sky was loud and empty.*

"I know," she breathed, leaning her brow to his. "I felt it too. Kept reaching and hitting silence. Hated it."

He lowered his head until the weight of him bracketed her, a shelter more than a wall. *We are not made for silence. Not you, Stormsinger. Not I.*

She laughed once—shaky, real. "I missed you," she said, and the words steadied as she spoke them. "I missed you so much."

Then remember this, Brontheus said, the bond settling around her like a cloak drawn tight. *Distance thins the thread. It does not cut it. Not while we breathe.*

Tessa closed her eyes. For a long moment, there was only the rough warmth of scale under her hands, the slow rhythm of his breath, the mountain wind combing the roost. The knot she'd been carrying loosened one cord at a time.

Bells drifted faint from the Keep—dusk, then deeper. She didn't move.

They call you, Bron observed, not quite a question.

"Let them," she murmured. "I'm where I need to be."

He huffed a small storm of air over her shoulder, affectionate. *Good. Stay, then. The world will still be there when you go back to it.*

She smiled into the darkening light. "Bossy."

Truthful, he countered, pleased.

They stayed until the sky went indigo and the first stars needled through. Only then did Tessa step back, hands trailing along his jaw one last time.

"I'll be back after," she promised.

You always are, Brontheus said, and the certainty of it followed her all the way down the path.

◈ ☽ ⚡ ☾ ◈

The Keep's corridors were cool and dim, the stones still carrying the night's chill. By the time they reached the outer walk toward the barracks, Val had peeled away toward the mess hall, leaving Wyatt and Cam side by side.

The air outside was heavy, though the sky was clear—a strange stillness that reminded Wyatt of the way the air feels just before lightning strikes. The memory of the Book's warmth lingered in his palm, and its strange, knowing light burned behind his eyes.

Cam broke the quiet first.

"Did it feel like... the Book knew you?"

Wyatt let out a slow breath, his voice low. "Yeah. Like something old already knew my name." His hand flexed unconsciously at his side. "And I didn't like it."

Cam nodded, her expression unreadable in the slanting light of late morning. They walked a few more steps in silence, their boots scuffing against the stone.

Finally, Wyatt spoke again, his words hesitant. "He talks to you a lot."

Cam blinked, glancing sideways at him. "Who?"

"Orren." He forced the name out like it tasted bitter.

A hint of quiet amusement curved her lips. "He talks to everyone."

Wyatt shook his head. "No. Not like that. Just..." He hesitated, then said it before he could stop himself. "Be careful, alright?"

He knew it wasn't jealousy—at least, not only that. It was fear of what Orren saw when he looked at her: the same dangerous brilliance Wyatt loved and didn't yet understand.

Cam didn't answer right away. There was no anger in her silence—only that soft, unreachable distance that made Wyatt's chest ache more than shouting ever could.

At the barracks, she slowed. "I should check on Tessa," she said, voice light but not quite warm.

Wyatt nodded, swallowing words he couldn't quite form. She turned to go, but after a few steps she paused.

Over her shoulder, Cam's eyes met his. For half a heartbeat, he thought she might close the distance between them—say something that would anchor him. Instead, she only gave that unreadable look and turned away. The echo of her laughter with Orren earlier burned sharper than the Book's heat in his palm.

Then she turned the corner, and Wyatt was left alone in the quiet walkway, the weight of the Book's glow still heavy in his memory.

Names held weight—and the Book knew his.

Chapter 13: Veins of Gold, Threads of Truth

The study smelled of ink, old parchment, and cold stone. Afternoon light struggled through the tall, narrow windows, casting thin gold bars across the floor. Cam paced along the edge of the war table, arms folded tight across her chest, boots whispering against the rug.

The Book of Unbinding lay on the table like a living thing. Black leather. Silver veins. Silent. Watching.

She could still feel the memory of its pulse in her palm from yesterday—the way the light had known her, the way it had reached for something in her she couldn't quite name. It left her stomach knotted, like standing too close to a storm about to break.

Valerie sat on a carved bench near the hearth, posture straight, eyes steady. She didn't fidget, didn't pace, didn't need to. Just being near her made Cam feel a little less like the air was pressing down on her chest.

In the corner, Alex knelt over an open chest of scroll cases, carefully stacking and unstacking them as he searched for one of Corin's requests. He fetched an inkwell next, then a fresh quill. His movements were careful, but his mind wasn't on the task.

Cam noticed the way his eyes kept flicking toward the Book, lingering too long, like he wanted to read it through sheer will. He hadn't said much since the rescue. He hadn't really smiled either. A soft, restless energy clung to him, and Cam felt it from across the room.

Something's wrong with him, she thought, but the words wouldn't form past the worry already knotting her chest.

The door opened with a creak, and Wyatt stepped in.

Cam's heart skipped before she could stop it. He looked the same as always—broad-shouldered, dark hair rumpled from wind, jaw set—but something in the way he carried himself made her chest ache. His gaze landed on her first, flicked away, and then found its way back again. He hovered just inside the doorway, as if unsure whether he belonged here.

"You're early," she said lightly, more to fill the silence than anything.

Wyatt's mouth twitched in the ghost of a shrug. He crossed the room to lean against the far wall, arms folded, fidgeting with the strap of his bracer.

The quiet settled heavy again. Even the fire in the hearth crackled softly, unwilling to disturb the tension.

Then the door opened once more. Kaden stepped in last.

Cam's pulse shifted. There was something about the way he entered the room—calm, almost solemn—as if he'd already known this was coming. His usually quick eyes were distant, and for a moment, he didn't speak at all. He just approached the table; gaze fixed on the Book.

Without a word, Kaden reached out.

The moment his fingers brushed the leather, light rippled across the cover, racing along the silver veins like molten gold threading through black stone.

The scrolls unfurled on their own, parchment edges snapping gently against the wood. Ancient sigils pulsed in soft, rhythmic light. A low hum rose from the Book, not in sound but in the bones of the room itself—Cam felt it in her chest, in her teeth.

She froze, hardly breathing. Wyatt straightened from the wall. Val's hand went to her dagger on instinct, then stilled. Even Alex stopped moving, his gaze caught in the glow.

The Book of Unbinding had awakened.

Golden veins crawled across the table, connecting the scrolls to the Book, pulsing like the heartbeat of something older than their world.

The hum from the Book filled the room, vibrating through Cam's chest like the deep note of a bell struck far away.

The scrolls lay open now, their ancient ink alive with a faint golden glow that pulsed in rhythm with the silver veins crawling across the Book of Unbinding.

Footsteps pounded the corridor. The door opened sharply, and Corin entered, Ben a step behind him. Both men froze mid-step at the sight of the illuminated table.

"You didn't wait for me," Corin said, though his voice held more awe than rebuke.

"It didn't wait for you," Val said evenly.

Corin moved to the table, gaze fixed on the glowing script. He extended a hand as though to touch the Book but stopped short, his fingers curling into a fist.

"It's warded," he said softly. "Intelligently. Not by strength, but by intent. This book and the scrolls are choosing who it lets in."

Cam swallowed hard, her heart racing in her ears. She could feel it—a subtle tug at the edge of her mind, like a current beneath her feet, pulling her closer. Kaden and Val stood within that same circle of awareness; their faces caught in the soft glow.

Alex stayed back by the hearth, half in shadow, his hands curling and uncurling at his sides. He didn't even try to approach.

The light along the scrolls pulsed once—then words began to rise from the parchment, as if etched by invisible fire. Cam's lips parted. Her throat felt dry, but she began to read, the words spilling like they'd been waiting for her voice:

"He who was made in hollow light
shall not be slain by blade nor fire.
For no death may touch
what lives only in absence."

Her voice trembled on the last word, and then Kaden's voice rose to meet it, low and steady:

"Thus was he cast
between the Breath and the Wound—
Bound not by death,
but by Balance."

The air felt heavier now, thick with the pulse of the Veil. Cam's fingers curled against the edge of the table as another line flared into life, and she spoke again, softer this time:

"...Only the one who carries
both Flame and Mercy
may unmake the echo."

A flicker of light traced her hand, and for a moment she felt a warmth in her chest that wasn't entirely her own.

Kaden's turn came next, his voice quieter, reverent:

"Not power, but healing.

Not force, but wholeness."

The golden light along the scrolls brightened, and the last lines coiled upward like smoke, trembling in the air before setting down on the parchment. Cam's voice caught as she read them:

"...When the Cradle calls her blood home,
and the Veil sings her name—
The Hollow shall be filled.
But beware:
If shadow touches the heart of the flame-bearer,
He shall rise again, not once—but forever."

The light dimmed, leaving the final words gleaming faintly on the page.

Cam lowered her gaze, pulse hammering. Her throat ached. She hadn't realized until that last line how her own voice was shaking.

The room was silent but for the soft hiss of the fire.

"That," Corin said finally, voice low and heavy, "is Veilbound script. Older than any text in the Academy vaults."

Ben crossed his arms, eyes sharp on the scrolls. "Older than anything the Capital would admit exists."

Wyatt shifted against the wall. His voice broke the stillness, blunt and unflinching:

"Is that about her?" His gaze landed on Cam like a brand. "Is it talking about Cam?"

Cam's lips parted—but no sound came. She didn't answer. She didn't have to. Cam didn't wait for Corin to speak again.

She couldn't breathe.

The words on the scroll were still glowing in her mind, their weight pressing into her bones. Her chest felt too tight, her skin too hot. She turned sharply and left the study without a word, boots pounding the corridor.

The stone walls felt like they were closing in.

Her magic was thrumming under her skin, demanding release, brushing the edges of her control. Not here, she thought, jaw clenched. Not in here.

She burst out through the Keep's outer doors into the cold mountain air. The sky was pale, washed in the weak light of late afternoon. Wind caught her hair and cloak, but it wasn't enough.

She ran.

Across the courtyard, past the training grounds, through the narrow path that led beyond the walls—until the stone beneath her boots gave way to the cliffs overlooking the endless drop below. She bent over, palms braced on her knees, trying to catch her breath.

Her thoughts came in jagged fragments, each one sharper than the last.

Was I chosen... or created? What if this has never been my choice?

The words from the scroll burned in her mind, coiling around the fear she'd tried to bury since the day she'd first felt the Veil answer her. Flame and Mercy. The Cradle. The Hollow shall be filled.

The first tear slipped hot down her cheek—and that's when the storm answered her.

Wind ripped along the cliffs, nearly knocking her back. Her hair whipped wildly across her face. Above, the sky darkened with gathering clouds, lightning flickering at the edges like an opening eye.

She gasped, clutching her arms, but it was already moving through her. Electricity coiled around her forearms in golden arcs, licking up to her fingertips. Her veins glimmered faintly beneath her skin, pulsing like the veins of the Book itself.

She sank to her knees, hands pressed to the cold stone, teeth gritted against the wild surge.

She could feel the Veil pulling at her, the same way it had the day she first touched it.

Only now, it wasn't asking.

The wind howled over the cliffs, tearing at Cam's cloak, but it was nothing compared to the storm inside her chest. Lightning curled up her arms, crackling at her fingertips. Her heart raced in uneven bursts, and every instinct screamed to either let go completely or bury it so deep it would never surface again.

Then, through the roar of wind and the pounding of her pulse—

A voice. Low. Calm. Ancient.

Camomile.

Her head snapped up. The storm around her fell away in an instant, the cliffs dissolving like smoke.

She stood barefoot on a battlefield of ash and broken stone. The air smelled of charred earth and rain, heavy with memory. And there—rising from the ruins—was Sylithra.

The dragon's obsidian scales gleamed faintly blue under the muted sky, threaded with veins of molten gold. Her massive wings drooped low, the edges cracked and scarred, as if she had carried the weight of too many wars. Her luminous eyes met Cam's, steady and mournful, and her voice filled the air and Cam's bones all at once.

Your power is not the danger, Sylithra said, every word a warm echo in the cold, ruined air. *Your fear of it is.*

Cam's knees felt weak. "I—" Her voice cracked. "I can't control it. I don't even know if any of this is really mine. What if they—what if I'm not—"

Sylithra's massive head lowered, so her golden-veined horns framed Cam like a crown.

Balance isn't submission. It's trust.

Cam felt her chest tighten, the words burrowing past fear to a place she didn't want to look.

You cannot wield your magic and fear it at the same time, the dragon went on, gently but unyielding. *You were born of choice, not design... even if they tried to control the path.*

A faint glow pulsed along Sylithra's wings, and the battlefield shimmered, as if the vision itself was breathing.

Do not let their chains live in your heart, Sylithra whispered. *You are not hollow.*

The wind from the real world brushed Cam's cheek again, and she realized she was crying, the tears hot even in the cold air.

The storm had finally passed, but the heaviness in Cam's chest lingered.

She sat on the cold stone ledge of the cliffs, frost clinging to the rock beneath her. The wind carried a biting chill, tugging at her cloak and hair, seeping into her bones until her fingers ached. Still, her thoughts were farther away—twisting and turning like the storm had been.

The glow in her veins had dimmed, but the echoes of Sylithra's words pulsed beneath her skin.

Was I really born of choice? she wondered, staring out at the endless horizon where pale winter light bled across the mountains. Or just a weapon shaped by others' hands?

Her fingers curled tightly around the stone, skin scraping against its icy crust.

I need answers. I need to know where I come from, what blood runs in my veins. Ben might know.

The thought felt like a lifeline—something solid in the swirling uncertainty.

But doubt crept in with it. What if knowing changes everything? What if it makes me less... me?

A gust rushed through the pass, carrying the sting of snowmelt and the sharp tang of pine. Cam drew a breath that burned cold in her lungs, trying to steady the tremor in her hands.

Then a voice—soft, familiar—cut through the silence.

"Cam?"

She looked up, startled, to see Wyatt approaching carefully, boots crunching over a thin glaze of frost. His breath misted in the air, and his eyes were full of something she couldn't quite place. Concern? Hesitation?

"Wyatt," she said softly, her voice rough.

He settled a few feet away, careful not to crowd her space. The wind tugged at his dark hair, and the cold sharpened the angles of his face. His eyes carried a weight she hadn't seen before, shadowed against the pale light of morning.

"I thought I might find you here," he said.

For a long moment, they just sat, the silence stretching between them—not uncomfortable, but full of things left unsaid. The wind whistled low across the ledge, rattling frozen branches clinging to the cliffside. A year ago, she would've walked away before he'd found her. But the storm had left her too hollow for pretending she didn't need the quiet company.

Finally, Wyatt broke it.

"That book... it knows you." His gaze flicked to her hands, veins glowing faintly beneath pale skin. "Like it's been waiting for you."

Cam nodded slowly. "It's... more than that. I felt it, deep inside. Like it was reaching for something I'm not sure I have."

Wyatt's jaw tightened. "You're not alone."

She glanced at him, surprise softening her features. "I'm not?"

He gave a humorless smile.

His eyes lingered on her a beat too long, something unspoken pressing in the space between them. Silence fell—thin and fragile, settling between them like frost. She felt it bite, sharp as the cold air, and knew if it stayed much longer, it would only deepen the distance.

The wind stirred along the ledge, carrying sharp flakes of snow that stung her cheek. Loose strands of her hair whipped across her face. Far below, the forest stretched in dark folds, muffled in frost, the stillness heavy enough that even the mountains seemed to be listening. Cam felt his unease coil in the quiet, but Wyatt didn't look at her.

When he spoke again, his voice was different—harder, edged.

"Does Orren talk to you as much as he talks to everyone else?"

Cam raised an eyebrow. The way Wyatt said it—tight, bitter—made her chest ache. His jaw was clenched, eyes fixed anywhere but her, like just saying the name tasted wrong in his mouth.

"He talks to everyone."

Wyatt's laugh was short, bitter, mist curling white in the air. "No. Not like that. Like he's... close to you. Like you're the only one he really listens to."

Cam frowned, studying him. "You don't like him."

"Not a bit." He looked away, voice dropping low, carrying like a breath of winter across the ledge. "Just... be careful. He's not who he seems."

She didn't think it was jealousy—not really. It was something heavier, quieter. Fear, maybe. The kind that comes from caring too much and not knowing how to say it.

Cam's heart stuttered, but she didn't say anything. Instead, she reached out, almost without thinking, and brushed a stray lock of hair from his forehead, cold against her fingertips.

Wyatt caught her hand, holding it gently, the warmth of his skin a contrast to the frozen air. For a breath, their eyes locked—everything unspoken in the space between them. That small gesture—the reach, the contact—cost her more than the storm had. But it felt right anyway.

Then Cam pulled back, standing with effort. Snow cracked under her boots as she moved. “I have to find Ben.”

Wyatt nodded but didn’t move. His breath fogged in the frigid air. “I’ll be nearby.”

She didn’t look back as she walked away into the winter stillness, but something in the way he stayed behind made her feel... less alone.

◈ ☽⚡☾ ◈

Cam found Ben in the armory, the rasp of steel against whetstone sharp in the cold air that seeped in through the stone walls. A lantern burned low, throwing long shadows across racks of spears and swords. Sparks flared with each careful pull, but Cam’s chest felt hollow, her thoughts twisting with everything she’d learned—or feared—since the Book had glowed beneath her hand.

“Dad,” she said softly, hesitating in the doorway. Her voice cracked on the word. “Can we... talk somewhere else? Somewhere private?”

Ben stilled, the whetstone pausing mid-stroke. He glanced at her, really looked, and in his eyes she saw recognition—he’d been waiting for this moment. Slowly, he set the sword aside and stood. His sigh carried years of words he hadn’t been ready to speak.

“Sure, kid,” he said quietly. “Let’s go.”

They crossed the snowy courtyard in silence, their boots crunching softly. The air was cold and sharp, their breath curling white against the darkening sky. When they reached the garden wall, Cam brushed snow from the stone ledge and sat, her fingers curling against the icy edge. Ben remained standing at first, the wind tugging at his cloak, before he joined her.

“I need to ask you something,” she said finally, her voice trembling. “Was I... made for this? Am I just a weapon in someone else’s story?”

Ben inhaled slowly, then let out a sigh that misted in the frigid air. It was the kind of sound that carried years of guilt, of choices deferred.

"Cam... your mother, Isabella, had an elemental alignment so rare the Capital quietly tracked her for years."

Cam's chest tightened. The words landed heavier than stone, sinking past bone into places she didn't want touched. Her hand drifted almost unconsciously to the woven pearl bracelet at her wrist—the only thing of her mother's she possessed. For a moment, an image stirred unbidden—not memory, not vision, just the ghost of a woman's face half-formed in her mind. Blue-gray eyes flecked with silver, the same eyes she saw in the mirror every morning. The rest of her features blurred away like mist, but the eyes stayed.

She blinked, breath catching, and glanced at Ben beside her. His hair, streaked heavily with gray now, still held the chestnut undertones that matched her own. The resemblance was quieter, but it was there. She was both of them—the mother she'd never known and the father who sat beside her now.

"They watched her?" she whispered, voice catching.

Ben nodded. "I didn't want to tell you. I thought... if you grew up away from it all, you'd be safe. No shadows. No chains. Just... your own life, for as long as you could have it."

The wind whistled softly over the wall, scattering flakes across her cloak. Cam stared at her hands, the veins beneath them faintly lit by the remnants of her earlier storm. "So, all this time... I didn't even know who I really was."

"I hid my own bloodline, too," Ben said, his voice rough but steady. "It's the only way I could bond with Skylith. The Veil notices blood, Cam. It feels power in the veins, and it never forgets."

Her fingers trembled against the icy stone. The Book had known her blood; maybe that was the point all along. "Then... what does that make me?"

Ben sat beside her now, close enough for warmth to bleed through the cold. "You were born out of love," he said firmly. "But you were born when the Veil was thin, and that matters. It noticed you. The world noticed you. That doesn't make you a weapon—it makes you a choice the world has been waiting for."

Tears burned in Cam's eyes before she could stop them. "So... I'm not a mistake?"

"Never," Ben said without hesitation. His gaze met hers, heavy with all the years he hadn't been there. "Your arrival wasn't planned. But it was whispered about—foretold quietly, in circles that feared and hoped in equal measure. Some prayed for you. Some feared you. But I..." His voice broke for just a heartbeat. "I only ever wanted to know my daughter—not a prophecy, not a weapon. You."

Cam swallowed hard, blinking against the blur of tears. Her voice came out small but certain. "Thanks... Dad."

It was strange, how saying the word didn't feel like surrender anymore. It felt like breathing.

Ben's hand rested over hers, grounding her against the cold. "You weren't built for this, Cam. But you might be the only one who can finish it. And no one—not prophecy, not bloodline—can take that choice away from you."

The winter wind curled around them, sharp and clean, carrying away the silence like a vow.

Chapter 14: The Blood Ledger

The chamber was quiet but for the steady pop of the fire and the scratch of his quill across parchment. Reports for Corin—patrol rotations, supply counts, a handful of disputes among the younger riders. All of it important, none of it able to hold his focus.

Ben set the quill down and pressed his hands over his face, dragging them back through his graying hair. The words on the page blurred into nothing. What lingered instead was Cam's voice, small but sharp as a blade:

'Was I made for this? Am I just a weapon in someone else's story?'

The memory of it pressed heavier than any report. He had seen storms break less suddenly, less violently, than the way those words had cut out of her.

A warmth stirred low in his chest, not his own—Skylith. Her presence slid through the bond, steady as the heartbeat of a forge.

You cannot write her answers in your ledgers, she rumbled, thought-voice flickering like flame. *No report will silence the question she carries.*

Ben leaned back in his chair, the wood creaking under his weight, and rubbed at his temple. "She's asking things I never wanted her to ask." His voice was low, roughened by exhaustion. "Things I can't undo."

And she hadn't asked through anger this time, but through trust—the kind that made him realize how much she'd stopped keeping him at a distance.

And yet, Skylith countered, a curl of heat brushing his mind, *she asks you. Not Corin. Not the others. You.*

That truth settled heavier than any rebuke. His daughter—the girl he had once tried to hide from the Veil itself—was looking to him for answers he wasn't sure he could give.

"She deserves better than this," he muttered. "Better than prophecy. Better than bloodlines carved up in ledgers."

Skylith's reply was quiet, but unyielding: *Then give her better. Not excuses. Not silence. Truth. Even if it burns.*

Ben's jaw tightened. He thought of Isabella, of the woven pearl bracelet that still circled Cam's wrist. He thought of the eyes that weren't his, the fire that wasn't his, but the weight of love that was.

He dragged the reports closer, forcing his eyes back to the neat columns of numbers. But the words refused to hold. The only thing that echoed was Skylith's certainty, pressing into the cracks of his doubt:

Stand with her in the storm, Forgeheart. Or lose her to it.

The quill trembled in his hand. He set it down again, the ink pooling where it touched the parchment. The fire popped, and the silence closed back in—heavy with truths he could no longer keep at bay.

◈ ☽ ⚡ ☾ ◈

The training ring shimmered with damp mist, sunlight catching on droplets in the late morning as Val spun them through the air. Threads of water coiled from her palms, fine as silk, then wove into the outline of a soldier's shape. For three breaths it held, an illusion laced with movement, before unraveling in a scatter of rain across the dust.

She stilled her hands, the water slipping back into silence. Her body was here, in the ring. Her mind was not.

From the far edge, Virellan stirred. Her scales rippled like stormfronts across the mountains, purplish-gray shifting with light, streaked in silver veins that glowed faint with static. She lowered her head, horns jagged and angled back, one chipped where battle had once marked her. Her silver-white eyes glowed, piercing and without pupils.

Stormheart, Virellan said, voice a low thunder rolling through Val's chest. *You bend water, but your thoughts bend elsewhere.*

Val exhaled slowly, fingers brushing her coat pocket. The packet was still there—parchment sealed in dark wax, edges worn smooth from her restless touch. She hadn't remembered it when she gave Corin the scrolls. Not until yesterday in the war room, when the Book's light had burned across the table and something in her mind jolted. Since then, the weight of it pressed like a stone against her ribs.

"I don't even know why I kept it," she admitted, her voice low. "It didn't look important. Just another scrap of the Knighthood's hoard. But I didn't hand it over. Not that night. Not even when I remembered."

Virellan's wings shifted, translucent edges humming faint with crackle. *Your hands do not keep what your heart has already judged useless. You knew, Stormheart, even if you will not name it.*

Val shook her head, tightening her fist around the packet through the fabric. "Then why did I forget? Why now?"

Because threads wait until the weave is ready, Virellan said simply. Her tail lashed once, lightning flickering faint across her scales. *This one was not meant for Corin. You carried it past that choice for a reason. You already know who it belongs to.*

The name surfaced before she tried to stop it. "Kaden."

Virellan's gaze stayed fixed on her, steady as the storm. *Yes. Earth steadies what water uncovers. Give it to him, and the thread will find its place.*

Val pressed the packet close, the wax seal cold under her palm. She didn't understand why she hadn't let it go before, but the truth settled in her chest now. Not hers. His.

She straightened, the mist thinning from the air around her. "The next time I see him," she said quietly, steady. "I'll give it to Kaden."

Good, Virellan rumbled, the sound rolling like distant thunder. *Storms do not keep what is meant for the earth.*

Val allowed herself the barest smile as she left the training ring, the weight in her pocket no lighter, but no longer hers alone to bear.

◈ ☽ ⚡ ☾ ◈

Dusk was approaching and the courtyard was thinning with footsteps when Orren lingered again, silver gaze following the circle as they dispersed. He didn't need to be seen to take stock—he never did. Watching was the work, and the habit.

For weeks, the pattern around her had tugged at him like an unfinished map. Cam at the center, Wyatt her tether, Kaden her counterweight. The shape was there, but the weave was not yet closed. He had written it once in his journal: Incomplete. Fractured.

Now, though—

Tessa walked beside Cam, shoulders squaring more firmly each day, Brontheus' presence humming steady in her stride. And Val... Val's quiet was different. He caught the way her hand brushed her coat pocket, guarded, like a weight she hadn't chosen to carry but refused to set down.

The air around them tightened, humming with the dragons' awareness.

There, Orren thought, a steady line forming where there had been absence. *The missing pieces.*

And yet... the map still didn't feel whole. The circle was stronger now, undeniable, but some part of him knew another thread had yet to be named.

He should have turned away then, written his report, filed their strengths as liabilities. Observe. Confirm. Report. Capture. That was the order.

But his feet didn't move.

It was her again—the girl they called chosen. He tracked the line of her profile in the fading light, the way her voice carried low when she spoke, how even her silences seemed to draw others nearer. He told himself it was vigilance, nothing more. That he only lingered because she was the variable in the pattern.

But the Veil between them whispered differently—a recognition he couldn't trace or trust.

And yet, as the courtyard emptied, he stood a moment longer, a faint tug he couldn't name threading quiet through his chest.

It felt, uncomfortably, like falling.

Not into her—not into anything so simple. Falling into the space she carried with her, the center she created without meaning to.

His chest gave a shallow hitch, the kind that came when balance shifted without warning. His feet stayed planted, but some part of him swayed all the same, as if the ground had tilted under his weight. Even his breath slipped out uneven, sharper than he meant.

He told himself it was vigilance, nothing more. A hunter reading the pattern of his prey. But the longer he stood, the less it resembled a hunt at all.

The courtyard lay empty now, quiet as the mountains themselves, yet the pull didn't fade when she was gone. It lingered, threading through his chest like a wire he hadn't seen until he was already caught.

Incomplete, his mind supplied—the word he had written in the margin weeks ago. Fractured. And yet, somehow, not without gravity.

Orren turned at last, cloak catching the wind. He left the courtyard behind, but the weight of that missing piece walked with him into the dark.

The Keep had long since fallen silent, save for the occasional crackle of embers in the hearth. Outside, snow whispered against the stone walls, blanketing the world in cold quiet.

But inside one chamber, the glow of flickering candlelight burned late into the night.

Kaden stirred from restless sleep and rose quietly, the weight of the day's revelations pressing heavy on his mind. The voices and faces of the group lingered behind his closed eyes, but it was Cam's—the way she'd carried the burden of old truths—that pulled at him most.

Drawn by a quiet urgency, he found Val and Cam still bent over scattered notes and faded parchments, piecing together the fragile remnants of the Book of Unbinding and the scrolls.

Val looked up as Kaden approached, offering a faint, tired smile.

"I kept something," she said, sliding a sealed packet across the table. "From the Knighthood vault. I had it hidden since the Capital captured us."

Her fingers returned to her notes, eyes focused but weary.

Kaden's gaze lingered on the packet for a moment—the cold weight of history pressing heavy in his chest—before he carefully broke the wax seal.

The faint crackle echoed in the quiet room as the smell of old parchment rose, and he unfolded the brittle pages.

The first line read like an accusation.

Lira Valehart – Echo Flame Candidate 3A

Status: Key Compatible.

Kaden's stomach clenched. He already knew the Capital tracked bloodlines, but seeing his mother's name written like a project, like an asset, made his pulse quicken.

He turned the page.

Ben Miles – Stabilization Potential – Auxiliary Line

Status: Deceased.

Kaden stared at the word. His grip tightened on the paper. They didn't even know the truth.

The old spell—Ben and Anthony's desperate gambit to keep Cam safe—had worked. To the Capital, Ben was dead. Anthony Lyte had been listed as Cam's father in the official ledgers, and the bloodline records had followed that lie.

But the next page...

Isabella Layton – Class: Singular

Acquisition Recommended – Candidate Merge: Lyte Line.

Kaden's breath left him in a slow exhale. He could see the plan, cold and calculated, etched in ink decades old.

Ben and Isabella were never supposed to be together. Isabella was meant to follow the Lyte line, clean and simple, her rare elemental alignment folded neatly into the Capital's plan.

But they had fallen in love anyway. Ben had lied about his blood, hidden his mage heritage just to bond with Skylith. For a while, it had worked.

And then Cam was born.

The ledgers didn't just track—they predicted. Planned. Designed. Her birth wasn't an accident to the Capital. She was a merge, the culmination of everything they were trying to create.

His eyes flicked to another file labeled "Valehart Twins."

Wyatt's file was marked "Unstable—Repressant Recommended."

Kaden's chest tightened. Even knowing the spell, even knowing the truth now, seeing it in writing chilled him.

Cam wasn't just a person to the Capital.

She was a blueprint.

A question gnawed at him—how much did she really know? And what would she do with the truth?

He glanced toward the empty corner of the room where Val and Cam had been earlier, but they had left some time ago.

Swallowing the heaviness in his throat, Kaden folded the documents carefully and rose.

He had to find Cam.

There were things they needed to talk about.

It didn't take him long to guess where she'd gone—he rarely had to. When the weight pressed too heavy, when silence became her shield, she always drifted to the same place. The watchtower had become her refuge, and because he knew her, he knew he'd find her there.

Still, as his boots carried him through the frost, he felt the faint tug of hesitation. Knowing someone this well could feel like stepping too close to a flame—comforting, but dangerous if he lingered.

The frost had silvered every stone, biting through his gloves as he approached. Mist coiled low over the forest, ghosting through the trees like the breath of some sleeping giant.

She stood with her cloak tugged tight around her shoulders, the wind threading her dark hair, staring out at the endless gray horizon.

He cleared his throat softly, voice low in the cold. "Cam."

She glanced back, and even in the weak light, he saw the strain around her eyes.

"I read it all," he said. His voice sounded like it belonged to someone else. "The blood ledgers, the experiments... they've been doing this for longer than I thought. A thousand years of planning, of watching bloodlines, of waiting for someone like you. Like... us."

Cam's lips parted, but no words came. She turned fully toward him, eyes shining with a mix of fear and disbelief. "So... they picked our blood like ingredients?" Her voice cracked. "Mixed and measured and just... waited?"

He nodded once, throat tight. "Yeah. But—" He took a step closer, his breath a faint cloud between them. "If you were made, it wasn't by them. They only tried to claim you after. You... you feel like something older. Bigger. Like the Veil remembered you before they even knew your name."

For a moment, neither of them spoke. The wind moaned against the stones. The truth lay between them, sharp and cold as the frost.

Cam's hands trembled at her sides before she reached out and took his, her grip firm but fleeting. "I don't want to be a project, Kaden," she whispered. "I just... want to be me."

There was no fire in it, only exhaustion—and a fragile honesty she rarely let anyone see.

"I know," he said. And he did. Maybe more than anyone.

For a heartbeat, the air shifted. The way she looked at him—raw, unguarded—felt like more than trust. It made something in his chest lurch, sharp and unfamiliar, as if the ground tilted beneath him.

He crushed the thought as soon as it formed. No. That wasn't what this was. Not for them. Cam was his anchor, his sister in all but blood. They had carried each other too far, seen too much, for it to ever be anything else.

Still, when he spoke, his voice came rougher than he intended. "I know. And you are. More than they'll ever be able to define."

After a long beat, she released his hand and turned away, footsteps whispering across the icy stone as she walked along the wall. Kaden stayed where he was, watching her disappear into the mist, the weight of a millennium pressing against his chest.

He leaned against the cold stone of the watchtower, letting the frost bite through his gloves, grounding him in the present.

A thousand years. A thousand years of Caerthalen playing gods with bloodlines, of people like his mother reduced to a line in a ledger.

He closed his eyes and saw the names again:

Lira Valehart – Key Compatible.

Wyatt Valehart – Unstable—Repressant Recommended.

Camomile Layton – Singular Merge.

Not people—entries.

He thought of Wyatt asleep in the barracks, unaware that his whole life was written like a caution in some long-forgotten project file. He thought of Cam walking into the mist, carrying a weight that was never supposed to be hers.

Kaden's stomach turned. He couldn't shake the feeling that all of this—their blood, their bonds, even their dragons—was part of something older, something that remembered them before they were ever born.

A shiver went through him that had nothing to do with the cold.

He pushed off the wall, thoughts already spiraling. He needed to write it all down before the dread swallowed him whole.

Kaden lingered a moment longer at the watchtower, the frost biting through his gloves, the weight of the ledgers pressing against his chest. The mist below curled and shifted, restless as his thoughts. At last, he turned from the wall, boots crunching over the frozen stones as he made his way back through the Keep's silent corridors.

The barracks were dark when he slipped inside the room he shared with Wyatt. It was dark except for a single candle sputtering on the desk, its light carving restless shadows across the walls.

Wyatt slept on, his breathing slow and steady beneath the heavy blanket, one arm hanging over the edge of his bunk. Kaden sat at the small desk, hunched over a scatter of papers, his own reflection flickering in the windowpane.

He scribbled everything he knew, his handwriting jagged and uneven:

Lira Valehart – his mother – the Capital's "Echo Flame Candidate."

Wyatt, flagged "Unstable—Repressant Recommended."

Cam, a merge the Capital claimed like they had built her themselves.

A cold shiver ran through him. They had all been pieces on the board long before they were born.

Kaden's gaze drifted to his brother, to the untroubled rise and fall of Wyatt's chest. Did Wyatt even realize how deep the Capital's claws went? That they had studied their blood like a weapon blueprint?

The memory of the Veilbind Fragment burned in his mind:

'Not power, but healing. Not force, but wholeness.'

If Cam was the answer... why did it all feel like a warning?

Kaden stared at the single document he couldn't bring himself to keep—the one with Wyatt's name scrawled across the top, cold ink declaring him "Unstable."

The fire in the small stone hearth was little more than embers. He fed the paper in slowly, watching the flames bite and curl it to ash. Wyatt shifted in his sleep but didn't wake.

The firelight flickered across Kaden's face, catching the sharp line of his jaw and the set of his mouth. A vow, silent and unshakable: They would never touch his brother. Not while he breathed.

He rose and crossed to the frost-edged window. Beyond the snowy courtyard, the mountains rose like jagged teeth against the starlit Veil. Somewhere out there, history was stirring, trying to remember itself.

If the world wanted to remember us as weapons... I'll make it remember us on our own terms.

◈ ☽⚡☾ ◈

The chamber was hushed but not silent. Wax dripped in slow beads down the candles, their smoke curling faint and bitter in the still air. The fire in the hearth had burned low, leaving only the occasional crackle and the smell of charred oak. Pages lay scattered across the war table, edges frayed, ink faded but stubborn.

Val rubbed her tired eyes, the words on the page blurring until she forced herself to focus. Cam had left for air an hour ago, but Val stayed, turning the parchment back toward the candlelight. The Book of Unbinding glimmered faintly, threads of silver ink catching like veins under skin.

Her gaze snagged again on the fractured lines they had skimmed too quickly earlier. She whispered them under her breath:

"Two Seals broken. Two yet bound. The Third in shadow, the Fourth in flame..."

Her brow furrowed. Slowly, the weight of it pressed down. "Not two seals total," she whispered, voice catching in the empty chamber. "Four."

She sat back hard, heart pounding. Four Seals. Four scrolls. The war table suddenly felt colder beneath her hands, the parchment heavier than it should be.

Val glanced at the door Cam had gone through, half-tempted to run after her. But no—Cam needed rest. They all did.

"This can't wait," she murmured instead, gathering the Book carefully into her arms. Her thumb brushed over the sigil, still faintly pulsing in her vision like an echo she couldn't blink away.

She blew out the candles one by one until only shadows remained, her own voice lingering in the silence:

"Four seals. Four scrolls. Corin has to know."

With that, she slipped into the hall, her steps quick and sure, carrying the truth straight to him.

Chapter 15: The Archivum

The courtyard was silver with frost when Wyatt stepped outside, breath misting in the sharp winter air. Snow dusted the walls of Haldrin's Keep, the sun just cresting the peaks. Kaden was already there, sitting on the low stone wall near the gate, cloak pulled tight but hood down, his hair tousled like he hadn't bothered to sleep.

Wyatt frowned, walking over. "You get any sleep last night?"

Kaden shook his head once, eyes on the pale forest beyond. "No. But I'm fine."

Wyatt didn't believe him for a second. He could see the tension in his brother's jaw, the way his hands flexed restlessly against the cold stone.

"You're not fine," Wyatt said, quieter this time. "You're doing that thing where you disappear into your head."

Kaden didn't respond right away. His gaze flicked toward the Keep, where Corin's messenger had just left. "We've been summoned. Corin wants us in the war room at noon."

Wyatt exhaled, rubbing the back of his neck. "So, we're doing this today."

Kaden stood, his movement stiff like the weight of last night hadn't left him. "Yeah. Today."

Wyatt studied him for a beat, unease stirring in his chest. Whatever kept Kaden awake last night wasn't leaving him alone now. He thought about asking—but the words stuck.

Some walls, he'd learned, his brother had to lower on his own.

The war room was quiet but heavy with the smell of burnt wax and old parchment. Morning light slanted through the high windows, catching on the sigils etched into the long oak table. Wyatt leaned against the doorway, rubbing the last traces of sleep from his eyes. Kaden was already seated, elbows braced on the table, looking like he hadn't closed his eyes all night.

Corin stood at the head of the table, his hands clasped behind his back, the Book of Unbinding open before him. Two Veilbind scrolls rested beside it, their unfurled edges curling like the breath of something alive.

"We were wrong," Corin said without preamble. His voice was calm, but there was a current beneath it. "The fragments and the Book don't speak of two seals. They speak of four."

Wyatt straightened. "Four?"

Corin's finger traced a line of faded script along the Book's margin, the sigil flickering faintly in response. "The Third and Fourth Seals. The text names the Forgotten Archivum—an old Caerthalen outpost east of Haldrin's Keep, left to rot with its secrets."

Val, standing just behind Cam, tilted her head. "I thought the old Archivum was destroyed during the last purge."

"So did Caerthalen," Corin replied. "Or so they claimed. But this—" he gestured to the sigil pulsing softly on the page "—says otherwise. The Book recognizes its echo. That means there are still records there... and likely, one of the missing scrolls."

A tense silence followed. Wyatt felt the weight of the words settle in his chest. Another scroll. Another piece of the truth waiting in the dark.

Ben's arms were crossed, his expression like stone. "If the Capital left anything behind, it wasn't by mistake. Places like that... they're built to keep secrets buried."

Wyatt glanced at Kaden, who hadn't said a word. His brother's eyes were shadowed, unreadable, but his fingers drummed once against the table before stilling.

Corin's gaze swept the group. "You will leave at first light. No one goes down there alone. If the Archivum still holds the Third Scroll, then what's buried in those halls could change everything."

The room seemed to hold its breath, and for the first time, Wyatt felt the faint pull of inevitability—like the ground beneath them was already tilting toward whatever waited in that ruin.

◈ ☽ ⚡ ☾ ◈

The courtyard was hushed under winter's weight, the snow softening every sound. The gray light of dawn approached, and Wyatt's boots crunched lightly as he crossed toward the path to the roost to check Sael's harness one last time.

Movement near the old fountain caught his eye.

Tessa sat on the frosted stone edge, her cloak drawn close, while Alex crouched in front of her. His hands wrapped around hers, thumbs brushing over her knuckles. Even from a distance, Wyatt could feel the intimacy of the moment—small and quiet, the kind that felt private even in open air.

"I'm not letting anything take me from you," Alex murmured, voice low but clear in the cold air. "We'll be together. Always."

Tessa's breath misted as she leaned forward, her forehead almost touching his. "Promise?"

"Promise," Alex said, steady this time.

Wyatt felt something twist in his chest. Maybe it was the way Tessa's shoulders eased for the first time in days—or maybe it was the way Alex's words rang a little too perfect, like a script he'd rehearsed. A thread of unease lingered, and Wyatt turned away before they saw him watching.

The path to the dragon roost climbed along the Keep's outer wall. Frost bit at his fingers, and the cold made his thoughts sharper, more restless. He found Kaden and Cam already there, the wind tugging at their cloaks.

"You ready?" Wyatt asked, scanning Kaden's face. His brother's eyes were rimmed in shadow, and the set of his jaw was too rigid.

Kaden shrugged like it was nothing. "Didn't sleep much. I'm fine."

Wyatt arched a brow. "You don't look fine."

"I said I'm fine." Kaden's tone was casual, dismissive—but his hand lingered a second too long on Sael's saddle strap, knuckles tight.

Wyatt let it drop. He wasn't sure which weighed more on his brother: the sleepless night or the secrets he wasn't ready to share.

Sael's tail flicked, smoke curling from his nostrils, while Sylithra's golden-veined wings flexed in the dim morning light, scattering frost into the air. Their unease whispered through the stone—dragons knew when old places were about to wake.

Cam stood with one hand pressed to Sylithra's muzzle, her dark hair tossed by the wind. Frost clung to the edges of her cloak, and the air around her felt... alive. Like the storm she carried inside was coiled just beneath her skin, silent but undeniable.

Wyatt's pulse quickened. He hadn't told anyone how much he noticed these moments—the quiet gravity in her stance, the way the world seemed to bend slightly toward her. And then there was Orren, always too close, always watching her in a way Wyatt couldn't stand. The thought of leaving for the Archivum with that gnawing jealousy in his chest made his jaw tighten.

Focus, he told himself. *Mission first.*

Cam glanced up as if sensing his presence, and for a fleeting moment, the tension in him eased. It wasn't just relief—it felt like his pulse had synced with hers for a heartbeat, one rhythm before the world remembered to separate them.

Ben's voice broke the quiet. "Ready?" He and Val were finishing the gear check—rope coils, satchels of salt and crystal charms, lanterns meant to cut through places where light didn't want to stay.

"Wards like these don't fade—they wait," Ben said as he handed Kaden a small satchel. "They'll taste your blood or drag up what you've buried, and they don't care which breaks you first."

Kaden's grip tightened on the satchel, the leather creaking under his hand. Wyatt caught the flicker in his brother's eyes—too sharp, too fast—before Kaden looked away. His jaw locked, like he was bracing against something Wyatt couldn't see.

Corin appeared last, cloak snapping in the wind, his gaze sharp on the horizon.

"Remember," he said evenly. "Do not linger."

The words chilled Wyatt, settling heavy in his gut.

They mounted in silence. The snow crunched under Sael's talons as the dragons crouched to leap. Wind bit at Wyatt's face, pulling at his hair, and the Keep dropped away beneath them. Mountains stretched pale and sharp against the horizon.

Whatever waited in the Archivum, it wasn't sleeping.

◈ ☽ ⚡ ☾ ◈

The flight east was silent but for the wind and the occasional rumble of dragon wings. Frosted peaks cut sharp lines against the pale winter sky, and every shadowed valley seemed to watch them pass. Wyatt leaned low against Sael's neck, the dragon's scales cold against his gloves, the rhythm of flight steadying his thoughts.

Below, the forest stretched dark and skeletal, its ravine webbed with frozen streams. When Ben raised a hand, signaling descent, the dragons angled their wings and dropped into the shadows.

The ravine swallowed them.

Skylith landed first, his weight shaking frost from the trees. Sael followed, talons crunching over the frozen ground, and Sylithra's golden-veined wings folded close as she coiled beside the cliffside, tail flicking. Virellan brought up the rear, scales glinting like tempered steel in the low light.

Wyatt slid from the saddle, boots meeting stone that felt... wrong. Too cold, as if it had been waiting.

The entrance wasn't obvious—just a jagged split in the cliffside, half-covered in ice and creeping moss. Ancient sigils were carved into the stone, faded but not dead. Wyatt felt them like a shiver at the base of his skull, as though the rock itself was whispering.

"Wards," Ben muttered, stepping forward. "They're old... but not gone."

Cam joined him, her hand brushing the stone. Val followed, the fragment's words on her tongue. Together, their voices wove the line Corin had given them, the syllables thrumming in the cold air.

The cliff shuddered. Light flared along the old sigils—first white, then faintly gold—and with a sound like stone exhaling, the entrance split wider. A breath of air rolled out, stale and heavy with the taste of iron.

"After you," Kaden murmured, but his voice was tight.

Inside, the Archivum was a skeleton of its former self. Shattered stone littered the floor, and the walls were charred with old sigils, some half-melted as if the place had tried to burn itself alive. Rusted chains hung from the ceiling, and farther down, Wyatt caught the glint of iron bars—cages large enough to hold a dragon... or something worse.

A prickle ran up the back of his neck.

He reached out, letting his hand brush the blackened wall. Cold bled into his palm—then something else.

A ripple, deep and wrong, ran through him.

Blood on marble. Screams swallowed by silence. A memory that wasn't his, thrumming through the stone like the ruin itself wanted him to remember.

Wyatt jerked his hand back, heart hammering. The air suddenly felt too close, too heavy—and every shadow seemed to lean in, listening.

Sael rumbled uneasily outside, and the sound carried through the stone like a drumbeat. Virellan hissed low, wings shifting, and even Skylith's heavy footsteps thudded in agitation.

"You feel that?" Wyatt muttered.

Cam's gaze flicked to him. Her hand lingered on the wall now, her brow furrowing as though she was hearing something he couldn't.

"It remembers," she said quietly.

Kaden's voice was sharper than usual, breaking the tension. "Then let's get what we came for and get out."

Wyatt swallowed, tearing his eyes from the blackened chains overhead.

The ruin breathed around them, not abandoned but alive, like it had been holding its silence for this moment.

It was waiting.

◈ ☽ ⚡ ☾ ◈

The ruin breathed wrong. Every draft slid too deep, carrying weight it shouldn't. Kaden slowed a fraction, lantern light slanting across chains that swayed though no one touched them. Shadows pooled thick in the corners, not his but close enough that his own stirred restlessly in answer.

He pressed them down, jaw tight. Not here. Not now.

But something in the dark pressed back, not foreign but familiar—like it knew his shape and waited for his shadow to answer.

The walls didn't just remember, as Cam had said—they recognized. Like the ledgers had, like the neat lines of ink that had turned his family into entries. His mother: Candidate. His brother: Unstable. Himself: Unmarked—yet never free, never unseen.

A faint sound slid through the ruin—not the groan of settling stone, not the clatter of falling rubble. Softer. Closer. Like something dragging a breath along the wall.

His shadows prickled in answer, coiling sharp against his skin as if to warn him. Shapes stirred at the edge of his reach, too fluid, too deliberate to be echoes.

Kaden clenched his fists until his gloves creaked. *No.* He pressed them down, refusing to listen. Listening too closely always left him skirting the edge of something he didn't want to name. Something that felt too much like the Veilborn.

He told himself it was nothing. Just ruin settling. Just stone.

And yet the unease crawled deeper, setting its hook behind his ribs and refusing to let go. The darkness slithered farther than torchlight could chase, curling like smoke through cracks in the stone. Even with his shadows suppressed, he felt it hovering at the edges—watching. Waiting.

His stomach knotted. He knew what it meant to be tracked, to be marked. And this place had the same patience as the hunters who had once stalked his family.

The thought came sharp, unbidden: *If the Capital had built a tomb for truth, they would have left something to guard it.*

Kaden flexed his fingers until his gloves creaked, forcing his breathing steady. He told himself it was just stone, just shadow. But the dread lodged beneath his ribs said otherwise. A shape lingered at the edge of his vision—faint, formless—but every time he turned his head, it slipped back into the dark.

He didn't speak. If he gave it voice, it would be real.

◈ ☽ ⚡ ☾ ◈

Their descent carried on, boots whispering over stone as if even sound feared to linger.

Wyatt stayed close to Kaden, his hand brushing the hilt of his sword, though he doubted steel would matter in a place like this. Cam moved ahead, lantern raised, guided by a pull he didn't fully understand—but felt all the same. Her light spilled across shattered sigils and walls that seemed to lean closer with every step, as if the Archivum itself were holding its breath.

The descent twisted through spiraling staircases and low corridors lined with rusted cages, chains swaying faintly in the drafts that crawled through the stone. Remnants of research tables clung to corners, their broken glass glinting in the lantern light. Wyatt's stomach turned. These weren't the tools of knowledge. They were the tools of control.

His earlier vision—the blood on marble, the screams swallowed by silence—clung to him like a shadow that wouldn't let go.

"Feels like the walls are watching us," he muttered, voice rough in the stillness.

"They are," Cam said softly. She glanced over her shoulder, the lantern catching the silver flecks in her blue-gray eyes, sparking like something alive. "Places like this... they remember."

Wyatt felt that look settle in his chest, sharp and unspoken.

Kaden's jaw tightened, but he didn't reply. His shoulders were rigid, heavy with the weight of thoughts Wyatt couldn't reach. He wanted to ask, to press, but the words stayed stuck in his throat.

Hours bled away in the dark, the only measure of time the slow guttering of their lanterns and the ache in their bodies. The Archivum gave no sense of day or night, only endless descent. By the time the passages widened again, it felt as if the day itself had been swallowed.

Then Cam slowed.

The corridor spilled into a circular chamber, its floor inlaid with black-and-gold stone cracked by time. At the center rose a mirrored obsidian pedestal, untouched by dust or decay. Faint sigils glimmered across its surface—blood-red and sharp-edged, alive in the lamplight.

Ben swore under his breath. "Trueblood wards. I haven't seen these since..." He stopped short, his jaw hardening.

Wyatt's pulse quickened. "Since the Capital?"

Ben only nodded, his silence answer enough.

"This is it," Cam said. Her voice didn't waver, but Wyatt felt the tension coil in the air like a bowstring.

She stepped onto the inlaid stone. The air grew heavier, pressing against Wyatt's skin, thick with a hum of magic that vibrated in his teeth. The sigils flared in answer, threads of color racing over the mirrored surface—gold, crimson, and icy silver-blue.

It was calling them.

"Together," Cam said quietly, lifting her hand.

Kaden hesitated only a heartbeat before placing his palm against the case. Wyatt followed, the cold biting into his skin.

The case split with a soft hiss, revealing the Third Veilbind Scroll. The parchment unfurled as though it had been waiting, ink glimmering faintly in the lantern glow.

Chapter 16: The Guarded Truth

The world held its breath—then light erupted, golden, crimson, and silver-blue, the colors coiling together like living veins.

Three lines pulsed brighter than the rest:

"Three shall awaken what was sealed in silence.

One who breathes storm, one born of twin flame,

And one who carries the wound that never healed."

The words crawled over Wyatt's skin, heavy as a chain. His breath caught.

Him. Kaden. Cam.

Whatever this place had been, it had been waiting for them.

Then the scroll shifted, and beneath it, a second scroll wrapped in blue silk appeared, as if the case itself was surrendering secrets. Cam lifted it carefully and unrolled it.

The second half of the prophecy shimmered into the cold air:

"One shall awaken who was never meant to sleep.

Born of hollow purpose and endless night,

he will carry what was left behind—

a crown of ash, a name unspoken.

The flame and the mirror will meet, and in that meeting-

A chill threaded down Wyatt's spine. He felt Kaden tense beside him, and for a moment, even Cam's breathing caught.

Before any of them could speak, something slid free from beneath the silk.

The third Veilbind fragment.

Smaller. Torn. Its edges jagged, as if it had been ripped away rather than sealed. The script along its surface flickered unevenly, weaker than the rest, but no less heavy.

Wyatt frowned. "It's incomplete."

Cam's voice was a whisper. "The rest... it matches what we found in the Knighthood ruins. The vault... four weeks ago. This is the continuation but it's not all there."

The chamber seemed to close around them, the air thick with the weight of what they'd awakened.

Whatever this prophecy meant... it was no longer just words on a scroll.

The chamber's glow faded slowly, leaving only the weak light of their lanterns and the faint shimmer of the newly uncovered scrolls.

No one spoke for a long moment. Even the air seemed heavy with the weight of the prophecy.

Wyatt forced himself to take a step back from the pedestal, but the words still crawled under his skin. Three shall awaken. Him. Kaden. Cam.

The words didn't feel like destiny. They felt like a verdict.

He glanced at his brother. Kaden hadn't moved. His shoulders were tight, jaw locked, eyes fixed on the floor like he could will the stone to swallow him whole.

"Hey," Wyatt said quietly, his voice echoing off the chamber walls. "What's going on with you?"

"I'm fine," Kaden muttered.

Wyatt's hand closed around his brother's shoulder, firm enough to make him look up. The shadows under his eyes were darker than ever, and his usual sharpness was dulled by exhaustion.

"No, you're not," Wyatt pressed. "You've been off since the other night. What's going on, Kade? You barely sleep. You won't look me in the eye. I'm not letting this go."

Kaden hesitated, his mouth opening—then closing. He raked a hand through his dark hair, exhaling sharply. For a moment, Wyatt thought he'd retreat into that wall of silence again. But finally, the words came out, low and raw:

"I read a blood ledger the other night that Val took from the knighthood ruins. I found a file on you."

Wyatt blinked. "...A file?"

"In the ledger," Kaden said, eyes flicking away. "Your name. Your... profile, I guess. The Capital keeps notes on bloodline subjects and potential candidates." His voice caught on the last word. "Yours was marked 'Unstable—Repressant Recommended.'"

The world seemed to tilt under Wyatt's feet. Unstable. The word burrowed into his chest like a shard of ice. The prophecy's lines throbbed in the back of his mind, and suddenly he could see himself in all the wrong ways—his power flaring when he couldn't control it, the anger he tried to bury, the way Cam sometimes looked at him like she wasn't sure what he might become.

"Unstable?" he repeated, the word scraping his throat. "What the hells does that even mean?"

"I don't know," Kaden admitted, his voice cracking with the effort of keeping it low. "But I wasn't about to let you see it. I burned it."

Wyatt recoiled like the words had hit him. "You... burned it?"

"I was protecting you—"

"Protecting me?" The sharpness in Wyatt's voice cut through the chamber's still air. "You think I couldn't handle it? You think I don't already know something's wrong with me?"

Kaden flinched, and for the first time in days, Wyatt saw the raw, unguarded exhaustion in his brother's face.

"It's not that," Kaden said finally, his voice quieter. "I just... I didn't want the Capital's words in your head. You're not what they say you are. I couldn't let you carry that."

Wyatt turned away, a tight ache winding through his chest. He didn't know if he was angrier at the Capital for the label... or at Kaden for keeping it from him. And maybe, just maybe, he was angry at himself—for fearing that the Capital was right.

The lantern's light flickered against the mirrored walls, their fractured reflections standing like silent witnesses between them. In every broken shard, Wyatt saw a version of himself he didn't recognize. Or maybe he did.

Wyatt swallowed hard. "You should've told me," he said finally, his voice low but sharp. "I don't need protecting. Not from you."

◈ ☽ ⚡ ☾ ◈

Wyatt's voice still rang against the mirrored walls when a sound slid through the chamber. Not echo—something else. A scrape, low and deliberate, dragging along stone.

The lanternlight shuddered. Shadows thickened in the far archway, too dense, too fluid to be natural.

Kaden's stomach dropped. He knew that presence. The same wrongness that had brushed his senses earlier—now pulling itself into shape.

A form peeled from the wall. Smoke and bone twined together, veins of pale fire running through a body that was neither whole nor hollow. Its face was a blur, mouth stretched too wide, eyes burning with a faint, silvery light.

"Veilborn," Wyatt breathed—then stopped.

"No, not Veilborn," Kaden whispered. His shadows bristled sharp against his skin. "Something *made*."

The creature's voice came like a breath dragged through water. *"Unstable. Candidate. Merge."*

The words weren't spoken; they were remembered, dredged from the Archivum's walls.

"You don't leave without paying," it rasped, voice grave and wrong.

And then it lunged. Straight at him and Wyatt.

It moved faster than shadow. Kaden shoved Wyatt sideways, blade flashing out, but the blow skimmed smoke and caught only bone. Cold fire seared across his arm, and the shadows under his skin snapped in warning.

Another shape slithered from the far wall—its twin, same twisted veins of light. Two of them.

Kaden's chest clenched. His shadows screamed danger, but he forced them down. Not here. Not now. Not in front of them. He wouldn't become what he feared.

The air wanted to use him—shadow seeking flame, flame seeking storm—and he forced it back, teeth clenched.

The first creature raked claws across the stone, sparks flying. The second struck low, straight for him. Kaden staggered back—too slow—until a blade cut across the thing's side.

Wyatt.

His brother's hand caught his shoulder, steadying him. The anger from before still smoldered in Wyatt's eyes, but the strike was clean, his stance unshakable. He would bleed first before letting the thing touch him.

"Don't you dare drop on me now, Kade!" Wyatt barked, shoving him upright.

Kaden swallowed hard, shadows bristling at the edges of his control. Even with Wyatt furious at him, that bond held—unspoken, unbreakable. And it scared him how much he needed it.

The air split with heat and cold as magic clashed. Ben's sword met bone, sparks scattering. Val cut the angle, snapping a ribbon of water across its knees. Cam's power answered on instinct, not flame this time but molten earth—violet-black and searing, rolling down the same line in a torrent that split stone and hissed against Val's water. For a heartbeat the two elements didn't just meet—they braided, water and earth spiraling into steam so sharp it seared the creature's face.

The mist glowed, alive, sparking like a thread of something greater. Something Cam still couldn't name.

Cam's breath hitched, but there was no time to question it. The second creature barreled into her. Claws raked her side, white-hot pain flaring, but even as blood dampened her coat, the wound pulled itself together faster than it should. Her fire burned it closed, her body knitting almost as quickly as it tore.

Too fast.

It didn't feel like her fire alone—something else steadied the burn, as if the others' magic had answered hers without being called.

She staggered, hand pressing to her side, half-expecting it to tear open again. But it didn't. The skin was whole. Uneven, raw, but healed. Her chest tightened—not with relief, but with unease.

Val's voice cut through the steam: "Again!"

Together, their magic lashed across the chamber, keeping the creatures off balance while Ben drove his blade deep and Kaden's shadows struck sharp as knives.

One creature reeled back, hissing smoke, but the second was relentless. It slammed into Kaden, knocking him to the stone. Wyatt's chest lurched—rage drowning the chill of fear.

He drove his blade through the thing's ribs, dragging it off his brother with a shout that tore his throat raw. It shrieked, smoke unraveling, and Ben's strike finished the job—splintering bone, fire flaring as it dissolved into nothing.

The last creature staggered, hemmed in on all sides. Cam's violet fire and Val's water braided again, steadied this time by Kaden's shadows lashing sharp from the floor. Ben pressed in with his blade, and Wyatt felt Sael's voice stir in his chest like thunder in his blood: *Together.*

For a heartbeat, he felt not only Sael—but Cam, Kaden, Val, even Ben—threads pulling through him like a single breath shared across five hearts.

Wyatt struck high, Kaden's shadows struck low, Val's water coiled, Cam's fire seared violet-gold—and for a breath, all five threads wove into one. A single strike, braided of flame, shadow, steel, and storm.

The creature screamed as it was ripped apart, dissolving into steam and smoke that burned away into nothing. Its shriek broke apart into ash and steam, the sound snapping off so suddenly that the silence rang louder than before.

Wyatt lowered his blade, every muscle trembling. They were alive—but the Archivum had made its price clear.

And the worst part? He knew this wasn't the last time they'd pay it.

The silence held, heavy as the smoke they'd torn apart. Wyatt swallowed hard, throat raw.

He turned from the others, footsteps heavy as he started toward the far end of the chamber, each step echoing like a break in the silence.

The chamber stank of scorched stone and shadow-burn, the silence after the fight louder than the creatures' screams had been. Wyatt's arms ached from the weight of Sael's borrowed flame, and his chest still hammered with the memory of Cam hitting the ground and rising again too quickly, skin knitting as if she'd never been torn. Kaden's blood on the floor burned sharper in his mind than any wound of his own. And over it all, the prophecy crawling through his veins, the Capital's label gnawing at his mind, and his brother's secret lodged in his chest, Wyatt had never felt more alone.

Silence pressed close after the fight, heavier than the creatures' screams had been. The air was thick with things unsaid. Wyatt's footsteps echoed as he climbed the crumbling stairwell alone, leaving the mirrored walls and their fractured reflections behind.

The climb felt longer than the descent. Lantern light guttered against the stone, shadows stretching with every turn of the spiral. Time thinned in the dark, marked only by the rasp of his breath and the ache in his arms. By the time the stairwell began to open, the gray light of dusk had already drained to indigo. What little glow clung to the horizon was bruised and thin, sinking fast behind the trees.

The Archivum's upper corridors were colder, the stale air biting at his lungs. He followed the draft until it spilled into the open night, and the forest's silence pressed in on him. The ravine stretched below, its trees skeletal against the snow. Wyatt looked up at the dark sky. A break in the clouds let the stars cut through, cold and sharp, before vanishing again. He drew a long breath, steadying his pulse, though his thoughts refused to follow.

The dragons waited in the clearing, coiled shapes of shadow and frost, steam curling from their nostrils. Sael lifted his head as Wyatt approached, a low rumble rising in his chest—not hostile, just... aware.

Wyatt sank onto a slab of broken stone, the cold leeching through his coat. His thoughts wouldn't settle.

Unstable.

The word clawed at him, catching on every memory he didn't want to face: the times he'd lost control, the flare of magic he barely understood, the flashes of anger that scared even him. He wondered if Kaden had seen it all along—if Cam had too.

He stared at his hands, half-expecting to see something in them—some mark of what the Capital thought he was.

Footsteps crunched softly over frost behind him.

"I saw you leave," Cam said. Her voice was low, edged with concern. "That was dangerous. Could have been more creatures."

He didn't look up at first, just listened to the way the cold wind caught in her voice. When he finally glanced over, she was already settling beside him on the stone, whole again, coat drawn tight against the night. No trace of the wound that had cut her a while ago. That should have eased him. Instead, it only twisted tighter—a reminder of how different she was, how far beyond him she might already be.

Cam caught his look, and for a heartbeat, the tension in her eyes eased. A small, wry smile tugged at her mouth.

"Yeah," she murmured, glancing back toward the ruin. "I think we got what was left in there."

The words weren't much, just a shard of humor tossed into the cold, but it was enough. Wyatt felt the corners of his mouth twitch, the start of a smile he couldn't quite hold back. Small. Brief. But real.

For a long time, only the forest breathed. The distant drip of melting ice echoed from the ravine walls.

"I saw it too," Cam said quietly. "In the scroll. Us. The three of us."

Wyatt's throat tightened. He wanted to ask if she was afraid, but what slipped out instead was sharp, cracked at the edges. "Feels like it's been waiting for me to screw up all along."

Cam turned her head toward him, the faintest furrow between her brows. "You're not what they say you are."

He almost laughed, bitter and quiet. "You don't even know what they say." The words came harsher than he meant, but he didn't pull them back.

"I don't have to," she said simply. "I know you."

Something in his chest eased, just a fraction. He hadn't realized how much he needed someone to say that out loud. Still, the jealousy burned—Orren's quiet watch, Kaden's steadied place beside her. Wyatt clenched his hands tighter in his lap, as if he could hold himself together by force alone.

After a beat, Cam looked down at her hands. "I think about it sometimes... if I was made for this. Not born. Like I'm just... some piece the Capital left behind to play their game." Her voice was soft, but steady. "But maybe that doesn't matter. Maybe we make it ours by choosing each other anyway."

Wyatt let out a short, shaky laugh, his words low. "Choosing each other... you make it sound so damn simple." His voice cracked, but he didn't care. "I'm not sure I'm someone worth choosing."

Cam's gaze lifted, steady, cutting through the frost. "You are. Even when you don't believe it."

The words sank into the quiet like the first hint of warmth after a long freeze.

Wyatt turned his head toward her, the faintest, unspoken gratitude in his gaze. He didn't know if he could believe in destiny—but sitting here with her, the cold and the fear felt a little more bearable.

The cold had settled deep into Wyatt's bones by the time footsteps crunched across the snow-dusted stone behind him. He didn't move.

Cam sat with him in the dark, the silence between them saying more than words could. Her last thought lingered like a quiet flame: Maybe we make it ours by choosing each other anyway.

He wasn't sure if she meant the prophecy, or their lives, or the pieces of themselves they were both afraid to face. Maybe all of it.

A voice broke through the quiet.

"Come on," Ben said as he approached. His tone wasn't sharp, but it carried the weight of command all the same. "You've all done enough for one night. Let's get you all home before the Archivum decides it isn't finished."

Wyatt turned to see the others emerging from the Archivum's mouth—Kaden with his hood pulled low, the sleeve of his coat still dark with half-dried blood, Val adjusting the satchel that held the scroll, Ben's lantern throwing harsh gold across their tired faces. The ruin behind them was silent now, its secrets spent, but its weight lingered on Wyatt's shoulders.

Cam rose first, brushing frost from her coat, and offered a hand to pull Wyatt to his feet. He took it without thinking.

The dragons stirred at their approach, as if sensing the shift in purpose. Sael's talons flexed against the frozen earth, steam curling from his nostrils. Sylithra lowered her head for Cam to mount, the faint gold in her veins pulsing like a heartbeat in the dark.

Wyatt swung onto Sael's back and cast one last look at the Archivum. Even buried in shadow, the ruin seemed to watch them leave.

They rose into the winter sky, the wind sharp against his face. The world below shrank to pale mountains and black forest, the path home stretching toward the distant lights of Haldrin's Keep. Wyatt said nothing on the flight back. He couldn't—not with Kaden just ahead of him, silent and rigid in Virellan's saddle, the sleeve of his coat still stiff with blood, and the weight of the scroll like a second heartbeat in Val's satchel.

Haldrin's Keep welcomed them with the glow of lanterns and the bitter bite of night air. Snow swirled in the courtyard as they dismounted, the echo of the Archivum's chill still clinging to Wyatt's skin.

Inside the war room, Corin and Ben moved with sharp efficiency. The third scroll was laid across the table, its ink glimmering faintly in the candlelight. Beside it, the Book of Unbinding thrummed softly, sigils along its spine responding to the new fragment.

"Another piece," Ben murmured, tracing the lines with a gloved hand. "And another warning we don't fully understand." His jaw tightened. "Places like that don't give up truths without taking something back."

Corin's eyes lingered on Cam, a quiet gravity in his expression. He motioned her aside, speaking low enough that only she could hear:

"If this fragment is right... you may be the balance, Camomile. But balance doesn't mean stillness. It means knowing what must be broken—and what must be kept."

Cam nodded once, but Wyatt saw the flicker in her eyes before she turned back to the table. She carried the weight of the words silently, as she always did.

The war room had emptied but for three. Corin stood with his hands clasped behind his back, eyes still on the fragment's ink. Cam lingered by the table, coat drawn close, the faint gold in her veins dim but not gone.

"It wasn't just Veilborn," Corin said at last, his voice low. "That thing in the Archivum... it was made. A fusion of shadow and the Hollow's corruption. Caerthalen's hand is in this."

Cam's jaw tightened. She glanced down at her arm, where only hours ago the creature's claws had torn deep. Not even a scar remained. Her fingers brushed the skin, testing it, as though searching for proof that it had been real.

"It shouldn't have healed that fast," she murmured.

Corin's gaze flicked to her, unreadable. "No. It shouldn't have."

Ben's stomach clenched. He wanted to speak—to reassure her, to tell her she was strong enough, more than enough—but the words stuck. What comfort could he offer when even he didn't understand what she was becoming?

Corin laid a hand on the scroll, his tone deliberate. "Whatever Caerthalen built down there, it was meant to guard truths they didn't want unearthed. And you, Camomile... you are healing like no ledger ever predicted. That is no accident."

Cam met his eyes for a heartbeat, then lowered her gaze. She nodded once, silent, and slipped from the room.

Balance. Corin had spoken the word to Cam, but it clung to Ben too. Balance meant more than prophecy—it meant every lie he'd told, every name he'd buried to keep her safe. Isabella. Anthony. Cam's whole beginning twisted into ledgers and secrets. He had thought love enough to shield her. Tonight proved otherwise.

Corin lingered a moment longer, his hand resting on the edge of the table where the scroll lay. "The creatures weren't accidents," he said, voice low. "Caerthalen doesn't leave guardians without reason. Whatever they were... we should assume there are more." His gaze flicked briefly toward the door Cam had gone through, then back to Ben. "Keep her steady. I'll see to the rest."

He gathered his coat and left without waiting for an answer, the door closing with a muted thud.

Silence settled, heavy and close. Only the faint shimmer of the Book broke the dark. Ben exhaled, leaning against the table as Skylith's voice stirred like fire through the bond—

Skylith stirred at the edge of his mind, warmth brushing against the cold coil in his chest. *You did not fail her, Forgeheart. She stands because you carried her this far.*

"And where do I carry her now?" he muttered, voice low in the empty room. "Into the fire? Into their games?"

No answer came but the slow pulse of dragonfire down their bond. Skylith's certainty was iron, but Ben's hands still shook as he gathered the fragments from the table. Prophecy didn't keep her hidden. Prophecy didn't carve false names into ledgers or burn the truth to ash.

That had been him. And still, it hadn't been enough.

He closed the Book with a soft thud, the sound final as a door shutting. Whatever balance meant—whatever Cam had to break or keep—he knew one truth already. He would stand in the storm with her, even if it burned him clean through.

◈ ☽ ⚡ ☾ ◈

Later, long after the Keep had quieted, Wyatt found himself in the tower overlooking the frozen expanse below. Snow drifted across the battlements, and the wind hissed against stone.

His mind replayed the prophecy, line by line.

Three shall awaken what was sealed in silence...

And one who carries the wound that never healed.

The words gnawed at him. His hands curled against the cold stone of the parapet, knuckles aching.

The wound.

His mind tried to fit it to himself—every flare of temper he'd buried, every moment he'd lost control, every shadow of doubt Kaden or Cam might have seen. The Capital had called him Unstable, and part of him feared they were right.

But no. His chest tightened as he shoved the thought back. That wasn't who he was. He wasn't a curse. He wasn't some wound left festering in the world. He wouldn't let them—any of them—define him like that.

And yet, denial didn't silence the ache. Not when Orren's shadow lingered everywhere—his quiet watchfulness, the way Cam sometimes seemed to listen to him. Wyatt hated that it burned so sharp, hated that he didn't even understand the root of it. Was it just jealousy? Distrust? Or something deeper, older, that kept him circling Orren like an open wound he couldn't close?

He drew a sharp breath, forcing the cold air deep into his lungs. It didn't matter. What mattered was Cam—and the truth that still cut whenever he looked at her. She hadn't chosen him. Not yet. And he couldn't make her.

He had to let her decide, even if every part of him ached to just *say it,* to strip the silence away and lay himself bare. But he stayed quiet, fingers digging into stone, because the choice had to be hers.

The prophecy whispered in the back of his mind, a chain he refused to wear.

He was not the wound.

He couldn't be.

And yet the thought clung, sharp as frost, refusing to let him go.

Chapter 17: Catalyst

The next day, Wyatt said little. Last night he'd sworn he wasn't the wound; daylight frayed the vow until it felt like thread in his fist.

The hallways felt narrower than usual, the vaulted ceilings heavier. He caught glimpses of Kaden across the war room, but his brother might as well have been a stranger.

He lingered in the doorway instead, watching Cam and Val bent over the Book of Unbinding. The two of them worked in soft murmurs, gold light from the sigils dancing across their faces. Their fingers skimmed the fragile pages, moving in a rhythm that didn't need him.

Wyatt's chest tightened—the same cold twist as by the ravine, when her skin knit whole and he'd felt further from her than ever.

Even now, the prophecy made space for him. Three shall awaken... the wound that never healed.

But he didn't know if he belonged inside it—

...or if he was the flaw in it.

He turned away before anyone noticed him staring, boots carrying him toward the empty courtyard and the bite of the winter air.

◈ ☽ϟ☾ ◈

High above, in the frost-bitten roost, Sael stirred. His rider's thoughts pressed through the bond in uneven pulses—tight, jagged, raw.

He rumbled low, exhaling a coil of steam into the cold. The sensation in his chest wasn't quite anger and not quite fear. It was hollow.

Wyatt did not reach back. The bond felt muffled, like a torch smothered under stone.

He pulls away again, Sael thought, curling his claws against the beam. *But the shadow is not his to bear.*

A second mind brushed against his own: Sylithra, soft and thunder-tinged.

The wound walks in another's shape, she murmured, thoughts rippling like distant lightning. *But even so... he carries the ache of it.*

Sael's tail flicked, unease shivering along the rafters. Yet he did not sever the touch. Sylithra lingered close, their thoughts overlapping for a breath too long, and in that stillness a warmth pulsed—quiet, steady, almost instinctive. Not his. Not hers. Something shared.

Then we guard him still, Sael answered, his thoughts like the roll of a gathering storm. *Even when he cannot guard himself.*

The wind shifted. Somewhere deep in the roost, the dragons fell still, their shared breath rising in slow, pale clouds. The air tasted of snow—of old bonds, of storms yet unbroken—and of things coming undone.

Far below, another rumble answered—Skylith, perhaps, or Virellan—subtle, acknowledging. Even the old ones felt the shift.

⟐ ☽ ⚡ ☾ ⟐

The training hall smelled of steel and cold straw, the kind of damp that sank into stone. Frost limned the windows, scattering the faint torchlight into shards across the floor. Cam's footsteps whispered as she entered, careful as if she were intruding on a sleeping beast.

Orren was already there.

He moved like a shadow wearing human skin, drawing a whetstone along the dagger's edge. *Shhhk. Shhhk.* Sparks caught the light and vanished before they hit the ground.

"You couldn't sleep either?" Cam asked.

Orren didn't look up. "Sleep and I... don't get along."

The words were soft, almost casual, but they left a chill that had nothing to do with the frost.

Cam hesitated by the rack of swords, fingers trailing along a hilt. "You train like someone's hunting you."

"Someone always is."

He turned the dagger in his palm, and for a moment, the silvered sigil on his wrist caught the torchlight. She'd seen marks like that before—burned into stone deep in the Archivum. Wards meant to keep dangerous things out... or in.

Cam's voice dipped to a whisper. "That mark. It isn't decoration, is it?"

His hand stilled. *Shhhk.* Silence.

"You really want to know?" he said finally.

"I asked, didn't I?"

Slowly, he slid the leather strap down. The sigil gleamed, thin and cruel, twisting like a snare around his pulse.

"It's a brand," he said. "The Capital doesn't waste bloodlines. When mage families fell, they kept the ones they wanted—and made things like me."

A soft hum stirred in Cam's magic, coiling tight around her ribs. "...made?"

His eyes flicked to hers, unreadable. "They trained me to track unstable magic. Snuff it out. Hunt the ones who break the rules."

"The ones like me," she said quietly.

"Yes."

The word landed like a knife laid gently on the table. Not swung. Not hidden. Just there, gleaming in the cold light.

"I've killed for them," he added, his tone flat. "People who didn't fit their neat little boxes. Hybrids. Wild magic. Anyone the Capital feared."

Cam's fingers tightened on the hilt. She didn't move.

"You should hate me," Orren said, voice low, dangerous in its calm. "It would be easier."

"I don't." She swallowed. "I can't trust you... but I don't hate you."

Something flickered in his expression—like a man seeing daylight through a crack in a door he wasn't sure he wanted to open.

"I didn't ask for this blood," he said, quieter now. "But I can choose where it leads."

For a moment, the hall seemed to hold its breath. Beyond the walls, a low dragon's rumble carried faintly through the Keep, as if Sael or Sylithra felt the tension threading through the bond.

Cam finally let go of the sword hilt. "Then choose better than they did."

Orren didn't answer, but the dagger in his hand caught the light again, its edge perfectly honed.

◈ ☽ ⚡ ☾ ◈

Morning crept through Haldrin's Keep like a reluctant guest.

Wyatt woke to the faint echo of Cam's laugh in the corridor—but it wasn't for him. It hit like a soft, dull ache. He lingered in bed longer than he should, staring at the frost gathering along the high stone window, the pendant under his shirt pressing cold and heavy against his chest.

He slipped through the Keep like a shadow that morning, moving in quiet corridors, ducking out of sight whenever he caught sight of Kaden. His only excuse—if anyone asked—was visiting the dragon roosts.

Frost clung to the stone like silver moss when he'd climbed to the roosts that morning.

Sylithra wheeled in from the gray sky, wings scattering snow across the courtyard.

Sael rumbled a greeting, low and resonant, but Wyatt didn't answer.

He pressed his hand to the dragon's scales for a heartbeat before retreating to the shadows.

Even Sael's warmth couldn't thaw the cold that had taken root in his chest.

By midday, he hovered in the doorway of the great hall, the smell of hot broth curling through the cold.

Cam and Val bent over open scrolls, murmuring with heads nearly touching. Kaden sat across from them, eyes tracking the script but not reading.

He paused just long enough to catch a flash of life he felt cut off from.

Tessa wrinkled her nose at an open scroll.

"I swear this rune is just a squiggle," she muttered.

"That squiggle," Val said dryly, "means 'honor.' Or possibly 'swamp,' depending on how you die."

Cam snorted a laugh, warm and unguarded.

Wyatt turned away before the warmth could reach him.

If I open my mouth, I'll break something between us. Maybe for good.

At dusk, Wyatt was in the training yard, hurling earth and light into frozen targets until the snow churned into dirt and shards of ice. Each strike echoed in his chest, dull and empty. He didn't look toward his brother, even when he felt the weight of Kaden's stare from across the yard.

From the yard below earlier, Tessa's voice had carried on the wind:

"If you drop that sword again, Alex, I swear—"

A clang had followed, then his muffled curse and her victorious laugh.

Wyatt lingered on the balcony for just a moment, the sound cutting against the winter silence.

He left before they saw him.

Above, Sael's low growl carried through the roosts, answered by Sylithra's mind-touch—a warm brush of wind and quiet, patient warning:

You can't outrun what waits in your blood, bright one.

Wyatt clenched his jaw and shut the link tight.

He didn't want their sympathy, didn't want the weight of destiny—or blood—pressing in.

The next afternoon, he retreated to the training grounds again, finding solace in the rhythm of blade and breath. The sky was a washed-out gray, the wind cutting against his face. He didn't hear Cam approach until her shadow crossed the dirt.

"You're avoiding him," she said softly.

Wyatt kept his eyes on the practice dummy. "I'm giving him space."

Cam studied him for a long moment, her voice almost a whisper when it came.

"He's your brother. Don't wait until the silence gets too heavy to break."

Her words landed the way '*You're not what they say you are*' had in the ravine—simple, and somehow heavier than comfort. It pressed like the prophecy itself, that line he couldn't shake: *the wound that never healed.* The pendant under his shirt felt heavier than ever, a weight he couldn't set down. And still, the ache twisted sharper when he thought of Orren's gaze lingering on Cam, silent and unreadable, too close. Was that what they saw in him too—a flaw, a fracture waiting to split? He clenched his hand tighter against the stone, refusing to name the ache or the prophecy for what they were.

Cam's shadow stretched against the snow as she stepped closer. She didn't press him with more words. She just reached, her fingers brushing his—light, certain, steady. Her eyes held his, unflinching.

The words sank into him like a blade finding its mark—not to wound, but to anchor. And then she let go, turning away, the hem of her coat tugged by the wind as she walked back toward the Keep.

Wyatt's hand lingered where hers had been, the ghost of her touch burning hotter than the cold air. His chest tightened, the knot of grief and fear shifting under the weight of her words. He pressed his palm to the stone wall, grounding himself.

She was right. He knew she was right. And gods help him, he believed her—because if there was anyone in this world who could cut through his walls, it was her.

He closed his eyes, letting the wind sting his face, and drew a long, steady breath. Stubborn or not, he couldn't carry this by himself. Not anymore.

When he opened his eyes again, the decision was already forming. He'd find Kaden—or, more likely, Kaden would hunt him down first. It was usually the latter. Either way, he'd break the silence before it grew too heavy to lift.

◈ ☽ ⚡ ☾ ◈

From the roosts, Sael watched his rider below, the morning light striking sparks from Wyatt's blade. The bond pulsed faintly—not muted as it had been in darker days, but steady, alive.

He sent a ripple of warmth toward Wyatt's mind, and this time it was not turned aside. Wyatt did not speak back, but the bond hummed in quiet acknowledgement.

He does not close himself, Sael murmured. *Not now.*

Sylithra stirred beside him, her coils pressed into the same alcove, their scales brushing where shadow met gold-veined dark. Her voice was a low current of storm:

He bleeds, but he breathes. And he rises.

Sael lowered his head, exhaling steam into the cold air.

Then he is stronger for it.

The two dragons settled, the winter wind weaving over their scales. And in the silence between heartbeats, a truth lingered unspoken:

Change was coming. It carried the taste of ash—and of light.

◈ ☽ ⚡ ☾ ◈

The wind at the top of the watchtower carried the sting of snow, sharp against Kaden's face. He spotted Wyatt immediately—silhouetted against the bruised sky, hood down, hair catching the cold light. He leaned over the parapet like the stones themselves were the only thing holding him up.

Kaden's boots crunched against ice, but his brother didn't turn.

"You've been avoiding me," Kaden said, voice catching in the wind.

A puff of white breath, the faintest snort. "You noticed."

"I noticed." Kaden moved closer, the stones numbing his fingers as he gripped the ledge beside him. "I also noticed you're freezing your ass off up here instead of talking to me."

Wyatt didn't answer. He just kept staring at the forest below, a black ocean under frost.

Kaden drew in a shaky breath. He had to say it. If he didn't now, the silence would swallow them whole.

"I need to tell you something," he said. "Two things, actually."

Wyatt glanced over, wary but silent.

Kaden's throat tightened. "First... Orren. He's not just some soldier. He's... from the Capital. Part of their old bloodline project. Like us." He paused, watching for a flicker of recognition, but Wyatt's expression didn't change—only his jaw tensed. "We need to keep an eye on him.

Wyatt grunted in acknowledgement.

"And second..." Kaden swallowed hard. "I found your name in the blood ledger. Subject Twenty-Seven. They wrote—unstable. Memory interference observed. Visions: powerful, dangerous."

Wyatt's shoulders went rigid. His eyes cut sharp toward Kaden, storm-dark.

"I remember. You said you burned it."

"Yes. I burned it," Kaden said quickly.

"Why?" Wyatt's voice was low, raw.

"Because if Caerthalen knew..." Kaden's throat bobbed. "They'd come for you. And I wasn't going to give them that chance. You're not a file. You're my brother. And they don't get to define you anymore."

For a long moment, all Kaden could hear was the wind and the hammer of his own heart.

Wyatt didn't explode like Kaden half-expected. He didn't shout or curse or shove him away. He just stood there, gripping the stone until his knuckles went white.

The wind tore between them, sharp and cold. Wyatt's jaw worked, storm in his eyes. Then his voice dropped, rough as gravel.

"If you ever find anything like that again... swear you'll show me. Don't keep it from me, little brother."

Kaden let out a breath—half a laugh, half a sigh. Somehow Wyatt could still pull that from him, even here. The promise wasn't much, but it was everything. They were all they had, and if they couldn't trust each other, then who could they trust?

"I swear," Kaden said, voice steady.

Wyatt pulled him into a rough embrace, the kind that was more shield than comfort. Kaden held on just as tight. For a moment, the cold didn't matter, and neither did the silence that had haunted them.

In the silence, Kaden realized the truth that scared him most:

It wasn't the Capital's words Wyatt feared.

It was the part of himself that almost believed them.

◈ ☽ ⚡ ☾ ◈

The war room at Haldrin's Keep was cold and close, its stone walls damp with winter. Three lamps cast halos of gold across the table, where the third Veilbind scroll fragment lay like a severed truth.

The group gathered around it in uneasy silence. Even the dragons outside were restless tonight—a low rumble echoed faintly from the roosts, vibrating through the floor.

Corin leaned over the table, his broad hands braced on either side of the parchment. His eyes, green and sharp as a hawk's, scanned the fractured runes.

"Three fragments," he said, voice a low grind of thought. "Three voices in a broken song. And still, the meaning hides."

Wyatt stayed near the shadowed wall, silent. Kaden kept close but did not touch him; their truce felt like thin ice over deep water.

Cam's thumb worried the loose leather strap at her wrist, the one that usually covered her mark. "The symbols repeat in the Book," she murmured. "But it's like trying to read a song with half the notes missing."

Val's finger traced the jagged script. "This line... 'Cradle...' and here, 'Breath'—" She glanced at Corin. "Could that be a place?"

Corin's mouth pressed into a thin line. "The Cradle Temple. Oldest story the mountains hold. They say it's where the first Unbinding failed."

Ben, standing behind him with arms folded, grunted. "Failed bad enough that the Capital erased it from the maps. If it's still standing at all."

The words hung heavy. The fire popped in the hearth like a bone breaking.

Then, softly, a new voice:

"I could help," Alex said.

Everyone turned. He sat at the far end of the table, shoulders hunched as if he hadn't meant to speak. Beside him, Tessa had been idly spinning a knife between her fingers, but she stilled, watching him.

"I've been reviewing the Academy cipher manuals," Alex went on, hesitant but earnest. "I might... see something the rest of you can't."

Tessa smiled faintly and leaned in, bumping his arm.

"He's annoyingly good at patterns," she said, trying to lighten the thick air.

Cam's gaze lingered on Alex, uncertain.

"Another pair of eyes couldn't hurt," she said slowly.

Alex nodded, but his hand tightened on the table edge. He stared at the fragment for a heartbeat too long, then at Cam, before looking away.

If anyone noticed the subtle calculation behind his eyes, they didn't speak.

Corin closed the Book of Unbinding with a soft, decisive sound. "Then it's settled. We keep decoding. The last fragment—and the Temple—will decide everything. Until then, we prepare."

Outside, the wind howled against the Keep's walls, and from the roosts, a dragon's low rumble rolled through the stone like a warning.

Alex nodded, silent, but the lamplight threw his shadow long across the table, reaching toward the fragments like a hand he hadn't lifted.

⟐ ☽ ⚡ ☾ ⟐

The wind off the cliffs behind Haldrin's Keep bit through Kaden's coat, carrying the sting of snow and salt. Below, the pine forest swayed like a black ocean, whispering in a language he almost thought he could understand if he stood still long enough.

He didn't hear Orren approach—he never did. One heartbeat the cliffs were empty, the next, the quiet soldier stood at his shoulder, arms loosely folded, gaze fixed on the same endless horizon.

"You're awake," Orren said at last, his voice almost lost in the wind.

"Couldn't sleep," Kaden muttered. He kept his eyes on the jagged tree line. "I keep wondering if... any of this matters. If we can change what we were made to be."

Orren's answer came after a long pause, soft but sure.

"Only if someone else believes we can. That's the difference between being made—" his eyes slid to Kaden, unreadable in the moonlight, "—and being chosen."

The words lingered, heavy as stone. Kaden didn't reply, but the truth of them stayed with him long after Orren disappeared into the shadows.

◈ ☽ ⚡ ☾ ◈

Later that night, the library was silent but for the soft hiss of snow against the window. Cam sat alone with the Book of Unbinding, her finger tracing the edge of the third Veilbind scroll fragment.

Her notes sprawled across the desk—crooked lines and half-sketched sigils, ink blotted where her hand shook. They weren't neat. They weren't finished. Just fragments, scattered like pieces of something she wasn't ready to name.

Fire: violet now. Always violet. Not just mine anymore?

Shadow with it. Should feel wrong. Doesn't. Feels like belonging.

Gold shimmer—appears when more than one element answers. Is it me? Or the others? Or both?

Stronger with Kaden. Air + shadow + my fire = storm that wasn't just ours.

Wyatt. Light + stone + my water. Gold again. Not clash. Not harmony either.

Val. Water + illusion + my fire. Gold flickered, faint but there. Stronger when she pressed harder. Like she could weave the edges tighter than anyone else.

Archivum—five of us together. Wyatt + Kaden + Val + Ben + me. Fire, shadow, steel, storm, stone. All threads pulled. Gold brighter than before. Not mine. Not theirs. Something else.

And the healing—

Shouldn't have closed that fast. Blood still wet on the floor but skin already whole. Fire knitting bone.

Was it mine? Or theirs? Or the threads pulling tighter?

Not accident. But not control either.

Like... threads binding themselves. Why?

Beautiful. Terrifying. Both.

And always back to them—

Kaden. His shadows bristling, his storm laced with mine.

Wyatt. His light, his stone, anchoring what should have come apart.

Three names repeating. Three threads no matter how many others join.

The prophecy said three. But the threads say more.

Which truth do I trust?

She stopped. The memory of the training yard, then the Archivum fight, stirred in her chest—the same wild hum threading through both, alive and almost sentient, as if it had known them better than they knew themselves.

Her hand stilled. She let the quill drop and pressed her fingertips absently against the nearest scroll.

And that's when it happened.

A soft pulse of gold ran along the scroll, flaring beneath her touch. The Book shivered—its text rippling, shifting—and then new lines of light curled into a sigil she had never seen before:

A sun wreathed in thorns.

Her breath hitched as the image burned into the page, and along the edges of the parchment, a map began to unfurl—delicate, fragmented, inked in the same faint glow.

It pointed west, threading through a jagged spine of mountains and a barren stretch marked with an outdated name in curling script:

The Shattercrest Wastes.

The name was old, half-forgotten, and the details would take days to decode—but her chest tightened with the weight of certainty.

Somewhere beyond that broken land, the Cradle was calling.

Chapter 18: The Quiet Ones Are Watching

Sleep never held her for long anymore—not with the Veilbind light still burning behind her eyes, not with the weight of what the others had brought back from the Archivum lingering in her chest.

Tessa sat up in the narrow cot, pulling the fur blanket tighter around her shoulders. The room was cold enough for her breath to smoke. Dawn hadn't quite reached Haldrin's Keep; the corridors were gray and still, holding the echo of last night's wind.

You dream too shallow, Brontheus murmured in the back of her mind, his voice like distant thunder. *Your body will break before your will does.*

"I'm not the one breaking," she whispered into the cold, though she wasn't sure if she meant herself or the group.

She padded softly to the small, slitted window and watched the sky lighten over the pines. Somewhere out there, beyond the frozen forests and mountains, was the Cradle Temple—the place they had whispered about after unrolling the Veilbind fragments across the war table. Even without seeing it, she could feel it like a pull in her sternum. A place older than the Capital. A place waiting for them.

She rubbed her arms, trying to shake the unease.

The others were carrying their own shadows:

Cam avoided everyone's eyes when she wasn't bent over the Book of Unbinding. Her fingers worried the strap that usually covered her mark, as if she could hold the magic in with leather alone.

Wyatt kept to the training yard or the watchtower, his silence heavy enough to fill whole hallways.

Kaden tried to move through the Keep like nothing had changed, but Tessa could see it—the tension in his jaw, the way his shoulders coiled tight whenever Wyatt was near.

And then there was Val.

She was quieter than the rest, orbiting the group with tired eyes and hands that never stopped moving—sharpening a blade, turning a page, twisting a ring on her finger.

Some days, Tessa felt like she and Val were the last threads trying to keep the others from pulling apart entirely.

Not leaders, not the ones carrying prophecies or dangerous bloodlines—

just the glue pressed into the cracks, holding on because someone had to.

Glue cracks when the storm grows, Brontheus warned. *You cannot hold them all.*

Tessa pressed her palm against the window ledge. "Then I'll hold as long as I can."

They were all avoiding each other, drifting like pieces of a broken constellation.

Tessa hadn't told anyone what she had glimpsed in the Veilbind light—how for a moment she thought she saw not just a sigil, but a shadow curling behind it. She didn't know what it meant, and she wasn't sure she wanted to.

A soft sound broke the quiet. From the northern roost, a dragon rumbled low and long, the kind of sound that vibrated through the stone walls and into her bones. She didn't need to guess which one. Brontheus.

A second rumble answered, distant and deep, carrying an undercurrent she didn't like to name.

The quiet ones are watching, Brontheus said, low and sure. *We all are.*

◈ ☽ ⚡ ☾ ◈

The yard still smelled of scorched air and wet stone. Frost clung to the edges of the walls where Kaden had left his mark, thin blades of ice cutting jagged patterns into the dirt.

Cam stood a few paces off, her palms open, chest rising quick with breath. Sparks jittered between her fingers—violet edged with gold—and for a heartbeat Wyatt swore the very air bent toward her.

Too much. Too unfocused.

"Hold it steady," he called across the yard, trying to keep his voice even.

The sparks slipped away in a scatter of dust, leaving Cam frowning at her hands. The silence that followed felt heavier than the winter air.

Kaden stepped forward, his boots crunching against the frost. His tone was quiet but direct. "What was that?"

Wyatt's jaw tightened. Trust Kaden to notice first. Not that he meant anything by it—Cam was family to him, nothing more—but with Orren's shadow still gnawing in Wyatt's mind, the knot of irritation came sharper than it should have. He crossed the space, quicker than he meant to, closing the gap between himself and Cam.

Cam kept her eyes fixed on her fingers. "I don't know. It's like... I'm trying to reach for something, but I can't tell what. Like smoke in the dark."

The words unsettled him. Cam never sounded unsure. He'd seen her wield fire with precision, lightning with wild joy, even coax water once under Corin's eye. But this—this wasn't any of those. This felt... unfinished. Dangerous, maybe.

A shiver slid down his spine.

Not wild, Sael murmured, cold certainty in his voice. *It is woven—magic, bond, fate. All threads of one cloth.*

Wyatt stiffened. His dragon's thoughts rarely intruded during training, and never like this. Across from him, Cam's head tilted slightly—just enough to tell him she'd heard it too.

"What does that mean?" he muttered under his breath.

Sael's answer coiled slow, like frost spreading across glass. *The threads remember. They wait only to be pulled.*

Cryptic. As always. Wyatt sent back to Sael, his teeth clenched against the chill threading his chest.

Cam lowered her hands, shoulders slumping. "See? Nothing. It just slips away."

But Wyatt knew better. He'd felt the shift in the yard, seen how the air bent toward her like a tide pulled by more than one moon. And the worst part was, Sael hadn't denied it.

He glanced at Kaden, who was still watching her too closely, suspicion flickering in his calm. For once, Wyatt didn't argue. He was just as unsettled.

◈ ☽ ⚡ ☾ ◈

Later that evening, Tessa sat outside the barracks, sharpening her dagger in the dim lantern glow. The scrape of metal on whetstone was steady, soothing, and the cold air cleared her thoughts better than the close walls of the Keep ever could.

Footsteps approached—soft, deliberate. She didn't look up until Orren's shadow stretched across her boots.

"You see more than most," he said quietly, voice almost blending into the night. "That's dangerous in a place like this."

Tessa paused, then lifted her gaze to meet his. "So is walking alone at night with clean hands and a shadow that doesn't match your steps."

For a heartbeat, the night held its breath. They locked eyes, and Orren's expression didn't change—but he didn't deny it.

Without a word, he turned and walked away, swallowed by the darkness between the torchlights.

Brontheus's growl rolled through her chest. *He smells of smoke still. Of forest. But tonight... there is thunder with no storm. That is not a thing that should be.*

Tessa's hand stilled on the blade. "*You're not making me feel better.*"

I do not mean to.

The whetstone slipped wrong against the dagger's edge, sparks flashing into the night.

Back in her small, cold room, Tessa lit a single candle and pulled out the journal she rarely showed anyone. On its last page, she'd sketched the rough map Cam had given her months ago—crumbling edges, dotted paths, the hints of places that didn't officially exist.

She circled the Keep with the tip of her charcoal, then hesitated, writing a single line in the margin:

"Trust is earned in silence, lost in noise."

A soft knock startled her. When she cracked the door, Alex was there, holding a bundle of firewood.

"You forgot the common room fire," he said with a faint, shy smile. "Didn't want you freezing up here."

She thanked him, and after he left, the room felt a little less cold. Alex was steady. Familiar. Safe—or at least safer than the shadows Orren carried with him.

Brontheus stirred faintly at the edge of her mind, not words this time but a rumble of discontent, the pressure of thunderclouds waiting to break.

"Not tonight," she whispered into the dark.

Her last thought before the candle guttered out was simple, heavy, and certain:

Cam isn't the only one being watched.

◈ ☽ ⚡ ☾ ◈

The Keep's shadows stretched long across the courtyard. Cam pulled her coat tighter as she crossed to the northern roost pathway. The air smelled faintly of snowmelt and smoke from the cookfires, soft and steady in a way that almost felt unfamiliar after the last few days.

She caught sight of Tessa leaning against the stair rail near the barracks, eyes half-lidded, hair messy from the wind. The other girl had barely spoken since dawn; her usual spark dimmed to a dull ember.

"You good?" Cam asked quietly.

Tessa gave a short shrug without looking up. "Just tired. Don't wait for me tonight."

Cam wanted to push, but she knew the signs—Tessa would talk when she wanted to. So she let it go and kept walking, though unease lingered in her chest.

At the roost gates, Wyatt was already waiting. His shoulders were tense; hands shoved deep in his coat pockets. He glanced at her, then looked away, the same way he always did when something weighed too heavy on his mind.

"You didn't say much earlier," he said at last. His voice was even, but not casual. "In the yard. With the magic."

Cam brushed a lock of hair from her face, trying to sound lighter than she felt. "That's because I don't have much to say. It's like trying to grab smoke. Something's there, but it slips out of reach."

Wyatt studied her but didn't press. Instead, they fell into step together, crossing the courtyard in silence.

Snow whispered beneath their boots, thin crust breaking over the gravel-packed path. The air carried the bite of winter—sharp, metallic, and clean. Their breaths curled pale in the lantern glow, vanishing into the gathering dark. The silence wasn't awkward, but heavy, as if the world itself were holding something back.

Cam couldn't stop replaying the training yard in her head. The sparks. The way the air had bent toward her. The way Sael's voice had cut through both of them—*It is woven. All threads of one cloth.*

Even now, the memory left her skin prickling. She hadn't asked Sylithra what it meant, and she wasn't sure she wanted to.

At her side, Wyatt's jaw worked like he was chewing on the same memory. He didn't look at her, but she knew. He'd felt it too.

The pull hit just before they reached the roost doors. Cam staggered a half-step, her chest tightening like someone had tugged a string buried deep in her sternum. Wyatt sucked in a sharp breath, head snapping toward her.

"You feel that?" he asked.

Cam only nodded.

The bond flared between them, sudden and bright, like a spark catching dry tinder. Not her link with Sylithra alone, not Wyatt's with Sael—but something overlapping, braided.

The threads remember, Sylithra's voice pressed into her mind, warm and certain.

The threads bind, Sael added, his tone cool and sharp as winter air. *As we are bound—so are you.*

Cam froze, breath catching. Wyatt's eyes met hers, wide with the same shock.

"What are you talking about?" she whispered.

Sylithra's voice was steady flame. *It means you must know. Sael and I are not only allies. We are mates. Newly bound, but certain.*

Wyatt's jaw clenched, anger sparking. "And you didn't say anything sooner?"

The sharpness in his voice cut through the air, but beneath it she caught something else—not just anger, but the echo of whatever Sael had named. It wasn't only his fury that shook her; it was the tremor of recognition, the same vast, unchosen thing that thrummed through her own chest.

Sael's reply rolled like ice cracking on a river. *There was no quiet moment. Only war. Only noise.*

Sylithra's warmth pressed close to Cam, gentling the storm. *But you are ready now. It matters that you understand. Our bonds shape yours. Flame to frost. Thread to thread.*

Cam's pulse jumped—but beneath the fear was recognition, like remembering a song she'd always known.

Her throat went dry. She knew of dragon bonds, of riders and their dragons—but this was something else entirely. Something she had no words for. She remembered Sael's words in the training yard, the strange spark that had unsettled her all day. Woven. Threads of one cloth. This was what he'd meant.

"Mates?" she managed, the word foreign on her tongue.

Sylithra's warmth curled through her chest. *It means the threads between us will pull tighter, Little Flame. It is our way. Do not fear it.*

Sael's presence brushed Wyatt's mind like wind over stone. *And perhaps one day, you will stop asking what it means and start living what it is.*

Cam glanced at Wyatt, his eyes storm-dark in the torchlight. For once, she didn't know if she was more afraid of the truth—or of how it made something in her chest feel inevitable.

She had expected training. She hadn't expected the ground itself to shift beneath her feet.

The roost doors groaned open, spilling cold air and the low rumble of dragons into the evening.

Sylithra's presence surged against her chest, eager, impatient, as if she'd been waiting for Cam to finally *see.*

Sael was already there, pale hide gleaming in the lantern light, his gaze fixed sharp on Wyatt. When the two dragons lowered themselves for mounting, Cam's heart thudded harder. Nothing about this felt routine anymore.

The moment Sylithra's wings unfurled, the bond stretched wide—wider than it had ever felt. Not just her tether to Sylithra, not just Wyatt's to Sael, but something overlapping, braided, shared.

Cold wind tore across the Keep as they launched, the courtyard falling away beneath them. Cam sucked in a breath, the air sharp as glass in her lungs.

For a heartbeat, Sylithra's mind brushed not only her own, but Sael's—and through him, Wyatt's. A flicker of vision that wasn't hers: snowfields far below, glowing pale in moonlight.

Wyatt swore under his breath. He'd seen it too.

This is what it means, Sylithra said, her voice a low burn. *Our bond shaping yours. Not command, not control. Thread to thread. Flame to frost.*

Sael's voice cut colder, steady as the stars above. *Two riders, two dragons. Four threads. Stronger woven than apart.*

Cam's hands tightened on the reins. She didn't know if she was afraid or exhilarated, but the air itself seemed to hum against her skin, every gust alive with possibility.

She glanced sideways. Wyatt's knuckles were white against Sael's harness, his jaw tight, but his eyes—dark and unsettled—met hers across the distance. And for once, she knew he felt exactly what she did:

The world had just shifted.

And there was no going back.

Chapter 19: Lanterns Before Dawn

The courtyard glowed like a pocket of stolen warmth against the frozen mountains. Lanterns drifted above on invisible tethers, their glass bellies lit in soft colors—amber, rose, deep blue—reflecting on the frost-dusted stones. Someone had strung old festival banners between the walls, faded but bright enough to pretend the world outside the Keep wasn't fraying at the edges.

Laughter rose with the heat from the firepit. Kaden spun Val in an uneven circle to the faint hum of a fiddle, her scarf flaring like a petal in the wind. Alex, predictably, had found the center of attention—juggling three bright apples near the flames, his grin catching the firelight. Tessa leaned against the stone bench beside Orren, clapping when Alex managed to catch one behind his back. Even Orren allowed the faintest curve of amusement to touch his mouth.

Wyatt lingered at the edge of the lantern glow, leaning against a cold wall, arms crossed.

He should be happy. Everyone else was smiling.

So why did it feel like something inside him was slowly unspooling?

The laughter and music were real, but they felt like they belonged to another life—a life where the air wasn't thick with secrets, where brothers didn't have to burn files to keep each other safe, and where prophecy didn't wait like a blade above their heads. He watched Kaden's head tip back in a laugh and felt the twist in his chest sharpen.

A lantern drifted overhead, its light washing his hands gold before moving on. For a moment, Wyatt thought of letting it go higher, into the dark—out past the mountains where no one could follow.

Cam had passed close to him, her hand skimming his arm in an easy, familiar touch. She smiled at him—bright, unguarded, the kind of smile that seemed to live in its own light.

And it struck him like it always did.

That smile.

He'd seen it before—years before she ever walked into his life.

Memory rose like a tide he couldn't stop:

A boy of twelve standing in a field of stars, the world hushed around him. The sky was endless and close, the constellations so sharp he thought he could pluck them from the dark. And there she was—hair the color of dusk, caught in a wind he couldn't feel. Her eyes met his, soft as a secret, and her voice brushed the edges of the dream.

Not yet.

Then she had turned, walking away into the starlight, leaving him reaching for something he didn't understand.

Wyatt refocused on the courtyard. The laughter, the music, the smell of firewood—it all felt thinner than that one, impossible memory.

Twelve years old. He had seen her face before he even knew what love was.

And now here she was—real, tangible, close enough to touch—and yet her light always seemed to drift just beyond his reach.

She had always been walking away in those dreams.

And tonight... she was walking toward someone else.

The ache that followed wasn't sharp. It was quiet, heavy, the kind that settled into his bones like winter. He tucked his hands into his coat and let the shadows have him, watching the lanterns rise until the world blurred at the edges.

Wyatt drifted along the courtyard's edge, the music and laughter distant now, like echoes through water. Lanterns bobbed overhead, scattering gold across the packed snow. Every face seemed softer in that light—except one.

Across the firepit, Orren sat with his usual stillness, a shadow in human shape. Tessa chattered at his side, her grin bright enough to fill the space he refused to.

Then, for the briefest moment, Orren tugged the leather strap on his wrist loose. The firelight licked across the skin beneath—faint, silvery, and cruel. A sigil-scar, curling in jagged patterns around the pulse point.

Wyatt froze.

Memory stirred, dark and uninvited.

A night when his mother's voice had been the only thing steady in a world that felt like it was breaking: *If you ever see a mark like this, Wy, you run. Mage hunters don't leave witnesses. They were made to erase what the Capital fears most.*

He had been just a boy, small enough to fit under the kitchen table, staring at the sketch she'd burned after. A curling brand like a chain around a wrist. And now, that same chain glimmered in the firelight across the courtyard.

Orren said something low to Tessa, his face calm, unreadable. The strap slipped back into place, the mark gone as if it had never been. But the image burned into his mind anyway, searing hot as iron.

Wyatt's hands curled into fists inside his coat.

This man wasn't just dangerous—wasn't just a soldier with shadows in his eyes.

This was the ghost of every story his mother had told, every fear she'd tried to bury under the floorboards. Of the hunters who had hunted their kind, caged dragons, and shattered bloodlines.

And he was sitting by the fire, like he belonged.

The mark on Orren's wrist burned in Wyatt's mind long after the man pulled his glove back on.

A mage-hunter's scar. His mother's warnings.

Wyatt drifted toward the far edge of the courtyard, where the shadows pooled between the stone arches.

Lanterns floated above, soft and golden, their reflections shivering in the ice patches on the stones. Light and music spun in the air, but none of it touched him.

The world had narrowed to a pulse in his ears and the bite of cold in his lungs.

That's when he saw them.

Cam and Orren stood near the northern archway, half in shadow, half in lantern light.

Her hand brushed his sleeve—a soft, instinctive gesture, the kind that said I see you. Her face was tilted toward him, lips moving low. The light caught in her eyes, turning blue to molten silver blue, and Wyatt's chest locked.

He couldn't hear the words, but he imagined them anyway.

"...you don't have to do this alone..."

"...I don't work for them anymore..."

The fragments meant nothing, and everything.

A thousand explanations could exist, but the cold, ugly thing curling under his ribs didn't care.

He wasn't afraid she'd belong to someone else; he was afraid she'd slip into a world he couldn't reach. Afraid she'd choose someone who didn't see her the way he did—not as the prophecy's weight or a soldier's ally, but as the girl whose laugh could shake frost off stone.

The music swelled behind him, a burst of glass and flute.

Wyatt turned away before the sound broke him open.

Maybe that made him selfish. Maybe it just made him human.

He didn't see Orren step back, shoulders locking, the mask sliding over his face again. He didn't see Cam's hand fall to her side, empty.

He only felt the cold of the stone wall under his palm as he left the courtyard, chasing the darker edges of Haldrin's Keep, where the wind could cut him open and no one would see him bleed.

The steps groaned beneath his boots as he climbed, each one heavier than the last. Lanternlight thinned with every turn of the spiral, until only shadow clung to him. His breath came sharp in the cold, matching the hammer of his pulse. By the time he reached the top, the night had swallowed the music whole.

The watchtower was colder than he remembered. Wind clawed at his coat, and frost bit his fingers as he leaned against the icy stone.

He didn't notice Val until she was halfway up the steps.

She paused in the doorway, her breath puffing white in the cold.

"I thought you might want this," she said softly, holding out a lantern already strung with a small loop of silver thread.

He hesitated before taking it. "Thanks."

Val studied him for a moment, her eyes gentle but tired. "You don't have to stay up here alone, you know."

"I know," Wyatt said, and it was the only answer he could give.

She squeezed his arm once—warm through the sleeve of his coat—and then retreated down the stairs without another word, leaving the faint smell of smoke and pine in her wake.

Wyatt lit the lantern. The flame quivered like it knew his heart wasn't steady.

Below, the courtyard pulsed with laughter and music.

Someone—probably Tessa—cheered at a burst of sparks from the firepit.

Cam's voice carried faintly, light and warm, and he swore he could pick it out even through the winter wind.

He closed his eyes.

Twelve years old. That field of stars. Her hair catching the wind. Her voice saying, "not yet."

He'd waited all this time for now, and somehow he still felt like he was standing on the wrong side of the glass.

Wyatt set the lantern on the ledge, watching the fire inside it reflect in his own eyes.

"Let her see me," he whispered. "The way I've always seen her."

The wind caught it, and the lantern rose.

Up past the battlements. Up past the dancing lights of the Keep.

Higher, until it was only a soft, trembling star among the others.

A low rumble stirred in the back of his mind—Sael, restless in the roost.

The dragon's unease thrummed through the bond like distant thunder.

Storm's coming, the thought whispered, though no words followed.

Wyatt stayed until the horizon bruised with pre-dawn, the music long gone, the courtyard dark.

And when he finally turned from the ledge, he felt it in his chest—

like the lantern had carried his heart into the sky and left only the hollow behind.

◈ ☽ ⚡ ☾ ◈

The festival light never sat right in his bones.

Lanterns bobbed overhead, soft and harmless, but to Orren they flickered like ghost-fires on a battlefield. The glow caught the edges of banners, laughter spilled across the courtyard, and all of it pressed against him like a memory he didn't want.

He kept to the archway's shadow, posture rigid, hands folded behind his back the way soldiers do when they're waiting for orders. If he stood still enough, maybe the noise would wash past him. Maybe the warmth wouldn't find a way under his skin.

But it always did. The scent of roasting meat curled through the air, too close to the smell of smoke. The fiddle's song twisted sharp in his chest, like a voice he could almost remember. He shut his eyes for a breath, forcing the images down: firelit faces, his mother's laugh, his brother's hand on his shoulder. Things that weren't his anymore. Things the Capital had burned out of him.

Cam found him. Somehow she always did.

"You're quieter than usual," she said gently. Her hand brushed his sleeve—light, instinctive, a touch that carried more warmth than he knew what to do with. "You don't like festivals?"

He should've lied. But the question cracked something open, if only for a breath.

"They remind me of what I lost," Orren said, his voice flat. "Family. Laughter. Things that don't come back."

Her brows knit, sorrow flickering in her expression. For a moment, she looked at him the way people used to, before the brand on his wrist, before the Capital carved him into what he was. She already knew what lay under the leather strap, had seen the brand for what it was. That truth sat between them now, sharper than fire, heavier than her pity.

So he stepped back. The air between them hardened, and the mask slid into place again. "It doesn't matter. I'm not here for lanterns."

Cam's hand fell to her side, empty. Her lips parted, as if to answer—but he was already gone, swallowed by the shadows beyond the archway.

◈ ☽ ⚡ ☾ ◈

Cam stood alone in the archway long after Orren's shadow slipped away. The lanterns overhead painted her in shifting colors—gold, rose, blue—but none of them felt like her. Not tonight.

Her hand still tingled from where it had brushed his sleeve. The memory of the training hall came back unbidden—the scrape of a whetstone, his voice flat as he bared the truth. *It's a brand. The Capital doesn't waste bloodlines. They kept the ones they wanted—and made things like me.*

She hadn't asked more. She hadn't wanted to. But now, in the glow of festival light, that mark haunted her—the leather strap, the cruel lines beneath it, the way his voice had sounded like he was reciting his own death sentence.

What did it mean, exactly? What had Caerthalen made him into? He hadn't said. Maybe couldn't. And the not-knowing pressed against her ribs, sharp as a blade.

The music carried faintly across the courtyard, warm and careless, but all she heard was his flat tone, that single word: *brand.*

Her chest tightened. She didn't hate him for it. She couldn't. But she didn't trust him either. Not yet. Not when the questions outnumbered the answers.

And yet... she still saw him. Saw the man who stepped back into shadow before she could reach him. Saw the weight he carried alone.

The lanterns drifted higher, their glow catching the frost. Cam tilted her head back, watching one rise, and for the briefest moment, she wished she could strip the leather from his wrist and demand the truth. But the fear stopped her—fear of what it would confirm, fear of what it would mean.

Instead, her thoughts betrayed her, drifting back to Wyatt as they always did. At least with him, she knew the shape of what she felt.

Bootsteps scraped faintly on stone behind her. She didn't turn until Kaden's voice broke the quiet.

"You okay?" His concern was soft, not sharp, a side of him few people ever saw.

Cam thought about telling him. She'd thought about it more than once. But fear always pulled her back, whispering close, reminding her what it cost to let someone in. So she gave the same half-smile she always did, the one that never reached her eyes.

"I'm fine."

Kaden's gaze lingered, steady, skeptical. He could read masks better than anyone. But, as always, he didn't press. He just nodded once, fading back into the lanternlight crowd until he was gone—like his shadows melting into dark.

His gaze lingered a fraction too long, as if memorizing the distance between them before it widened again. But the weight of his gaze stayed, pressing her thoughts right back where they always went—toward Wyatt.

Movement caught her eye. Up the far steps, half-shrouded in shadow, Wyatt climbed the watchtower, his shoulders stiff, his head bowed. She felt the pull in her chest before she even named it: not magic, not prophecy. Just him.

Her breath caught. She should go after him. She wanted to. But her boots stayed rooted to the stone.

Her thoughts orbited back to Wyatt—the way they always did when it came to him—messy, dangerous, too close to the places she didn't want to bleed. The way he looked at her like she wasn't just fire and fate. The way he stood between her and danger without ever asking anything back. The way his silence still managed to feel like loyalty.

She had told herself it was gratitude. Friendship. Something she could hold without fear. But tonight, watching his figure vanish up the stairs, the truth pressed sharper.

Maybe it had always been more. Maybe she was already in love with him.

Her chest tightened, and Anthony's face rose unbidden—the man who had raised her, then torn from her life in a single brutal moment. The grief never left. It only shifted; a scar she didn't dare test. She'd lost one father. She couldn't risk losing someone she loved again.

So she held it back. Held it all down.

But another truth whispered through anyway: She owed him an explanation.

Not yet. Not tonight. But soon. Because he deserved to know why she hadn't acted on what was already there, why she let silence stand between them.

A lantern drifted overhead, its glow soft against her face. She tilted her head up once more, eyes tracing its rise until it disappeared into the night sky.

Her lips moved in a whisper only she could hear.

"I don't want to lose you too."

And as the lantern vanished into the dark, she felt it carry the words with it—up past the battlements, into the stars.

◈ ☽ ⚡ ☾ ◈

High above the courtyard, four minds brushed in uneasy rhythm.

Sael's silver gaze tracked Wyatt's retreat into the watchtower, the bond pulsing with storm-dark unrest. Sylithra coiled near him, her warmth bleeding into the cold night, pressing calm that didn't reach far enough.

Sylithra's thoughts brushed his—warm, insistent. *The bond strains*, she warned. *If they do not speak, the silence will do it for them.*

The threads fray, Brontheus growled, thunder in his chest. *Too many voices pulling apart.*

Virellan did not answer in words, only loosed a breath of frost across the cliffside. Yet her silence was heavy, edged like ice about to crack.

Below, the humans laughed and danced, lanterns bobbing as if the world could be light again. But the dragons felt the deeper truth: every flame was a tether. Every rising spark tugged at bonds already strained. What was bound pulled tighter. What was hidden pressed against its cage.

The quiet ones were watching. And in the shadows between stars, something else was too.

Chapter 20: The Day the Sky Waited

Cam woke before the sun, the air of her small stone room sharp with winter.

Her breath misted in front of her face, and for a moment she just watched it curl and fade like smoke.

Outside her window, the world was silvered and still.

The first light of the solstice crept over the mountains, catching on drifts of snow and the frozen river far below.

A single bell tolled from the distant village, the sound soft and solemn—

a tradition to call the day into being.

Down in the courtyard, the remains of last night's lanterns glimmered like ghosts.

Some were half-buried in snowdrifts, their paper shells crumpled but still faintly aglow.

Others had caught in the pine branches, swaying with the wind,

like strange little spirits that refused to leave with the night.

Cam wrapped her arms around herself, the weight of the prophecy settling heavier than the blanket had.

It wasn't just the solstice. It wasn't just the Book of Unbinding or Sylithra's whispers in her dreams.

Something about this dawn felt like standing on the edge of a moment that couldn't be undone.

Down the hall, the Keep was already stirring.

Wyatt passed her doorway once, silent and withdrawn, his eyes fixed on the floor as if thoughts weighed more than armor.

Kaden followed later, his movements tight and restless, a storm trapped under his skin.

Only Val and Tessa seemed steady, moving through the morning with quiet purpose—

tending the fires, straightening the tables, acting like the thin glue holding all of them together.

They fell into step together, boots clicking softly against the cold stone as they made their way through the quiet hall.

The chill of the solstice morning clung to the air, their breaths misting faintly as they passed tall, frost-laced windows.

Outside, the pale winter light spilled in soft silver and pink hues over the mountains—a beauty that felt almost suspended, like the world itself was holding its breath.

By the time they reached the war room, the Keep was hushed in that rare morning stillness.

Lantern light flickered against the walls, and the smell of cold stone and old parchment wrapped around them.

Inside, Val stood near the window, her fingers absentmindedly tracing a worn rune carved into the sill. Wyatt's silhouette was shadowed against the far wall, silent and still, his gaze fixed on the ancient Book of Unbinding resting on the table between them.

Cam approached slowly, her eyes drawn to the tome as if it might reveal answers on its own.

She hesitated, breath catching in her throat. The pages seemed to shimmer faintly in the soft light—alive with something older than memory.

Her fingertips brushed the parchment, and the surface pulsed, faint and rhythmic like a heartbeat beneath her skin.

One page, blank the day before, now bore a fresh line of text glowing faintly:

"The One Who Sees in Flame."

Her pulse quickened, a mixture of awe and dread swirling inside her. The Book was no longer just words and symbols—it was calling to her.

Kaden's footsteps echoed softly behind her, breaking the heavy silence. He smiled, though there was an edge of nervousness she hadn't seen before.

"Looks like the book doesn't like me much," he said with a half-joke, reaching out and touching the page.

The faint pulse flickered beneath his fingers, more subtle this time.

He glanced quickly between Cam and Wyatt, and for a moment, the quiet between them felt charged—a silent acknowledgment that they were all caught in the same unfolding mystery.

Then Corin entered, his presence steady and somber. His eyes swept the room, lingering briefly on the twins standing nearest to the Book of Unbinding. The winter light caught in their dark hair, and something in his expression softened—like a private note surfacing in his memory.

"Ah—before I forget," he said, voice calm but carrying. "Happy birthday, you two."

Kaden blinked, startled, then gave a crooked smile.

"Right. Thanks."

Wyatt only inclined his head, quiet as ever, though his eyes shifted briefly toward Cam. She caught the look and felt something twist warm in her chest—small, private, fleeting.

Corin's gaze lingered on them a moment longer before he said quietly,

"Sometimes, the prophecy doesn't ask who is worthy. It asks who is willing."

The words settled over Cam like a heavy fog.

She swallowed hard, feeling the solstice light outside fade to a colder, more fragile glow.

The day was waiting. And so was she.

The book's heartbeat faded under Cam's fingertips, leaving her own pulse loud in her ears. Corin's words clung to her ribs like frost. No one spoke for a moment. Even the fire in the war room seemed to quiet, its soft crackle swallowed by the cold stone walls.

Val leaned over the table, tracing a careful circle around the new line with her gloved finger.

"It feels like it's... waiting for something," she murmured. Tessa hugged herself, her gaze darting between the book and Cam.

"Or someone," she said. "I don't like how it looks at you."

Wyatt made a small noise in his throat, almost a growl, but said nothing. Kaden only leaned back against the table, his arms folded, watching all of them like he was trying to keep them from splintering.

When Corin finally turned to leave, the others began to drift as well.

Val moved toward the hearth, pulling Tessa with her to warm their hands.

Wyatt followed Kaden into the hall, their boots echoing like a fading heartbeat.

Cam lingered at the doorway, suddenly restless. The fire felt too close, the room too heavy with the weight of things unspoken.

"Going out?" Tessa asked, tilting her head.

"Just for air," Cam said, forcing a faint smile.

The courtyard was colder, quieter, lantern light spilling over stone as she stepped through the gate. A gust of pine and frost met her as she crossed the snow-dusted ground and followed the northern wall. Lantern strings swayed in the wind, their glass catching the pale afternoon light.

That's when she saw him—Orren, perched on the wall, sharpening his blade against the horizon. The steel caught the weak solstice sun, and for a heartbeat, he looked like part of the winter itself.

Cam's boots crunched softly in the snow as she slipped back through the outer wall.

The Keep felt different in the late afternoon light—muted, like the whole world was holding its breath for the solstice.

The smells of pine smoke and frost followed her inside.

Even surrounded by warmth and familiar stone, she felt like she was standing on the edge of something vast—like a step forward could send her into a storm she wasn't ready to name.

She'd spent so long building walls out of fire and silence. But the walls didn't feel safe anymore—they felt lonely.

Her eyes drifted to the stairwell that led to the watchtower.

Without thinking, her feet carried her up.

The sun bled out slowly over the snow, turning the mountains to molten copper.

Cam stood at the top of the watchtower, her fingers curled around the cold stone, as if the whole Keep might drift away if she let go.

The world felt suspended—caught between breath and heartbeat.

Wind tugged at her hair, carrying the smell of pine smoke and frost. Somewhere below, the courtyard lanterns swayed, their faint glow winking through the violet dusk.

Magic hummed in her bones. She could feel it in the air, straining at some invisible seam.

Even the dragons were restless; low rumbles and shifting scales brushed the edges of her mind through the bond-link, like thunder pacing behind the clouds.

The Veil is thin tonight, Sylithra's voice murmured, soft as snowfall. *Your flame is waking. When the stars align, you must choose where to burn.*

Cam shivered. Not from the cold—though it sank into her fingertips—but from the certainty that she was standing inside a hinge in time.

All day the truths had stacked against her chest: Orren's confession, the book's pulse, Corin's quiet warning.

And now the sky itself seemed to be waiting for her to answer a question she couldn't yet name.

A soft sound below caught her attention.

Wyatt.

He was leaning against the courtyard wall, half in shadow, face tipped up toward her.

He didn't call out. He didn't have to.

Their eyes met through the dimming light, and something in her chest tightened—like a string pulled taut between them, vibrating with words she wasn't brave enough to speak.

Even from this height, she could feel him—an echo through the bond, faint but steady, like warmth under frost.

She wanted to go to him, wanted to ask if he felt it too—the world holding its breath, the future tilting.

But the words stayed trapped, heavy with everything that might change if she let them out.

The wind rose, scattering snowflakes like sparks around her. The last rim of sun slipped behind the mountains, leaving the world awash in deep silver and blue.

Lanterns flickered to life in the courtyard below, one by one, like new stars being born.

She lingered until her fingers went numb against the stone, the cold sinking into her bones.

The sky deepened to indigo, stars shivering into view one by one. She didn't move. Didn't speak.

It felt like if she stayed just a little longer, the night might whisper the answers she was too afraid to ask.

Far below, the Keep settled into quiet.

She waited, the world holding its breath with her. If the Veil was waiting, then so was she. But waiting wasn't enough. Not forever.

◈ ☽ ⚡ ☾ ◈

Val lingered as the others shifted, her hand still resting on the table where the Book pulsed faintly. The air felt brittle, like one more word might splinter it. Cam had slipped out a while ago, restless, and Wyatt had gone only minutes later, muttering something about the cold air waking him up.

That left the room thinner, quieter. Kaden leaned against the table; arms folded like a wall he hoped no one would test. Tessa stood near the hearth, shoulders hunched, her usual spark dimmed to embers.

It struck Val, suddenly and sharply, how thin they'd all become. Not in body, but in thread. Pulled taut, fraying, held together by nothing more than stubbornness and silence.

Tessa had said it once to her—that she and Val were the glue in the cracks. Tonight, she felt it. The weight of keeping them steady. The ache of pretending she didn't notice when even her own hands shook.

Her fingers traced the table's edge, grounding herself against the grain of old wood. The candlelight trembled there, reflecting in small gold arcs, and she breathed until the room steadied again.

Still, her gaze drifted—unwilling, but certain—toward Kaden. He was watching the others, not her, but there was a line in his brow she recognized. A mirror to the one she carried. The thought unsettled her. Or maybe steadied her. She couldn't tell which.

And then it came—strange, subtle, like a shift in the air. Not sound. Not sight. Just a pulse. A quiet hum threading beneath her ribs, too faint to name, too fleeting to hold. It wasn't sound or sight, but the way her chest tightened as if someone had plucked a string threaded through her ribs.

She blinked, her breath catching. By the time she tried to grasp it, it was gone.

But Kaden's head lifted sharply, as if he'd felt it too.

◈ ☽⚡☾ ◈

It hit him like a ripple, faint but certain—something shifting under his skin, answering a hum he hadn't known he was waiting for.

Not sound, not sight, just a hum. A thread pulled tight, then gone before he could name it. He glanced toward the table, toward Val, and for an instant he could've sworn her breath caught too.

Kaden's eyes followed her as she moved toward the hearth, Tessa at her side. Val bent to warm her hands, her jet-black hair catching in the firelight. She looked steady. She always did.

But he'd seen the truth in her eyes when she thought no one was looking—the same tired shadow he carried himself. And gods, he admired her for carrying it anyway. For carrying them all.

He didn't bother to hide that he was watching. Let her see it, for once. Let her see that someone was watching her back, even if she didn't ask.

Her gaze flicked up, caught his, and for a moment the crackling fire faded. There was only the warmth between them, fragile but real.

He didn't move closer. Not yet. But he didn't look away either.

◈ ☽⚡☾ ◈

The wind thinned in the high peaks, sharp enough to sting even their scales. Tenebrin rode it in silence, wings stretched long and sure, his shadow spilling dark across the snowfields. Beside him, Virellan climbed through the currents, her frost scattering into the air like glass shards caught in sunlight.

Their thoughts brushed—not just coordination, not just flight—but something deeper, a thread they had felt before they ever shared a sky. It had pulled faintly in the past, quiet and patient, waiting.

Before tonight, it had only been a pull, faint and patient, waiting. But now, with one shared breath, the thread tightened into something undeniable—not new but chosen.

Now, it tightened.

Not with force, not with fire, but with consent—two wills leaning into the same current. A recognition. A choice.

The bond settled between them, not new, but acknowledged. Like a flame banked until the moment both chose to feed it.

And in the stillness of that choice, echoes stirred—Val's steadiness like frost-thread through Virellan's chest, Kaden's storm-shadow thrumming faint against Tenebrin's wings. The riders could not name it yet, but the dragons felt the brush of it: their bond reflecting through human hearts, tugging threads that had already been there.

Rare, Tenebrin thought. Rarer still that humans might feel what should belong only to dragons. Coincidence? Or fate weaving tighter than even dragons could name?

Neither spoke further. They only flew, side by side, shadow and frost carving the same sky. The choice had been made, and it was theirs alone.

Chapter 21: When the Veil Sang Their Names

Snow whispered across the stones as Wyatt climbed the watchtower.

He hadn't meant to—he'd tried to walk the other way, to linger in the courtyard where lanterns bobbed like fallen stars in the snow.

But that pull in his chest wouldn't let him go.

Ever since he'd looked up earlier and seen Cam standing on the tower against the fading light, something in him had been tethered.

He'd wandered the grounds, told himself to give her space, but his steps kept circling back here—until the only place left to go was up.

The stairs were cold under his hands as he gripped the stone rail, breath misting in the winter air.

When he reached the top, the world opened around him in silver and shadow.

The Keep below was hushed, lanterns flickering softly across the snow like a constellation that had fallen to earth.

And there she was—Cam—standing at the edge, her hair catching starlight, wind tugging it into soft waves.

For a heartbeat, he froze.

He'd held this inside for weeks—no, longer. Years, if he was honest.

His throat tightened, and for a moment, he almost turned back.

Instead, he stepped closer, boots whispering against the snow.

"Cam..." His voice was rough, catching in the cold. He hesitated, breath fogging, before the words slipped out in a quiet rush.

"I've... I've been dreaming about you since I was twelve."

The words felt fragile, absurd, and yet truer than anything he'd ever said.

"I didn't even know what it meant back then. I'd just... see you. In starlight. Walking away, always just out of reach."

He swallowed, voice softening.

"And then I met you. And it felt like I'd been waiting my whole life without knowing why."

Cam's eyes glimmered with lanternlight, her lips parting like she might speak—then she bit them together, hesitating.

"I..." Her voice wavered, the cold and the weight of the moment catching in her throat. "...I kept my distance because every time I let someone close, I lose them. My father. My home. Everything. I thought... if I stayed quiet, if I didn't feel too much, maybe I wouldn't lose you too."

Wyatt's chest ached, sharp and warm all at once. He stayed still, letting her finish.

"I can't keep pretending I don't—" She stopped herself, swallowed, and tried again, barely above a whisper. "...You've always seen me. Even when I tried to hide. And that scares me more than anything else... because I don't want to lose this. I don't want to lose you."

The wind rose between them, lifting soft streams of snow into the starlight.

For a moment, the whole world seemed to hold its breath. The wind hissed over the stone, carrying their breath into the night.

Wyatt's hand lifted, and this time he let his fingertips ghost along her cheek, gentle and certain.

She leaned ever so slightly into his touch—and their fingers found each other, brushing in the frozen air.

The instant their fingers touched, cold air sparked with Cam's magic.

Wind curled around them in sudden, swirling gusts, lifting snow like silver dust. A deep, rhythmic pulse thrummed through Wyatt's chest—like the Veil itself was breathing.

The world tilted.

◈ ☽ ⚡ ☾ ◈

Stone and snow and lanternlight bled away in a blinding flash—and then there was nothing but the pull of the vision.

The world shifted into shadow, a jagged battlefield framed by cracked canyon walls.

She saw Val, Tessa, and Kaden—their faces taut with strain, backs bent under the pressure of a fight slipping away. Veilborn, twisted and snarling with dark veins pulsing beneath their skin, lunged suddenly toward Wyatt.

"No... not again. Not him—" her mind screamed as golden light flared from her hands.

Her scream tore through the void, raw and desperate, a beacon cutting through the dark.

The battle blurred around him, the chaos seeming to slow and stretch—each moment deliberate, measured. He saw her running towards him hand outstretched.

The cliff edge crumbled away taking him with it, a ripple of time tugged him sideways, pulling him away from the edge of death.

Beneath his feet, cold stone steps materialized, rising like a stairway from nothingness.

Together, yet apart, they stood on the vast staircase of the Cradle Temple—distant but unmistakably connected.

The sky above was clear and endless; the battlefield below vanished like smoke.

Their voices whispered in unison across the void between them:

"We're not lost. Not yet."

Behind Cam, a sigil blazed briefly—a symbol of delay, not death.

Wyatt recognized it from Corin's notes, the fragile hope they had been clinging to.

◈ ☽⚡☾ ◈

The cold air crashed back into their lungs as the vision faded, sharp and sudden, like a winter gust. The watchtower felt impossibly still again—just as it had been before, save for the faint snowflakes settling silently on stone.

They stood there, fingers inches apart, the space between them charged and aching with what had just passed.

Cam's shoulders shook slightly. Silent tears traced cold paths down her cheeks, catching the wavering lanternlight. Wyatt's own body trembled—not just from the chill, but from the weight of the shared truth hanging between them.

"Wyatt... Y-you died," she whispered, voice brittle, breaking through the quiet.

He swallowed hard, keeping his gaze fixed on her.

"I don't think I did," he said low, voice rough but steady. He wanted to believe it—needed her to. "Not like that."

For a long moment, neither spoke. The world beyond the tower seemed to hold its breath with them.

They both knew—this vision wasn't just a glimpse. It was a warning. A call to fight for every moment they still had.

Her voice cracked, raw and trembling. "Wyatt... I've been scared... I still am. Every time I let someone close to me; my mother, Anthony... I lose them. And I can't..." She stopped, her voice cracking raw. "I can't lose you too."

Her words cut through him sharper than the vision. Not a confession. A fear.

Wyatt's hand rose anyway, slow, trembling, until his fingers brushed her cheek.

"You won't," he whispered. "Not if I can help it."

He exhaled slowly, a warmth threading through the chill in his chest. "I see you. I always have."

His fingers traced the delicate line of her jaw, the soft heat of her skin beneath his palm. His thumb brushed gently over the corner of her mouth, a silent question lingering in his gaze.

She froze for a heartbeat, the world narrowing to the single point where his hand met her skin. The silence between them trembled. Every breath felt borrowed.

Then—slowly—she leaned into it.

Cam drew in a shaky breath, eyes fluttering closed. Her breath caught as she tipped her face toward his. Her hands rose hesitantly at first—one resting lightly on his chest, the other curling to thread fingers through the curls at the nape of his neck, pulling him closer without a word.

And then she kissed him.

The world seemed to tilt, the cold fading to the edges of his awareness. The taste of snow and salt filled his senses. His breath caught, sharp, before melting against hers.

The space between them dissolved.

Their lips met—not from certainty, not from ease—but from the terror of almost losing him. From the truth she couldn't bury anymore, even if she couldn't yet name it.

The kiss was soft, desperate, edged in fear, and Wyatt met it gently, letting her set the pace. Snow whispered around them, their breath fogging in the cold, and he thought only: she chose to stay. For now, that's enough.

When they broke apart, her forehead rested against his. She was still shaking, still afraid—but she hadn't run.

Wyatt felt the tension in her body melt into him, every beat of her fear and longing pouring into that trembling connection. His hands cradled her face, anchoring her to the here and now, while the cold night wrapped them like a quiet witness.

Wyatt rested his forehead against hers still. He understood then—it wasn't love she couldn't name. It was the terror of it. The terror of losing it.

Cam's eyes fluttered open—blue-gray with flecks of silver that caught the lantern light. She looked at him like she wanted to say more but couldn't. Not yet.

She drew back half an inch, breath trembling between them, as if unsure whether she'd done something irrevocable.

Wyatt's hand stayed where it was, steady against her cheek.

Then she moved—just the smallest shift—but it was enough.

Her hand slid to the back of his head, fingers curling in his hair, and the world narrowed to her and the heat between them.

For a second, neither of them moved. Just breathing—her heartbeat brushing against his chest, his thumb tracing the pulse in her throat.

Then he closed the space.

One hand tangled in her hair, the other settling at her waist, holding her like she might vanish if he wasn't careful. The kiss that followed was not calm, not a promise—they both knew that. It was fear and relief and defiance all tangled together. A way of *saying I can't lose you* without daring to speak it aloud.

Snow whispered down around them, catching in Cam's lashes. She pressed closer, tilting her head, her free hand sliding up to cradle his cheek, as if holding him there could keep the vision from stealing him away.

Wyatt answered her urgency with steadiness. He let her pour the ache of almost-losing him into the kiss, and he anchored it, holding her as if to remind her: I'm still here. I'm not gone yet.

The second kiss was deeper, unspoken words spilling into the space between them—every hesitation, every "not yet," burning into the plea that neither wanted to lose the other.

She pressed closer, tilting her head, her free hand tracing the line of his jaw as if memorizing him.

Her lips moved with a soft urgency against his, answering a question they'd both been asking in silence for months. Not a promise, not yet—but a need, raw and undeniable.

When they finally broke apart, foreheads touching, neither spoke.

Their breaths fogged in the winter air, and Wyatt thought he could still taste the echo of her fear, tangled with the fragile promise of something more.

For a moment, the world felt perfectly still—just the sound of their breathing, the whisper of snow, the echo of everything unspoken.

The silence that followed wasn't empty. It hummed—soft, electric—as if the air itself had memorized them.

They were both still breathing too fast, the kind of rhythm that didn't know whether it came from fear or relief.

Cam's fingers lingered against his jaw, her thumb brushing lightly over his skin. Her voice was soft, almost shy after the storm of emotion between them.

"...Happy birthday, Wyatt."

The words landed like an ember in his chest, quiet but searing.

A small, unsteady smile tugged at his lips. "Best one I've ever had."

Above them, the stars burned against the longest night, and Wyatt understood what it meant to wait. She hadn't chosen yet. Not fully. But she hadn't run either.

And for him, that was enough, for now.

That quiet truth carried them down the tower steps and through the still barracks halls, snow clinging to their boots. At her door, Wyatt had meant to leave—meant to give her space—but Cam's hand lingered on the latch, her voice low, almost uncertain.

"Stay. Just... stay."

Nothing more. No explanations, no expectations. And he hadn't needed any. He followed her inside, meaning only to sit for a moment. She had curled up beside him, head resting against his shoulder, and before long her breathing slowed, even and steady. He'd told himself he would go once she drifted off—but then her hand slipped against his chest, holding on as though she couldn't let go.

So he stayed. And somewhere between listening to her breathing and memorizing the weight of her leaning into him, sleep found him too.

◈ ☽ ⚡ ☾ ◈

The Keep slept beneath a veil of snow, its lanterns flickering like faint embers in the dark.

Far above the stone walls, Sylithra crouched on the edge of the outer parapet, her wings furled tight against the cold.

She had felt it—the flare from the watchtower.

A ripple through the Veil itself, gold and raw and young, born not from triumph but from fear.

A bond bracing against loss. Fragile, but burning.

The thought was not words but instinct, threading through her chest and into the deeper currents of magic that wove the world together. She lowered her head, golden eyes catching the faintest gleam of starlight, and listened.

Wind swept over the Keep, carrying scents of frost, dragonhide, and human warmth. Beneath it all pulsed the low hum of the Veil, disturbed but not yet broken.

Not yet.

Brontheus stirred distantly, curious, while the others slumbered on. Only Sylithra kept watch, knowing what the vision had whispered—the shadow curling at the edges of the night.

Hollow light rises. Balance trembles.

Her claws tightened against the frost-rimed stone. The humans below lay wrapped in breath and warmth and trust, but she felt the truth beneath it: their closeness was a lantern held against a storm.

Snow began to fall again, soft and steady, erasing the marks her claws had left behind. She turned her gaze to the stars, waiting—because even lanterns can be blown out.

◈ ☽ ⚡ ☾ ◈

Wyatt woke to soft gray light and the slow rise and fall of Cam's breathing.

For a moment, he didn't move—didn't dare. Her head rested against his shoulder; one hand curled loosely against his chest like she'd fallen asleep holding onto something she couldn't let go.

He thought of the kiss—of both of them, really—and how it had felt less like an answer and more like a vow born of fear. She'd seen him fall. He'd seen her fight to reach him. They hadn't kissed because they were ready, but because the thought of losing each other had been unbearable.

And yet, instead of leaving, she had asked him to stay. That was all. And he had—without question.

Cam stirred but didn't wake, her lashes trembling faintly against her cheek. Wyatt smiled, memorizing the silver-flecked shadows under her eyes, the way her hair fanned across his arm. She wasn't running. Not last night. Not this morning. That was enough for him.

By the time they slipped from her room and made their way to the hall, the Keep was alive with muted morning activity. Val and Tessa were already passing steaming mugs of tea to Kaden, and Corin leaned over a map, brow furrowed as always.

No one looked twice at them. Of course they didn't. Cam and Wyatt had spent months circling each other in quiet companionship; nothing about them walking in together seemed strange.

But the difference thrummed beneath Wyatt's ribs, silent, invisible, just for them. They sat closer at the war table than usual, elbows brushing when they leaned in to study the map. They traded fleeting glances that said more than words ever could. When Cam reached for a quill and her fingers brushed his, Wyatt felt the same pull he'd felt under the starlit tower.

Mutual protection had become instinct now—unspoken, natural. And though no one in the room noticed, Wyatt carried the warmth of that night in his chest like a secret lantern, bright enough to outshine the weight of the vision.

◈ ☽ ⚡ ☾ ◈

The Veil had tugged at him before, but never like that night. A pull sharp enough to stop his breath mid-step, as if the world itself had snagged his chest on an invisible hook. Cold spread under his skin, threading bone and blood until he couldn't lie still. He'd risen, followed the pull without thought, boots crunching soft across the courtyard snow.

The hum grew stronger near the watchtower. Not melody—discord. A vibration that scraped against his ribs, too close to pain. His fingers had twitched at his sides, itching to summon air, to steady the imbalance pressing in from nowhere.

Then he'd looked up.

Lanternlight caught on snow, scattering it into pale sparks. And there they were. Cam and Wyatt, standing too close to be called distant, yet not close enough to name what hung between them. Their hands, their breaths, the way Cam tilted toward him—it was all written plainly, the thing Wyatt had carried since childhood.

Kaden hadn't felt jealousy. Not once. His bond with Cam had never strayed from trust, from the kind of sibling weight that didn't need words. Seeing them only confirmed what he'd always known: that she was his brother's before either of them could admit it.

But the Veil told a different story.

The shift hadn't been soft. It didn't hum of fulfillment or fate catching up. It clawed, twisted, forced itself into his senses like a storm that wouldn't break. Whatever had stirred in that tower wasn't just them—it was bigger, older, the kind of thing Corin's notes whispered about in margins and half-finished warnings.

Kaden had stayed long enough to feel the wrongness settle deep. To see Cam's shoulders shake, Wyatt's hands steady her, their lips find each other in the hush of snow. To feel the Veil itself recoil even as they clung tighter.

He'd turned back toward the barracks, the hum gnawing at him with every step.

And now, in the war room, with maps stretched wide and firelight flickering across their faces, the memory pressed sharp in his chest. He glanced at Wyatt, then at Cam. They sat close, steady in ways the others didn't notice—but he felt it again. The hum. The scrape.

The Veil was shifting. And whether they were ready or not, it was already tying their fates tighter.

Chapter 22: Echoes in the Walls

Beneath Caerthalen's gilded spires, the Concord Chamber brooded in flickering half-light. Obsidian-veined walls swallowed the fire from the sconces, and the Heartshard pulsed faintly in the center of the crescent table—its silvered veins whispering of the Veil, listening to every word.

Lord Arven Corthal, commander of the Knighthood, leaned forward, jaw tight.

"She has slipped our grasp twice. The Outpost. The Arena. Now she trains under Corin Veyr himself. Every day she lives, she grows stronger. I say we end this before the world remembers what the bloodlines truly are."

Across from him, High Magister Selvara Odrin of the Academy traced one long finger over the obsidian surface, her tone sharp but calm.

"End this?" she echoed. "And discard the only living key the prophecy still acknowledges? Killing her risks unmaking the tether entirely. The Cradle was never a place—it is her blood. We sever that, and we may sever the Veil itself."

Corthal's mouth twisted.

"Better no tether than a weapon we cannot control. I will not see another Valehart rise unchecked while the dragons stir. If she ascends, the Knighthood falls. And she is not alone—Wyatt and Kaden Valehart train beside her, dragons at their backs. They are as great a threat as she is."

A new voice joined, low and measured: Chancellor Deyric, his eyes glinting in the dim firelight, his tone carrying a weight that silenced the room.

"You speak of threats, Lord Corthal, but you forget she is not untested." He paused, letting the silence stretch. "I have seen... glimpses. She has been brushed by the Veil and lived. No assassin will succeed where the Veil itself could not."

The chamber chilled, though only Kaelith, the ancient soul coiled within Deyric, knew the truth: he had tested her many times. He had drawn her close to the threshold, slipped her into the Veil for the briefest heartbeat—and she had returned. Scarred, but alive.

The council would never understand that strength.

"Assassins may fail," Selvara admitted, "but inaction is worse. She is already becoming a symbol. The prophecy's echo stirs the lower provinces. Dragons flock where she treads. And we have confirmation that Ben Miles—her father—is aiding her. A man who concealed his bloodline to claim a dragon the Knighthood could never tame. That creature still flies free."

Corthal's fist struck the table.

"Then we end it. Her. Her father. The Valehart twins. All of them, before the rebellion swells past the point of control."

The murmurs rose, a storm of cold resolve and fraying patience.

When the vote came, the council's decision was final.

The Chancellor's opposition was noted—but overruled.

Corthal's voice cut the air with the finality of a blade:

"Then it is agreed. She dies before the next season turns."

In the dim candlelight, the Heartshard gave a single, almost imperceptible pulse.

Kaelith, silent within Deyric's frame, smiled where no one could see.

Let them send their knives.

He had other plans for the girl who could open the world.

◈ ☽ ⚡ ☾ ◈

The halls of Haldrin's Keep breathed in low whispers, a language of stone and shadow. Torches burned low, their flames barely holding against the draft that coiled through the narrow passages. Far below, a ward thrummed faintly, its pulse a distant, steady heartbeat.

Footsteps stirred against the frost-kissed floor—soft, careful, measured. The spy moved as though the Keep itself had learned to accept their presence, its walls no longer warning of the intruder that slipped through them night after night.

They've grown predictable.

Even the dragons slept too soundly now, wings tucked tight, smoke curling lazily from their nostrils. No challenge. No threat. Not tonight.

The spy paused at a narrow window slit, letting moonlight slice across gloved hands. It was a ritual, this stillness. The chance to listen. To measure the rhythm of the place—and the people who thought it theirs.

Even she doesn't flinch anymore when I enter a room.

The thought lingered, quiet as the snow.

She looks past me now, like the others. Like I belong here. Good.

The spy turned down the east corridor, boots whispering against cold stone, passing the shuttered doors of sleeping allies. Allies in name, but not in truth. Every laugh shared by the fire, every map studied side by side—it was a careful mask. A pattern of belonging.

Let them think the storm sleeps.

But the Arena had changed everything. The spy could still see it—her power tearing loose, the air alive with raw Veil-light, a force that bent the world toward her will. She had not just fought that day; she had declared something older, louder than any council decree.

It was never about breaking her, the thought came, sharpened by memory. Only bending her. But storms do not bend. They tear down the walls we build to contain them.

And the walls of the Capital had heard.

The message had come as all orders did—silent, sealed, carrying the weight of inevitability:

Before the season turns, the girl must die.

The spy had read it without surprise. Perhaps with something close to regret, quickly buried.

This was the shape of loyalty. This was survival.

The spy's path ended at a darkened archway overlooking the training yard. Snow had drifted against the far wall where wind funneled in from the mountains, tracing faint silver lines in the moonlight. The Keep slept. The rebellion dreamed it was safe.

They are starting to believe I've chosen their side, the spy thought, letting the cold air wash over them. *That is enough.*

Their gaze lifted toward the black horizon where mountains swallowed the stars. Soon, they would fly west. Soon, the plan would end where it had begun—in silence and blood.

By the time they see me for what I am, it will be too late.

The spy turned and vanished into the dark, leaving nothing but the quiet hum of the Keep behind.

The spy lingered in the shadowed archway, silent as the wards' soft hum filled the hall. Beyond the cracked door of the war room, Kaden and Val were still awake, bent over the Veilbind scrolls, muttering about fragments and half-translations. The lantern light caught on the edge of Kaden's jaw, sharp with exhaustion, while Val traced one line over and over with her fingertip as if the pattern itself might surrender its secrets.

Kaden's eyes flicked to Cam and Wyatt—once, sharp—then returned to the scroll. Not longing; inventory. He'd marked a change. The spy filed it with other small shifts: who reached first, whose shoulders eased when the other entered. Patterns like these told you where to cut.

Just inside, Camomile Miles-Layton had fallen asleep in a chair, her head tipped against Wyatt's shoulder. He was awake, always watchful, one hand draped over the hilt of his dagger. Earlier that evening, the two had sparred in the yard, and the memory still clung to the spy—a flare of power when her magic slipped past her restraint. Wind and light in the same heartbeat. For a moment, she had been... magnificent.

A dangerous thought.

The spy's lip curled in something between disdain and reluctant awe.

Too loyal. Too raw. Too untamed to be theirs.

Further down the hall, Tessa leaned lightly against her companion—chatting, laughing softly, the easy sound echoing in the stone corridor. She rested her head briefly on Alex's shoulder, and he smiled without looking away from the floor. Almost natural. Almost. None of them looked toward the shadows. None of them sensed the quiet watcher who weighed the room like a blade in hand.

They think the storm can be trusted now, the spy thought, and the words carried a bitter edge. *But storms don't bow forever. And some storms... are meant to break.*

The spy lingered at the end of the corridor, letting the quiet of the Keep settle around them. Behind, the group remained as they were—unaware, unguarded.

Cam still slept against Wyatt's shoulder, soft and warm in the lantern glow. Kaden and Val's hushed voices drifted from the war room. Down the hall, Tessa murmured something that made Alex's smile twitch just slightly, the picture of contentment.

They looked so sure of their little world. So certain of their bonds and their safety.

The spy's lips curved—not with joy, but with the same practiced shape they'd worn in countless reflections. Hollow. Measured. A mask that knew its part.

Before the season turns... the cradle will open.

And with that thought, they turned and disappeared into the quiet, leaving only the flicker of torchlight where they'd stood.

Chapter 23: Of Names and Bloodlines

The sun was sharp but cold, turning the courtyard snow into a patchwork of glitter and mud. Wyatt's boots scuffed the edge of the sparring circle as he ducked under Cam's swing. The wooden blade whistled past his ear, close enough to ruffle his hair.

"Too slow," she teased, a faint smile tugging at her lips even as her breath puffed in the cold air.

"Too reckless," he shot back, stepping into her guard. Their weapons cracked together, and the sound rang off the stone walls.

Above them, Sylithra and Sael perched along the rampart, the dragons as still as carved statues. Only their eyes moved—slitted, bright, always watching.

Cam lunged again, faster this time, and Wyatt felt his own rhythm rise to meet hers. They'd grown used to each other in this dance—her sudden bursts of speed, the flicker of wind in her movements, his steady blocks and counters. He could read her now. Almost.

A sharp gust swirled snow into their boots as she spun, and he barely dodged the strike that followed. The wooden blade stopped an inch from his side, and Sael let out a low, rumbling growl from the wall.

Cam froze, tension rippling through her shoulders.

"Sorry," she said, lowering the blade immediately. The apology was quiet, genuine.

Wyatt straightened, rolling his shoulder with a soft grunt. "It's fine. You didn't hit me." He let a small grin break the moment. "Almost doesn't count."

Her mouth quirked upward, but her eyes flicked toward Sael. The dragon had already gone still again, but the reminder lingered—how closely they were all being watched, not just by dragons but by the weight of everything they carried.

They dropped onto the edge of the sparring circle, boots crunching in the half-frozen dirt. Their breath came in slow clouds. For a few heartbeats, they didn't speak—only listened to the muted bustle of the Keep, the distant clang of steel from another yard, and the low whisper of the wind over stone.

Wyatt glanced sideways at her, catching the brown in her hair where the sun hit it, the flecks of silver in her blue-gray eyes when she finally looked his way. His pulse slowed, steadying with a kind of quiet he'd only ever found next to her.

Wyatt leaned back on his hands, the cold from the packed earth seeping through his gloves. Cam sat beside him, still catching her breath, hair falling in a loose wave over one shoulder. The silence between them wasn't heavy. It just... held things. Things he wasn't sure he should say.

He exhaled through his nose and broke it anyway.

"Corin's my uncle," he said, voice low.

Cam blinked, startled, turning toward him. "Your... uncle?"

"Yeah." He traced a finger over the dirt between his boots. "Our mom—Kaden's and mine—was Lira Valehart. She didn't want anyone in the Capital to know. Said our name was dangerous enough without dragging Corin into it. So we grew up... hidden, I guess. In plain sight but still hidden."

Cam didn't interrupt. She just watched him, eyes steady, like she understood that these words didn't come easily.

"Kaden doesn't talk about it much," Wyatt went on, voice quieter now. "But it's there. Always there. It's strange, carrying a legacy you didn't choose. Like you're walking a path someone else laid for you, and no matter what you do, you're just... following their footsteps."

He let the words hang, heavy in the cold air. A part of him wanted to take them back, tuck them behind the walls he'd built. But he wanted her to know him—beyond the fights, beyond the plans, beyond the weight of visions and prophecy.

Cam's voice, when it came, was soft. "You can trust me. Even with the pieces you hide."

She didn't reach for him immediately. Instead, her gloved hand brushed the dirt near his, close enough that the warmth of her presence seemed to hum in the space between. Not comfort. Solidarity.

After a beat, she asked quietly, "What was your mother like?"

Wyatt's chest tightened. He stared at the dirt between his boots, the memory sharp as winter air.

"She was... warm," he said finally. "But she carried this weight all the time. Like she knew the Capital would take everything if she let them. She ran from it her whole life."

He hesitated, thumb brushing the hilt of his training blade.

"Sometimes I wonder if I'm doing the same thing. Running... or maybe just walking a path someone else set for me."

Her words settled into the cold air like a vow.

"If it's fate, then let it be fate," she added, softer now. "But if it's love... then let it be a choice."

Wyatt's chest tightened, and for the first time in weeks, the weight he carried felt a little less like a burden and more like something he could bear—with her.

Wyatt glanced sideways, catching her profile in the pale light. A stray lock of hair had fallen across her cheek, and without thinking, he reached to brush it back. His fingers hovered for a breath—then stopped, curling into his palm.

Cam turned her head just enough to meet his gaze, eyes glinting like frost catching sun. She didn't smile, not fully, but something soft and certain flickered there—like she'd heard the words he hadn't said.

Neither moved closer. Neither needed to.

The wind stirred around them, carrying the quiet weight of promises not yet spoken.

Wyatt let the silence stretch, the weight of Cam's last words settling into something quiet but certain between them.

A crunch of boots on packed snow drew his attention. Corin and Ben were crossing the courtyard, their conversation low and clipped. Ben carried a bundle of practice blades under one arm, his brow furrowed as he listened.

Corin slowed when his gaze fell on the two of them sitting side by side at the edge of the sparring circle. For a long breath, he simply studied them—his green eyes sharp, thoughtful, distant in that way that always made Wyatt feel like he was being measured against something unseen.

"What binds the blood," Corin said at last, his voice carrying easily in the still air, "may also unbind the world."

Ben paused mid-step, glancing at him, but Corin didn't elaborate. He only held Wyatt's gaze for a heartbeat longer before moving on, the crunch of their boots fading toward the hall.

Cam frowned slightly, brows drawing together. "What was that supposed to mean?"

Wyatt didn't answer right away. He stared after his uncle, a cold twist settling in his chest. "With Corin," he said finally, "it usually means more than it sounds like."

Cam tilted her head, puzzled, but let it drop—for now. The quiet settled again, heavier than before, carrying the echo of words neither of them yet understood.

Cam finally rose, brushing the dust and snow from her gloves. Wyatt followed, slower, his joints stiff from the cold and the long sparring session.

As Cam rose to leave, Sylithra's wings shifted gently, the dark scales catching the light with a slow, deliberate movement—an echo of Cam's own poised tension.

Sael's pale eyes remained fixed on Wyatt, calm and steady. When Cam turned back toward Wyatt, Sael's gaze flickered to her, soft and knowing—like a quiet acknowledgment between trusted companions.

When Cam brushed Wyatt's hand in farewell, both dragons moved almost in unison—tails flicking with a subtle grace that spoke of deep bonds and silent understanding.

Sael stepped lightly between them, not with a challenge, but as if to share their presence, grounding the moment.

Cam teased with a smile, "He's worse than Corin."

Wyatt smiled back, voice low and warm. "He only guards what matters."

A moment passed between them—a quiet, weighty understanding. Unspoken but real.

◈ ☽ ⚡ ☾ ◈

The war room was hushed but for the scratch of quill on parchment. Scrolls sprawled across the table between her and Kaden, lines of ink twisting like a maze that refused to open.

He leaned over the page, lips moving faintly as he sounded out a fragment under his breath. His grip on the quill was steady, almost rigid, like even the letters might break formation if he let them.

"You're staring too hard," Val said, folding her arms on the table. "The symbols won't confess just because you glare at them."

One corner of his mouth tugged upward—there and gone. "Worked on you, didn't it?"

She blinked, startled, before she caught the faint humor in his tone. A rare thing, and sharper for how little he gave it away.

"Mm. Maybe," she allowed a smile ghosting at the edges of her lips.

He bent back over the scroll, but she found herself watching him instead—the precision of his movements, the way his shoulders never really loosened even when he joked. Everything about him was contained, disciplined, as if he'd taught himself long ago that letting go wasn't safe.

And still, she thought, it anchored her. The steadiness in him. The way he stood like stone even when exhaustion shadowed his eyes.

Trust wasn't simple. But in that quiet, Val wondered if it could be built—slow, steady, like the work of his careful hands.

◈ ☽ ⚡ ☾ ◈

Tessa found Orren sharpening a blade in the courtyard. The rasp of steel against stone echoed steady and unhurried.

She folded her arms, leaning on the wall. "You polish it like you think someone's watching."

His gaze flicked up briefly. "Someone usually is."

Tessa raised a brow. "That's unsettling."

"Truth usually is."

His tone was flat, clipped—like everything about him, precise to the point of unnatural. She studied the way his movements never wasted energy, how his eyes tracked shadows more than people. He didn't move like someone who belonged to them.

"You don't fit here," she said, smirking, though her voice carried more weight than she meant.

He slid the blade home with quiet finality. "Belonging's overrated."

For a moment, his eyes lingered on her—steady, unreadable. Tessa felt a chill run down her spine, though she forced a shrug and pushed off the wall.

"Good thing I'm not asking you to," she tossed back, lighter than she felt.

As she walked away, her pulse thudded harder than it should have. She told herself it was annoyance, nothing more. Still, the rasp of steel stayed with her long after she'd gone.

Dangerous. Fascinating. Probably both.

◈ ☽ ⚡ ☾ ◈

From across the courtyard, Ben had slowed his pace. Cam and Wyatt sat close along the edge of the sparring circle, their conversation quiet, their posture eased in a way he hadn't seen before.

He didn't need to hear the words to know something between them had shifted. It was subtle—the way Wyatt seemed anchored in her presence, the way Cam's eyes softened when she looked at him—but it was there.

Ben felt the knot in his chest loosen. Not because he was ready to stop being protective—he doubted that would ever happen—but because for weeks he'd wondered where Cam's heart might land. He'd seen Orren lingering at the edges of her path, and while the man was capable enough, Ben had never quite decided whether to trust him.

Wyatt, though... Wyatt had already bled for her. And he'd do it again without hesitation.

The sight pulled a quiet memory to the surface—Isabella's laughter, the way her hand fit into his when they were young, long before the weight of war had settled over them. That same spark was there now; in the way Cam and Wyatt seemed to fit beside one another.

It was a dangerous thing, loving someone in times like these. It made you a shield—and a target. But maybe, Ben thought, watching them, it also gave you a reason to keep standing when the rest of the world tried to break you.

He adjusted the bundle of practice blades under his arm and kept walking, hiding the faint smile that threatened to break through. Whatever storm was coming, he'd stand between them and the worst of it.

Just like he'd promised Isabella he always would.

Chapter 24: Fractures

The air in the Keep had changed. Tessa felt it most in the pauses—between sparring drills, in the quiet stretch of corridors where wind slipped through the stones. Strategy still filled their days, blades still rang in the yard, but beneath it all the silence pressed heavier. And Orren was always there, like a shadow that refused to stay in the corner.

She caught him once in the strategy alcove, seated alone at the stone table. A disc of etched metal lay in his palm, faint runes spiraling across its surface. He worked it with slow precision, thumb turning, breath steady, until it flared with a brief, cold glow. The light died quickly, but not before it tugged gooseflesh up her arms.

Tessa leaned against the doorframe, arms crossed. "Anti-magic?"

Orren's head lifted, his eyes meeting hers without surprise. For a heartbeat he only studied her, then he stood and crossed the space between them. He didn't explain. Didn't ask. He simply pressed the disc into her hand.

The weight of it was colder than she expected.

"You trust me with this?" she asked, trying for lightness, though her voice betrayed the edge under it.

"I trust that you can learn," Orren said. His tone was flat, but his gaze lingered, sharp enough to feel like a test.

She fumbled through the runes the way she'd seen him do it, cursing when the light sputtered and died twice in a row. The third time it caught, a faint glow flickering across her palm. The satisfaction came quick and startled, curling her mouth into a grin she didn't mean to show.

"Didn't know you could teach."

"Didn't know you could listen," he replied. For an instant, the corners of his mouth threatened something almost like a smile.

Orren didn't walk away after. He only lingered letting the disc stay in her palm.

He stayed close, and she caught herself checking for him without meaning to. Annoying. Unsettling. Harder to ignore than she wanted.

When he finally stepped back, she realized she was breathing steadier than she meant to. She told herself she was only humoring him. Yet she couldn't ignore the way he kept orbiting near her and her friends, like a shadow choosing its place.

◈ ☽ ⚡ ☾ ◈

The wind bit against Cam's face as she pivoted in the sparring ring, boots scraping against the packed earth. Snow clung in the cracks where the sun couldn't reach, glittering in the light that bounced off the mountainside. Below, the valley stretched into haze and frost, the sky sharp and blue as a blade.

They had been training since sunrise. Every spar blurred into the next—Tessa's quick jabs, Kaden's measured strikes, Val's sharp, efficient movements. The air was thick with the metallic tang of sweat and the low rumble of dragon breath; Sylithra and Sael crouched along the ridge, watchful and still, while Brontheus prowled the edge of the circle, his claws leaving trails in the frozen dirt.

Cam refused to stop. Her muscles burned, her fingers trembled around the hilt of her training blade, but she waved off Val's offer to switch partners.

"Another," she said, voice clipped.

"Fine by me," Orren said as he stepped into the ring. His face was unreadable, that same quiet smirk flickering at the corner of his mouth. Since the solstice, they hadn't spoken much. Cam could feel the unspoken weight in the air between them—the understanding that he was dangerous, that the others didn't trust him, and that she couldn't afford to.

"Don't hold back," she warned, raising her blade. "I won't."

He tilted his head, as if amused, and lunged first.

Steel met steel in a quick, testing clash. Orren was fast, sharper than most of the mage riders she'd trained with at Haldrin's Keep or on the cliffs beyond. He pressed her with precise strikes, probing for weaknesses, and she countered with quick footwork and flashes of lightning that cracked against the cold air—not enough to hit him, just enough to keep him wary.

He almost had her once—his blade whispering just past her ribs—but she rolled with the momentum and came up behind him, the tip of her blade to his back.

"Dead," she said.

Orren's smirk widened slightly as he lowered his weapon in acknowledgment. "Not bad."

But there was something in his eyes when he stepped away. Not anger. Something quieter, unreadable.

Cam barely had time to shake off the tension before Wyatt stepped into the ring. He didn't say anything. He never did, not when the earth was already speaking for him.

Wyatt's boots sank slightly into the dirt, his stance solid, unshakable. He wasn't fast like Orren, but every motion carried weight. When he blocked her strike, the impact vibrated up her arm—like hitting stone. His patience was unnerving. He didn't chase her. He didn't lunge. He just waited, reading her, letting the rhythm of the fight settle like silt in water until he decided to move.

And when he moved, the earth seemed to move with him.

Cam grinned, exhilaration sparking in her chest. She lunged, testing him, and he caught her wrist in a gentle but immovable grip, twisting the blade from her hand with careful precision. She froze, caught in the space between his calm strength and the cold wind whipping their hair.

Tessa's voice rang out from the edge of the circle.

"Oh, for the love of the Veil—just kiss her already!"

Heat flushed up Cam's neck. She jerked back a step, shaking Wyatt's grip loose, the blush on her cheeks stark against the cold. The motion sent her practice sword slipping from her hand, clattering against the frozen dirt. Wyatt didn't press; he only let her retreat, his eyes steady, calm as ever, though his jaw tightened just slightly.

Cam crouched quickly, fingers brushing the hilt as she muttered under her breath, "You're next, Tessa. And I'll use a real sword, not a practice one."

When she straightened, she caught the faint twitch at the corner of Wyatt's mouth. He didn't laugh, didn't tease, but the quiet curve of it told her he'd heard—and understood—it was meant for him.

The laughter from Tessa's outburst still hung lightly in the air as the group settled back into rhythm. The brief break had loosened tight muscles and eased the tension threading through them all.

Cam wiped a bead of sweat from her brow, her breath steady, heart still quick but calm now. The warmth of the sun felt good against her skin, and the familiar weight of the training blade in her hand grounded her.

Around the circle, riders rotated through light sparring—Wyatt exchanged quick blows with Val, their movements fluid and measured, while Kaden and Tessa kept a steady, easy pace.

Cam's eyes flicked to the edge of the ring where Alex lingered, watching with an expression she couldn't quite read; part casual, part calculating.

He stepped forward smoothly, nodding to her. The playful air shifted just enough to make the moment feel deliberate.

Without breaking stride, Alex drew his practice blade, sliding easily into the sparring ring.

At first, it felt routine.

"Ready to lose again?" Alex teased, a sly grin tugging at his lips.

Cam smirked, stepping into stance. "You're dreaming."

Their blades clashed in a rhythmic dance—light, teasing strikes at first.

But as the sparring wore on, Alex's jokes faded.

"Getting slow, Cam? Or just saving energy for the big fight?" he said, voice low, eyes sharp.

Cam's smile tightened. "You should worry about your own speed."

That was when the air changed. His next strike carried a shimmer of frost—subtle, but real. Ice spread faintly along the practice blade as it glanced off hers, cold burning through the wood.

Cam's pulse spiked. *Magic—he's using magic.*

She caught the frost with an earth-flared block, her voice snapping out before she could stop it.

"Not here, Alex. Not with practice blades."

The dragons watched from the ridge—Sael pale and still as carved stone, Tenebrin a shadow coiled in silence, Brontheus prowling like a storm held on a leash, Virellan gleaming faintly in the sun. They saw everything, but only one moved.

Sylithra's claws scraped the stone, a low growl curling from her chest as her molten eyes locked on Cam. The sound thrummed through the tether between them, sharp and protective, like a warning meant only for her.

The instinct came before thought. Earth surged up through Cam's chest and into her arms, an invisible shield flaring across her skin. Alex's next swing hit the barrier with a crack of frost against stone, shards splintering across the dirt.

Her own blade shoved through the clash, heat rising in her chest. "Enough, Alex," she snapped.

But he didn't stop. His eyes had gone sharper, colder. Another flare of ice laced the ground near her boots, forcing her back a step.

Cam's earth rose again, steady this time, grounding her like bedrock. She let it channel through her arm, swept his strike wide, and in the same breath disarmed him—his blade clattering to the frozen dirt.

The others stilled, the air thick with more than frost now—suspicion, unease, something brittle enough to break.

Silence fell heavy.

Alex froze, chest heaving, frost steaming faintly from his fingers. For a heartbeat his eyes met hers, dark and storming, and he looked less like the boy she'd sparred a hundred times and more like a stranger.

Kaden, standing nearby, narrowed his eyes, voice low. "You used magic."

Wyatt stepped forward, concern threading his voice. "Cam. You alright?"

She nodded quickly, hiding the flicker of unease. But her fingers twitched involuntarily, the memory of frost still clinging to her skin.

Across the ring, Orren's gaze lingered on Alex, watching his every move with a sharp, unreadable intensity.

Cam watched Alex stalk off toward the lower halls, jaw tight, shoulders rigid. The echo of steel on stone and the faint sting of cold still rang in her bones. She exhaled, wiping her palms on her training leathers, trying to shake the chill he'd left behind.

Tessa caught the look on Cam's face and felt something twist in her chest. Without a word, she jogged after Alex, her boots scuffing the stone as she disappeared into the stairwell.

◈ ☽⚡☾ ◈

The air was cooler in the lower corridors, the mountain wind sneaking in through high, narrow windows. She found Alex beneath the overlook, leaning against the weathered stone rail, his gaze fixed on the jagged line of peaks. His fists rested on the railing, knuckles white.

"You walked out fast," she said, breathless from the chase. Her voice carried a note of teasing at first but worry threaded beneath it.

Alex didn't move. Didn't even look at her.

"She's not yours to prove something against," Tessa said, arms crossing instinctively. "And she's not why you're angry."

His jaw flexed, silent.

"You're mad she survived without you," Tessa pressed, voice softening. "That she doesn't need you the way you thought she would."

That earned her a glance—a flicker, sharp and unreadable—but still no words.

Tessa's chest tightened, but she forced a small, wavering laugh. "You know, you don't have to win against her to matter. You already matter. To me."

For a heartbeat, the wind filled the silence. Alex's lips curved in a faint, practiced smile, the kind that didn't reach his eyes. It felt like a wall more than a bridge.

Tessa hesitated, then touched his arm lightly. "I'll see you at dinner?"

He gave a single nod. Nothing more.

She turned to leave, but something pricked at the edge of her awareness. The corridor felt heavier than it should have, shadows stretching long against the stone. Tessa shook it off, telling herself it was nothing more than the mountain wind slipping through the arches. Still, her pulse skipped as she walked back toward the upper halls, the echo of Alex's silence following her like a shadow.

◈ ☽⚡☾ ◈

The sun angled low enough to throw long shadows across the sparring ring. Cam's lungs still burned from the last bout, breath ragged and bright in the cold. Around her, the others moved with the measured tiredness of people who'd trained too long—muscles set to memory, conversations thin and practical.

Tessa had rejoined them from the lower halls, Alex nowhere in sight, her jaw tight with whatever words had passed between them. Sparks still clung faintly to her fingertips, as if the argument lingered in her bones.

Then Kaden's voice cut through the yard, quiet and tight. "Where did you get that?"

Cam followed the line of his stare and saw it—the dark spiral of sigils climbing the skin above Orren's wrist, clean and deliberate as ink. Her own breath seemed to stall.

Wyatt's jaw clenched beside her. "That's not a scar," he said, low enough that the snow swallowed it. "That's a hunter's mark."

The words fell like a thrown stone. For a second, the world narrowed to the small circle of cold between them and Orren, and she saw the way Val's hand curled white around her hilt. Her face went pale as old grief and new fury tangled together.

"Not a hunter," Val breathed. Her voice was tight, brittle, shaking as much from memory as from rage. "Not one of them."

Orren didn't flinch. He only let one shoulder roll, as unruffled as if they were discussing weather. "I was a mage hunter," he said flatly.

Something in the yard cracked, like thin ice giving way.

Kaden's voice cut sharp through the ring.

"Once a mage hunter, always one. You think we'll let you stand at our backs?"

Val's hands trembled on her blade, but her voice was steady, cold. "He doesn't belong here. Not with us."

Tessa's sparks crackled in the air, her jaw tight. "We end him now before the Capital uses him against us."

Wyatt said nothing, but his silence was heavier than all their words. His blade angled low, steady, like he was waiting for the first strike to fall.

That was the moment Cam realized they weren't bluffing. They were ready to kill him—now, together, without hesitation. And if she let them, if she stood still and let them cut him down in cold blood, it would send them down a path none of them could return from. She could almost see it, the echoes of what they might become.

Her feet moved before she even thought, carrying her forward, blade loose in her hand, her body between Orren and the only people she'd ever trusted.

Kaden's response was the first blade. It was a movement too quick to be thought—drawn, leveled, the point aimed straight for Orren's chest. Tessa's shout followed, raw and furious. "You lied to us. You lied to her—"

Wyatt moved next, but not with a blade; his hand came for his dagger, and his face went hard as flint, and something like fear flickered under the anger in his eyes.

Cam didn't think. One moment she was still on the edge of the ring, the next she was squared against her friends, hands out stretched towards them, heart banging an animal rhythm in her throat.

"Stop!"

Val's eyes snapped to her—pain, betrayal, accusation all cut in the same line. "Cam—" she started.

"No. You don't get to do this here," Cam said, before she could unpack the cascade of fear and reason that had driven her forward. Her voice sounded too loud in her own ears. "You don't get to kill him before he's had a chance to—"

"A chance?" Tessa barked. "He has the mark. He hunts people like us."

The circle tightened. Kaden's arm trembled with the force of the blade in his grip. Wyatt's eyes flicked from Orren to Cam, his silence pressing on her chest harder than words.

Orren's hands were empty. He watched them all with that same stillness that had made Cam trust him when nothing else did.

"You think I chose it?" His voice was quiet, stripped of defense. "I did what I was told to survive."

The sound of leather sliding, of blades cutting loose from sheaths, the soft metallic cough of edges checking—the yard thrummed with readiness to end it. For a moment Cam tasted the iron tang of panic, the way the air seemed to press tight against her ribs.

She thought of every night he'd stood watch, every careless silence, the way he'd let danger pass without reaching for the kill, and something else under that—a restraint she couldn't name.

Her voice came out steadier than she felt.

"If he wanted me dead," she said, and the words snagged the air, "I would be."

The reaction was immediate and raw. Val's hand trembled so hard the hilt bit into her palm. Tessa's mouth was an angry line. Kaden's blade wavered fractionally. Wyatt's eyes locked on Cam in a way that made heat pulse through her.

"He's had every chance," she went on, shoulders squared to buy herself courage. "You don't have to trust him. But you trust me. If he proves false—if he ever turns on any of us—then I'll kill him myself."

Silence broke like thin glass. Sael lowed in the ridge above, a rumble that was almost a warning. Sylithra shifted along the parapet, wings feathering the air. Brontheus's claws scraped stone, his breath rolling like stormwind. Tenebrin's wings flared once, shadow spilling across the yard, while Virellan's scales rippled faintly, a shimmer of unease that thrummed through Val's chest. The dragons were answering their riders' fear—threaded tethers humming like struck wire.

Kaden lowered his blade a hair. Val's face was a map of wounds. Tessa's fists unclenched, not in forgiveness, but because the violence that had been about to unfold had been—by a hair—held back.

Wyatt didn't speak. His look cut through her, not anger at Orren, but a question: *Why put yourself between us? Why choose him?* And beneath it all, she saw something like fear—raw, unguarded, for her.

Orren's expression remained unreadable. He didn't beg. He didn't ask for mercy. He only nodded once, the motion small and almost private, and stepped back into the shadow where his mark ran like a dark river across his skin.

The group frayed at the edges but did not snap. Cam's heart still hammered. Her hands shook where they hung at her sides. She hadn't realized she'd moved until she felt the cold press at her back and heard Wyatt's breath a fraction too loud.

She had no certainty. Only this: the rightness of the choice to stand between them, to let whatever trust he might earn be earned in the open—not with a blade in the dark.

Wyatt's voice came at last, low and rough, aimed only at Cam. "You put yourself between us." No anger, not yet—but the raw edge of something that hurt worse.

The others' silence pressed in, sharp as drawn steel. She met their eyes one by one—Kaden's fury, Val's grief, Tessa's sparks trembling at her fingertips, Wyatt's silence like stone—and for the first time, she spoke not to defend Orren, but to them.

"I saw the path you were about to take," she said, voice raw but steady. "And I won't let you go down it. Not like this. Not in cold blood."

Above the dragons stirred as one—Sael's low rumble, Sylithra's restless wings, Tenebrin's hiss through the cold air, Brontheus stamping the frozen dirt, Virellan's tail lashing against stone. They mirrored their riders, unsettled, dangerous, waiting.

Then the crunch of boots broke the silence. Corin emerged from the colonnade at the edge of the yard, Ben a step behind him, both carrying the weight of men who had been watching far longer than the rest of them realized.

Corin's voice cut through the tension, measured but carrying iron. "We will not act hastily."

It wasn't just command—it was reprieve. Even Kaden's blade dropped another fraction, though his eyes still burned. Val looked away, lips pressed thin, and Tessa's fists unclenched with a snap of sparks.

Corin stepped further into the circle, his gaze steady on Orren. "He'll be questioned. Watched. Bound if need be. If his loyalty is false, it will be proven soon enough."

Ben shifted the bundle of blades in his grip, his voice like steel ground against stone. "Until then, he doesn't breathe without one of us knowing. I'll see to it myself."

No one argued. But the silence that followed said none of them trusted it—not yet.

Cam steadied herself on the scent of smoke and dragonhide and knew, with a quietly anchoring certainty, that whatever came next, she had chosen to hold everyone or hold nothing. She'd given the others the one thing they could not take away: the knowledge that she would stand between them and the blade, and that if he broke her trust, she would be the one to see it done.

She felt the weight land like a stone—leader, shield, or traitor; whichever they named her, she'd chosen.

◈ ☽⚡☾ ◈

The stone walls pressed close in the chamber. No windows, no light but the lantern burning low on the table. Orren sat with his hands loose on his knees, back straight, as if posture alone could keep the cold from sinking deeper.

His thumb drifted over the spiraling mark on his wrist. At first he didn't even notice he was doing it. The skin was raised, familiar, carved into him as deep as bone. The others had looked at it like it was a death sentence. And maybe it was.

The echo of the training yard clung like frost. Kaden's blade flashing for his heart. Tessa's sparks snapping, furious. Val's face—white with grief, her fury trembling on the edge of her blade. Wyatt's silence heavier than steel. He had seen his death in their faces and accepted it. There had been no fear—only the inevitability of a weapon meeting its end.

And then she had been there.

Camomile Miles-Layton, planting herself between him and the circle that would have cut him down. Her voice steady, her shoulders squared, her fire turned on them instead of him. "You don't have to trust him. But you trust me."

His thumb pressed harder against the mark now, no longer unconscious, but deliberate. As if he could grind the inked lines into dust. As if he could force them to answer him. He could still hear her words. Not defense. Not mercy. Something else entirely.

The Capital had shaped him into a blade, honed to strike without question. But in that moment—when she chose to shield what she did not trust—something inside him fractured. The weapon faltered. And he didn't know what was left beneath it.

The interrogations had followed. Ben, Corin, a captain with a scribe's ink-stained hands. Questions thrown like arrows, patient and merciless. Orren hadn't lied. He hadn't needed to. The truth was damning enough: he had not finished the mission the Capital had set. He had not taken her.

And now, after the yard, after her voice, after her standing where no one else would, he knew he never would.

The lantern hissed, guttering low, shadows climbing the stone. Orren's fingers lingered on the mark as if it might remind him what he was. But all it gave him was silence.

He didn't understand her. He didn't understand why she had chosen him—just that she had. And it was breaking him in ways the Capital never could.

Chapter 25: Silent Threads

Morning light crept through the tall, narrow windows of Haldrin's Keep, scattering in fractured beams across the long tables. Dust hung in the air like suspended sparks, catching the light with each shift of breath.

Kaden traced a finger down the margin of the scroll in front of him, careful not to smudge the crumbling ink. He could feel the weight of the words before he could even translate them. Prophecy had a way of pressing on his chest, as if every line expected something from him.

Across from him, Val turned another page of the Book of Unbinding. The parchment gave a soft sigh, brittle against her gloves. Her motions were deliberate, almost ceremonial, as though handling the book was an act of devotion.

"It's like the magic wants us to see it," she murmured. Her eyes caught the faint green flecks in the light as she studied the page. "Like it's tired of being forgotten."

Kaden's jaw flexed. He thought of his mother, Lira Valehart—the weight she'd carried, the legacy she'd hidden, and how even now, in the quiet of a library, he felt like her choices were shackled to his spine. He hadn't chosen this bloodline, or the dragons that seemed to sense it before he could.

And layered over that memory—Cam, standing in the sparring yard, blade lowered but body squared, shielding Orren. *Shielding him.*

The way her words had cut through them*: If you trust me, then trust me now.*

Kaden trusted her. He always would. But the image still burned in his chest—because Cam might be right, and still Orren could be exactly what his mark declared him to be.

Tenebrin's presence coiled close, shadow and wind threading with his thoughts. The dragon had seen too—Cam's fire flaring in the yard, the moment she put herself between blade and hunter.

She burns for more than herself, Tenebrin murmured. *But flame can blind as well as light the path.*

Kaden swallowed hard. Trust in her was easy. Trust in Orren was another matter.

Trust in her. Suspicion of him. No way to reconcile it.

Val shifted in her seat, quill tapping once against the parchment. Tension edged her movements; the same tension Kaden had seen since the yard. He knew she hadn't forgiven Cam for stepping in front of Orren. She might never.

His gaze flicked to the far window where sunlight pooled on the stone. For a heartbeat, he imagined he saw a faint golden shimmer—like the Veil breathing. He blinked, and it was gone.

"Yeah," he said finally, low and rough. "Maybe it is."

The silence settled again, but it wasn't empty. It pulsed, the same way the old mark on Cam's wrist had pulsed that night when she thought no one was watching. A secret he couldn't unsee.

He remembered the council chamber months ago—how the elders had spoken of it in clipped voices, as if the mark itself was dangerous to name. He had never asked Cam about it. Maybe out of loyalty, maybe out of fear. Now, with prophecy bleeding into every page, silence wasn't an option anymore.

Soon, he would ask her.

Because whatever that mark was, it wasn't just a scar. It was a tether—and tethers only ever snapped at the worst possible time.

Wind stirred faintly in his chest, Tenebrin's tether brushing against his thoughts. *You trust her. That is enough. Do not let the shadow of one man unmake the circle.*

The words pressed steady as stone, but Kaden couldn't let them settle. His gaze fixed on the glyph, and on the silence coiled tight in his chest.

◈ ☽ ⚡ ☾ ◈

The hall hummed softly with the low murmur of voices and the clinking of utensils, but Kaden had felt none of the comfort that should have come with shared meals. The air was tight, heavy with things left unsaid.

Cam sat beside Wyatt, their hands brushing once—too quick to be accidental, too fleeting to be bold. He noticed the slight stiffening in her posture, the way her gloved fingers twitched near the leather strap that hid the mark on her wrist. Wyatt's gaze caught hers for a moment, steady but unreadable. Neither of them spoke, as if afraid to break the fragile calm.

Across the table, Alex watched them like a storm gathering behind calm eyes. His jaw had been tight; lips pressed in a line that said everything without words. Kaden felt the weight of that look like a physical thing pressing against his ribs.

He's angry, Kaden thought. *Or worse, jealous. But he masks it too well.*

His own eyes flicked to Cam's wrist, the hidden mark stirring beneath her skin. Silent questions clawed at him: How long had she been carrying this secret? How many more secrets?

Val caught his gaze and gave him a small, knowing look—no words, but all the warning he needed.

And over it all, Orren's shadow had lingered. He hadn't even needed to speak; his presence had been reminder enough. The hunter's mark had been plain, the memory of Cam stepping between him and their blades even plainer. Trusting Cam had been easy. Trusting Orren still felt like playing with fire.

Cam sighed heavily and met Kaden's eyes with quiet steadiness. "No matter what's between us... this—what we're up against—is bigger than all of it."

Wyatt nodded, his eyes briefly meeting Kaden's. Everyone else tensed but there had been something unspoken in that glance—a mixture of resolve and caution.

Kaden swallowed the tightness in his throat. The threads binding them all were growing taut—and soon, they might snap.

Their group rose from the table—Wyatt, Cam, Kaden, Val, and Tessa gathering their notes and heading toward the war room. The air had been thick with unspoken thoughts as they pored over maps and scrolls, reviewing what they had learned and what still needed unraveling.

After a while, the others began to disperse to their duties before dusk fell, leaving Kaden and Val lingering in the dimming light of the war room.

Val broke the silence, her voice quieter than he'd ever heard it. "You carry too much, Kaden. You'll break before the rest of us if you don't let someone share the weight."

Kaden offered a tired but warm smile. Their hands met briefly—a quiet reassurance—before Val turned to leave.

Alone now, Kaden reopened the Book of Unbinding, his mind settling on the pages and on the mark on Cam's wrist.

I have to ask her soon, he thought. *Before someone else does.*

◈ ☽ ⚡ ☾ ◈

Val paused at the door to her quarters, fingers curled tight around the iron latch. The barracks hall was quiet, only the faint murmur of wind threading through the stones. She should have gone inside, let the day dissolve into rest, but her mind kept circling back—back to the training yard, to Cam stepping between them and Orren.

Her chest tightened. Cam's fire had burned steady, unshaken, shielding him when every blade was poised to fall. The others had seen it as blindness. Val had seen it as betrayal.

A pulse of calm pressed faintly at the edge of her mind. Virellan, ever watchful, coiled in the back of her thoughts.

Stormheart. Let it go. The dragon's voice was soft thunder, low and steady, trying to anchor her against the storm rising in her chest.

But Val couldn't. Not this time.

Her thoughts slipped further, down a path she rarely allowed herself to tread. She was ten years old again, knees tucked beneath her at the kitchen table, the smell of woodsmoke and ash clinging to her clothes. Her parents had stood across from her, faces gray with grief but set with something colder.

'Your brother is gone.'

The words had landed like stone, but worse had followed.

'He was killed by a mage hunter.'

Her father's voice had been quiet, bitter. Her mother's eyes had brimmed with tears, but not for the son she'd lost—for the shame of his defiance. To them, he had been a traitor to the Capital, his crime unforgivable: wielding more than one element.

But Val had known better, long before Cam entered her life. She too could wield more than one element. And her brother had made sure she knew how to use them—made sure she understood what it meant, even if their parents didn't.

Virellan stirred again, her tether brushing Val's thoughts like the steady weight of wings. *Stormheart, his death was not your fault. Do not let the wound command you.*

Val clenched her jaw. The scar had grown with her, jagged and unspoken, carved deep by silence and by the wound her parents never named again. But no calm, not even Virellan's, could quiet it.

And now Cam had stepped in front of Orren—a man marked with the same sigil.

Val let her hand fall from the latch. Her boots carried her down the hall, out into the cold.

The training yard lay empty by dusk, only the echo of sparring blades lingering in the stone. Cam stood near the edge, brushing snow from her gloves, when Val found her.

"My brother," Val said, before she could think better of it. The words felt like pulling glass from her throat. "He was killed by a mage hunter."

Cam stilled, her blue-gray eyes lifting, flecks of silver catching the fading light. There was no pity in her face—just listening.

Val's jaw tightened. "Do you know what he is, Cam? What Orren is?"

"I know enough," Cam said. Her tone was steady, not sharp, but it stung all the same.

"Then why let him live? Why let him stay like he belongs?" Val's voice cracked on the last word, raw with the scar she couldn't hide.

Cam didn't argue. Didn't even raise her voice. "Because if we cut everyone down before they prove themselves, we'll end up as blind as the Capital."

That was all. No more, no less. Cam turned and walked away, leaving frost crunching under her boots.

The words landed heavier than Orren's presence ever had.

Val stood alone, staring out over the yard. Orren crossed it below, moving with the same unreadable stillness as always. On the battlements above, Wyatt leaned against the stone, his posture steady as the cliffs themselves. One hand rested near the hilt at his belt, not gripping, but close enough to speak for him. His gaze tracked Orren with the same quiet, implacable weight he gave to anything that threatened Cam.

Not trust. Not hatred. Just suspicion, heavy as stone.

Val's chest tightened at the sight. Cam's circle thought she was blind for stepping in front of him—for shielding him when they all had blades drawn. But Val knew Cam wasn't blind. That almost made it worse. Because if Cam could see Orren clearly and still chose to defend him, then what did that say about the rest of them? About her brother's death? About the scars that still bled in silence?

Her throat ached, her grip on her gloves biting into her fingers. That was when Virellan's voice stirred through the tether, calm as rain softening a storm.

Stormheart, breathe. The wound is yours, not hers. Do not let it cut you twice.

The words settled like mist in her chest. Virellan's steady presence pulsed at the edge of her awareness, scales cool against her grief, the low rhythm of her breath wrapping Val like a shield. The dragon's wisdom wanted to anchor her—remind her that Cam's choices did not rewrite her brother's death, nor bind her scars to Orren's mark.

But Val's exhale trembled, half-caught between relief and refusal. The wound was still raw, and no counsel could change that. She clung to her anger because it was easier than letting go, easier than accepting that Cam might see something in Orren worth saving.

For all Cam's fire, for all her conviction, she didn't see. Not really. Not the depth of the scar her brother's death had carved, not the way Orren's mark tore it open every time.

Virellan rumbled softly, like thunder withheld. The tether whispered calm, but it slid over Val like water on stone.

Instead of easing her, it unsettled her more.

If Cam wouldn't see what he was—or if she saw and still chose him—maybe Wyatt would.

Chapter 26: The Mark and the Map

The morning was silver-bright and quiet, meltwater threading the stone paths and the scent of pine cutting through the last breath of winter. Cam stood near the edge of the courtyard where the dragons were roosting, her fingers tightening the last strap on Sylithra's harness. The great dragon rumbled low in her chest, wings shifting once with a sound like falling silk.

She could feel it still—the weight of their mistrust. Val's clipped silences. Tessa's sparks too quick to flare. Wyatt, steady as stone, but distant. They hadn't forgiven her for stepping between them and Orren. Maybe they never would.

And still, she would do it again.

"Cam."

She turned. Kaden stood behind her, arms crossed, boots damp from snowmelt, his expression unreadable. His tone was too calm. Too direct.

"I saw it again. The mark. On your wrist."

Her hand twitched, tugging her sleeve lower, but too late. The strap had slipped, and the air between them tightened. The mark beneath it prickled faintly, as if aware it had been named.

"I think I deserve to know what it is," he said.

Cam's throat closed. She could lie. She almost wanted to. But Kaden's eyes weren't angry—just afraid. And that fear broke something in her.

"It's a tether," she said quietly. "At least... that's what I think. It showed up after I went into the vault at the Academy. Where the Book of Unbinding was locked away."

His brow furrowed. "That book...?"

"There was something in there. A presence. Dark. Old. I thought I was imagining it, but then the mark appeared, and Corin confirmed it wasn't just some magical burn. Ben knows too. And Wyatt." Her voice faltered. "I was going to tell you. I just—"

"You waited," Kaden said, voice even. "Until I had to ask."

Cam looked away, guilt rising like tidewater. "It scares me. I didn't want to put that on anyone else."

He nodded slowly. No anger. No accusations. Just disappointment—heavier than any fury.

He turned and walked away without another word.

His steps were measured, too even, the way he always moved when he was holding something in. he didn't look back. Not once.

Cam stood there long after he was gone, the harness forgotten in her hands. Sylithra nudged her shoulder gently, a low, questioning hum vibrating through her jaw.

Little Flame, Her voice coiled through Cam's mind, deep and steady, like fire banked beneath stone. *The fear is not the danger. The silence is.*

Cam blinked hard, then fastened the last buckle.

The sun was climbing. The others would be waiting. But still, the cold under her ribs lingered.

The mark tingled beneath the strap—cold, restless. Not for Kaden. For something else.

Later, after Cam's flight training was done the sky opened above the cliffs, and two dragons streaked through the thinning clouds, their wings carving the wind with dazzling precision. Meltwater sparkled as it flew off scales—pale-white and obsidian-dark.

Wyatt whooped as Sael dove beneath Kaden's path, the two of them sparring midair, magic crackling in layered threads—Wyatt's golden light grounding against Kaden's controlled swirls of air and shadow.

Cam watched them from the stables below as she and Val sorted rations while Tessa complained about the scent of preserved herbs. For all the playfulness above, she felt the fracture beneath it—the same fault line that hadn't healed since the yard. Even in laughter, the threads binding them all were stretched too tight.

"You chose to bond a dragon that smells like a lightning storm and burnt moss," Val teased.

"I thought that'd cancel out the smell of dried eel paste," Tessa shot back.

Cam laughed, the sound slipping out too easily. For a heartbeat, it felt like things had turned. Like maybe they had come through the solstice with enough light left in them to keep going.

But the laughter was fragile. She could feel the strain beneath it—the hard edge of Val's tone, the way Wyatt hadn't joined them, the silence that seemed to cling after every joke. It was a reprieve, not a healing.

And beneath her sleeve, the mark cooled again, as if mocking the illusion of peace.

◈ ☽ ⚡ ☾ ◈

Tessa leaned against the shadowed arch of the war yard, arms folded tight across her chest as she watched Orren cross the stones below. He moved with that same unnerving stillness—silent, unflinching, like he belonged more to the cold than to the people around him.

She wanted to hate him cleanly. Wanted it simple. Just the mark on his hand, the silence of a hunter, the reminder that he had been forged to destroy everything she fought for.

But she hated herself for noticing the cracks. The way he lingered just beyond their circle, never pushing closer. The way his eyes had softened, barely, when Cam had stood between him and their blades. He hadn't even raised a hand that day. No defense. No strike. Just stood there, waiting, as if he had already accepted his end.

What kind of man accepted death that easily?

Her nails bit crescents into her palms. She had been starting to let her guard down, almost believing he was more than the mark carved into him. But that was the danger. Letting him look human.

As if pulled by the weight of her stare, Orren slowed. His head turned, eyes lifting toward the shadows where she stood. He stopped mid-stride, boots planting square on the stone.

For a heartbeat, they held. His gaze was steady, unreadable—stone and shadow—but there was something under it, fleeting as a breath. A weariness. Maybe even regret. It flickered, then was gone, leaving only the mask behind.

Her chest tightened. She tore her eyes away first, forcing her shoulders back into the arch until the stone pressed into her spine. The mark on his hand burned in her mind, and she told herself she hadn't seen anything else. Couldn't have.

She hated him for that, too. For not looking away. For letting her be the one to break.

Brontheus stirred, the tether humming low and electric through her veins. *Stormsinger... do not chain yourself to his choices. His silence is not your wound.*

Her throat ached. Sparks danced at her fingertips, dimming only when she pressed her hands hard against the stone. She wanted to believe Brontheus. She wanted to hate Orren cleanly. But the question lingered, crackling in her chest like stormfire, dangerous and unresolved.

◈ ☽ ⚡ ☾ ◈

The roost sat high above the cliffs, open to the wind. Below, the vast sprawl of the Karethwyn Forest stretched to the horizon, a sea of dark green broken by rivers of silver meltwater. Wyatt sat on the stone ledge, knees braced, the cold biting through his gloves. Sael's pale coils rested behind him, the dragon's chest rising slow and steady, a living anchor against the sharp air.

The tether hummed faintly. Patience. Steadiness. *Wait.*

But waiting didn't ease the echo in his chest. *'I saw a path you were about to go down. And I won't let you go down it. Not like this. Not in cold blood.'*

Cam's words. Cam's fire. Cam stepping in front of him when Orren had stood there, marked, unarmed, waiting.

His hand found the pendant at his chest. The sigil pressed warm against his palm, but trust didn't erase the sting. She had chosen to shield someone else—when Wyatt's blade had been raised.

Bootsteps scraped against the stone stair. Wyatt didn't move until her shadow spilled into the roost.

Cam stepped into the light. The wind tugged loose strands of her dark hair, silver flecks catching in her blue-gray eyes. She hesitated, just long enough to make his chest ache, then came to sit beside him. Not close, but close enough.

"You stood for him," Wyatt said, low. The words tasted like frost.

"I don't take it back," she answered. Her voice was steady, but quiet, like she knew how close the edge was. She looked out over the forest, then back at him. "And if it had been you standing there—if it had been your blade raised—I would have done the same. I won't let you go down that path. Not like this."

Her words didn't tremble, but her eyes did. Just the faintest flicker, silver catching like a crack in steel. Wyatt saw the breath she held too long, the way her shoulders tightened, the way her hand hovered as if she'd reach for him and thought better of it. She was breaking under her own choice—he could feel it, even if she wouldn't say it.

Wyatt swallowed, jaw tight. The wind pulled at his coat, carried the scent of pine and thaw. "You make it sound simple."

"It's not," Cam admitted. Her gloved hands clenched against her knees, the strap at her wrist stretched taut. "It hurts. I know it does. But I couldn't let you do it. I couldn't watch you turn into something the Capital would've wanted you to be."

The silence between them was heavy, stretched thin as glass. Sael shifted, lowering his great head until one gleaming eye caught the fading light, a quiet presence pressing through the tether.

Trust her.

Wyatt turned at last, catching Cam's hand before she could pull away. His thumb brushed the edge of the strap that hid her mark. "I don't like him," he said, rough, honest. "Maybe I never will. But I trust you."

Her breath hitched—too sharp to be hidden. Her lips parted, like she had words and no air to give them. Her eyes flickered, silver catching like a crack in steel, and Wyatt saw it—the moment she faltered under the weight of her own choice.

Before she could turn away, his other hand lifted, brushing a loose strand of hair back from her face. His knuckles grazed her cheek, gentle, grounding. For the smallest breath, she leaned into it. Her eyes closed, her cheek warming against his hand, as if the touch steadied her more than his words ever could.

And gods, it undid him. Because it wasn't the first time.

The solstice night returned sharp and vivid—the heat of her lips against his, the way her voice had broken when she'd asked him to stay. He hadn't slept after that, not truly. Not when every breath had been filled with the knowledge that she wanted him near, even if fear kept her from saying it again.

He wanted it still. Wanted her still. But not by accident, not by desperation. He wanted her to choose it, to choose him, without the weight of visions or the shadow of war pressing her to it.

Then, just as quick, she drew back—not coldly, but carefully. A soldier re-fastening her armor. She nodded once, fierce and fragile all at once, the fire in her tempered by something rawer.

And for a moment—just a moment—with the forest sprawling endless below and Sael humming low like the earth itself, the weight between them eased. Not gone. Not healed. But carried together.

◈ ☽⚡☾ ◈

It was midafternoon when everything shifted.

The war room glowed with lanternlight and rustling parchment. The Book of Unbinding remained stubborn, but sometimes glyphs would flare faintly beneath Cam's touch—just enough to make her hope.

She caught Wyatt's eyes across the table once. His smile came easier now, but there was distance in it, like a line neither of them dared cross. The warmth of their moment in the roost still clung to her—the way his hand had steadied hers, the brush of his thumb against her wrist, the way she'd leaned into him before she'd remembered herself.

Her chest tightened. She hadn't meant to. Hadn't planned to. But gods, it had felt steady in a way nothing else had. And it wasn't the first time.

The solstice night returned sharp and heavy. His lips against hers. Her voice breaking when she'd asked him to stay. She wondered now if that had been a mistake. Not because she didn't want him there—she always wanted him there—but because the weight of the vision they'd shared had been crushing. A temple of molten light, a hand reaching and never touching. The future they'd glimpsed had bled into that kiss, into her plea for him not to leave.

And now? Now she was scared of how much she needed him, when the others still questioned her choices. When even Wyatt, steady as he was, had looked at her with hurt in his eyes after she'd shielded Orren.

Val's quill scratched harder than it needed to, her lips pressed tight. They didn't say it aloud, but Cam felt it anyway: the doubt, the wound of her choice. She didn't regret it. Not for Orren. But she hated the weight it left between her and her circle.

Her sleeve itched where the mark pulsed faint and cold, as though it had felt the tension too.

Then Alex's voice cut clean through her thoughts.

"Hey. This mark."

He tapped a faded outline near the western cliffs on an old Eldvale map, his tone casual.

Cam blinked, leaning in. Her own handwriting marked the margin in ink: Shattercrest Wastes. A note she'd written weeks ago, chasing a half-vision from the vault, not knowing where it pointed.

"It used to be called that," Alex said smoothly, as if he'd read her thoughts. "Shattercrest. Before the records were updated a century ago. The Eldvale mountains are the same range."

Her chest tightened. Of course. That was why she hadn't been able to find it.

Val leaned closer. "If there's a temple there, it's buried under centuries of stone and ice. We'd be walking into the unknown."

"Or flying," Kaden muttered, though his jaw was tight. "Unknown is still a risk."

Tessa crossed her arms, sparks whispering faintly over her fingertips. "Risk? It sounds like a trap. The Capital renames places for a reason—half the time it's to bury what they don't want us finding."

Wyatt spoke next, voice low and even, but his eyes never left Cam. "If this place holds the rest of the prophecy, we can't ignore it. But we can't walk blind, either. Not after everything."

Alex shrugged lightly, too smooth. "Prophecy doesn't finish itself. You wanted answers—this looks like one."

Cam felt every eye turn toward her. The silence pressed harder than any blade, all of them waiting. She thought of Val's raw anger, of Kaden's suspicion, of Wyatt's steady hurt. She thought of Orren, standing unarmed while their circle nearly cut him down, and how her choice to shield him had already split fault lines in their trust.

And she thought of that solstice kiss, of Wyatt's hand steadying hers, of the way she had wanted him close in the dark. The mark beneath her strap pulsed cold, biting against her wrist—as Alex's voice lingered in the room.

She straightened, her voice steady. "It's worth the risk."

Excitement stirred, lifting the edges of weariness. Corin approved the expedition with caution, five days' flight west.

Alex stood beside Tessa, arm draped over her shoulders, but his eyes lingered on the map—on the cliffs where old magic waited.

The mark pulsed once more, colder still.

And Cam wondered—just for a heartbeat—if she had agreed to Alex's path instead of her own.

Chapter 27: Fractures and Faith

The thaw came slow to Haldrin's cliffs. Meltwater traced thin lines down the stone, darkening the courtyard paths, and the air carried the sharp bite of pine where winter's grip had loosened. Ben stood at the barracks arch, arms folded, watching the circle move among the stables.

They worked in silence that wasn't silence—boots scraping, buckles fastening, supplies shifting into neat stacks—but beneath it all ran the weight of a fracture still unhealed. Val spoke less than usual, her humor edged. Tessa sparked too easily. Wyatt's steadiness carried distance in it, and Kaden's gaze lingered too long on Cam, measuring her with suspicion he hadn't voiced.

The wound was still there.

Ben remembered when it split open. He and Corin had been on their way to check the ration stores when the noise from the yard stopped them. He saw the circle ringed around Orren, blades and magic ready to fall, and then Cam—his daughter—stepped between them.

She'd raised her hands, voice steady, and refused to move.

He had felt it then, sharp as a blade through the ribs: Isabella's fire in Cam's stance, Isabella's mercy in her defiance. The same unshakable resolve that had drawn him to her mother years ago, the same defiance that had cost Isabella everything. Gods, it had hurt to see it again—but pride rose through the hurt.

Cam hadn't let them become executioners. Not even when it would have been easier.

Ben dragged in a breath, the cold cutting clean through his chest. He could hold on to the anger, let it fester like frost between them. Or he could follow Cam's lead—let healing matter more than hurt.

He chose healing.

That evening, the war room filled with the rustle of parchment and the weight of decision. Corin bent over the old map, ink smudging beneath his hand as he traced the western ridges. Eldvale mountains—dangerous, renamed, buried in history.

"Five days west," Corin said, marking the line clean. His voice carried no hesitation, though the caution in his eyes was sharp. "Four days of preparation."

Ben nodded once, steady. "Then west it is."

If Isabella had stood here, she would have made the same call. And Cam—gods help him—was proving herself her mother's daughter more with every step.

Ben exhaled, loosening his arms at last. Through the courtyard arch, he caught a glimpse of Val in the stables, bent over the packs with her jaw set tight. She moved briskly, but her silence was louder than any words.

The circle would need more than maps and orders. They would need to begin mending.

◈ ☽ ⚡ ☾ ◈

The scent of thawing pine clung to the stables, mingling with leather oil and wet hay. Meltwater threaded the stone walk in silver seams; the last grains of snow sulked in the shadowed corners like forgotten ghosts. Val crouched over the packs and sorted without looking at Cam for as long as she could manage: vials rattling softly into their padded slots, clean cloth rolled tight, needle-cases counted and tied.

Cam worked beside her in the quiet. When Val did glance over, she caught the hitch of a strap around Cam's wrist—the way her fingers lingered there as if the leather were colder than it should be. Val looked away first.

She had told herself that day in the training yard, Cam had stolen a choice from all of them. The edge of it still lived under her tongue, salt and iron. But days had a way of sanding anger down to size. Every time Val replayed the moment—Cam's hands raised, Tessa's fury held in check, Orren's stillness—something else surfaced through the sting.

Cam had taken the weight because no one else would.

Val tugged a buckle perhaps harder than necessary; the leather complained. She would not trust the hunter. Not now, not ever. But Cam? Cam had never turned away when things were worst. If Cam said the weight was worth carrying, then Val would help carry it.

"Ugh." Tessa's voice scowled before she did, then she ducked under the lintel and scrunched her nose. "It smells like wet fur and moldy oats."

Val caught the soft, betraying flicker of a smile at the edges of Cam's mouth and buried her own. She lobbed a linen roll at Tessa. "You think the Veilborn care what we smell like?"

"Chosen to suffer, apparently." Tessa stepped around a drift of straw as if it were a trap. "If I stink like goat in Eldvale, I'm blaming you both."

"Then fly fast enough no one notices," Val said, letting the dryness of it cover the softening in her chest.

Cam laughed—quick and unguarded—and the sound loosened something Val hadn't noticed she'd been holding. As Tessa's laughter bounced back into the courtyard, bright as a spark in thaw, Val let herself breathe.

Outside, the wind picked up and carried Tessa's joy with it, racing out across the ridges.

◈ ☽⚡☾ ◈

The next morning broke blue and sword-bright—the kind of sky that begged for wings. By the time Brontheus vaulted from the roost ledge, Tessa's heart had already leapt; wind knifed her cheeks, icy and alive, and she laughed without meaning to, the sound cracking like a clean strike of thunder.

Below, the peaks spread in a map of stone and melt, rivers throwing silver through the cuts. To her right, Tenebrin rode a rising current like a shadow learning to fly; to her left, Sael flashed pale-white where the light caught him. Ahead, Sylithra cleaved the air with terrible grace. Cam settled into the dragon's rhythm as if born to it, and Wyatt slid into her line without a word.

Formation found them rather than the other way round: Tessa and Brontheus dipping low to test the air, Kaden's path threading steady through crosswinds, Val banking wide to cover the arc. For a breath—a long, bright breath—Tessa thought, We're not whole. But we're not broken either.

She whooped and leaned flat, letting Brontheus skim the cliff face before they climbed in a spiraling surge that set every nerve alight.

On the overlook far below, a figure stood with arms folded, small as a nail in the stone. Still. Watching.

The laugh thinned in Tessa's throat. Orren. Always watching. Always measuring. Waiting, maybe, to see which thread would fray first.

Brontheus rumbled, storm-deep. *We fly*, he told her, and she bared her teeth at the wind in answer. When they landed, the joy still buzzed in her skin, but sharper at the edges. Somewhere beneath the din of tack and bootsteps, Ben's voice cut out through an open war-room window—low, precise, already counting the costs.

She shook sweat from her hair and followed the sound.

◈ ☽⚡☾ ◈

By the third day of preparation, maps had bred across the table like ivy. Inked ridgelines stacked into a snarl; dotted routes threaded between hazards no one would see until too late. Kaden stood shoulder to shoulder with Corin and traced the western approaches with his eyes, tallying ambush points, windward walls, the way a valley could look like mercy and close like a fist.

Val leaned in across from him, finger pressed to a choke point. Cam stood just off his right shoulder, quiet, the strap at her wrist drawn neatly tight. Alex hovered a pace behind her, eyes made for listening. Kaden chose to act as though the man wasn't there.

"West," Corin said, quill ticking lightly. "There's no better corridor. Just a careful one."

Kaden had already chosen it twice in his head. He nodded once, then shifted out of the map's immediate pull. "Cam," he said quietly, and tilted his head toward the door.

She hesitated, then followed him into the dim hallway beyond. The walls here smelled of dust and old oil, lanterns guttering faintly against the stone.

Kaden stopped where no one else could hear. "We can't start distrusting each other now," he said, voice even. "If you thought he deserved to live, I'll believe you."

Her shoulders eased by a hair—but his gaze didn't waver.

"But the mark..." His eyes flicked to her wrist, where the strap hid it clean. "I had to see it myself. Had to put it together. You didn't tell me."

Cam's breath caught; she tugged the strap tighter as though it mattered. "I was going to. I just—"

"You waited." His tone stayed calm, but there was no mistaking the weight in it. "Until I asked. Do you understand what that feels like? To know you trusted others with it but not me?"

Her throat tightened. "I wasn't trying to cut you out, Kaden. It scared me. I thought if I said it aloud, it would make it more real—and you already carry so much. I didn't want to give you another reason to doubt me."

He studied her face for a long moment, then let out a breath through his nose. "I understand. Fear makes silence look like safety." His jaw shifted. "But it still hurts, Cam. It matters that I had to find out on my own."

Her eyes burned, silver flecks catching like seams in stone. "You're right. I should have told you."

Kaden reached out and set a hand on her shoulder—not sharp, not accusing, but grounding. "Then tell me now if there's more. Anything else. No silence between us. Promise me that."

She nodded once, fierce and reluctant and true. "No silence."

He let his hand fall away, the air between them still heavy with things unsaid. For a moment, he searched her face—looking for cracks, for lies—but found only the same stubborn weight she always carried.

"I'll hold you to that promise," he said, softer now. Then he turned away before she could answer, before the ache of it could deepen.

The corridor opened onto the courtyard. Cold air struck him first, sharp enough to clear the tangle in his chest. Dusk had turned the stone to violet glass, the evergreens bowing under thaw, their branches whispering with melt.

By the wall, Wyatt stood with his coat drawn tight, gaze fixed west as if trying to pierce the mountain line. Kaden lingered at the threshold, the silence behind him pressing heavier than the chill. For half a breath he almost turned back—almost.

The guilt followed him out, small but sharp. He told himself he'd given Cam space. He told himself it was the right choice. But he wondered if leaving her there with her promise still raw between them had been another kind of silence.

He turned down the steps and crossed the dim courtyard, boots catching on thaw-slick stone. At the far edge, Wyatt never moved, gaze fixed west as if carved there. Kaden didn't break the stillness.

He walked on toward the barracks, letting the door shut softly behind him, leaving the courtyard—and his brother—to their keeping.

◈ ☽ ⚡ ☾ ◈

The Keep's door thudded shut, soft but final, and Wyatt caught the edge of his brother's retreat as Kaden crossed the courtyard without a word. Head down, stride tight, shoulders carrying something he hadn't shared. Wyatt's jaw clenched, but he didn't call after him. Some silences couldn't be broken by force.

He stayed where he was, coat drawn close, shoulder braced against the cold wall. Sael's tether pulsed steady in his chest—low, grounding, patient—but beneath it ran another current. Faint. Unsettling. A pressure rolling from the west like air before a storm.

Minutes passed in that violet stillness. The evergreens whispered with meltwater, shadows stretching long across the stones. Then the door opened again.

Cam stepped out, hood drawn, her gaze already angled west as if she hadn't noticed anything else. Wyatt knew she hadn't seen him in the shadow of the wall; her stride carried her straight toward the courtyard's open center.

She stopped there, shoulders squared, the fading light catching in her eyes. Smaller than he'd ever let himself think of her, and yet unbearably steadfast.

Her hand tugged once at the leather strap on her wrist, the motion small but sharp against the stillness, as if she could hide the mark by tightening it further.

His hand brushed the pendant at his chest. He thought of crossing the space between them, of saying the trust still stood even after the fracture. But jealousy had teeth, and words had weight, and silence was easier to keep.

So he only watched—his brother gone, Cam standing her ground, and the west whispering closer with every breath.

◈ ☽ ⚡ ☾ ◈

Haldrin's halls settled into the late hour with the ease of an old fortress: timbers speaking softly, a far-off door finding its frame, the last of the kitchen's heat sighing into stone. In the war room, lanternlight washed the map table in gold and shadow. Corin sat alone, the quill between his fingers poised above the western ridges.

He could name most of the noises the Keep made at night. Tonight, something else threaded them—light as a pulse at the wrist, insistent enough to make the hairs lift along his arm. Not vision, not yet. Just the weight that came before it. The mind's hand drawn toward a door it had not decided to open.

He thought of the circle. Val's silence softening into sardonic steadiness at Cam's side. Tessa's laugh in the thin blue air, reckless and necessary. Kaden's blade-true pragmatism, choosing trust without pretending it was easy. Wyatt's restraint—jealousy caged and breathing but caged.

And Cam, with the weight under her ribs that made her stand straighter rather than bend.

Fractures and faith. In another life, he had mistaken control for care. Tonight he set the quill down and placed his palm flat on the map instead, the paper cool and faintly rough beneath his skin. Ink gleamed where the line to Eldvale darkened and disappeared into the mountains.

The prickle along his foresight sharpened—no picture, just pressure, like air before a storm.

Corin breathed out and did not chase it. He acknowledged the pull, the whisper at the edge of things, and let the knowledge do what it would.

Out beyond the ridges, past what ink could show, the west began to whisper.

Chapter 28: When the Mark Listens

The stones still held the day's chill, slick with a skin of frost that caught the moonlight in pale shards. Ben tossed Cam a wooden blade.

"Last night to stretch before you throw yourself at an ancient temple," he said, voice dry as ever. "Might as well remember which end stabs."

She caught it easily, mouth quirking. "Don't need to stab if I melt their eyebrows off first."

The joke landed sharper in him than it should have. Too much like Isabella—light words hiding the fear underneath. He masked the ache with a grunt and stepped forward.

They fell into rhythm, the soft slap of wood against wood echoing off the courtyard wall. Her stance was solid, but he saw the slip in her footwork, the way her hand twitched toward the leather strap at her wrist. The mark again. Always the mark.

"They still don't trust me," she said after a few exchanges, the words sharp with more weight than her blade.

Ben parried once, twice, then lowered his weapon. "They trust you more than they want to admit. They're angry because you didn't let them be executioners."

Her jaw tightened, but she didn't deny it.

He drew in a breath. "Your mother would have been proud of you for that—choosing mercy, and for not letting your friends turn into something they'd never come back from."

The way Cam's eyes flickered at Isabella's name told him the words had struck deep. Her fingers pressed against the strap again, tugging as if the leather could bury what it bound.

Ben shifted his weight, blade resting loose at his side. "Kaden told me about the mark. Why didn't you tell him yourself?"

She hesitated, and when she spoke, her voice was low, brittle as frost.

"I tried. But every time I thought about saying it, the words felt like a blade. And Kaden... he already carries too much. I couldn't make him bleed for this too."

Ben stilled, her words striking too close to an old memory. Isabella had hidden her wounds the same way—thinking silence was a shield when it was only a weight that grew heavier.

Cam's hand twitched toward her wrist again. Her voice dropped, almost swallowed by the frost-bound air.

"It's like it's listening," she whispered.

"Listening to what?" Ben asked.

Cam's fingers twitched against the strap. "I don't know but it feels like an ear pressed to the door of my veins. Waiting."

From the shadows at the courtyard wall, Skylith stirred, amber eyes glowing faintly as she watched. Overhead, a deeper shape cut against the stars—Sylithra wheeling wide arcs above the forest, her presence steady as a watchfire.

A low rumble pressed into Ben's chest through his bond. *Strength is not silence*, Skylith's voice whispered, molten and steady as fire in the deep. *And secrets are not mercy.*

Cam's head jerked slightly—she'd heard it too. Her gaze flicked to Skylith's silhouette in the shadows, then up toward the circling dragon, and back to Ben, eyes wide and unsettled.

From Sylithra, another voice braided through, darker and steadier. *The danger is not her power, but her silence.*

Ben lifted his blade again, grounding himself in motion. "They're right," he said, softer than before. "Fear doesn't excuse silence. You can trust him with the truth—even when it cuts."

Her eyes glimmered, silver catching like a seam in stone, but she gave a small nod.

Cam hesitated, fingers finding the edge of the strap—but this time she didn't tighten it. She only breathed, slow and steady, and let her hand fall.

She nodded. "No more silence."

"Some burdens find the strongest backs," Ben added. "That man—Orren—he carries scars of his own. They can damn him. Or save him. But you choosing mercy wasn't wrong."

For a heartbeat, he thought of Isabella again—how she had stood in front of danger without flinching, how mercy had cost her everything but also made her unforgettable. Pride and fear tangled in his chest until he could hardly separate them.

Skylith shifted in the shadows, talons scraping stone low and sharp, the sound carrying like a warning. She felt the wrongness in Cam's wrist—a whisper that didn't belong.

Ben exhaled slowly, forcing the fear down. He lowered his blade slightly, voice rough.

"If this mission gets bad, you run."

"Not happening, Dad."

Her reply came quick, sharp, and so familiar it pierced him with memory—Isabella's defiance all over again. *Gods, don't let me lose her the way I lost Isabella.*

He let the ache sit, pride and fear tangled so tightly they were one. Then he raised his blade into guard once more.

"Again. Until you remember which end stabs."

This time, the smile she gave him was quick and sharp, and for a moment it was Isabella's all over again. It hurt—and it healed.

◈ ☽⚡☾ ◈

The courtyard at dawn smelled of thaw and leather. Meltwater threaded between flagstones, hooves and claws shifting as packs were buckled down. Harnesses creaked. The air was sharp enough to sting, carrying the promise of height.

Cam adjusted Sylithra's saddle straps until a shadow fell across her. Wyatt crouched without asking, tugging one of the packs straighter. His fingers brushed hers; steady, callused, familiar.

"Thanks," Cam murmured.

Wyatt gave a small smile—quiet, private, only for her. "You saved us, you know. That day."

Cam blinked. "Saved you?"

"You kept us from crossing a line we wouldn't have come back from," he said, voice low. His gaze flicked toward the gate. "Not everyone wants to admit it."

His smile pulled one from her too—small, unguarded. She didn't look away this time. For once, it was easier to meet warmth than to brace for it.

Her chest tightened, but before she could answer, his jaw set. "He's watching you."

Cam followed his glance. Orren stood at the gate, arms crossed, eyes sharp as a blade. For a moment, she braced for distance, but Wyatt didn't step back. He stayed beside her, solid as the wall at her back.

Orren pushed away from the post and crossed the courtyard. His movements were measured, no wasted motion. He stopped just close enough that his voice carried.

"You kept me alive," he said, tone even, unreadable. "That's a debt I can't pay. Not yet."

Cam held his gaze. "I didn't do it for a debt."

Her breath tightened, and before she could stop herself she asked, "Why didn't you fight back? That day. You just stood there."

Something flickered across his face—too quick to name. His jaw worked once before he said simply, "Some battles aren't meant to be fought."

It wasn't an answer, not really.

His eyes flickered—first to Wyatt, then toward Alex across the yard, quiet and intent by the tack. He leaned in closer. "Not all doors should be opened just because you're the key."

"Then why give me a key at all?" Cam asked.

Orren didn't answer. His stare slid to Tessa as she mounted Brontheus and lingered just long enough for Cam to notice. Then he turned and fell back to the gate, watchful as stone. It wasn't the look he gave prey, or even threat—it was sharper, quieter, as if he were measuring her for something she couldn't name. The unease crawled under her skin and stayed there, even after he turned away.

◈ ☽ ⚡ ☾ ◈

Tessa saw it all from Brontheus's shoulder: the look Orren gave Cam, the way Wyatt didn't move from her side, the way Orren's eyes brushed over her too—sharp, unsettling. It snagged in her chest like a pebble in her boot.

Why did it always feel like he was measuring her? As if he knew something she didn't. As if she were a page he meant to read and fold away.

She told herself it was only habit—hunter's instinct. But habit shouldn't make her pulse skip.

Then Alex's voice cut through the clatter of tack. "I'm coming."

Kaden's head snapped up, sharp as a blade. "We don't need you."

"You'll slow us down," Val added, her scowl as precise as her words.

"I won't." Alex's tone was calm but harder than usual, like steel drawn just far enough to glint. His gaze didn't falter—it slid west, beyond the Keep, to the jagged horizon. "You'll need someone who can move quiet, find routes no map shows. That's me."

Kaden bristled. "Or someone who can disappear when things turn."

"That's not fair," Tessa cut in before she thought better of it. Her voice carried sharper than she intended, and every head turned. She forced a smile, brittle at the edges. "He's a good scout. Extra eyes won't hurt."

Kaden's jaw worked. "Good scouts don't keep secrets."

"Neither do brothers," Tessa shot back, heat rising under her skin. The silence that followed was heavier than Brontheus's saddle.

Wyatt, quiet at Sael's flank, finally shrugged. "Doesn't make a difference to me. If he keeps pace, he keeps pace."

Cam only watched, unreadable. When she gave the barest nod, the argument was finished. Alex inclined his head in thanks, but his eyes never left the mountains. Already there without them.

As the last straps were checked, Tessa caught movement at the edge of her vision. Orren was leaving through the main gate, coat dark against the pale morning. He didn't look back, but she felt the weight of him anyway, like a shadow stretched long behind her.

She told herself it was a relief. She didn't believe it.

Brontheus shifted wings catching the wind as Tessa settled into the saddle. She turned at the extra weight—Alex had swung up behind her, smooth as if he belonged there.

He leaned in, voice low and steady against her ear.

"You and me, Tessa. They trust you, so they'll trust me. That means we can go anywhere."

A shiver rippled down her spine. The words should have steadied her, but they landed strange—too certain, too sharp beneath the softness. She told herself it was only the chill of dawn, or the strangeness of having him pressed so close. After all, they were together, weren't they? He'd chosen her.

She smiled, small and unguarded, and gripped the reins tighter. Brontheus rumbled low in his chest, storm-breath humming against her ribs, but she hushed him with a pat.

Behind her, Alex's gaze never wavered from the horizon. West. Always west

Brontheus vaulted from the courtyard, wings punching sky, and the ground dropped away in a blur of stone walls and pine tops. The circle rose with her—Sylithra cutting a black-gold arc through the dawn, Sael a pale streak in the sun, Tenebrin dark as smoke, Virellan gleaming storm-bright.

The first hour was only wind and sky: leather creaking, air tearing her hair loose, Cam's laugh carried sharp and bright across the currents. Tessa leaned into Brontheus's rhythm until her muscles burned with it. Every downstroke thrummed through her bones, storm-deep and steady.

Stormsinger, his voice rumbled in her chest, low as thunder beneath the wind. *You breathe with me, and the sky obeys.*

"I'm breathing," she whispered into the rush, though her throat was raw with cold air. She spread her arms wide for a reckless heartbeat, and her laugh broke against the wind like lightning.

By midday, the world had flattened into a sea of green. The Karethwyn canopy stretched endless in every direction, broken only by the glitter of rivers or the shine of hidden lakes. Clouds dragged shadows over the treetops; the horizon looked the same no matter where she turned. Hunger gnawed, but she ignored it. There was only rhythm—wing over wing, the warmth of Alex steady at her back. He didn't speak much, only shifted when she did, guiding their balance like he'd flown there all his life. She told herself it was comfort, even when Brontheus's growl stirred faint and low at the contact.

The sun angled west, and by dusk they spiraled down toward a narrow clearing where pines had opened just wide enough for five dragons. Talons churned earth and needles, branches snapping under downdraft. The air smelled of sap and smoke even before they struck flint for the fire.

They built it quick, their movements quiet with fatigue. Sparks leapt against the dark trunks, smoke threading through the pines.

"Not bad for a first day," Wyatt said, tossing Kaden a strip of dried meat.

"Not bad," Kaden allowed, catching it without looking—his gaze already sweeping the tree line.

Val stretched her legs toward the flames. "If no one fell off their dragon, I'll call it a victory." Her lips curved faintly as she added, "Though I hear some of us have a history with that..."

Tessa snorted, nearly choking on her water. Cam's eyes narrowed, but the corner of her mouth twitched, betraying her.

"Once," she muttered, heat rising in her cheeks. "It happened once."

Wyatt smirked into the firelight. "And I caught you."

"And I'm the one who teleported both of you onto Sael before you hit the trees," Kaden added, tearing a bite of dried meat. "You're welcome."

"Gods," Cam groaned, dragging her hand down her face. "You're never going to let that go, are you?"

"Not a chance," Tessa said cheerfully, jabbing the fire with a stick.

"Especially when it makes me sound like the responsible one," Kaden said dryly.

That broke a ripple of laughter from the circle—even Val's sharp edges softened, her chuckle low but real. Cam rolled her eyes, but her smile caught in the firelight, reluctant and warm.

Tessa caught it—the way Cam's laugh came easy now, not forced or careful like before. It sounded like someone learning how to belong.

Brontheus shifted, eyes half-lidded in the glow. *The sky tests you,* he murmured inside her, storm-deep and knowing. *But storms forge what stone cannot.*

Tessa tucked the words close, letting them steady her as the fire snapped, sparks climbed into the night, and the forest pressed black and endless around them.

The forest woke damp and silvered, mist lifting from the pines as the dragons shook dew from their wings. Harness buckles clicked in the chill, breath fogging in the air. When they lifted off again, Sylithra and Sael cut a long, sweeping parallel through the sky, their wingtips riding the same currents. Cam and Wyatt didn't speak across the link, but Tessa saw it in their bodies: the way one shifted and the other followed, seamless as breath. Even Brontheus felt it, his chest rumbling beneath her.

Threads find each other, he told her, voice storm-low. *Even when frayed.*

By late afternoon, the canopy below had turned shadowed and endless, the sun slanting low through haze. A storm flickered far on the horizon, lightning faint and silent, as though the sky were reminding them what it held back.

They landed in a clearing lined with spruce and set the fire quickly. Sparks leapt high when the kindling caught, the smoke clinging sweet with resin.

Wyatt handed Cam a log. Their hands brushed, and Cam laughed—quick, unguarded, the sound slipping free before she could catch it.

Tessa froze, the sound tugging at something raw inside her. Not jealousy, not exactly. But the ache of seeing something shift, something opening, and knowing she couldn't shape what it would become.

Kaden pretended not to notice, though his mouth pressed flat. Val raised a brow at the sound, then looked away, sharp but unreadable.

Tessa forced herself to poke the fire, her grin a little too bright. Alex was across from her this time, not behind—kneeling by the flames, passing dried meat across the circle like it was nothing. When his hand brushed hers as he gave her a strip, his smile was soft, certain.

"You'll keep them laughing, Tessa," he said low enough for only her to hear. "That's worth more than you think."

Warmth caught in her chest, startling, and she told herself it was comfort. But Brontheus shifted behind her, eyes narrowing, and the tether in her ribs thrummed uneasy.

Morning broke bright and hard on the third day, sun cutting through the mist in sharp bands as the dragons rose. The forest rolled on forever beneath them, green broken by the silver thread of a river. By evening, when they landed in another clearing, Tessa's legs ached from hours in the saddle, and Brontheus rumbled low with fatigue.

Val and Kaden had a scroll stretched between them, heads bent so close their hair nearly brushed. Their voices moved in low rhythm—routes, choke points, odds of ambush. It wasn't just strategy; it was cadence, a language only the two of them seemed fluent in. Tessa watched the way

Val's brow eased, how Kaden's sharpness softened when he spoke with her. The sound of it was steady, almost soothing.

Tessa sat just outside the circle of firelight, leaning back into Alex's shoulder. He asked a question now and then—about the terrain, about the pace—and she answered without thinking, grateful for the steadiness of his voice. His warmth pressed along her back, anchoring her in the flicker of the fire.

But when the flames caught his face, carving his features from shadow, his eyes weren't on her. They were on the mountains, black and jagged against the stars. West, always west.

The next day stretched gray and thin, clouds dragging low over the forest. The air bit colder as they flew, the canopy thinning in places where rock pushed through, a sign the Eldvale foothills were drawing closer. Conversation had dwindled to nothing; even laughter felt spent.

By the fire that night, shadows leapt long against the trees. Tessa caught the motion before she caught the meaning—Cam rubbing her wrist again, slow circles over the strap as if soothing something underneath. The firelight caught the movement and held it, insistent, until Tessa's tongue burned with the question she didn't ask.

Wyatt sat close enough that his shoulder brushed Cam's, but his gaze stayed on the flames. Val and Kaden were quieter than usual, the scrolls untouched between them for once. Even Alex kept to the edge of the firelight, his face unreadable in the shifting glow.

Brontheus rumbled storm-low in his chest, the sound vibrating through Tessa's ribs. From the other side of the clearing, Sael shifted where he lay, pale coils gleaming faintly in the firelight, a low hiss leaking from his throat as if he scented something wrong. Sylithra's head lifted for a breath, golden eyes fixed on Cam before she lowered her muzzle again, but not all the way—watchful.

Tenebrin twitched his wings, the shadows clinging too long to his scales as though the night itself bent uneasy around him. Even Virellan, steady as stone, loosed a sharp exhale and pawed once at the earth before resettling.

The circle pretended not to notice. Or maybe they truly didn't. But Tessa felt it—all of it—through Brontheus's tether, storm-unease sparking like flint under her skin.

She reached back to stroke the ridge of his jaw, swallowing her question like ash. Some secrets were too heavy to pry loose.

The air grew thinner on their fifth day, metallic on Tessa's tongue. Brontheus's wingbeats slowed as they climbed, his body quivering with the strain, but he didn't falter. None of the dragons did. They pressed on together, steady as a tide.

By the time they made camp, the firelight felt like a gift.

Val jabbed her spoon into the pot with theatrical offense. "Kaden, this isn't stew—it's something they'll write ballads about. Tragic ballads."

Kaden snorted, flicking a coal into the fire with his boot. "Better than the salt-bricks you call bread. At least mine's edible."

"Edible if you hate yourself," Val shot back.

Wyatt leaned back on one elbow, voice low and dry. "I'd rather take my chances with the Veilborn than whatever that is."

Cam laughed, quick and bright. "Oh come on, it's not that bad."

Wyatt arched a brow. "That sounded like mercy, not honesty."

"Mercy's a survival skill," Cam said, still smiling.

Tessa laughed then too—loud, unguarded, spilling out before she could hold it in. The sound tangled with the others', warm and sharp in the cold night air. For a moment, it was almost like before. Before Orren. Before fractures. Before trust had turned into a wound.

She leaned into Alex's side, letting the warmth at her shoulder steady her.

Alex smiled faintly, but his eyes weren't on her. They were fixed on the horizon, west beyond the firelight.

The laughter thinned as night settled heavier around them. The mountains loomed darker, jagged against a sky washed with stars. The fire sank low. One by one, voices faded.

When sleep finally claimed her, silver fell like rain—liquid light that hissed when it struck stone. Dragons roared, but the sound was muffled, trapped behind glass. The silver bled into gold, the two colors folding into each other, blinding in their fusion.

For a heartbeat, it shone brighter than day.

Then the brilliance collapsed. Darkness surged in, swallowing both whole.

The ground cracked beneath her, splitting wide, and she jolted awake with her heart pounding like a war drum. A hot trickle slid from her nose. She wiped it with the back of her hand and saw red against her skin, thin and bright in the moonlight.

Brontheus's eyes were already on her, storm-deep and unblinking, as if he had seen the dream too.

Chapter 29: Darkness Beneath the Stones

The dreams were worse than before.

Not just smoke and chains this time, but fire licking at the edges of stone—heat so real it blistered his lungs even in sleep. Cam was there, shackled, her scream carried like thunder across the smoke. He reached for her, but his legs locked stiff, like the dream itself had bound him.

And Kaden—Kaden was there too now, his wrists scored raw by iron, his eyes burning with shadows that weren't his own. Some nights, Wyatt found him shackled at Cam's side, defiance in his face even as the chains pulled tighter. Other nights, the space where his brother should have been was empty, as if the vision hadn't decided whether to damn him or spare him.

Always, both of them slipped farther away no matter how he clawed toward them.

This time, the smoke cracked open, and a shape rose through it—black stone carved into a temple, its walls scored with sigils that flared in brief light. Behind Cam, one symbol blazed sharp enough to sear his sight. Not death. Not release. A mark of delay, like time straining at the edge of a rope.

He woke with his chest hammering, sweat cold on his skin. Dawn pressed gray fingers through the mist, and the camp was quiet save for the groan of dragons shifting in their sleep. Wyatt dragged in air, but the dream clung to him like frost.

Cam lay curled against Sylithra a few paces off, hair tangled across her cheek, her hand twitching faintly as if even her sleep wasn't free. The sight cut him raw—want pulling him one way, dread the other.

"You had another one," came a voice.

Wyatt startled. Kaden sat against Sael's flank, a waterskin in hand, his eyes too knowing.

Wyatt nodded once, jaw tight.

"Wanna talk about it?"

"No." His voice was raw, breathless.

Kaden crossed the space anyway, pressing the waterskin into his hand. Wyatt drank; the water cool but not enough to ease the weight in his chest.

"Was it about her?" Kaden asked.

Wyatt's silence was answer enough. He feared if he spoke it, it would carve the dream into truth.

Kaden's voice softened into the tone he used for no one else. "I'm always here if you want to talk, Wy. You know that."

Wyatt nodded, not trusting his throat. His gaze drifted back toward Cam, and something in him ached at the sight. The others were beginning to stir now—Val rolling her bedroll sharp and neat, Alex moving with that quiet, deliberate efficiency. Morning had come, but the dream still clung like smoke in his lungs.

◈ ☽ ⚡ ☾ ◈

The air felt thinner here, sharp with a cold that scraped at her lungs. Val tightened Virellan's straps, the dragon growling low as her wings twitched in restless complaint.

"You feel it too," she murmured, pressing her palm against her scales.

The thought pressed back through their bond, steady as stone but edged. *The silence is wrong. The stone remembers.*

Val's frown deepened. She glanced across the camp. Cam and Wyatt avoided looking at one another, though every time Cam's gaze slid his way, Wyatt's followed after. Kaden moved with his usual sharpness, though Val saw the tired edge at the corners of his mouth. Tessa forced brightness into her voice as she packed, Alex's presence shadowing her movements more than steadying them.

The fracture between them had dulled, but it hadn't healed.

Virellan's growl deepened, and Val pressed her hand firmer to the dragons shoulder. "It's not them, is it?" she whispered. "It's the mountains."

The dragon's thoughts slid against hers again, colder this time. *Stone does not forget. And it does not welcome.*

Val swallowed and straightened. "Then it can choke on us," she muttered, loud enough for Kaden to hear.

His head lifted, a smirk tugging faintly at the corner of his mouth. "That's one way to look at it."

"Only way," she shot back. "Fear's not going to do us any favors."

Kaden hummed in agreement, but his gaze flicked toward the mountains again, sharp and uneasy.

Val swung into Virellan's saddle, the leather cold against her palms. The silence pressed heavy, not from their circle but from the cliffs themselves—as if the air between the peaks were holding its breath.

◈ ☽ ⚡ ☾ ◈

They flew hard that day, the air thinning as the ridges drew higher. Cam's shoulders ached from holding Sylithra steady against the crosswinds, but her mind ached worse.

Sleep had given her nothing but lightning—forks cracking across the sky, silver flashes burning behind her eyes, rocks splintering loose from cliffs before she could move. She woke with the echo still in her blood and hadn't told anyone. Not yet.

The Eldvale Range rose like a wound against the horizon—jagged cliffs jutting from a dull sky, their edges sharp enough to cut the clouds. Meltwater dripped from black stone into cracks far below. The wind didn't whistle here. It keened, long and thin, like the mountains themselves were mourning something they'd never get back.

Sylithra's descent was silent, her gold-veined eyes pinned to the ravine's shadow. Cam slid from the saddle, boots striking stone that felt colder than snow.

Sael cut a pale arc and touched down beside them; Wyatt dismounted, his gaze brushing Cam's—quick, unthinking—before it slid back to the dark.

Virellan wheeled once and dropped to the ledge, wings snapping tight. Her growl rolled deep in her chest, nostrils flaring as if the air itself soured on her tongue. Her scales twitched in restless shivers.

Brontheus followed, talons scraping; Tessa's storm-bright grin faltered the instant her boots met stone. "This place..." she muttered, brushing her palms on her trousers. "Feels like the air's watching."

A shadow swept long across the cliff as Tenebrin glided in last, folding his dark wings close with a whisper of silk. Kaden slid down from the saddle, eyes already on the broken pass, his jaw set.

Val cut Tessa a sharp look, though her voice held steadier than her eyes. "Then keep your sparks close. If the stone wants to stare, let it blink first."

Alex came up a step behind Tessa, quiet as ever, but Cam caught the way his gaze measured the shattered archways. "Veilbind sigils," he said, almost to himself. "But not carved to shield. To choke."

Kaden's head snapped toward him, suspicion flashing like a blade. "And how would you know that?"

Alex didn't blink. "Because that's what they look like when they've failed."

The silence that followed pressed heavier than the wind. Cam's unease prickled sharper. *That didn't sound like a guess. It sounded like memory.*

The wind here doesn't move, Cam thought. *It waits.*

From deep within her mind, a whisper brushed the bond: *The stone remembers. It does not welcome.*

Sylithra's tail lashed once. She did not look away from the black mouth of the pass.

They saw the temple only when the last curve of cliff fell away. It crouched at the valley's center, half-buried in black rock and choked with dead vines. The obsidian walls caught the melting snow's thin light in broken reflections.

The great doors had collapsed outward, splintered and scattered as though something had pushed out from within. Around the archway, Veilbind sigils had been carved deep into the stone—protective once, but now jagged, their edges torn and warped, as if carved to scream.

"This place feels wrong," Cam murmured. "Like it's pretending."

She should have called for Kaden to check the runes. Instead she trusted what she felt—the pulse beneath her skin, the thread that said listen.

Wyatt's gaze swept the shadows, his hand hovering near his weapon.

Beside him, Kaden's voice came low, tight:

"Feels like something's watching through the stone."

Inside, the air pressed heavier. Their torchlight didn't stretch far—it wavered as though something unseen pressed against the flame.

Pillars rose around them like ribs, holding up a skeletal hall. Dust hung suspended, unmoving. The mark beneath Cam's leather strap throbbed—not glowing but listening.

Her pace slowed. Wyatt's fingers brushed hers, unthinking. She hesitated—old reflexes whispering to pull away—but she didn't. She let the touch stay, a tether in the dark.

Val had gone still near the wall, her gloved hand tracing the curve of a mural. A circle of kneeling figures. Above them, a black triangle, sharp lines radiating downward like chains.

She flinched—eyes widening as though she'd seen more than what was carved. Her voice trembled when she spoke:

"They didn't build this to worship... they built it to contain."

The sound came next—low, almost imagined. Not a growl. Not the groan of stone. A hollow breath, too slow for anything living.

Kaden's steel was in his hand before anyone else moved.

Cam stepped closer to the inner doorway, her palm finding the cold stone. It drank the warmth from her skin like snow drinking blood.

This wasn't elemental cold.

This was cold that remembered.

"This isn't a temple," she said, her voice thin but steady. "It's a tomb pretending."

The wall shivered under her hand. Dust drifted down in a single, slow line.

Outside, Brontheus's growl echoed off the cliffs. Sael crouched low to the ledge, eyes fixed on the temple's heart.

Cam tore her hand back—but the mark had left its shape on the stone, faint and glowing, before fading to nothing.

"Whatever's beneath us... it knows we're here."

Chapter 30: The Maw Opens

Jagged shadows stretched across the ribbed stone hall as the group descended deeper into the temple. The stone swallowed sound, every footstep echoing too sharp and too thin. The air pressed heavy, acrid with the sting of burnt metal, like breath caught in a forge too long choked of air. It didn't smell like worship. It smelled like something caged.

Fissures cracked across the walls like veins, vents carved into the stone that whispered with faint drafts. Pillars rose like broken ribs, holding up a ceiling that groaned with every shift of weight. Nothing about it felt holy. Nothing about it felt safe.

Cam rubbed her wrist again, slow circles over the leather strap like the mark beneath it ached. Kaden's eyes caught the motion, and unease stirred low in his gut.

"This place..." Tessa's voice cracked against the silence. "Doesn't even feel alive. It feels... emptied."

Val's lip curled as she brushed her hand against the wall, stone grit breaking under her glove. "No. Not emptied. Bled dry."

Wyatt's eyes swept the dark, shoulders tight, hand hovering near his blade. "Doesn't matter what it was. Whatever it is now, it wants us in here."

Kaden's gaze flicked back to Alex, who had been walking too quietly, every step too measured. His eyes weren't on the group at all—only the far doors behind them. Before Kaden could call it out, Alex's shoulders tightened. Then, without a word, he bolted.

"Alex!" Kaden barked, but Alex didn't look back. His footsteps rang sharp against stone, retreat echoing down the hall. For a flicker, Kaden's gut twisted—not from fear, but from the precision of it. Too sharp. Too certain. Like Alex wasn't fleeing in panic at all but running a path he already knew.

Confusion ripped through the circle, heads snapping toward the sound, but they didn't have time to follow.

Because Kaden saw it then. The cuts in the floor. The vents. The way the narrow halls all pulled toward this point. His pulse kicked hard.

"They built it to funnel us here."

The words had barely left his mouth when the stone trembled. Dust rained down in soft trails, followed by the deep groan of something ancient shifting in its sleep. A hollow roar began to swell, rising through the cracks beneath their boots.

The chamber opened before them, not a sanctuary but a maw carved into the mountain itself. The far wall split into a broken archway where light spilled thin and jagged onto a ledge beyond.

Then chaos erupted.

Howlers poured from the dark, their bodies snapping with too many joints, eyes burning crimson red. Wraithbeasts slithered between pillars, their limbs dragging like half-forgotten corpses. Mirebats tore down from the ceiling in a shriek of wings, shadows thrashing against torchlight. And deeper still, Veilborn flickered in and out of sight—half flame, half void, their forms unfinished, their hunger endless.

Outside, the dragons answered with thunder. Their roars ripped through the bond, wings cracking air like war-drums as they beat back the creatures swarming the cliffside.

Then it came.

The dragonlink snapped open, not asked for, not gentle—forced wide like a storm tearing through every mind. Kaden staggered as voices and visions flooded in at once. Sael's fury. Sylithra's warning. Brontheus's storm-crack snarl. Virellan's growl laced with ice. Their riders' hearts beating in his skull alongside his own. Cam's fear, sharp and bright as glass. Wyatt's pain, low and dragging. Tessa's sparks flaring uncontrolled. Val's iron pulse bracing against the dark.

They were all inside his head. All of them at once.

And beneath it, Kaden felt the truth coil cold in his chest. They hadn't just been attacked. They'd been separated on purpose. The monsters didn't strike wild—they struck with precision, cutting the circle into pieces. How did they know?

He slashed and teleported, blades cutting through shadow-flesh. But every time he carved a path forward, more poured in, herding him back, shoving him away from the others.

The stone cracked. A pillar fell. The ground itself seemed to claw them apart.

Kaden's gaze snagged on light—a broken exit, sunlight spilling through dust. Hope. He pushed toward it, teleportation bursts ripping him across the floor, heart pounding.

Through the blur of stone and smoke, he caught flashes of the others—Tessa fighting toward the same break, her lightning snapping off the walls as Brontheus's storm roared in his head. Val wasn't far, fog curling off her palms. They were all driving toward the light. Toward each other.

But the monsters knew. He could feel it in the way they pressed, precise, deliberate. They wanted the circle apart.

Cam staggered through the open, her face bloodied but her eyes unbroken. Veilborn light slashed at her heels, but she drove forward anyway, every strike a refusal to fall.

Wyatt followed hard after, limping but relentless, his blade tearing through a pair of howlers that closed too fast. The pain in him bled sharp through the link—ragged, searing—but his will burned hotter. Kaden felt it in his own chest, the sheer refusal to let Cam face the storm alone.

Together, they forced their way into the spill of daylight, barely standing but standing.

Kaden lunged to follow, teleporting past a snapping maw, only to be slammed back by a Veilborn's claws.

"Wyatt!" Kaden shouted, but the howls swallowed his voice.

A Veilborn lunged between them, all jagged void-light and claws. Kaden swung—steel hissed through air—but the impact forced him back into the dark.

The cliff, the light, Wyatt; all torn from view as the temple closed around him.

◈ ☽ ⚡ ☾ ◈

The chamber was chaos—stone splitting, shadows pouring from every crack, shrieks tearing the air. Sparks bled from her palms in wild arcs, each strike lashing through the dark like a whip of stormfire. Brontheus thundered inside her chest, a storm given form.

But beneath the fury, the memory cut sharper: Alex's shoulders tightening, his footsteps ringing against stone, and then—gone. No word, no look back. Just gone.

It burned through her, betrayal knotting into rage. He'd promised *you and me*, and the second it mattered, he'd bolted for the doors. Left her to the dark.

The dragonlink pressed tight around her skull, every breath and heartbeat not just hers. Cam's fear spiking sharp. Wyatt's pain dragging low. Val's iron steadiness holding. Kaden's shadows tearing forward. All of them tangled together, storming through her veins until she couldn't tell where she ended and they began.

The creatures struck with precision, driving them apart, cutting them down corridors of dust and falling stone. They knew. They *wanted* the circle divided.

"Not happening," Tessa snarled, her voice raw with sparks. Lightning screamed from her hands, searing a cluster of mirebats to ash. She forced her way toward the thin shaft of daylight cutting across the chamber, every strike fueled by fury—at the monsters, at the stone, at Alex's retreat.

A blur of motion kept pace at her flank. Val, her braid loose and eyes like glass knives, fog steaming from her palms as she sent wave after wave rolling between them and the horde. Every exhale was frost, every step beside Tessa iron-solid.

Val's voice cut sharp through the link, iron-edged but steady. *"Don't break. Don't scatter. Hold the line."*

"I'm holding!" Tessa roared back, though her chest heaved with effort, lightning carving every word.

Brontheus surged with her, storm-bright eyes searing the dark. *Storms do not bow. And neither do you.*

Her teeth clenched, her body shaking with strain, but she pressed on. Through dust she glimpsed Cam staggering into the light, Wyatt beyond her, bleeding but still fighting, and Kaden's shout tearing through the bond before the Veilborn's roar drowned it out.

The way was closing, the stone clawing back its silence. If they didn't break through now, they wouldn't at all.

◈ ☽⚡☾ ◈

The first thing Val saw wasn't the monsters. It was the stone itself—veins splitting wider, cracks blooming with every tremor. The temple wasn't failing. It was breaking by design.

Virellan's growl surged down the bond, the sound a storm under her ribs. They want us apart, Val thought, even as the dragonlink hammered her skull with everyone's panic and pain. Cam's fear, Wyatt's stubborn fury, Kaden's sharp focus, Tessa's crackling rage—all braided with the dragons' voices, a cacophony barely held together.

She forced it into shape the only way she knew: strategy. She scanned the chamber—pillars falling, debris narrowing paths, the creatures driving them into splinters instead of a circle. "They're cutting us off on purpose!" she shouted, water pooling quick in her palms before she slashed it wide. The stream flared into the shape of another her, a phantom-double that darted left, drawing a pack of howlers into a frenzy.

Tessa's lightning flared wild on her right, Kaden's teleportation strikes snapping like shadows on her left. For a heartbeat, they fought like one body—until the link stabbed her with something colder.

Alex. Running. His retreat still echoing in her memory—his back to them, his silence like a blade. Fury flared sharp in her gut, but it was tangled with hurt. He hadn't even looked back. Not at Tessa. Not at any of them.

A Wraithbeast lunged, claws dragging sparks off the stone. Val snapped her hand up, the air warping into a shimmer of water-light. The beast's strike split harmlessly through her illusion, long enough for Kaden's blade to cut it down. She hissed a curse, pulling more water into her grip, shaping it into a blade that cut clean through a Mirebat as it dove too close.

The chamber convulsed with another roar, Veilborn flickering in and out between shadows. One lunged—half-light, half-void—and Tessa's storm-crack slammed into it before Val could move. The smell of ozone and burning stone seared her throat.

Step by bloody step, the three of them drove forward. Water shimmered into false shapes around Val, illusions darting in and out of the fight to confuse their attackers. Monsters fell, more poured in, the ground itself clawing at their boots. Her lungs burned, but the door was there—the broken arch, daylight bleeding through. Hope.

They pushed into it together, backs to one another, blades and lightning cutting a path. Sunlight struck Val's face like a slap, but the fight didn't end. The creatures spilled after them, shadows gnashing against the light.

Then the link surged again—stronger, sharper. Cam's voice, ragged, unmistakable:

"Alex... what is going on?"

◈ ☽ ⚡ ☾ ◈

Wyatt burst through the fractured archway seconds after Cam, the crush of battle still clawing at his heels. Shadows snapped at his back—howlers lunging from the dark, claws raking across stone as he spun and struck. One caught his arm, tearing through the sleeve, hot blood slicking his skin. Another slammed him against the wall, claws scoring deep into his ribs before he drove steel through its throat. The pain flared sharp, but he shoved it down, forcing himself after her into the open air.

The mountain wind hit like ice. It cut through his torn sleeves, through the dark streaks of blood across his clothes. His lungs heaved, every breath ragged. Behind him, the temple seethed—howls, shrieks, stone breaking under too much weight. Dragons roared outside, thunder in his skull through the link.

But all he saw was her.

Cam.

She fought ahead of him, staggering but unbroken, each strike a defiance against the tide. Her fear, her fury, her fire—they pressed through the dragonlink like shards of light. Val's grit. Tessa's storm-bright rage. Kaden's sharp, iron focus. All of them were there, knotted together in his chest. He clung to that bond, even as pain dragged at his every step.

Then, in a sudden surge of shadow, he lost her. A wall of howlers crashed between them, their snarls ripping through the link until all he felt was pain and panic not his own. Dust swallowed her figure, her fire snuffed from sight. His chest seized as dread clawed in—he couldn't see her, couldn't hear her. He shoved, slashed, staggered, but the creatures drove him sideways, herding him step by step toward the cliff's edge.

"Cam!" he roared, but the battle swallowed his voice. The emptiness where she should have been threatened to break him more than the wounds already bleeding him dry.

The wind shifted then.

A strange ripple passed through the air, cold and electric—an echo of the vision that had haunted his dreams since the solstice. The memory was sharp and clear: Cam, bleeding and reaching; the screaming wind tearing at their souls; the terrible fall.

It was no longer just a dream. It was unfolding here. Now.

A Veilborn lunged out of the swirling shadows, claws slashing for Wyatt's back. Instinct flared—the seasoned fighter he was—Wyatt spun, deflecting the strike with the flat of his blade, but the force slammed into him, driving a deep, burning ache through the other side of his ribs.

Before he could steady himself, another Veilborn burst from the shadows behind him, teeth bared. Wyatt ducked low, rolling hard and driving his blade upward in a brutal arc. The creature's howl was cut short as it collapsed.

The first Veilborn, enraged, attacked again with frenzied claws. Blood slicked the stone as Wyatt grappled and finally drove his blade through its heart. Both monsters lay still, but the price was heavy.

Pain flared sharply through his whole body, blood seeping hot and fast through his torn armor. His breath hitched, ragged, every inhale a fight against the darkness closing in. He dropped to one knee, the strength in his legs giving way.

The world swam, shadows blurring at the edges, yet his eyes locked stubbornly on Cam. Her face stayed clear, the one truth his mind refused to blur—his only anchor in the storm. His fingers brushed against the cool weight of the pendant at his neck, a silent reminder of everything he fought for.

Instinct and desperation pulled at him. If this was the end, he wanted to leave her something real—something to hold onto when he couldn't be there.

His trembling hand moved slowly, almost unwilling, toward the chain around his neck.

Blood slicked his fingers as he fumbled the family pendant, the cold metal slipping in his grasp like a fragile lifeline.

A silver pendant rested against his palm now, its design etched in fine lines—a hooded, faceless figure framed by curling filigree, one hand cradling a swirl of blue mist, the other a jagged streak of gold. It was the Valehart family sigil, a symbol of balance passed down through generations.

It was meant for her—meant to be hers. Not just a token, but a promise. A future he hadn't dared say aloud.

Suddenly, the memory came crashing back—the quiet morning in her room, Cam curled beside him, eyes wide as she turned the pendant over in her hands.

"It's beautiful," she'd whispered.

Wyatt's voice had been soft, almost shy.

"It's my family sigil," he'd told her.

Cam's eyes lifted to meet his, filled with wonder.

In Valmira, to propose to someone, you gave them your family sigil. The pendant was more than metal and history—it was a vow, a promise of forever. He'd thought about giving it to her—really thought about it. Not out of fear she'd refuse, but because the weight of that promise was terrifying. It meant everything.

Now, his chest burned with pain sharp enough to steal his breath, each heartbeat a hammer. His vision blurred, shadows pooling at the edges.

He squeezed the pendant, desperate to hold onto something real. To hold onto her.

But his fingers faltered.

The pendant slipped free, tumbling through blood and dirt.

Through the chaos, Wyatt caught sight of her—bleeding, staggering, but still fighting her way toward him.

For a heartbeat, the world narrowed to just her and the wind between them.

It struck him—sharp as the first time he'd seen her in a vision years ago: sunlight in her hair, her head lifting as if she'd been waiting.

But that day, she hadn't truly seen him.

Now, on the cliff, she did. And gods, if the world meant to take him in the next breath, he wanted that to be the last thing he felt.

He forced his eyes open against the pull of darkness, and there she was—Cam, fierce and unbroken, cutting her way through the chaos toward him. Her hand was outstretched, reaching, just as in the vision that had haunted them both for weeks.

For a heartbeat, hope burned sharp and bright. He almost believed he could rise, that if he reached back she would catch him, hold him, save him.

Then—she faltered. A shadow slammed into her side, dragging her stumble short. His chest clenched with panic, but the blur of battle swallowed the sight before he could see her rise again.

Their gazes locked anyway, across the storm of dust and blood, tethered by something deeper than the wound splitting him apart.

"Cam—" His voice broke, raw and trembling.

But the abyss rising to claim him wasn't the cliff's edge—it was the black fog closing around his mind. Unconsciousness clawed at him, cold and merciless.

Every shred of will screamed for one more breath—for one more second with her. But his body betrayed him. Darkness didn't fall; it rose, cold and merciless, swallowing the light where she stood.

Chapter 31: The Traitor Wears Silver

Cam staggered out of the temple's fractured mouth, smoke and dust clawing at her throat. The mountain air hit cold and sharp, but there was no time to breathe—two howlers lunged from the rubble, all snapping jaws and sinew. She swung up her blade, catching the first across its neck, black ichor splattering her face as it dissolved into shadow. The second slammed into her before she could turn, claws tearing across her cheek and shoulder. The world spun as she hit the ground hard, stone biting into her palms.

Sylithra's voice cracked sharp through the bond: *Up, Little Flame!*

For the first time, the command broke at the edges—urgency fraying into something raw.

Up, Little Flame—please.

Cam shoved to her feet, spitting copper. Pain burned down her face where blood dripped into her eye. She parried the howler's second strike, blade skimming so close it sliced across her arm. She staggered but drove her sword home, sending the creature into smoke.

No reprieve came. From the side, a Veilborn flickered into being—half-flesh, half-void. Its jagged blade raked across her ribs before she could fully turn. White-hot agony split her side, tearing a cry from her throat. She stumbled, clutching the wound with her free hand, blood seeping fast and hot.

Still, she kept moving. Always forward.

The slope opened before her, battle chaos raging through smoke and screams.

Cam staggered up the rocky terrain, each breath a jagged shard sawing through her ribs. Ash clung to her tongue; iron burned the back of her throat. Stone dust swirled where the wind knifed across the ridge and shoved the smoke into ugly spirals. Her palm pressed tight against the wound at her side—heat slick, rhythm sickening.

Run, Sylithra whispered, sharp as a flare inside her skull. *Run, Little Flame.*

"I can't," Cam rasped, even if her lungs had no air to spare. "Not without him."

Shadows shifted ahead. A Veilborn broke through the haze—spindled limbs, blade-arm slick with void-light. Cam brought her sword up; the impact rattled her bones to the elbow. Another lunged from the left. She pivoted, steel catching, heel slipping on gravel; she drove her blade across the first creature's chest, and it collapsed into black vapor that smelled like burnt cold.

The second raked her ribs. White heat split her nerve from skin to spine. She nearly folded. Didn't. She set her teeth, shoved forward.

Silver flashed at the cliff's edge.

Not sunlight. Not steel. *Him.*

Alex stood there, untouched by blood or ruin, as if the battle had been arranged for his view alone. The haze curled around him like it shifted to make room.

Cam's breath caught, her heart tightening painfully as memories surged back—the vision she had shared with Sylithra after bonding*: Figures coated in shadow, faces hidden beneath dark helms. But one stepped forward—clad in silver. The traitor wears silver.*

"It was you," she whispered, disbelief scraping her raw.

For an instant she saw a dozen small nights at once—Tessa's laughing shoulder against his, Val's brow arched but letting him sit, Wyatt giving him space without trust, Kaden's jaw tight in the firelight—and Cam herself, refusing to be the hinge that slammed shut. She'd made room. She'd let him close. Guilt and fury braided until they hurt more than the gash in her side.

Betrayal has teeth, Sylithra growled across the link, molten and low. *But so do you.*

Cam took a step. Her voice barely held steady as she stepped forward, the sharp sting of fury rising. "Alex... What... what is going on?" she demanded. "What have you done?"

His eyes were too calm. "It was always going to end this way," he said softly. "I'm sorry" He spoke low into a communication sigil; words not quite meant for her ears: "Orders confirmed."

"Orders?" Her voice tore. "What orders?"

Alex's eyes hardened, and his voice dropped to a bitter whisper. "The first ones I broke... the second I saw how he looked at you." He looked at her with cold contempt; voice laced with something cruel. "I'm loyal to Caerthalen. And you? You were never meant to exist."

Cam's throat closed. "Alex... I thought we were friends," she said, voice breaking.

For a moment, something flickered in his expression—pain, maybe—but it died as quickly as it sparked.

"No," he said, quieter now, almost to himself. "You were a mistake I thought I could believe in."

He met her gaze one last time, eyes gone hollow. "But you was never my friend."

The last of whatever she'd kept aside for him snapped. She lifted her sword—but silver swallowed him whole, light collapsing in a single silent breath. He was gone.

Ash. Silence. The tight, ugly ring of *'I let him in'*.

Her chest heaved. She wanted to scream, to set the mountain on fire with what he had just done to them—what he had done to Tessa.

The battlefield wavered. Smoke bent wrong, shadows stretching long, as if the world itself tilted with his betrayal. Her stomach dropped, vision swimming—not from blood loss, but from the knife lodged somewhere deeper. For a heartbeat she could hardly tell which way was up. Then the pull slammed into her chest, thin and bright as wire.

Wyatt.

Her head jerked up, eyes burning. Smoke veiled the slope; shrieks tangled with the scrape of stone; the world juddered as if the mountain were breathing wrong. She spun—left, right—heart pounding too loud to hear her own name. The bond was a storm of panicked threads, each voice crowding the next: Val iron-steady, Tessa a crackle on the edge of breaking, Kaden sharp and moving, dragons roaring so hard the air shook.

Find him, Sylithra urged, fierce as a strike. *He is there.*

There. A break in the smoke.

Across the fractured incline, Wyatt staggered into view—bloodied, battered, moving. Determination held his shoulders square even as his leg gave a little under him. Time warped; the solstice vision blitzed across her mind—the hush of golden light, the terrible stillness of a moment waiting for a choice. Here the sky was a bruise and the wind screamed through cut stone, but the tether was the same.

"WYATT!" she cried, voice raw enough to bleed.

He turned toward the sound—toward *her*. Stone cracked under his boots, thin fissures webbing out like frost.

She ran. Lungs burning, side on fire, she ran. She slashed a shadow from the air; a second; her blade hummed with each kill. Blood smeared hot across her fingers where she held her side, but she didn't care. A few more strides—two—one—

A snarl from her right. A howler lunged low. Claws hooked her ankle.

Cam went down hard. Stone tore her palms open. Her sword clattered; panic flared—*not now, not now*. She kicked, heel smashing muzzle, and dragged steel up in a brutal arc, the blade splitting its skull. It dissolved in a cough of ash and frost-burn.

Up, Sylithra snapped, fury like heat in the marrow. *Bite and burn.*

Then the ledge gave way.

The crack wasn't a sound at first but a feeling—stone shifting out of conviction. The ground under Wyatt fractured, edges shearing. The shelf dropped a handspan, then another. Pebbles sluiced into the void. He fought for purchase—boots scraping, heel gouging stone—but the cliff unstitched beneath him.

Cam shoved to her feet, breath tearing, sprinted. Hope punched her chest so hard it hurt. She reached—closer, closer—

For a heartbeat, their fingers almost touched.

His eyes locked to hers. Raw. Defiant. Full of everything he hadn't said. His mouth shaped her name.

The ledge tore, and he fell.

"WYATT!!!"

Her scream ripped the sky. She hit her knees so hard the pain stabbed up her thighs, fingers clawing broken rock until her nails bloodied. The abyss took what crumbs she had to throw at it—grit, breath, broken prayers—swallowing all of it.

The dragonlink convulsed with her grief.

Tessa's voice knifed through—high, ragged, *no no no*—

Cam felt the cry distort through the dragonlink, the sound warping into broken static before her mind could even register it.

Val's denial slammed iron-hard against the void. *Hold—Cam, HOLD—*

Kaden's refusal burned hot, a brand pressed to bone. *Not him. Not now.*

Sael's roar thundered so deep it rattled the ribs of the mountain; Brontheus keened storm-low; Virellan's cry cut thin and bright; Tenebrin went knife-quiet, silence like a blade.

Sylithra's fury exploded through Cam's veins, white-hot, uncontainable.

Through the link, Cam felt the thunder of Sylithra's heart—each beat a wingbeat, wild and terrified, slamming against her own ribs.

Lightning broke from her in a ragged crown, cracking the storm-dark sky. The mountain groaned—old stone shifting, the Maw waking deeper, wider.

The world spun. Shattered.

Cam didn't feel the ground when it hit her. Didn't feel the blood sliding warm down her ribs. Didn't feel Sylithra's voice break from a command into a plea.

She felt only the absence where Wyatt should have been.

Because he was gone.

Chapter 32: Not Him

The world shattered around her.

A shockwave slammed into Cam, pitching her backward. Her body crashed against the jagged mountain wall, head snapping back with a sharp crack. Stars bloomed behind her eyes, and silence screamed in her ears.

Blood trickled into her vision, warm and salty. Limbs trembled, betraying her. She fought to crawl forward, every movement a dagger of pain.

"No... Wyatt..." she rasped, voice raw, desperate.

No answer came. Only the harsh wind, swirling ash, and distant screeches of unseen creatures. The mountain seemed to breathe wrong, each groan of shifting stone a cruel echo of the moment she had missed him.

She stumbled, driven by something fierce and broken. Black stone and shattered cliffs stretched before her, but no sign of him.

Again, she screamed: "WYATT!" The sound echoed hollow, swallowed by the mountain's cold breath.

Her storm flickered, lightning sputtering with her faltering heartbeat. The dragonlink thrummed faint with the others, but Wyatt's silence was a wound in it.

Her fingertips brushed something cold buried in the dirt. Her pulse faltered as she caught the faint gleam—Wyatt's pendant.

Her chest clenched. *If I stop... I won't get up again.*

She left it behind.

Her strength drained fast—head spinning, blood loss and grief clouding every thought. But stubbornness clawed her upright one last time. She pressed shaking palms against the ground, forcing her legs to lock, to carry her just a few steps more.

Little Flame, Sylithra's voice trembled, not sharp this time but pleading. *Stay, please—stay.*

Cam lurched forward, body burning, vision smeared with blood. Every nerve screamed to give way, but she refused—until the world tilted, and her knees buckled.

Solid arms caught her before she hit the stone. Strong, steady.

Through the haze, she recognized not Wyatt's familiar warmth, but Kaden's firm grip.

It's not him.

Bitter fury and despair warred in her chest.

I was supposed to catch him. Where is he?

Her world slipped into darkness.

◈ ☽⚡☾ ◈

He had seen it coming in the split-second before it happened—her body swaying too far forward, blood streaking down her side, her knees giving at the cliff's edge. For one breath, it looked as if the mountain meant to claim her too. His chest seized. *Not her. Not again.*

He lunged, arms wrapping around her just as her weight tipped toward the abyss. The momentum nearly dragged him with her, boots skidding on loose stone, but he anchored himself, hauling her against his chest. His own ribs screamed with the effort, but he didn't let go.

Through the dragonlink, Kaden's voice was steady but laced with panic. "I've got you, Cam."

Her pulse thudded faint and shallow beneath his fingers, her skin clammy with blood and dust. His own hands shook as he held her upright, fury and grief tangling hot in his throat.

He scanned the broken cliff, searching for his brother. Nothing. No movement, no cry. Just the void yawning below, whispering what the link had already shown them all.

Not him. He can't be—

The ground cracked again, stone shrieking as the Maw split wider. Shadows poured from the fractures, Veilborn screeches carrying on the mountain wind. The temple was dying—collapsing in fire and ruin—but Kaden couldn't tear his gaze from the cliff's edge.

The dragonlink burned with Cam's grief, so raw it nearly knocked him to his knees. Val's silence pressed iron-hard against it, Tessa's sparks hissed with denial, Sael's roar rattled the mountain. They were all unraveling.

But Cam was slipping fast. He eased her down, pulse weakening, her lashes clumped with blood.

"Stay with me," he whispered, though his voice cracked. His chest felt hollow, as if holding her meant letting go of Wyatt all over again.

◈ ☽ ⚡ ☾ ◈

Val's legs nearly gave when she saw Kaden hauling Cam back from the cliff's edge, her body limp against him. For one terrible heartbeat, she thought he'd been too late—that the mountain had claimed them both. Her lungs seized like stone had dropped into them.

The link screamed with grief—Wyatt's absence ringing sharp and endless—but it didn't feel like one voice. It was weight, crushing from every side: Tessa's panic sparking wild, Kaden's fury jagged as broken glass, the dragons' roars rolling like thunder through her ribs. The pressure of it nearly forced her to her knees.

Her eyes dragged unwillingly toward the ledge, but she couldn't make herself look down. If she looked, it would be real. So instead, she fixed on Cam—blood soaking through Kaden's gloves, her skin pale as ash.

"No," Val whispered, the word so thin it almost vanished. "Not her too."

Virellan's growl pressed into her chest, low and storm-steady. *Hold. If you fall, they fall with you.*

Her hands shook, but she shoved them forward anyway, weaving streams of water into jagged shapes. Illusions darted through the haze—phantom doubles of herself that pulled howlers off course, momentary shields that bought Kaden seconds. Every drop of focus went into keeping the creatures at bay, giving them even a shred of space to breathe.

Her throat ached with unshed screams. Tessa's grief crackled like static beside her, threatening to splinter her own control, and Val bit down hard until she tasted iron. The urge to follow Wyatt into the abyss pressed heavy on her chest, but she clung to her dragon's command. Her job was clear: hold the line until they got out.

◈ ☽ ⚡ ☾ ◈

Tessa stood frozen, breath jagged, hands sparking uncontrollably. The dragonlink had forced it all into her skull—the silver betrayal, the cliff's collapse, Cam's scream—and it was too much.

Alex. The memory of his back seared silver in the dark burned behind her eyes. He hadn't stumbled. He hadn't been dragged. He had chosen to leave. To leave them. To leave *her*.

And now Wyatt—

Her chest split open at the thought. She'd known him since she was sixteen, when her storms first broke loose and nearly burned the outpost to the ground. He hadn't mocked her or flinched from her sparks—he had steadied her hand, told her she wasn't broken, just *loud*. Along with Kaden, he had become the brother she hadn't known she needed. Her family. Losing him now felt like the sky itself had fractured—like she was falling through the storm with nothing to catch her.

Her throat locked so tight she thought it might split. She wanted to scream, to tear the whole mountain open with lightning, to make the world feel even a fraction of the way her chest did—raw, hollow, breaking apart.

But the battle didn't care about grief. Veilborn and shadow creatures swarmed, jaws snapping, claws scraping against stone.

Val's voice cut sharp beside her: "Focus!" Her tone carried steel, but grief pressed under it like weight. She had felt Wyatt's absence hit like a blade through the dragonlink too—iron cracking, steadiness gone. Her hands shook, but she still shoved them forward, water weaving into jagged streams that burst into illusions. Phantom doubles darted into the fray, pulling howlers off course, buying Kaden seconds to breathe.

Tessa's lightning lashed wild, answering the creatures with ragged fury. "We trusted him," she choked, sparks flaring uncontrolled, burning fissures into the stone. "We *trusted* him!"

Brontheus's growl rumbled through her ribs, storm-deep and grieving. His fury tangled with hers until she shook with it, every strike cracking the air.

The grief wasn't quiet—it was a storm breaking loose, jagged and violent, impossible to hold. And the storm inside her wanted to rip free, to burn everything down.

Val's voice slammed into her again, iron and unyielding—but this time it broke a little around the edges: "Hold the line, Tess. *Hold.* Or we will lose her too."

Her friend's steadiness was an anchor, but not because it was unshakable—because it shook the same way hers did, grief and rage threaded through every word. Together they struck—lightning and water cutting side by side, illusions and sparks holding the swarm back, just barely.

◈ ☽⚡☾ ◈

The temple groaned, stone splitting like ribs under a giant's hand. The Maw was opening wider, fire bleeding through the cracks.

Kaden's fingers traced frantic runes into the dirt, a gate sparking into life before them. His hands trembled, but his will held firm. "Stay with me," he whispered to Cam again as the light spread into a shimmering arch.

The dragons circled close, their grief-stricken rumbles low and mournful. Brontheus's chest heaved with sorrow. Sylithra curled tightly, golden veins dimmed to a mournful dusk. Sael's roar still carried, though Wyatt's silence in the dragonlink tore at them all.

As Kaden lifted Cam, a glint caught the corner of his eye—Wyatt's pendant, half-buried in the dust where he'd fallen. Panic gripped him, but survival left no room to stop. His heart screamed to dive for it, to cling to that last piece of his brother, but Cam was slipping.

Together, they vanished through the gate just as the mountain roared and the temple crumbled into oblivion.

On the other side, in the cold silence of an abandoned fortress court yard, the group collapsed.

Cam lay unconscious, blood loss severe. Kaden lowered his forehead to hers, whispering fiercely:

"I've got you. I won't let go."

But through the quiet dragonlink of dragons and riders, one truth echoed painfully clear:

Wyatt was gone.

Chapter 33: Ashes of the Cradle

The map room smelled of dust and old fire. Ben moved slowly, his fingers trailing the spines of rolled parchment until one snagged his attention. He didn't know why—only that the unease gnawing in his gut wouldn't let him stop.

Sleep had been broken the night before. Not by his own memories, but hers.

Cam.

The dream still clung to him: her silhouette framed against a cliff, blood streaking her face, her shoulders bowed but not broken. Grief had hollowed her eyes, but defiance burned there too, fierce enough to sting his chest even in sleep. It hadn't been his foresight. It had been hers—a storm so raw that it had ripped backward through the bond of blood, striking him where he couldn't ignore it.

You felt her, Skylith murmured, her voice a low ember in the back of his mind. *Not the future. The present bleeding into you.*

He pressed a palm flat against the table, breathing hard. "I know."

She had felt like her mother in that moment—when Izzy's grief had made the Veil itself shudder. Ben closed his eyes, steadying against the weight of it.

The map unfurled beneath his hands, parchment creasing at the edges. His gaze followed the jagged black ink of the Eldvale range. Everyone said the cradle temple had been there. The records, the whispers, even Corin's fragments of vision. But his hand hesitated, drifting north. The coastlines, the ridges, the frozen spine of land that most forgot existed.

He remembered walking there once. Not alone. Isabella at his side, weeks before Cam had even taken her first breath. She had insisted the temple mattered. That it was older than the Capital's lies. He had believed her.

And then the years had buried that memory. Not with peace, but with blood. Years spent chasing ghosts, hunting betrayal across battlefields and shadows. Too many faces, too many nights. Age and guilt fray edges—names slip, places blur, and sometimes you forget the things that matter most until they rise like ghosts.

But now, with Cam's grief ringing in his skull, the ghost had become a blade.

"It wasn't west," he muttered, tracing north with a trembling finger. "Gods, it was never west. It was north."

Skylith rumbled through their bond, a sound of agreement threaded with sorrow. *And they are walking straight into it.*

His breath caught. If he was right, then his daughter and her friends had flown not into discovery, but into a snare.

The door creaked open behind him. Corin's presence filled the room, quiet but edged like drawn steel.

"You feel it too," he said, not asking.

Ben glanced up, meeting the strategist's gaze. "The cradle temple... it's not where we thought. Isabella and I saw it in the north, years ago. I don't know why it slipped from me until now. But I think they've been led into a trap."

Corin's expression didn't shift, but the air seemed to still around him. "An hour ago, I had a vision. Not one I trust. It was fragmented, veiled—just stone collapsing, shadows rising, and a scream I couldn't place. But it hasn't left me." He exhaled slowly, controlled. "I have learned to listen when unease lingers."

Ben frowned. "Then you think—"

"I don't think," Corin cut in softly, a rare crack in his usual calm. "I know something has gone wrong." His hand hovered over the table, not quite touching the map. "But visions lie, Ben. Or worse—they tell the truth too late."

Before Ben could answer, the communication stone flared hot at his belt. Kaden's voice shattered the silence, ragged with panic.

◈ ☽ ⚡ ☾ ◈

The Ember Fortress loomed from the cliffs like a scar—carved into the black rock, its broken gates yawning open as if it hadn't expected visitors for centuries. The air here carried the bite of stone and ash, every breath harsh and dry.

Kaden staggered through those gates first; Cam cradled in his arms. Blood had soaked through her tunic, staining his own. Her head lolled against his chest, breath shallow, pulse faint.

Val and Tessa rushed in behind him, their boots echoing off stone as they entered the ruin's shadowed halls. The fortress felt abandoned, hollow, a shell of old wars and colder memories. Dust and silence clung thick in the air, broken only by their uneven breathing and the distant rumble of dragons outside.

The first chamber they found still held a long, cracked stone table, its surface scarred by time and fire. It wasn't meant for this—it had once borne maps, weapons, maybe councils of war—but it was flat, solid, and it would have to serve.

Val was suddenly at his side, reaching for Cam. Her face was pale, but her voice cut steady.

"Let me—your arms are shaking."

He didn't argue. His muscles screamed from carrying her, his ribs raw, but letting go felt like tearing himself in two. Together, they lowered Cam onto the stone. Her body looked far too small against it, far too still.

Val's hands moved fast, water shimmering as she cleaned and bound the worst of the wounds. Kaden tried to steady his breathing, to ignore the way her fingers trembled even as she worked. He forced himself to focus on the pulse at Cam's throat, faint but there. It was the only anchor keeping his chest from breaking wide open.

Kaden fumbled for the communication stone, his throat raw.

"Corin," he rasped. "It was a trap. Alex was the spy."

A beat of silence. Corin's voice came, quiet but sharp:

"Understood. Are you all safe?"

The words lodged in Kaden's throat. He couldn't say it. His jaw clenched, his shoulders trembling. Finally, the truth tore free.

"We lost Wyatt."

Silence.

Not the silence of a broken stone or a severed link—this was heavier, breathing between them. Kaden could almost feel it pressing through the channel: Corin's foresight gone sharp and cold, Ben's grief like a held breath too jagged to release. For a heartbeat, no one spoke. The weight of it said more than words ever could.

Then Ben's voice came, rough with grief but steady enough to cut steel.

"Kaden... Cam. Is she..?"

Kaden's gaze dropped to her—blood soaking through bandages, her chest rising shallow and uneven. His throat worked, but no sound came for a moment. Finally, he forced it out, raw.

"She's alive. Barely."

Ben's exhale rasped across the stone, jagged with both relief and fear.

"Where are you?"

"The Ember Fortress," Kaden said. "I couldn't bring them to Haldrin's Keep. Alex—he escaped. If he reports back, the Keep's compromised. I couldn't risk it."

A pause, long and heavy. Then Ben's voice came again, grim with resolve though grief underpinned every word.

"You were right. If he slipped through, Haldrin's not safe for any of us. Open a portal, Kaden. We'll regroup. Abandon the Keep. Everything we can carry comes with us—the rest we leave behind."

Corin's voice followed, quieter, heavy as stone breaking.

"So it begins."

◈ ☽⚡☾ ◈

Val's hands didn't falter as she tightened the binding on Cam's ribs, but her eyes burned with unshed tears. Blood slicked her fingers, warm and sticky, refusing to be staunched no matter how tight she pulled the cloth. She blinked hard, biting her lip until it split, copper filling her mouth—anything to keep her focus steady. If she let go, even for a heartbeat, Cam would slip further away.

"Stay with me," she whispered under her breath, though the words were for herself as much as for Cam.

The dragonlink screamed with grief, Wyatt's absence ringing through it like a snapped tether. The weight of it pressed against her ribs until she thought she might crack. She wanted to scream, to let the storm inside her out, but she shoved it down—bound it tight. Virellan's voice growled steady through her chest: Hold. If you fall, they fall with you.

So she held. She kept her hands moving, water weaving into thin streams that cleared blood away, let her see where to press and where to bind. The motions were steady, but her vision blurred, and her throat locked with the ache of unspoken grief.

At the edge of her hearing, she caught Kaden's voice—low, rough—speaking into the communication stone. Corin's reply, Ben's too, muffled by distance. She didn't take it in, couldn't. All that mattered was the shallow rise and fall of Cam's chest beneath her hands. The rest of the world could have burned to ash, and she wouldn't have looked up.

Tessa dropped to her knees beside the table, her hand covering Cam's for a fleeting heartbeat before it slid away, trembling. Her shoulders shook, sparks flashing at her fingertips, but her voice forced itself out—thin, breaking, but still there.

"She can't lose him. Not him too."

The words lanced through Val like a blade. Not just because they were true, but because they echoed her own thoughts—raw, unsaid, festering in her chest. Not him. Not Cam. Not any of them.

Her eyes burned hotter, but she blinked it back, setting her jaw.

"Focus," she hissed, though her own voice cracked. Her hands only pressed harder, as if sheer force could keep Cam's pulse beating, could keep her tethered to them all.

Kaden's throat worked as he swallowed against the lump lodged there. Then he dropped to his knees beside them, the communication stone slipping from his hand to clatter uselessly against the floor. Val felt him breaking as he knelt there, his grief jagged and sharp in the dragonlink. His shoulders hunched forward, fists pressed hard against his eyes as if he could force the tears back.

Tessa's shoulders shook uncontrollably as she reached out, laying her hand on his shoulder. Instead of shrugging her off, Kaden turned and pulled her close, their grief spilling into the link like a wound torn wide. His hands shook so badly Val's heart lurched. For a moment, she watched both her friends unravel, clinging to each other in silence heavy enough to crush bone.

Exhaustion screamed through every nerve, through all of them, but Val kept her hands on Cam, steady and unyielding. She didn't dare falter. She didn't dare let go.

◈ ☽⚡☾ ◈

Orren had been moving crates when Ben's voice cut sharp across the hall.

"Hail. With me."

He set the weight down without a word, wiping dust and ash from his gloves as he crossed to where the older man stood over a half-rolled map and a communication stone still glowing faintly. Ben's jaw was set, his expression carved from grief and iron. Orren had seen commanders wear that look before. It meant something had broken—and there was no undoing it.

"What's happened?" Orren asked, tone clipped, steady. But something in his chest tightened, as if he already knew.

Ben's eyes flicked to him, sharp and unyielding. "The Cradle Temple. It was a trap. Alex was the spy."

The words hit like a blade sliding between ribs. Alex—the quiet one, always near the circle's fire, always listening. Orren's mouth tightened, though he kept his face unreadable. "And the others?"

"They're alive," Ben said, voice rough, the sound of someone holding too much back. His hand pressed hard to the edge of the table. "But Wyatt... we lost him."

For a breath Orren said nothing, though his jaw worked tight. He hadn't known the man long, but he'd fought beside him, watched him move like stone and light through chaos. He didn't need the bond to feel the absence—though faint threads brushed him anyway. Not his. Never his. Yet something tugged faint and raw across his chest, a grief that wasn't entirely his own. He shoved it down, unsettled.

Ben's eyes stayed fixed on him, as if measuring what he'd do with this truth. "I'm telling you this because you owe my daughter a life debt."

The words stopped Orren cold.

'Daughter.'

He masked his reaction with silence, but inside, the thought slammed into him harder than any order ever had. He had suspected—once or twice—the way Ben's eyes lingered on her, the way his voice roughened when he said her name. But to hear it named...

His voice came low. "Then it's true."

Ben didn't flinch. "It's true. And if you mean to honor that debt, you'll stand with us now. Not the Capital. Not their chains. Us."

Something shifted inside Orren at those words. Mage hunter. Soldier. Weapon. That's what the Capital had carved him into. But here—Ben's blunt truth, the circle's grief, Cam's storm strong enough to shake mountains—it pressed against a place in him he hadn't let himself feel in years.

"I'll stand," he said at last, quiet but certain.

Ben gave a single sharp nod and turned back to the maps. "Then help me hold this together. We're evacuating the Keep. Everyone goes through the portal before the end of the day. No exceptions."

Orders followed—shouting runners, shifting supplies, dragons landing heavy against the cliffs—but Orren's thoughts kept circling back. Cam's face in the firelight, defiant even when fear gripped her. Kaden's iron focus, Val's steady edge, Tessa's sparks. A circle the Capital would have broken without hesitation. A circle the Capital feared.

And him, standing here—not as their hunter, but as something else.

For the first time, he wasn't Orren Hail, mage hunter of the Capital, the pale fang.

He was just Orren. And maybe that was enough.

So he moved through the chaos with new purpose. He steadied a child's trembling grip on a pack, adjusted the straps of a soldier's armor, shifted a crate onto his shoulder as if it weighed nothing. Calm. Efficient. Chosen.

Orders followed—runners dispatched, soldiers called, families gathered. Dragons moved first, wings stirring dust as they filed toward the portal. Their cries carried heavy across the cliffs, mourning layered into every sound. Then came the people: soldiers with worn packs, families clutching children, elders leaning hard on canes. Not chaos, not panic—just the slow, heavy press of inevitability. Betrayal had found them, and now safety meant leaving everything behind.

Orren moved among them, steadying grips, adjusting armor straps, shifting crates onto his shoulder as if they weighed nothing. He didn't have to bark orders; he wasn't that man anymore. Instead he kept pace with them, one pair of hands among many.

The portal pulsed in the courtyard of Haldrin's Keep, its edges glowing like molten glass. Each figure who passed through stretched long in its light, then vanished into the field beyond.

And then Orren stepped through.

The air shifted, cooler, sharper—the field outside the Ember Fortress unfolding before him. Dragons shook themselves free of the magic's veil, wings rattling the grass flat, their cries rolling across the tree line. The circle's bonded dragons waited just beyond the fortress gates—Sylithra, Brontheus, Virellan, Tenebrin—watching with grief-etched eyes. Sael was there too, but his silence pressed heavier than thunder.

He no longer bothered with crates or straps. Instead, he watched the faces—soldiers who'd once stood tall now moving like shadows, children clutching charms as if they'd keep the world from breaking further. He had herded people before, but as prisoners, as spoils of the Capital. This... this was the opposite. These people weren't bound. They chose to walk through the fire and follow. And that realization unsettled him more than silence ever could.

When his gaze caught Kaden—blood-stained, pale, half-collapsed from strain—he stilled. Tessa stood rigid at his side, glaring at Orren as though he were the enemy, and to her, he was. Cam and Val were nowhere in sight, and unease prickled sharp under his ribs. Kaden leaned hard against the wall, hands trembling, Tessa bracing him as if she could lend what little strength she had left.

Orren's jaw tightened. He didn't need to ask, but his silence held the question all the same.

He lingered until the last refugee had crossed. Then, with a single firm gesture, he carved a rune into the stone, sealing the portal behind him. The path back to the Keep was gone.

◈ ☽ ⚡ ☾ ◈

The chamber was still by the time the last rays of light vanished. The portal's glow had left a ghostly afterimage in Kaden's eyes, and his entire body shook with the effort it had taken to hold it open. His palms were raw, the rune-burn still etched faintly into his skin, and every nerve screamed with exhaustion.

Tessa collapsed first. She slid down the wall beside him, sparks still flickering uncontrolled from her fingers as silent sobs racked her chest. She pressed both hands to her mouth as if she could smother the sound, but the tremble in her shoulders betrayed her. Kaden had felt her magic fray while they'd anchored the gate together, wild and raw with grief, and now it cracked loose in tears.

He swayed where he stood, half-collapsed himself, the world pitching dangerously with each breath. If not for the stone wall bracing his shoulder, he wasn't sure he'd still be upright. He was starting to see a glint of gold running through his veins beneath his skin—residue from too much magic.

Too much magic, he thought. He'd carried too much—his fury, their grief, Cam's weight in his arms, and the silence where his brother should have been.

The inner door scraped open. Val emerged, blood streaking her hands up to the wrists, her braid torn loose around her face. She leaned against the frame, drawing one ragged breath before speaking.

"She's stable," she said softly. Then, quieter, almost to herself: "For now."

The words steadied and broke Kaden in the same heartbeat. Relief slammed into him, sharp as a blade, but it didn't ease the weight crushing his chest. Val's gaze flicked toward him, and her voice carried a thread of worry.

"She isn't healing like she usually does. It's... too slow."

The meaning landed heavy. Cam's physical healing usually closed wounds with terrifying speed, her body refusing to break for long. But now—nothing but shallow breaths, colorless skin, and blood drying where Val had stitched. Something deeper held her under, and the thought hollowed Kaden's stomach.

He clenched his jaw until it ached, forcing himself not to look at Tessa's shaking shoulders, not to think of Wyatt. If he gave in—if he let it take him—none of them would stand.

Later, in the chamber where Cam lay pale and almost broken, Kaden stood at one of the narrow window slits carved into the fortress wall. The forest stretched black and endless below, the stars sharp in the spring sky. And beyond, far beyond, the mountains where Wyatt had fallen.

No sound reached him. Only stillness.

Behind him, the room was thick with the weight of vigil. Cam lay on a rough pallet, her chest rising shallowly, her hair matted with blood and ash. Val sat beside her, hands folded so tightly in her lap the knuckles gleamed bone-white, her bloodstained sleeves sticking to her skin. Tessa had curled against the far wall, her eyes swollen, sparks still twitching across her fingertips as if grief refused to quiet inside her. Neither spoke. They only watched Cam's breath, waiting, fearing it might stop.

Kaden opened his mouth—just once, just to break the silence—but no words came. His throat locked. What could he say? That he should have seen what Alex was? That he could have done more to save them? The truth would tear them apart even more. So he closed his mouth again, and their silence grew louder, heavier than any scream.

I was supposed to bring us all back, he thought bitterly. *I should have—*

His hand curled on the windowsill, knuckles white, nails biting stone. But beneath the grief, something else took root. A spark. Small, dangerous, unyielding.

If there's even a chance... I'll find you.

On the pallet, Cam stirred. She shifted restlessly, her breath uneven, and murmured one broken word into the darkness.

"Wyatt..."

The sound was a knife. And a plea.

Then the dragonlink rippled.

Sylithra's mourning hum carried through the stone, deep and aching. Brontheus keened low, sparks dancing off his scales like lightning-tears. Tenebrin prowled restlessly along the cliffs, wings half-spread, shadows dragging long and uneasy.

But Sael... Sael was only silence.

Not gone—not yet—but distant, frayed like a thread stretched too thin. The dragons recoiled from it, unable to anchor to what they could no longer feel. The absence hollowed through the link so sharp Kaden gasped, bracing a hand against the wall. Val pressed her fist to her chest as if the silence had punched straight through her ribs. Tessa flinched, her tear-streaked face lifting toward the sound that wasn't there.

Even Cam stirred, murmuring his brother's name again in her sleep.

The silence bled into all of them, trembling like the echo of a scream too far away to hear.

Kaden shut his eyes against it, jaw clenched until it hurt. He let the grief burn through him, but he did not drown in it. He couldn't.

Because if Cam's storm had taught him anything tonight, it was this... threads only break if you let them.

When he opened his eyes again, the vow was steel in his chest.

I'll find you, brother. For me—and for her.

Chapter 34: Aftershock

The Ember Fortress felt silent—too silent for a place that had only just been filled with life hours ago.

No laughter drifted through its halls; no dragon calls echoed from their makeshift roosts. Even the fire, guttering faintly in its sconces, sounded like a dying breath. Shadows stretched long across the stone, turning the fortress into a tomb that still pretended to hold the living.

Tessa pushed open the infirmary doors.

Cam had been carried there a few hours ago, after the chaos of Haldrin's Keep and the scramble of settling refugees. Val and two of the healers had worked without pause to keep her steady, but steady wasn't the same as better. The bandages had been changed, the bleeding slowed, yet her skin was still too pale, her breathing still too shallow, as if every breath was being borrowed.

Val bent over her now, hands sure but face tight with exhaustion. Cam lay motionless beneath her care, pale against blood-streaked wrappings. Bruises marred her temple, ribs, and shoulder. Strands of dried blood clung to her hair like dark threads.

Tessa's fists curled at her sides. She didn't cry. Her voice came out flat, scraped raw.

"Tell me what to do."

Val didn't look up. She pressed a cloth to Cam's shoulder and only nodded toward a basin.

Tessa obeyed. She dipped another cloth, cool water stinging her raw knuckles, and pressed it gently to Cam's brow.

And then the memories crashed in.

Wyatt, standing across from her in the training yard, his grin quick and reckless, like he believed nothing could touch him. That grin had annoyed her as often as it had steadied her—he knew it too, damn him—but now she would have given anything to see it again.

Alex's voice followed, quiet, almost fragile: I'd never hurt her. I swear it. A vow she'd wanted to believe. She remembered his eyes when he'd said it, earnest and trembling at the same time. She'd vouched for him. She'd defended him. And still, it had been lies.

Then the moment when everything split apart: stone crashing, blood spraying, Cam's scream tearing through the dragonlink like glass shattering inside her skull.

Her stomach twisted. Her hands trembled over Cam's skin.

Not now, she told herself fiercely. She needs me first.

When Val murmured for fresh bandages, Tessa moved quickly, silently, as though speed might undo the ache clawing at her chest. But when she stepped back, when Cam's lashes didn't flutter, when her breathing stayed shallow—Tessa fled the room.

Her boots struck sharp echoes along the corridor. She couldn't stay still; she couldn't breathe in that silence. Sparks leapt at her fingertips, snapping bright and angry in the shadows.

Stormsinger, Brontheus rumbled, his voice a low thunder across her mind. *You carry the storm too close.*

"I vouched for him," she whispered, words burning like sparks. "I let him come. And now Wyatt is gone."

Blame will not mend what is broken, Brontheus answered, steady as stone. *But it will break you if you let it.*

Her chest tightened, rage twisting with guilt until it pressed against her throat. She braced a hand against the cold wall, dragging in a breath. The stone bit her palm, grounding her just enough, but it couldn't stop the tears. She tried to swallow them down, tried to blink them back, but they spilled hot and silent anyway, cutting down her cheeks faster than she could wipe them away.

She pressed her forehead to the wall for a moment, eyes squeezed shut, the storm in her chest threatening to burst free. Her shoulders shook once—sharp, angry, unwilling to admit it was grief at all.

She forced herself upright. Another breath. Then another. Her hand closed into a fist until the sparks dimmed. Only then did she push back through the door.

Val was still bent over Cam, but her eyes flicked up when Tessa entered. They caught on the streaks down her cheeks, the redness in her lashes. For a moment, Val's hands stilled. Then, without a word, she reached across the cot and laid her hand on Tessa's shoulder.

The weight of it was steady, grounding. No comfort offered, no lie spoken—just presence. If Val opened her mouth, Tessa knew she would break. She could feel it in the tremor of her touch. And Val couldn't break. Not yet.

Cam still didn't stir.

Tessa leaned against the cot, throat raw, lashes wet.

"Don't die too," she whispered hoarsely. "Please... not you too."

◈ ☽ ⚡ ☾ ◈

Outside, Brontheus prowled along the fortress ledge, talons grinding sparks from the stone. His green-black wings unfurled, the membranes catching stray lightning that arced and hissed across the cliff face. The storm within him churned restless, coiled too tight, answering the storm inside his rider.

He lifted his head toward the distant mountains, where thunder pressed heavy in the clouds. The air was thick with iron and rain, but beneath it he tasted something sharper—grief bleeding through the bond, bitter as ash. It clung to him, pressed into his chest the way it pressed into hers.

Farther along the ridge, a pale glow shimmered against the stone—Sael, wings tucked close, his eyes fixed on the horizon as if staring hard enough might call his rider back. His bond to Wyatt was frayed to silence, nulled but not severed, and the weight of it hung heavy in the dragonlink.

Beside him, Sylithra coiled low, her scales veined with gold fire that pulsed faint and irregular, like a heart struggling to beat. Each flicker dimmed too quickly, then returned in stuttering bursts, as if even her light had grown shallow. Her rider's mind was sealed in darkness, and the Cradle-blood dragon pressed close to Sael, her presence a quiet anchor against the void.

Brontheus rumbled low in his chest, tasting their strain through the shared tether. Storm and flame, light and silence—they leaned into one another because they had no choice. And he, too, pressed his strength outward, letting his storm roll wider, trying to steady them as much as his own rider.

Stormsinger, he thought, sending the word into Tessa's mind. *You hold the storm until it breaks you. But you are not alone in it.*

◈ ☽ ⚡ ☾ ◈

The balcony air stung her skin, sharp as glass. She shoved through the archway, lightning biting between her fingers, sparks hissing each time her pulse spiked. The storm inside her needed somewhere to land, and the night air was the only place it wouldn't tear her apart.

Bootsteps followed.

She stiffened before turning. Orren stood in the shadows of the arch, as if he hadn't meant to find her but had anyway. His gaze flicked to her hands where sparks hissed, then to her face.

Tessa's jaw tightened. "Come to deliver judgment?"

He didn't move closer. "Didn't know I needed to."

Her chest burned. "Say it, then. I failed. I trusted him. Wyatt's gone because of me."

His eyes sharpened, but his voice stayed calm, almost infuriatingly so.

"You think you cornered the market on mistakes? You're not the only one who let him in."

That hit harder than she wanted. Her laugh cracked bitter. "I should've seen it."

"Maybe." He tilted his head, studying her like he was measuring the storm beneath her skin. "Or maybe you wanted to believe. That's the difference between you and me—you still do."

Her breath hitched, anger snapping bright. "Don't pretend you know me."

His mouth curved—not a smile, not kind, but something sharp. "I don't. Not yet."

Lightning flared in her palm before she realized it, the storm begging to loose itself. His gaze flicked down, not afraid, not flinching—just steady. That steadiness unsettled her more than fear would have.

They stood like that, storm and stone, neither giving ground. And for one raw heartbeat, Tessa hated how much she wanted to close the space between them—whether to strike him or grab hold, she couldn't decide.

So, she turned from him, each step sharp as she climbed the stairwell. She didn't look back though she could still feel Orren's gaze on her. The air grew colder, thinner, until the night opened before her at the top. The sky was bruised with storm, heavy with clouds, lightning flickering faint and sharp.

Brontheus thrummed steady in her chest, storm pressing against her ribs. His voice rumbled low in her mind: Stormsinger... the storm is not your end. It is your beginning.

Tessa gripped the stone rail, breath trembling as the storm flared alive in her veins. She whispered into the night, bitter and quiet:

"Next time... I *won't* be fooled."

Chapter 35: What Cannot be Undone

The Eldvale mountains loomed cold and vast, their peaks crowned in snow. Ben had walked these ridges in another lifetime—back when patrols were routine, when dragons still wheeled freely above the cliffs. But tonight the range felt wrong. Hollow. Empty. Like the stone itself remembered what had been torn from it.

The wind cut sharp across the cliffs, carrying no sound but the crunch of boots on ice and the rasp of breath. Every echo seemed swallowed too quickly, leaving only silence.

Behind him, Orren moved with quiet efficiency, scanning each ledge, each dark crevice as though discipline alone could force the mountain to yield its secrets. Ahead, Kaden pressed forward with frantic determination, his jaw tight, his eyes darting to every shadow as if sheer will could make his brother appear.

Ben's chest ached. He knew what it was to lose—and to keep losing. He had seen it hollow men out, had felt it himself when Isabella's absence carved through him. Watching Kaden now, shoulders rigid with a hope already curdled into desperation, something inside him broke.

He shifted his gaze to the sky, where Skylith's shadow circled against the clouds. Her grief pressed through the bond—not her own, but Sylithra's, carried across the tether the dragons shared. The sorrow was vast and heavy, laced with a quiet terror that bled from rider to dragon to rider again. Through Skylith, Ben felt it like a bruise pressed into his ribs: the ache of Sylithra's mourning for Cam, who hovered between life and death.

And when Cam woke, she would feel this loss all over again. Wyatt's absence would gut her as surely as it was breaking Kaden now. Ben didn't know how she would survive it—if she even could.

For a fleeting moment, he wished he could shield her from it, just once, even if it meant bearing it alone. But some wounds couldn't be carried for another.

He swallowed the thought and pressed on. The mountain gave nothing back. No tracks. No blood. No body. Only silence.

◈ ☽ ⚡ ☾ ◈

Night pressed heavy against the Valthorne peaks, the sky a bruise of shadow and dim starlight. Sylithra crouched low on the fortress ledge, wings furled tight, her chest glowing faint through scales veined with gold. The light pulsed unevenly—too faint, too slow—like a heart struggling to remember its rhythm.

Beside her, Sael stood sentinel, pale wings folded close, his eyes fixed on the horizon where no dawn stirred. His silence pressed into her like stone—immovable, sorrow-weighted—but beneath it, she felt the fracture of something raw.

Sylithra closed her eyes. She pushed her fire outward, pouring it into the bond with her rider, weaving warmth into the fragile thread that stretched between them. It quivered like a bowstring drawn too far, straining against an unseen pull.

Stay. Do not drift, Little Flame. Hold fast.

But the current pressed back, cold and vast, pulling, pulling. Her fire guttered. The tether slipped in her grasp.

Her head lowered, pressing against the stone as a low rumble spilled from her throat—a name, broken, weighted. A name that carried silence where once there had been light.

Sael shifted, his pale gaze flicking toward her. He did not speak, but he pressed his presence against hers, layering silence atop flame until the bond steadied by a hair's breadth.

Together they anchored. Together they resisted.

Sylithra rumbled again, low and steady, though her chest burned with the effort. To others it would sound like dragons keeping vigil in mourning. But beneath, she wove her fire into a single thread, fighting the unseen pull that sought to unmake it.

And she held. Gods, she held.

◈ ☽ ⚡ ☾ ◈

Flickering wardlight painted the infirmary walls in pale gold, shadows stretching long across the stone. The air smelled of crushed herbs and ash from the torches, sharp enough to sting. Every breath Val took felt thin, like her chest was carrying smoke instead of air.

She sat at Cam's bedside, salve cupped in one palm, smoothing it gently across bruised skin. Her fingers moved with practiced steadiness, but beneath the rhythm her hands ached from holding too much tension. She could not let them shake. Not here. Not in front of Cam.

The healers moved around her at first, binding cloth, whispering low-spoken incantations to ease pain. One by one, they slipped out as the night deepened, leaving Val to the silence and the steady rasp of Cam's breathing. It wasn't enough. Her chest still rose too shallow, her lips still too pale. Every breath seemed borrowed from some place that would soon come to collect its debt.

Val brushed damp hair back from Cam's brow, telling herself she was checking for fever. The truth was she needed to touch her, to prove she was still warm, still here. Just barely.

Then Cam stirred, caught between waking and oblivion. Her lips parted.

"...Wyatt..."

The name broke something clean through Val's chest. It was soft, almost soundless, but it cut all the same. She bowed her head for a moment, blinking hard, swallowing against the thickness in her throat.

Across the cot, Tessa sat rigid, posture sharp as if holding herself together by sheer force. Her eyes didn't lift from the floor. Her face was carved in stone, but Val could feel the heat of her guilt rolling across the room like fire.

The hours dragged. Wardlight flickered. The hush pressed so heavily it was almost a sound itself. Val sat with her grief coiled tight, her hand never leaving Cam's, afraid that if she let go, the tether might snap.

Finally, Tessa's voice broke the silence, low and raw.

"If I hadn't vouched for him... if I hadn't let Alex come... Wyatt would still be here."

Val turned her head slowly. For a moment, her throat closed with words she couldn't speak. She could have said you couldn't have known, but the lie would taste like ash. She could have said Wyatt chose his path, but grief wasn't reasoned away.

So instead, she reached across the cot and set her hand over Tessa's. Her own hand trembled faintly before she stilled it.

Her voice was quiet, rough at the edges.

"*We all trusted him.* That's what makes it hurt."

The words dropped into the stillness like stones in water, sinking deep, rippling out.

And Val didn't pull her hand away.

For a long moment, the only sound was Cam's fragile breathing, the faint hiss of wardfire in the sconces. Val eased her hand back at last, flexing her stiff fingers. She rose quietly, carrying the empty bowl to the basin. The water had gone tepid, tinged pink from the salves and blood she had already washed away tonight. She dipped her hands in, rubbing the mixture from her skin until the sting of herbs bit her knuckles.

She let the water run off her palms, stared into the basin as ripples spread across its surface. For a heartbeat, she wished the ripples could carry their grief away with them.

The door creaked.

Val looked up, droplets sliding down her wrists.

Kaden stepped inside, shoulders slumped, pale with exhaustion. His eyes looked raw, rimmed red as if sleep had abandoned him days ago and grief had taken its place. His movements were slow, almost hollow, but his presence filled the infirmary like a shadow.

He moved wordlessly to Cam's side and stood there for a long moment. Val watched the muscles in his jaw clench as his gaze fixed on Cam's still form. His lips moved, whispering something she couldn't catch, a vow meant only for her. The sound was too soft to reach, but the way his throat bobbed after told Val it had cost him everything to say it.

Then he leaned back against the wall, posture collapsing as if even standing was too heavy a burden. His hands trembled faintly, the tremor betraying what he might have otherwise hidden. His breathing was uneven, shallow pulls of air that never seemed to fill his chest.

Val's heart ached at the sight. Kaden had always carried himself with sharp, clever confidence—the kind that sometimes brushed close to arrogance. He was the one who challenged her plans, who made her argue harder, sharpen her edges, keep her footing. But now? Now all of that had been stripped away, leaving only grief. She wanted to speak, to reach for him, but before she could gather the words, he pushed off the wall and slipped out the door.

Her own breath caught. She looked at Cam—still unmoving, lips parted as though whispering Wyatt's name even in dreams—and then at Tessa, still stone in her chair. Quietly, Val excused herself and followed.

The corridor was hushed, lit only by guttering sconces. Her boots echoed soft against the flagstones as she trailed the sound of Kaden's retreat. Each step carried her farther from the smell of herbs and ash, into air that thinned with cold. The fortress walls seemed to breathe around her, old stone holding its silence like a secret.

By the time she reached the stairwell, the draft slipping through the cracks was sharp enough to sting. She pulled her coat tighter, climbed, and pushed through the final archway.

The night air struck colder still on the balcony cut into the mountainside. Wind swept sharp across the stone, tugging at her coat until it snapped and whispered like restless wings. Above, the sky bruised heavy with storm clouds; below, snow-dusted peaks stretched into endless shadow.

On a distant ledge, Brontheus shifted, wings tight against his back, his eyes glowing faint in the dark. His presence mirrored Tessa's grief, restless and unstill.

Kaden leaned against the wall, shoulders hunched, breath fogging quick and uneven in the freezing air. His lips shaped a single name—Wyatt—over and over, like a prayer or a curse, though no sound carried. Each time his mouth formed it, Val felt the ache deepen in her chest, as if the name itself hollowed the night around them.

She approached softly, boots crunching against frost. She laid a hand on his shoulder.

He turned suddenly, pulling her into a tight embrace. It was not graceful. It was desperate. His arms locked around her as though he would break without something to cling to. The dam finally gave way.

His voice cracked against her hair, torn ragged from his throat.

"I went back... Ben and Orren went with me. The temple's rubble. The cliffs are gone. There's nothing. No body. No sign..."

The words splintered, frayed into the cold air. His chest heaved against hers, his breath sharp with anguish, the sound of someone unraveling.

Val's own control wavered. She tightened her hold on him, pressing her cheek to his shoulder, anchoring him even as her own eyes stung. He was shaking so hard she could feel it rattle through his frame, and she knew she was shaking too. They were both breaking, but they held to each other because the alternative was to fall apart alone.

"Nothing," he whispered again, softer this time, the word shattering into silence.

Val closed her eyes. Her fingers clenched into the fabric of Kaden's coat, holding fast even as the cold air cut sharp into her lungs. She thought of Wyatt then—not as Cam's protector, not as Kaden's brother, but as her friend. She remembered his steady grin in the sparring yard, the way he caught her elbow when she faltered, the quiet moments when his light steadied her without trying. He had believed in her strength even when she doubted it. And now he was gone.

The memory stung, sharp and sudden, and for a moment she felt the loss as raw as Kaden must have.

The cracks in her steadiness spread wider. She held Kaden tighter, not just for him, but for herself. If she let go, she wasn't sure either of them would stand.

Something shifted in the silence—subtle, but certain. Not love, not yet, but the recognition of it somewhere far ahead. Kaden had always met her strength with sharpness, with challenge. Tonight he met it with grief, and she answered it with her arms around him. A fragile seed planted in ruin.

They stayed like that in the wind, silence heavy as the mountain itself, grief pressing down with every gust. Val lifted her gaze over Kaden's shoulder to the black horizon, the mountains a jagged maw against the storm-dim sky.

Some wounds can't be healed, she thought, the truth bitter as snow on her tongue. *But we survive anyway.*

And for tonight, survival was enough.

Chapter 36: Damage Report

The Ember Fortress command hall burned with torchlight, each flame casting long shadows against the cold stone walls. The chamber was crowded now—mages and warriors from Haldrin's Keep, civilians too young or too old to fight, dragon riders posted like sentinels while their bonded circled the cliffs above. The fortress had been half-empty only days ago. Now it thrummed with uneasy life, buzzing with the low hum of voices, the clatter of armor, the coughs of the wounded.

Corin stood at the center, directing with quiet authority. One group to the lower barracks. Another to the kitchens. The injured down to the healers. To anyone watching, he was composed, steady—the still point in the storm.

But his mind was elsewhere.

On the table before him lay a casualty list, its ink barely dry. Not Haldrin's Keep—that had been evacuation, not slaughter—but other outposts, ambushed in the chaos Alex's betrayal had sown. Corin's hand hovered over the names, fingers tightening as they found one written in neat, merciless letters: Wyatt Valehart.

His throat closed. He traced the name once, barely a touch. A boy he had raised into a man. The light in Kaden's eyes. Gone.

For a moment, memory broke through the commander's mask. He saw Wyatt at twelve, grinning too wide after sneaking out of drills; at fifteen, bruised but refusing to yield; at twenty, quieting a hall with nothing but his certainty. He had believed the boy would outlive him. He had wanted that more than foresight could promise.

Corin slipped a hand into his coat and drew out the Veilbind scroll, unrolling it just far enough to reread the line that haunted him:

"Born of hollow purpose and endless night."

The words glared back like a wound. Kaelith's shadow loomed larger than ever, and now Wyatt's loss—this boy, this man—was tangled into that cost. Corin exhaled through his teeth, low enough no one could hear.

"We've bought time," he murmured to the dark. "But the cost... it's more than I feared."

He rolled the scroll shut and tucked it away. Duty still called.

Commanders came in shifts, each bearing burdens heavier than the last. Enemy scouts sighted near the passes. Raiding parties probing their defenses. Casualties mounting in the outer outposts, lists of names read aloud with voices grown hoarse.

Corin listened, his jaw tightening with every account. The Eldvale temple: rubble. Two border outposts: overrun. Each report pressed deeper into him, though his face betrayed little. A flicker of narrowed eyes. A stiffening of shoulders. Small cracks no one lingered on.

"Rest while you can," he said at last, voice even. "Tomorrow we rebuild again."

They saluted and withdrew. The hall fell quiet, torches spitting low flame into the emptiness.

Corin braced his hands against the map-strewn table. The inked lines wavered in the torchlight, rivers bleeding into shadow. For a moment, the mask slipped, leaving only a man with grief too sharp to speak aloud. His foresight whispered in the back of his mind—fragments, warnings—but none of it had saved his nephew. None of it could promise Kaden, Cam, or the others would live to see what came next.

He bowed his head. Just one breath, stolen for himself. Then he straightened again.

The rebellion needed its strategist. But tonight, he was also an uncle with empty hands.

◈ ☽ ⚡ ☾ ◈

The air of the infirmary still clung to him when he shoved through the war room doors—the sharp tang of herbs, the faint crackle of torches, the sight of Cam pale and still beneath her blankets. Three days, and she had barely improved. Every shallow breath had sounded like a clock winding down.

He had stood there too long, watching Val tend her with quiet steadiness, watching Tessa fold in on herself in guilt, watching Kaden slip in like a ghost, only to vanish again. He had wanted to reach for her—his daughter, his last tether—but he hadn't. Because if he touched her and she didn't stir, he wasn't sure he could bear it.

Now that weight spilled over.

The smaller war room felt too tight, the air too close. Ben paced the length of it, fists clenching, breath harsh. He had spent years swallowing anger, burying it under discipline, but tonight it broke free.

"They never should've gone," he muttered, then louder, voice shaking with rage. "They *never* should've gone! This wasn't supposed to happen."

The words ricocheted off the stone walls, raw and jagged. He slammed a hand against the edge of the table, the impact rattling the maps pinned there, inkpots shivering against the wood.

Alex. His name burned like ash in Ben's mouth. Betrayal cut sharper than any blade, and it had cost them everything. Wyatt—gone. Cam—broken, still fighting for her life. The rebellion—bleeding from wounds it could not afford.

He dragged both hands through his hair, pulling until his scalp stung. His voice cracked into something closer to despair. "We were supposed to protect them. I was supposed to protect her."

The words rang hollow. He could still see her face as he had left it—lashes dark against her skin, lips faintly parted around breaths that seemed borrowed from someone else. He could still hear the catch in her chest, the fragile rattle that made him feel powerless.

The weight of command pressed on him too, but unlike Corin's, Ben's armor was anger, not calm. He wanted something to strike, someone to blame, but the enemy was too far, too vast, and the fault—at least some of it—lay with him.

Forgeheart, Skylith's voice thrummed through the bond, low and steady, warm as the hearth fire of her name for him. *Do not let grief hollow you. I am here.*

Ben closed his eyes, pressing his palms flat to the table as if he could push the weight into the stone. "I should've protected them. Gods, I can't lose her too."

You have carried more than any man should bear, Skylith murmured, her tone a rumble of flame contained. *But you are not alone. Not while I breathe.*

His breath hitched, the anger cracking into silence. He leaned on her presence, steady and vast, the way he had countless times before. For the first time in days, he let himself take a full breath.

But the question still gnawed at him. Quiet, bitter, almost whispered into her flame:

"If this is what it takes to survive... what will we lose next?"

◈ ☽ ⚡ ☾ ◈

The wind carved cold across the Valthorne Mountains, lifting snow from the ridges in silver sheets. Skylith soared at the forefront, her wings scattering moonlight over jagged peaks. Behind her, Tenebrin's shadow-threaded form cut silent and swift through the air. Brontheus wheeled higher, his storm-slick wings trailing faint arcs of lightning. Virellan flew lowest, scales a stormfront gray with silver streaks, glowing like veins of lightning when the moon caught them.

Together they circled the Ember Fortress, a ring of vigilance around the fragile lives inside.

Through Skylith's chest burned the weight of her rider's grief. Ben carried it close, as he always had, but now it pressed heavier than flame: Wyatt's silence in the dragonlink, Cam's stillness on her cot, the years of burden already etched into his bones. Skylith felt it all, the way fire feels the shape of its hearth—contained but never diminished.

Her gaze swept eastward. Beyond the horizon, deep in the hidden folds of these mountains, lay the Ember Cradle—the last true nest of her kind. No human eyes had seen it in centuries. Perhaps one day Cam would, for the girl carried dragon-song in her marrow and could hear what no other mortal could. But for now, the cradle remained veiled, sleeping, as if waiting for its time.

Skylith's thoughts drifted back to the fortress. To Ben. To all of them. A low rumble stirred in her chest, more to herself than to anyone else. They need us more now than they ever have before.

The other dragons minds stirred in answer. Tenebrin's shadows pulsed agreement, Brontheus's storm rumbled low and steady, and Virellan sent a sharp flicker of silver light across the bond. Different voices, different elements, but the same truth carried between them.

Their riders were breaking. And the dragons would hold them until they could stand again. Until fire, shadow, storm, and light rose again.

Chapter 37: The Thread Breaks

Darkness.

Then light—strange and silver, sky spread wide like molten glass. Stars hung sharp above, fractured like broken shards. The ground beneath her feet cracked and splintered, lines racing outward like veins of a mirror breaking.

Cam stood at the center, disoriented. The air was too thin, too bright, and when she breathed, it stung like ice. Her lungs seized, pulling nothing.

Something flickered at the edge of her vision.

A line of light—so fine she might have missed it if it hadn't moved. It stretched out from her chest into the silver haze, trembling like a living thing.

A thread.

It hummed faintly, warm against the cold of the place, neither solid nor entirely light. Cam frowned, lifting her hand without thinking. Her fingers passed through it at first, tingling sharply—then caught.

The sensation jolted her. Not pain. Not comfort. Recognition.

Her grip tightened instinctively and she pulled—not hard, not gentle, but certain. As if she were steadying something that mattered. The thread pulsed once beneath her fingers, answering.

Then nothing happened.

No shift. No voice. The thread slipped from her grasp, dissolving back into the light as though it had never been there at all.

Cam's breath hitched. Unease curled low in her chest, sharp and sudden, but before she could follow the feeling—

A voice drifted across the emptiness. Low. Familiar.

"You fell too soon."

She turned.

A figure stood in the silver haze, indistinct—yet she knew the set of his shoulders, the tilt of his head. Wyatt.

Her chest lurched. She staggered toward him, each step pulling the cracks wider beneath her feet. "Wyatt!"

He reached too, arm outstretched, fingers straining toward hers. For a heartbeat, she believed—if she reached far enough, hard enough, they'd touch.

But their fingers never met.

The silver light flared, blinding. She reeled, gasping, clutching at her throat. Her body refused the breath, and suddenly she felt the weight of herself—the pain in her ribs, the ache of broken flesh, the drag of wounds that hadn't healed. The waking world tugged at her, sharp and cruel.

Her lips moved without sound. A name, over and over. Wyatt.

The ground quaked beneath her. The cracks spidered wider, opening into black void. She stumbled, caught between reaching for him and being torn backward by the invisible pull of her own body.

"Don't go—" Her voice tore from her throat, raw, desperate.

The sky split. Light tore from shadow, the silver world shattering into blackness. Through the rent, she thought she heard another voice—a rumble like Sylithra's, muffled as if pressed against thick glass. *Little Flame... hold fast...*

The words tangled, half-formed, broken before they could reach her.

Her fingers grazed air where Wyatt's hand should have been. He blurred, dissolving like ash in wind. But even as he vanished, it didn't feel like an ending. Not final, not severed. It was like watching a thread pulled just out of reach—still there, still humming, but lost to her grasp. That was why she couldn't let go. Why she wouldn't believe.

And then the ground collapsed.

Cam fell.

Silver fractured into black, shards spinning past her like glass in a storm. Each fragment caught a memory: Ben's hand steady on her shoulder, his voice telling her she was stronger than she believed. Wyatt's laugh in the sparring yard, bright and reckless. Sylithra's eye, gold-veined and vast, leaning close to whisper *Little Flame.*

They spun around her, too fast to hold. She reached for one, then another, but each shattered in her grip, turning to dust.

Her body screamed with every impact she didn't feel—ribs tearing, lungs burning, blood roaring in her ears. The weight of her injuries dragged her down like chains, pulling her deeper.

Through the void, voices frayed and tangled. Ben calling her name. Wyatt shouting something she couldn't hear. Sylithra's rumble breaking through like distant thunder.

Hold fast.

The words cracked like lightning, but the current swept her farther still.

Her chest seized. She gasped, lips shaping the only name that remained.

"Wyatt—Wyatt—Wyatt—"

The void swallowed the sound.

And then, with a wrenching force, the fall stopped.

She slammed back into herself.

The fall didn't end so much as rupture.

Cam's body slammed back into itself with a force that stole breath and gave it back all at once. Her lungs convulsed, dragging in air like drowning water. She jolted upright with a ragged gasp, drenched in sweat, trembling so violently the cot rattled beneath her.

Pain seared through her ribs, her shoulder, every torn sinew and bruise, but it was nothing compared to the hollow blaze in her chest. Her heart beat too fast, too hard, as if trying to claw its way out. The scream from her dream hadn't stayed behind—it followed her, lodged beneath her ribs, demanding release.

"Easy—Cam, you're safe."

Val's voice, soft and steady. A hand pressed to her shoulder, anchoring.

Cam didn't hear it. Couldn't. The world was too bright, too sharp, every breath a knife in her throat. Her chest heaved once, twice, and then the scream tore free.

It wasn't a cry. It wasn't even a sound meant for human lungs. It ripped out of her whole body, raw and keening, a broken horror so deep the ward sconces guttered with its force.

Her bond convulsed.

Sylithra's fire flared erratic and pained, gold veins flashing as though her very heart had cracked. Skylith answered with a roar that split the cliffs, grief-laced flame scattering sparks into the night. Sael's silence pressed in like ice, hollow and searing, an echo of a bond gone mute. Brontheus bellowed against the storm, his grief rolling like thunder that rattled stone. Tenebrin's shadows lashed outward, restless, sharp with unease. Virellan's silver-streaked wings flared wide, a tremor of lightning shivering through his frame.

Cam couldn't hear them, not truly—but through her, every dragon's grief braided together, pulled tight, as if her scream had torn open a path none of them could close.

Val's hand on her shoulder stilled, as if the weight of that sound froze even her. Tessa bowed her head low across the room, fists clenched white. The air itself seemed to tremble, every surface holding the echo. Dust sifted from the beams overhead, wardstones humming low as though the fortress itself had flinched. For a heartbeat, it felt as if the mountain remembered her grief too, carrying the sound down into its bones.

Cam's throat burned, but still the scream tore on—long past where her breath should have given out—until it collapsed into a ragged sob. Her body folded inward, clutching at her ribs as though to hold herself together.

The sound lingered after, caught in the stone and the dragons' bonds alike, a cry too deep to belong to one voice alone.

Cam's chest heaved, raw and burning, her body folding inward around the pain as though clutching it close could keep it from tearing her open again.

Val leaned closer, steady in a way Cam couldn't stand to see. Her hand pressed gently to Cam's shoulder, grounding. "Breathe. You're here. You're safe."

The word *safe* shattered something sharp inside her.

Cam flinched back, clutching the blanket to her chest like armor. Her eyes burned with salt, her throat raw and torn, when footsteps thundered in the hall.

The door burst open.

Ben was first through, eyes wide, chest heaving as if he'd run the whole fortress to reach her. His gaze locked on her—alive, upright, screaming—and relief warred with fear in every line of his face. Kaden was right behind him, his expression pale and raw, caught between grief and desperate hope.

"Cam—" Ben's voice cracked, too many words trying to push out at once. He stopped short at the sight of her trembling, wild-eyed, clutching the blanket like it was her last defense.

Kaden froze too, his hand half-lifted toward her before it faltered. His mouth worked soundlessly, as though her name were lodged in his throat.

Cam's voice broke, rising sharp and desperate into the charged silence.

"He's not dead. *I'd know*. I didn't see it—I would have seen it!"

The words hung between them like a blade.

Val's hand hovered in the air, useless. Ben's breath caught. Kaden's jaw tightened, his eyes dark and wet, but no words came.

The silence that followed was worse than denial.

Cam's chest stuttered, breath breaking on a sob. "Say something. Any of you—say it."

But no one did.

The weight of their silence pressed in on her harder than the wounds in her body. It wasn't just grief twisting inside her—it was certainty fracturing, a bond she thought unbreakable suddenly cast into doubt. The conviction she clung to—that Wyatt lived, that she would have felt his death—was hers alone.

And in that moment, she knew. No one else believed her.

The weight of it pressed until the cot seemed to tilt beneath her, the room spinning even though she hadn't moved. Her breath came shallow, her fingers twisting the blanket against her chest as if the cloth alone could anchor her.

Val drew back slowly, her hand hovering in the air a moment longer before lowering, her expression unreadable. Then she turned away, busying herself with the basin, with tidying salves that didn't need tidying. Tessa stood too abruptly, the scrape of her chair loud against stone, and crossed to the far wall, shoulders taut, her silence as sharp as a blade.

The room grew heavier by degrees, silence thick as smoke. One by one, they slipped away—Val with a glance too careful, Tessa with none at all. Even Ben, who had burst in moments ago, lingered only long enough to press a hand to the doorway, his jaw tight, before he left without a word.

The door closed.

Only Kaden remained.

He didn't speak. He just lowered himself into the chair beside her cot, elbows braced on his knees, hands clasped tight. His presence was quieter than she'd ever known it to be—no sharp wit, no clever observation, just silence. She barely noticed him at first, her own thoughts drowning her.

Her chest ached, her mind spiraling. *They don't believe me. They think he's gone. They're already letting him go.*

Cam's gaze drifted, unfocused, until a flicker caught at the corner of her eye. A silver glint against the blanket.

Her breath stuttered. She reached with trembling fingers, pulling the small object free. Wyatt's pendant.

The chain slid through her trembling hands, knotting against her fingers. She clenched it tight, knuckles straining white, the metal edges biting into her palm until the sting bloomed sharp. She welcomed it. Needed it. Because the pain was real, and he had touched this. Worn it. Breathed with it against his skin.

Her chest hitched. A sob clawed at her throat, but she swallowed it down, pressing the pendant so hard into her hand she thought it might break. *No. Not gone. Not gone.*

Her mind reeled back. Anthony—her father. His death had gutted her; left her staggering under a weight she hadn't believed she could bear. That grief had been a blade, sharp and sudden. It had cut, it had bled, but she had survived it. Somehow.

This was different.

This wasn't a wound to heal. It was a thread snapping. A part of her tearing loose, unraveling in the silence left behind. She couldn't stitch it back. Couldn't knot it closed.

Her thoughts spun—memories flashing like sparks in dry tinder. Wyatt laughing under his breath when she tripped in training and pretending not to notice when she flushed. Wyatt's voice low and steady when her fire slipped out of control, his calm anchoring her back from the brink. Wyatt's hand on her shoulder, wordless, enough. Always enough.

Gone.

Her chest hollowed. She pressed the pendant to her lips, the metal cold and unyielding, and whispered into it as though he might hear.

"I would have known. I would have felt it. Don't let them be right."

No answer came. Only silence.

The weight of the pendant dragged heavy against her chest, as if it carried not just metal but the absence of him—the gaping absence that nothing could fill.

A flicker of fear threaded through her certainty. What if she was wrong?

Beside her, Kaden shifted. His voice came low, raw in a way she had never heard from him before.

"He wanted you to have it." His voice roughened further, barely more than a breath. "And I want to believe you're right."

Her throat tightened. She looked at him, really looked, and saw the tears he wasn't quick enough to hide, slipping down his cheek before he turned his face away.

She was terrified she was wrong—that the thread she clung to was only her own desperation unraveling.

But Kaden's eyes betrayed him. He wanted to believe her. She saw it in the set of his jaw, in the grief that mirrored her own. He wanted her certainty to be true, wanted Wyatt's absence to be anything but final.

And for one fragile heartbeat, their grief aligned: her fear against his hope, both of them clinging to a thread neither could let go.

She clutched the pendant to her chest, knuckles white. The thread inside her still felt frayed, half-broken, but for the first time since waking, it wasn't only hers to hold.

◈ ☽ ⚡ ☾ ◈

The days blurred. One bled into another until she couldn't tell where mourning ended and survival began.

At first, Cam tried—whispers of answers, murmurs to questions—but even that dwindled. Her voice faded into nods or silence until people stopped asking.

She sat in the firelit halls and watched the flames without warmth. At night, she curled on her cot with the pendant clenched so tight her knuckles whitened, her hand aching by morning. The metal bit her skin, sometimes drawing blood, but she held on anyway. It was the only proof she had left.

Food lost its taste. Bread turned to ash on her tongue. Water choked her throat. She chewed and swallowed because they told her to, not because she wanted to.

Even Sylithra dimmed in her mind. Not gone, not severed—but hushed, as if grief itself pressed against their bond and muffled her fire. Cam could still feel her warmth, but distant, like heat through stone. *Little Flame*, Sylithra murmured sometimes, her rumble low and steady. *Do not drift too far*. The words anchored her just enough to keep breathing, nothing more.

And sometimes, when the silence threatened to consume her entirely, Sylithra reached deeper, not with fire, but with memory. She would show Cam the glint of scales turning gold in the dawn, the smell of pine rising on mountain winds, the weightless lift of wings beating against sky. Fragments of life. Fragments of belonging. They weren't demands, weren't arguments. They were reminders: *Here. Still here.*

And then there were the others. Skylith, Brontheus, Tenebrin, Virellan—threads of voices that slipped into her mind unbidden. They didn't offer comfort; they offered truth, the kind dragons never softened.

Grief is flame. Burn or be consumed.

Storms tear or cleanse. You must choose which.

Shadows linger whether you face them or not.

Even the unbonded dragons near the Ember Cradle murmured at the edges of her mind, strange and distant, their tones like echoes through stone. She could not silence them. She could only endure them.

When people came, they carried their grief like coats.

Val sat beside her cot one night, weaving fresh cloth in her hands to keep them busy.

"You don't have to carry it alone," she said softly.

Cam turned her face away. "I already am."

Val's hands stilled, the bandage limp in her lap, but she said nothing more.

Tessa came during the day, pacing the room like a caged storm. Sparks popped at her fingertips as she muttered, "If I'd seen it sooner... if I hadn't vouched for him..."

Cam whispered, flat, "Stop."

But Tessa didn't. Couldn't. Her guilt clung like smoke, and when she finally left, it followed her out the door.

Ben tried too. He came late, when the fortress had gone quiet. He stood in the doorway, shadows cutting his face into sharp lines.

"I lost you once, when I had to hide you," he said, voice gravel rough. "And then I spent five years searching for you. I won't lose you again, Cam."

The words landed sharp. Not the part about hiding—she had known he had kept her hidden for a reason—but the rest. *Five years.* He had searched for her. Long before she had known to search for herself, he had been scouring the world for her.

Her chest tightened, grief twisting with something stranger, heavier. She clutched the pendant harder, the chain biting deep into her palm, but said nothing. Not because she had no words—because words would break her.

Ben's hand curled at his side. He left without another word.

Even Corin came, though rarely. He stood tall and still at the foot of her bed, hands clasped behind his back.

"Camomile," he said once, his voice as measured as in the war room. "The living cannot afford to follow the dead."

She lifted her eyes to him then—just once. "Maybe I don't want to live in a world without him."

For the first time, Corin faltered. His jaw tightened, his gaze flicked away, and he left her to the dark.

Cam gave them nothing else. No words, no comfort. She had none to offer. They left carrying more weight than when they had entered, and she sank further into silence. Around her, the fortress kept moving. Boots thundered down halls, new voices filled the chambers, maps and orders changed by the day. Refugees made homes of empty rooms, dragons wheeled restlessly over the cliffs. The world lurched forward, reshaping itself around loss. Only she remained unmoving, as if grief had rooted her in stone.

Only Sylithra and Kaden lingered.

Her dragon's presence remained steady in the background, never pushing, never demanding—simply there, a pulse of fire that refused to go out, even when Cam wanted everything to dim. And Kaden mirrored that in the waking world.

He didn't push either. He'd sit near her, not close enough to touch, not far enough to be dismissed. Sometimes he brought maps or scrolls, spreading them across the table just to have something between them.

Once, he tried a joke—dry, edged with his usual wit. "You know, if you're going to stare at fire this much, you'll end up learning prophecy by accident."

She didn't laugh. She didn't even smile.

His smirk faltered, eyes tightening as if the ground beneath him cracked too. But he didn't leave. He stayed.

Because he understood. Not because he tried to—but because he was breaking too. She saw it in the hollows beneath his eyes, in the way his shoulders curved inward as though holding too much.

And still, even with him, she felt the barrier rising. The thread that had once bound her to all of them frayed thinner each day.

There had been a thread between them once—bright and sure.

Now it dangled loose, cut and fraying.

And she didn't know if it would ever be tied back together.

◈ ☽ ⚡ ☾ ◈

Two weeks later, he still remembered the scream.

It hadn't been a sound—it had been a fracture in the world itself. He had felt it through Tenebrin, their bond crackling with panic. He had felt it in the stone under his boots, in the marrow of his bones.

He hadn't been there when it happened. He had been in Haldrin's Keep, gathering maps and scrolls for Corin before they abandoned the place entirely. The halls had been cold, empty, wrong. And then the silence had split. The scream had torn through him so violently he thought the walls would fall.

He had teleported back without thinking, ripping himself across distance to reach the Ember Fortress. By the time he arrived, she was still screaming, the sound rattling through the fortress stone, through the dragons, through him.

It had silenced eventually. But the echo had not. Sometimes, in the quiet of night, he still heard it—faint as if carried on wind, raw as if tearing out of her again. It haunted him in dreams, clawed at the edges of his waking thoughts. The world hadn't felt right since.

Now he stood in the forest outside the fortress, watching the dragons carve slow arcs across the sky. Tenebrin's shadow-threaded wings cut against the clouds, a steady rhythm grounding him in the present. The air was sharp with pine and frost, but Kaden barely felt it.

You've been silent too long, Tenebrin rumbled in his mind, voice deep as the caves beneath the mountain.

Kaden's jaw tightened. "What is there to say?"

The dragon's shadow pressed close, both presence and anchor. *You fear breaking her. But she is already breaking herself. Threads cannot hold if both ends pull away.*

Kaden closed his eyes, the words settling like stones in his chest. He thought of Cam, clutching Wyatt's pendant like it was life itself. He thought of her silence, her eyes that no longer met his.

And still—beneath the silence—there was something else. A spark he hadn't expected.

When she had whispered, raw and broken, that Wyatt wasn't dead... part of him had wanted to shut her down, to say she was wrong, to save her from the slow death of false hope. But the words had stuck in his throat. Because he wanted to believe her.

He wanted her to be right.

Wyatt was his brother. He had felt his presence beside him since the day they were born, a thread woven tighter than blood alone. That thread had snapped two weeks ago—or should have. Yet somewhere inside, Kaden still felt it, faint as breath in winter air, a pull he couldn't explain.

And now Cam held that same hope. Broken, desperate, unshakable.

Maybe that was why he hadn't walked away when the others had. Because clinging to her belief was easier than facing the hollow truth the world wanted to hand him.

He pressed a fist against his ribs, breathing slow, controlled, though his voice cracked when he whispered, "If you're alive, brother, give me something. Anything."

Tenebrin's presence stirred, shadow-warm and steady. *Hope is not weakness, Shadowborn. It is the only thread that keeps her here. And you, too.*

He opened his eyes to the sky. The dragons wheeled above, watchful, tireless. His gaze dropped back to the fortress, to the faint glow of wardlight in the high windows where Cam sat in silence.

She hadn't pushed him away—not completely. But the barrier between them grew higher each day, and he didn't know how much longer he could stand at its edge.

Still, he stayed.

Because if her thread frayed apart, he wasn't sure his would hold either. Because some part of him still felt it—that faint pull in the dark, fragile but alive. *If he let go of her, of that hope, he feared the last piece of his brother would vanish too.*

Chapter 38: Signs in the Sky

The training ring smelled of scorched air and smoke. Sparks leapt restless from her fingers, lightning skittering over her knuckles as she swung again. Tessa's blade cracked into the wooden post with a hollow snap, splinters raining to the floor. Not enough. Nothing was ever enough.

She swung again. Harder.

The post split, but her fury didn't. It only built, humming sharp in her chest, demanding release.

A shadow shifted at the edge of the ring.

She didn't need to look to know who it was. Orren. Silent, still, watching. He always watched, as if she were a threat to catalog, not a person.

Fine. Let him watch.

She spun, lightning sparking down her arm, and hurled a bolt straight at his chest.

He slipped aside with a blur of motion, the bolt cracking against the stone wall where he'd been standing. Smoke curled between them.

"Whoops," she said, smirking, though her voice was sharp enough to cut.

"Does that make you feel better?" His tone was maddeningly calm.

"Yes," she snapped. "Actually, it does."

He sighed, as though the weight of her storm was nothing more than inconvenience. Then he stepped into the ring. "You really want to do this now?"

"You're the enemy." Her sword rose, firelight running along its edge.

"Not anymore." He stooped, picked up a blade from the rack, testing its weight like it was a formality. His eyes never left hers. "But if you need me to be..." He raised the sword into guard. "Then I will."

The clash was immediate. Steel on steel, sparks scattering with every strike. She fought like the storm itself—wild, relentless, hurling lightning into each swing until the air burned ozone.

But he was steady. Composed. Each of her wild strikes met with precision, each furious lunge turned aside with ease that only stoked her rage higher. His breath came steady, measured, as if her storm was nothing more than weather he had already endured. That calm unsettled her more than his blade—it was infuriating, dangerous, and for one reckless moment she hated how unshaken he seemed.

"You're sloppy," he said, deflecting a blow with the barest twist of his wrist. "You fight with rage, not skill."

"Better rage than nothing!" she spat, swinging harder, lightning screaming down her arm.

He parried again, calm cutting sharper than steel. "You blame yourself for trusting Alex. And now you can't trust anyone. Or maybe you don't want to."

Her chest seized. The words hit like lightning in reverse, burning her from the inside. She lunged harder, reckless. "Shut up!"

Orren twisted, ducked, and drove her sword off course, stepping inside her guard. His voice cut low, close. "Because trusting leads to getting hurt. Or maybe—" their blades locked, the metal vibrating between them, "—you just like carrying the weight because it makes you feel important."

The words landed like a blow. For a heartbeat, her grip faltered, shame burning through her throat. Rage filled the crack before it could spread.

She shoved him off with a snarl, lightning cracking down her arm so hard the stone underfoot smoked. Her voice came sharp, venomous. "And what about you? Empty weapon on a leash. You don't carry weight—you wait to be told where to strike."

His expression flickered, the smallest crack in that infuriating calm. Enough to make her chest twist in something far too close to satisfaction.

"Thought so," she hissed, lowering her blade. The storm in her chest still raged, but she wouldn't let him see how deep his words had cut.

But Orren wasn't finished. He stepped forward again, raising his sword in challenge, not retreat. "You're angry at me because it's easier than forgiving yourself. You want me to be the enemy because then you don't have to admit the truth."

She froze, fury warring with something colder.

He pressed the point, his voice still infuriatingly calm: "And now you can't trust anyone. Not them. Not me. Not even yourself."

The storm in her chest cracked. Her throat locked, shame and grief tangling in the back of her mouth. For one reckless instant, she wanted to kill him. To silence him.

She lunged. Lightning screamed down her blade, her strike sharp enough to kill.

But he was faster. Their swords collided, sparks flaring into the night, and in one sharp movement he wrenched her blade off course. His edge came to rest low against her side, steady, controlled.

"And still," he said softly, "you didn't take the kill."

Her chest heaved, blade trembling in her grip. He could've killed her. She could've killed him. They both knew it.

The realization twisted her stomach in knots. Worse than that, though, was the spark that flickered in the clash between them—not rage, not hatred. Something she refused to name.

For a heartbeat, she hated him for sparing her—because it left her wondering why. That thought twisted sharp, and she shoved it down deep, burying it where she wouldn't have to face it.

She stepped back like his nearness burned. Jaw tight, eyes fierce. "You're still the enemy."

She stormed from the ring, lightning snapping at her heels, not daring to look back. Because if she did, she was terrified she'd see that spark again.

The heavy doors slammed behind her, her storm still crackling across her skin. The fortress corridors should have swallowed the heat of it, but instead the air felt heavier, charged in a way that wasn't hers.

Her steps slowed.

A strange stillness pressed in—too still. No shouts from the barracks. No clatter of boots in the hall. Even the torches burned with a strange, wavering light, their flames bending sideways though no draft stirred.

She paused at a narrow window cut into the wall.

The mountains beyond should have been steady under pale spring evening light, but the horizon... shifted. A thin tremor rippled across the sky itself, faint as a hairline crack beneath glass. Silver threaded through it for the briefest instant, there and gone, like lightning frozen mid-flash.

Tessa's breath caught. Her storm quieted, sparks guttering against her palms. She pressed her hand to the stone sill until her knuckles ached.

Whatever anger had burned her moments ago dimmed into something colder, heavier.

The enemy she'd been fighting in the ring suddenly felt smaller.

The world itself was breaking.

The halls of Ember Fortress were too quiet.

Val knew the rhythm of the place now—the steady tread of boots, the clang of steel in the yards, the echo of voices drifting through the stone. Even in grief, even in rebuilding, a fortress carried sound. But this morning, the silence pressed heavier than stone, settling into her teeth and bones until each step seemed too loud.

She turned a corner toward the library and stopped short.

Cam stood at the window, motionless. Her hair hung loose around her face, catching pale light, her fingers worrying the chain of Wyatt's pendant until it caught and twisted against itself. Her eyes didn't move. Glassy, fixed on the horizon, as if the world beyond the walls had taken her and refused to give her back.

"Cam," Val said quietly.

Nothing.

Not even a blink.

Val's chest tightened. She wanted to reach for her, to shake her free from whatever silence had caught hold of her, but she didn't. Instead, she followed her gaze, stepping closer to the window.

At first, she saw nothing. The mountains were steady, peaks still dusted in snow, forests dark at their base. But then the tree line shivered. Branches creaked—not swaying with wind, but bending unevenly, as though pulled by unseen strings. A vibration hummed low through her ribs, her teeth. Wrong.

She pushed through the library doors and stepped out onto the balcony, the cold stone biting through her boots.

And then she saw it.

The sky itself rippled.

Faint at first—like heat-haze bending air above stone—but then sharper, a fracture spidering across the pale blue dome. It stretched thin, a hairline crack, and a faint silver pulse bled along it, alive, searing against the eye.

Val gripped the railing hard enough to ache. Her breath left her in a whisper.

"...but... the solstice... it passed."

The Veil shouldn't have thinned again. Not until the next turning of the year. Not now.

The Breath wavers. The Veil thins even more.

Virellan's voice coiled softly into her mind, silver-streaked and solemn.

He is rising.

Her heart lurched. The name didn't need to be spoken. Kaelith. The Hollow Prince.

Val turned and nearly ran through the halls. The silence followed her, crawling at her heels, until she reached the heavy oak door carved with ward marks. Corin's study.

She knocked once, sharp, and pushed through.

The room was dim but alive with clutter. Scrolls lay unrolled across the broad table, weighted with stones, their margins marked with Corin's tight, spare script. A map of the Valthorne Mountains sprawled beneath them, ink bleeding with annotations. Sigils chalked across the hearthstones pulsed faint, holding the cold at bay.

Corin stood at the table, hands braced against the wood, head bent over a scroll. His eyes flicked up as she entered, and whatever words he'd meant to speak faltered when he saw her face.

"The sky," she said, breathless, chest tight. "It's—"

"I know." His voice was low, grim. He had already felt it. Perhaps before she had.

"It fractured," Val pressed. "I saw it. Silver along the break—like it was alive."

Corin's jaw tightened. He looked older in that moment than she had ever seen him, lines carved deep into his face by more than years.

"It isn't time," he murmured, almost to himself. "Not yet... unless—"

He cut himself off, shaking his head.

"Unless what?" Val demanded.

His gaze flicked to her, sharp but shadowed. "Unless something has broken the pattern. A shift large enough to loosen what should have held. Prophecy doesn't move without cause."

Val's pulse hammered. She thought of the scream. That raw, world-splitting sound that had torn from Cam's chest two weeks ago, echoing through stone, through the dragons, through her own marrow until it felt as if the mountain itself would split.

Her voice caught. "Do you think—" She swallowed. "Do you think it was her?"

Corin didn't answer.

Not yes. Not no. Just silence. She realized he was afraid.

But his hand reached for a small leather-bound book half-hidden beneath the maps. He uncapped a pen and wrote a single line in the margin before closing it again, too quickly for her to read.

Val's stomach twisted. Whatever he'd just written, he wasn't going to share it. Not yet.

She turned slowly toward the door, the air thick in her lungs.

When she slipped back into the library, the window gaped pale with light. The balcony doors were still ajar, curtains whispering in a wind she hadn't felt before.

Cam was gone.

Val froze, a cold weight coiling in her chest.

Something had changed. She could feel it in her bones, in her bond with Virellan, in the very air of the fortress.

And Val couldn't help but wonder if it was Cam's scream that had fractured the world—and if what they were seeing now was only the beginning of its echo.

◈ ☽ ⚡ ☾ ◈

The fortress walls held the chill long after the sun had risen. Lanterns sputtered against the gloom, their flames bending in unseen drafts, shadows stretching across stone worn thin with centuries. Somewhere deep in the foundation, the wind moaned low through cracks like a wounded animal.

Ben hadn't been able to sit still since Val had returned pale-faced from Corin's study. The words she'd carried with her—the Veil had fractured, silver alive across the sky—had settled into his chest like a weight he couldn't dislodge.

And all he could think of was Cam.

He hadn't forgotten the scream.

Two weeks hadn't dulled it. It wasn't the sound of her voice that haunted him—it was the way it had broken the world around them. A scream that rattled stone, silenced every dragon in their roost, turned the marrow in his bones to ice.

It had torn open an old wound he had carried for twenty years. Isabella had died when Cam was only three weeks old. He hadn't been there when it happened—had been led astray, too far to save her when it mattered. He never heard her last cry, never had the chance to reach her in her final breath. That silence had hollowed him for decades. And when Cam's scream ripped through the fortress, it was like the echo of what he'd missed—the sound he imagined Isabella would have made if he had been there to hear it. Only this time, he had heard it. And he would never forget it.

He searched the fortress first—the library, the wards, the high halls where refugees whispered—but found only empty corridors and echoing silence. His gut pulled him outward through the narrow pass that wound between sheer cliffs toward the mountain shelf the dragons had claimed as a makeshift roost.

The air was sharper here, cold and metallic with the tang of stone. And there she was.

Cam sat pressed against Sylithra's side, the obsidian curve of the dragon's wing half-folded around her like a living wall. The girl's shoulders hunched forward, her face slack and pale, fingers clenched white around the silver chain of Wyatt's pendant. The metal caught faint light with every tremor of her hands, a heartbeat she could still see when she couldn't feel her own.

Sylithra's low rumble vibrated through the stone, not aggressive, but warning—protective. Her molten gold eyes slit open to regard Ben as he stepped closer, then closed again with a sound almost like grief.

Ben stopped at the edge of the wing's shadow. For a moment, he considered speaking—telling Cam she shouldn't sit in the cold, that she needed rest, food, warmth. But the words died before they reached his tongue. She didn't need orders. Not now.

Instead, he saw Isabella. Clear as if the years between hadn't passed. The way she used to sit by the fire in their cottage, hair haloed gold in the lamplight, holding Cam as a baby wrapped tight in blankets. She'd hummed sometimes, low and steady, a sound more soothing than any words. He hadn't realized until too late how much he depended on that sound, that steadiness. And when she was gone, the silence had been unbearable.

Now here was Cam, wrapped in Sylithra's wing instead of her mother's arms. Silent. Fragile. And if he let himself look too closely, he saw Isabella in her—saw the same tilt of the head, the same stubborn set to the mouth when grief had hollowed her out.

The memory tore at him. He had lost Isabella. He had spent years searching for answers in her death, then five more searching for Cam. He could not lose her too.

He lowered himself to the ground with a quiet grunt, settling his back against Sylithra's scales. The dragon's warmth seeped into his spine, steady and alive. For a long stretch, the only sound was Cam's ragged breathing and the deep, patient rumble beneath them.

Ben closed his eyes, forcing his own breath to slow, to match Sylithra's. He let the silence do the work; let it tell her that she wasn't alone.

When he finally spoke, it was low, steady, almost swallowed by the mountain air.

"You don't have to move yet. I'll stay."

Cam didn't respond with words. But after a long moment, she tilted her head—barely, the smallest shift—enough to let him know she'd heard, that she permitted his presence.

Ben rested his hand briefly against Sylithra's scales, feeling the dragon's pulse thrum beneath his palm. Strong. Certain. It matched the rhythm in his chest, tethering him to the present when everything else felt like it was slipping away.

Above the cliffs, the sky hung pale and fractured. The silver line still lingered, thin but undeniable, a scar across the heavens. Ben stared at it, jaw set, the weight of it pressing down harder than stone.

The world held its breath.

And in the silence, he felt it—something vast and patient watching back, waiting for the moment to break through.

His mind drifted back to Isabella—how he hadn't been there when she needed him, how her death had left him chasing ghosts and shadows for decades. He hadn't saved her when it mattered. That silence had haunted him every day since.

But this time, he was here.

This time, he wouldn't let go.

Cam wasn't alone—and he swore, silent and fierce, that she never would be again.

Chapter 39: Flame Without Anchor

The Ember Fortress lived, but hollowly. Boots still struck stone, maps still shifted across tables, dragons still swept the sky—but all of it sounded dim, like the whole world had been padded in ash.

Every dawn and every dusk, Kaden opened a portal to the Eldvale Mountains. The spell burned in his veins, more draining with each repetition, but he did it anyway. Sometimes he joined the search parties, combing the cliffs and river valleys himself. Sometimes he only held the gate wide enough for others to pass through, standing in the doorway of distance and praying they'd bring something back.

But every day, the portals opened on nothing.

No trail. No wreckage. No sign of Wyatt at all.

And each evening, when the searchers returned, the silence was worse than the fatigue in their faces. It was absence that came back through his gates—absence heavy enough to make him dread the next sunrise, when he'd have to open them again.

He had grown to hate the act of closing the portal most of all. Watching the mountains seal shut, knowing they still hid only emptiness, left his chest colder than the stone beneath his boots.

He felt the weight of it most in the spaces where sound should have been.

Cam drifted through the fortress like a shadow, a smaller gravity pulling around her wherever she went. She didn't speak much. She didn't have to. The silver pendant at her chest did it for her, turning under her fingers until the chain bit skin. Once, Kaden had caught her lips moving silently against it—as if she were whispering to Wyatt through the metal. He'd turned away, unable to watch.

Tessa refused the silence. She filled it with the shriek of lightning in the ring, or the thunder of Brontheus's wings, hunting the horizon as if it had insulted her personally. She came back blistered and breathless, sparks still snapping at her fingertips, and went again before anyone could ask if she'd eaten. Her rage was a shield, loud enough to keep grief at bay.

Val bled ink. She buried herself in fragments—the Book of Unbinding, stray lines of Veilbind, Corin's marginalia devoured and cross-scored—writing until the candle wicks drowned in their own wax. Every time Kaden passed her, her eyes were red, her jaw locked tight, as if sheer will might pry answers out of parchment.

And he kept watch. Someone had to. Someone had to be the surface that didn't crack.

It's not that we're breaking, he thought, pausing in a corridor where the light went thin and cold. It's that we're cracked... and pretending we're not.

Every day, Corin grew more silent when the riders reported back. Every day, his pauses before dismissal stretched longer. Kaden knew what it meant. Sooner or later, Corin would call off the search. Declare Wyatt lost, shift focus to the war they could still fight, the enemy they could still see.

But how could they fight what was rising, if they couldn't even keep their own threads from snapping?

He pressed his palm against the stone wall. It pressed back, colder than it should be in late spring. The fortress itself felt caught in the same waiting silence, as if the mountain knew the decision was coming.

When he finally pushed off and moved down the corridor, his feet carried him toward the library. Toward Val's ink-scattered table, toward Cam's silence, toward the one thing still holding them together: the prophecy fragments.

Because if the search ended, prophecy was all they'd have left.

The library doors had groaned faintly as Kaden pushed through. Hours had passed since then.

The map-table was a wreck of parchment and ink, scrolls unrolled and weighed down with whatever stones and blades they'd found to keep the drafts from scattering them. Wax puddled thick at the edges of the lanterns. Smoke clung to the beams like cobwebs.

Val sat stiff-backed at the head of it all, fingers ink-stained, the quill scratching until her hand cramped. Kaden had taken a place across from her, sorting, stacking, discarding, hunting for any fragment that wasn't already wrung dry. He wasn't built for this kind of work—his patience frayed fast—but still he stayed.

The hours wore on. Cam hadn't moved much at all. She sat at the far end, half in shadow, eyes hollow and fixed not on the words but on the silver at her chest. The pendant glinted faintly each time her fingers turned it. Sometimes he thought he saw her lips move against it, whispers swallowed before they could form.

He'd caught Val watching her more than once, eyes tight, as if she wanted to speak but swallowed it back. The only sound was the scratch of ink, the occasional crackle of a candle drowning in its own wax.

By the time Val's quill stilled, the silence had already grown unbearable. Her hand hovered uselessly above a parchment, trembling once before she stilled it.

At last, she spoke. Her voice barely more than breath.

"If the flame-bearer falls... the gate shall remain open. The Hollow will have no end."

The words hung, heavy as stone.

Kaden felt the silence choke the room. He didn't look at the scroll—he looked at Cam.

Val did too.

Cam sat hunched, fingers curled around the pendant so tightly the chain creaked. Her shoulders shook once, barely. But she didn't lift her head. Didn't say a word.

She didn't have to. The prophecy had already named her.

Kaden's throat locked. He forced his voice out anyway. "We need to find him. Or we lose everything."

The iron in his words rang too hard, too sharp.

In the back of his mind, Tenebrin stirred in the bond, a faint, uneasy tremor—the way a hawk's shadow slides over a field and everything small goes still. Not fear. Not yet. But the shape of it. The dragon's voice was low, shadow-thick, cutting like frost through marrow:

We cannot find the dead.

The words coiled around his ribs until he could barely breathe. He ground his teeth, refusing to answer, refusing to let the thought take root.

Val shut her eyes. When she opened them again, her voice was steadier, but her gaze slipped past Cam as if she couldn't bear to meet it. Her whisper barely carried across the table.

"...We may already be too late."

She thought Cam couldn't hear her.

Kaden did. His chest ached as he stared at Cam—at the fragile, stubborn line of her shoulders, at the way she clung to that pendant like it was breath itself. She hadn't let go of Wyatt. She refused.

And he couldn't let go either. Not yet. Not while she still believed.

For a few heartbeats, nobody moved.

The lantern hissed softly, its flame guttering against the draft that snuck through the high windows. Shadows stretched long across the maps, swallowing the silver threads of ink as if the words themselves didn't want to be read.

Kaden's pulse thundered in his ears, but the room itself was too quiet—quiet enough that he could hear Val's shallow breaths, the grind of Cam's fingernail against the pendant chain, the low hum of Tenebrin coiled in the back of his mind.

Then the door groaned.

Ben stepped inside. Shoulders tense, eyes sharp, hollowed by too many sleepless nights. His presence hit like a change in air pressure—everyone felt it. He didn't glance at the maps or the parchment, didn't ask what words had just been spoken. His gaze fixed on Cam.

She felt it. Kaden saw the faint stiffening in her shoulders, the way she angled her body a fraction away, as if the firelight itself burned sharper under his stare. She didn't look up. She only pressed the pendant harder into her palm, silent as stone.

The look in Ben's eyes hurt to watch—grief sharpened to a weapon, anger barely leashed. It wasn't the look of a father seeing his daughter. It was the look of a man staring down the one thread he was terrified of losing next.

Across the table, Val's breath caught. She didn't speak, but her quill snapped clean in her fingers, ink bleeding across her palm. She dropped it quickly, as if hoping no one had noticed—but Kaden did.

The silence thickened. Scrolls lay abandoned, their words like open wounds no one dared prod further. Val busied herself with stacking parchment she didn't need to touch, her motions clipped, desperate. Cam didn't move at all. Kaden had the sense she was holding herself rigid so she wouldn't shatter into pieces in front of them.

The session unraveled like frayed cloth. One by one, they drifted toward the door, but Ben didn't leave. Not yet.

He caught Kaden's arm as he passed. His grip was hard, fingers biting through cloth, his voice roughened like gravel under pressure.

"If Corin had acted sooner—if anyone had—we wouldn't have lost him."

Kaden's gut twisted. He tried to steady his voice, tried to be the surface that didn't crack. "Blame doesn't bring him back." The words came out too fast, too sharp.

Ben's mouth tightened. It wasn't argument so much as closing a door. "Neither does waiting."

He let go and left, taking a chunk of the room's air with him.

Kaden stood there, arm tingling where Ben's hand had been, staring at the door as it breathed shut.

A fracture line, he thought. Not new. Just deeper.

◈ ☽ ⚡ ☾ ◈

Evening pressed gold against the window. The light caught dust motes in the air, slow-turning, like the world itself had grown tired. Fire snapped in the hearth, small, effortful sounds—the kind that said it was running out of wood.

Cam sat on the edge of her cot in her new quarters. They had moved her from the infirmary once her body had mended enough, given her a room of her own in the Ember Fortress. She had barely noticed the wounds while they'd closed over the past month; they hadn't mattered, not compared to the hollow inside her. A part of her had wondered—once, briefly—why she hadn't healed as quickly as she always had before. Why her body felt slower, heavier, like it too resisted mending. But the thought had passed. She didn't care enough to follow it.

The pendant turned, turned. Her thumb traced the rim until the metal warmed, until the imprint of it lived in her skin when she let go. She didn't let go often.

Nights were worse. Every time she closed her eyes, she dreamed of him. Wyatt. He was always there, always near—an outline in the corner of her vision, a voice carried thin through too much distance. Sometimes she woke with the sharp, desperate certainty that he was sitting on the edge of her bed, head bent, waiting for her to notice. Her breath would catch; her chest would fill—and then the space beside her would be empty. Every time. Empty.

Other nights were worse still.

In those, she watched him fall. Again and again, the image burned behind her eyelids: his hand reaching, her own outstretched but too far, her feet locked to the stone as the distance yawned between them. She would scream in the dream, her throat tearing, her chest a furnace of fire and terror. And she would wake the same way—screaming into the darkness, heart pounding so hard she thought her ribs might split.

Not like that first scream, the one that had shaken stone and dragon alike. Smaller, but sharper. Personal. As if her body was reminding her that the fall hadn't ended.

And every time, silence rushed in after. Heavy. Absolute. The kind of silence that made her wonder if the world itself was waiting for her to break.

Someone stood in the doorway.

She didn't have to look to know the shape of him, broad and tired, shadow long against the stone. Ben. She felt the hush that came with him now—the way he carried silence like armor. The way his love had sharpened into something edged with fear.

She didn't turn. If she did, something might crack that wouldn't mend.

I'm still here, she thought. The words pressed hard against her ribs but wouldn't rise to her mouth. He is too. She held to that even when it hurt, especially when it hurt.

Ben's presence lingered in the threshold. He didn't speak, didn't step inside. The fire crackled low, a failing heart. For a long time, that was all.

At last, his shadow shifted, retreating down the hall. His silence stayed behind, heavy as stone.

The fire spat once and surrendered to ember.

Cam lay back without lying down, spine pressed to the wall, knees drawn tight, pendant cool again in her hand.

Hold, she told herself. Hold, hold, hold.

But the word didn't feel like strength.

It felt like not drowning.

Little Flame.

The sun had set, washing the sky in bands of yellow, rose, and bruised violet. The colors softened the sharp ridges of the mountains, softened even her own obsidian hide until the gold threading her veins gleamed like embers buried in ash. Not fire, not fury—just a glow that waited. Banked.

Her wing curved close, talons sunk deep into the stone shelf of the roost. Stillness wrapped her, but it was not silence. The bond thrummed through her chest like a second heartbeat, raw and uneven. Grief and hope, so tightly woven together in her rider that even Sylithra could not tell where one began and the other ended. The ache bled into her, filled her lungs with a weight she could not expel.

And she was not the only one who felt it.

Through her tether with Sael, she tasted the echo of his own storm—ice-hollow, fire-seared. He carried the same wound, because their riders carried the same loss. The bond was a bridge, and across it grief traveled freely.

Around her, the mountain held its breath.

The weave stirred wider. Tenebrin's shadow-warm coil brushed against her senses, circling ever watchful. Brontheus pricked sharp, restless as storm-winds snapping taut banners. Virellan's silver hum slipped like a river through the threads, steady, cooling. Skylith answered faint and far, a low forge-note buried in flame and iron. And deeper still, older than them all, the great ones who slept under stone shifted in their dreams and were still again.

"*I'm still here, Syl.*"

The voice brushed soft as smoke, not in her mind but through the bond, thin and tremulous. Cam. It wasn't much—just breath against silence, the shape of words spoken into darkness. But it was enough.

Sylithra lowered her head, steam curling from her nostrils in slow plumes. Sometimes the only word that mattered was the simplest one. She closed her eyes, letting the ember-glow in her veins pulse back across the bond—steady, unyielding.

I know, Little Flame.

The silence between them wasn't empty anymore. It was shared.

The fortress breathed uneasily in the dark. Torchlight bled across the stone, throwing long, uneven shadows. His boots carried him without asking, past the training ring where sparks still scarred the floor, past closed doors where whispers stilled the moment he passed.

On the stair, he found Val. Her braid sagged loose over one shoulder, strands pulled free where she'd run ink-stained fingers through it too many times. She pressed the heel of her palm against her brow, then scrubbed at her eyes as if sheer force might erase the exhaustion carved into her face.

"You're still at it?" Kaden's voice was low, careful in a way he didn't use with most people.

She startled faintly, then shifted the scrolls in her arms like they might hide her fatigue. "Words don't stop just because we do."

Kaden leaned against the wall, crossing his arms. He watched her for a moment longer than he should have. Val carried silence differently than Cam did—it wasn't empty, it was weight, bound and ordered until it bled through the cracks anyway.

"You look like you're trying to wring blood out of parchment," he said finally.

Her mouth tugged into something halfway between a smile and a grimace. "Better than sitting still."

The quiet stretched between them. The only sound was the slow gutter of the torches and the soft shuffle of her boots against the step.

Kaden exhaled, jaw flexing. "She's not ready." His voice came quieter than he intended, rough at the edges. "To accept it. Wyatt."

The name lodged in his throat, heavy as stone. Saying it felt like setting it in place.

Val's eyes flicked to his, sharp for an instant, then softened.

"She has to choose it," he went on, softer still. "We can't force her."

The words sounded practical, but they weren't the whole truth. Not the part gnawing at him. Because he wasn't ready either. He couldn't be. Not while Cam clung to her certainty with both hands, pendant chain biting her skin like a lifeline. If she believed Wyatt still lived, then Kaden could almost believe it too. He couldn't say that aloud. Not to Val. Not when the world already looked at him like he was reckless enough without feeding a ghost of hope.

Val shifted the scrolls against her chest, parchment flaking under her nails. Her attempted smile landed crooked. "I wasn't going to try." She let out a breath, then added, "We keep breathing. We keep reading. And we don't let Ben run alone at the dark."

A huff broke out of him—something not quite laughter, not quite surrender. "You read my mind."

"I read your feet," she said, glancing down the corridor Ben had stormed through earlier. Her face sobered, all humor stripped clean. "He's a step away from breaking something that won't fix."

Kaden's jaw worked, throat dry. He thought of Cam again, silent in her grief. Of Val, red-eyed but steady. Of Ben, cracking under the weight. Of Tessa, who refused silence the way a storm refused stillness—lashing lightning at stone, flying Brontheus until her hands blistered, rage loud enough to keep grief from swallowing her whole. And of Corin, standing always at the edge of it all, stoic as carved granite. The man never cracked, but Kaden saw the pauses stretch longer when reports came in empty, saw the way his foresight shadowed his eyes darker each day.

The whole circle was straining at different seams, and someone had to keep track of the threads before they snapped.

"I'll stay close."

"And I'll stay loud enough to be heard." Val lifted a scroll like a shield, her expression wry but tired. "Go. Rest. I'll wake you if the words change shape."

Words did that now—shifted when you weren't looking. Or maybe grief just bent them.

By the time Kaden made it back to his quarters, the fortress had gone almost silent. Torches hissed low in their sconces, throwing narrow bars of light across the stone floor. His boots felt heavier than they should have. He'd spent the evening walking the corridors until the stone itself seemed to pulse under his palms, as if trying to answer questions he hadn't asked out loud.

He'd stopped outside Cam's door more than once, listening to nothing. He'd passed the training ring where Tessa's scorch-marks still blackened the stone and felt the echo of her storm coiled like a threat under his own skin. He'd looked toward Corin's study, the door shut tight, the faint glow of sigils leaking around the frame, and thought of how even Corin's foresight couldn't keep them from coming apart.

On the way down the stair, he saw Val asleep at her desk in the library alcove, head pillowed on her arms, scrolls spread like fallen feathers around her. He almost woke her, almost offered to carry her to her cot, but the sight of the ink on her cheek and the quill still in her hand stopped him. She needed her walls as much as he did. So he left her there, the faint scratch of her breathing fading behind him.

His own chamber waited in the eastern wing, small and spare, stone holding the day's cold. He didn't light a lamp. Didn't need to. Moonlight stretched in from the high, narrow window and laid a thin wound of white across the floorboards.

He sat on the edge of his cot for a long time, elbows on his knees, staring at his hands as though they belonged to someone else. Every dawn and dusk he opened gates to emptiness. Every night he tried to believe tomorrow might be different. He wasn't sure how much longer the repetition could hold.

When sleep came, it didn't come gently. It slipped over him without permission, like a soft-handed thief.

He stood—or didn't—inside a place without weight. Cinders drifted like thought. There was no sky to pin them to, no ground to tell him he was falling. Only the hush of unmade things.

Light threaded the dark in silver strands. Some went slack. Some tightened, singing quiet notes he felt in his teeth more than in his ears.

A voice found him there, near and distant at once, as if carried down a long corridor of bone.

"I'm not gone..."

He turned hard enough to lose his balance on nothing, heart a hammer against a wall that wasn't there. "Wyatt?"

The strands shivered. One brightened, then failed. Another pulled faintly, like a caught breath.

Through the bond, something stirred: a low, resonant hum from Tenebrin—subtle, questioning, real. The dragon felt it too. Not a memory he'd fed the bond. Not grief looping back on itself. Something.

"Where?" Kaden demanded, to the dark, to the voice, to the thread that had tugged once and then lay quiet. "Where are you?"

Ash moved. That was all.

He woke with a sound in his throat that wasn't quite a word, palms cold, ribs held by a fist he couldn't see.

The room knew he was awake and didn't care. Moonlight made a thin white wound on the floorboards.

"I can't..." he whispered to nobody. "I can't let go yet."

He lay back and stared at the ceiling until it remembered how to be a ceiling. Dawn would come. He would put on his voice and his hands and go be the version of himself that didn't shake.

The wrongness lingered—not hope, not certainty, just the refusal to cut a thread because it had gone quiet.

He closed his eyes and held it anyway.

Chapter 40: What They Carry

The war room looked less like strategy and more like aftermath. Scrolls sprawled in disarray, half-rolled, half-torn, ink bleeding where quills had snapped under frustrated hands. Maps stretched across the table, marked in slashes of charcoal—lost keeps, fallen outposts, safehouses crossed out like graves.

Corin sat hunched at the center, the Book of Unbinding open before him, though his eyes had not truly touched its pages in hours. Firelight guttered low in the grate, casting restless shadows that deepened the hollows of his face. He spoke at last, his lips shaping the fragment that had circled his mind since dawn:

"The Hollow shall be filled."

The words clung to the air like frost. Heavy. Patient. Unanswered.

His hands spread against the map-scarred table until his joints ached. He had prepared for this—years of fragments, foresight, tracing threads until his vision blurred. He had prepared for Veilborn, for the Hollow Prince, for Balance itself.

But not for them.

His mind reached back unbidden—not to these walls, but to Haldrin's Keep before it fell. Wyatt had leaned against the banister there once, grinning with that easy warmth that made even the hard-edged veterans unclench their jaws. The man's laugh had carried down the stone hall, chasing shadows from corners, chasing dread from hearts that had forgotten how to breathe freely.

That sound was gone now. Replaced by a silence too deep to ignore.

Not silence, no. The scream.

A month past, he hadn't been in the infirmary, hadn't seen her when it tore loose. But the fortress had felt it. The dragons had gone silent. The wards had quivered. Corin himself had staggered where he stood, as if the sound had reached through stone to seize him by the spine. He hadn't needed to be told whose voice it was. No one but Cam carried power that could split the world.

And it haunted him still. Some nights he woke with the echo clamped around his chest, ribs aching, lungs refusing breath. Prophecy had never warned him of that. Nothing had.

"I should have read deeper," he whispered. "Should have seen the trap."

But foresight was never certainty. It was glimpses, flickers, shapes half-formed in mist. He had always known that. He had simply chosen to believe it was enough.

Memory answered him, not his own voice but one he carried still. Lira's. Not sharp, never sharp, but steady as tide on stone. His little sister had always spoken with a wisdom that felt older than her years, a clarity that left him both proud and unsettled.

"Balance isn't strategy, Corin. It's choice."

She had told him that once, when he was still sharpening plans and playing with futures like pieces on a board. He had laughed it off then. She had been right, of course. She often was.

His head bowed, hair falling into his eyes. "Then why did I choose wrong?"

The fire gave no answer.

He pushed up at last; every motion weighted and left the war room behind. The corridor beyond breathed cold, wards trembling faintly along the stone as though even their lines feared to hold. His steps slowed when he reached the frost garden—a small courtyard open to the night, the air silver-thin beneath the stars. Once, when they had first arrived, it had been little more than ruin: stone beds cracked, ivy strangling dead stalks, frost clinging stubbornly where life refused to grow.

Now, against all expectation, it breathed green again. Shoots of grass threaded between flagstones, pale blossoms opened shyly to the starlight, and the air smelled faintly of living things. It looked less like a ruin, more like a place remembering what it had been.

Cam sat there, curled against Sylithra's flank. The dragon's vast wing arched close like a shield, gold-veined scales glowing faintly in the dark. Cam's hand moved once, brushing the black scales like someone tracing the edge of a lifeline.

Corin's chest tightened. He had called her fulcrum, keystone, balance incarnate. He had told himself she was strong enough to carry the weight because she had to be. But strength like that was borrowed, not endless.

Now she seemed half-absent, a ghost of herself wandering the edges of her own skin. Her eyes no longer sought the horizon; they sank into it. Even her silence was different—it wasn't the contemplative stillness he had once admired in her, but an emptiness, the kind that devoured sound instead of holding it.

He wondered, not for the first time, if he had mistaken endurance for resilience. If he had convinced himself that prophecy could replace the marrow a person needed simply to keep breathing. He had built his strategies on her shoulders, blind to the fact that shoulders could bow.

Here—she was not prophecy. She was a woman who laughed in storms. A woman who grieved in silence. A woman who now carried grief so heavily it made her appear transparent, as though the world might look right through her and forget she had ever been.

And he—he had forgotten the difference.

His fingers found the nearest wardline scratched into stone. It faltered, the sigil stuttering, nearly guttering out before his practiced touch coaxed it back. His hand trembled as he traced the mark, the flame inside his chest unsteady as the fire in the war room had been.

"Balance," he whispered. "Yes. But not if it costs their hearts."

◈ ☽ ⚡ ☾ ◈

After weeks at Ember Fortress, Val swore she could smell the ash from Eldvale on her coat—the ghost of burned Veilborn flesh and steel, the memory of everything they'd been through and lost. Haldrin had been emptied by betrayal. But it was Orren who'd kept the evacuation from turning into chaos.

She remembered the way he'd moved through the fortress that night—quiet, efficient, unshaken while everyone else drowned in panic. His orders were calm, measured. People listened. She had listened.

And still, every time she looked at him, she saw what he had been.

Mage hunter.

The word alone made her stomach tighten.

She crossed the courtyard, papers clutched tight to her chest to keep the wind from tearing them free. The sky had begun to fade toward dusk; a thin strip of orange pressed between the peaks. The heat of the day was fading fast, the kind of chill that crept down from the stone and settled into her bones.

Orren was by the armory steps, kneeling beside a stack of gear crates. He was repairing the clasps on a supply chest, movements sure and deliberate, sleeves rolled to his elbows. The scar that ran along his forearm caught the light—a thin, pale line that looked too much like the ones left by restraint cuffs.

Val hesitated a few paces away. She hadn't meant to stop.

He glanced up, noticing her in the reflection of the metal clasp. "Need something?"

The question was calm, but it carried weight—like he already knew she didn't want to be there.

"No," she said quickly, then—too quickly—"Corin sent me to check the inventory lists."

A lie, but not entirely. It sounded better than I can't stop watching you.

Orren nodded once, returning to his work. "It's under control."

"I know." She lingered anyway. "You've been... organizing things since Haldrin."

He gave a faint, humorless smile. "Somebody had to."

She hated the flicker of gratitude that stirred. He was the reason they had gotten out without losing anyone. She knew that. Everyone did. But the knowledge clashed with everything she had been raised to believe about his kind. Mage hunters did not save people like her; they marked them, bound them, burned them. One had killed her brother. She still remembered the look on his face before he had been killed.

She adjusted the strap of her satchel to hide the tremor in her hand. "You didn't have to stay with us. You could've gone back."

He paused, looking up this time. The torchlight caught in his eyes—gray, distant, but not cold. "And do what? Keep hunting people for doing what they were born to do?"

The bluntness hit her harder than she expected. She stared at him; words caught somewhere between disbelief and something that almost felt like understanding.

He reached for another clasp, tightening it, but when the crate shifted slightly, Val stepped forward on instinct. "Wait—" She bent to steady it, and their hands brushed.

Her pulse snapped like a wire. She flinched back before she could stop herself.

Orren froze. The motion was subtle, but she saw it—the way his jaw set, the flicker of guilt in his eyes before he turned slightly aside to give her space. "Old reflex," he said quietly. "For both of us, I guess."

Val's throat ached. "You don't have to—"

"I know," he cut in gently, setting the clasp aside. "But I understand."

The silence that followed wasn't sharp this time. Just heavy. The kind that comes from too many truths unsaid.

Val swallowed hard, trying to find something solid to stand on. "You knew," she said finally. "About the others. About me."

His gaze lifted to hers, steady. "I did."

"And you didn't tell anyone."

"I'm not that man anymore."

She wanted to believe him. Gods, she almost did. But old terror had a long memory.

She shifted her weight, forcing herself to meet his eyes. "If I ever think you're lying to us..."

"I wouldn't blame you," he said, tone flat but without resentment. "But I won't give you a reason to."

Something in her chest cracked open—small, reluctant, real. The wind hissed between the stones, carrying the smell of oil and pine sap. She nodded once, almost to herself.

When she turned to leave, he didn't stop her. Just went back to work, quiet as before.

At the archway, she glanced back. Orren was still kneeling in the torchlight, hands steady, face unreadable. But the sight didn't fill her with dread anymore. Just a wary kind of peace.

Maybe people could change.

Maybe even the ones who weren't supposed to.

◈ ☽⚡☾ ◈

The trees beyond the fortress crouched under mist. Every branch dripped with dew, the air heavy, listening. A hunter learned to hear silence as much as sound, and tonight, silence screamed the loudest of all.

Orren moved like a shadow through the undergrowth, bow slung at his back, blade loose at his hip. Two others from the fortress trailed at a respectful distance—quiet men who knew his steps set the pace. Their packs were meant for meat, hides, and bones to be salted and smoked, stored for the next winter that already waited with its teeth.

But the forest wasn't the only thing pressing close. His thoughts crowded too, each one a ghost he couldn't shake.

Tessa's storm haunted him most. He had watched her earlier on the cliffs, Brontheus pacing behind her, refusing to fly no matter how she coaxed. Lightning had flickered along her arms until the air itself had snarled. The night before she had turned that storm on him, words spat like sparks, rage lashing sharp. He had answered in kind, colder, cutting. That should have ended it. Should have repelled him. But instead, it unsettled him in ways he didn't want to name. Chaos should have pushed him away. With her, it didn't.

Val was easier to read. She bled herself into ink and parchment, burying grief in lines of prophecy until her eyes burned. Orren knew the trick. Exhaustion left no room for silence, and silence was where grief breathed. He understood her choice.

Kaden was different. Orren had seen him in the library, jaw set, hands steady, always within reach of Cam. Hope clung to him like frost that refused to thaw. Hope he shouldn't have. Hope Orren almost envied.

Ben's grief had curdled sharper. He carried it in his shoulders, in the way his voice cut when he spoke Corin's name. Orren had heard him mutter blame into the stone walls—if Corin had acted sooner, if someone had moved faster, if anything had been done differently. Anger gave his grief an edge, but edges cut both ways. It was the look Ben gave Cam that Orren remembered most—fear sharpened into possession, love turned into something that hurt to watch.

And Corin—the commander who tried to wear foresight like armor. Orren had passed him once in the frost garden, wardlines guttering under his hand. The man's face had been stone, but his eyes had turned upward, raw, searching the Veil as if it owed him an answer. He carried strategy like a shield, but Orren had seen the cracks. Stoicism couldn't hide guilt forever.

And Cam... she was the thread that bound all of them, and she looked more ghost than girl. Orren had seen her asleep in the library once, curled small in a chair, pendant clenched so hard the chain cut her skin. Even in dreams, she twitched, lips moving like she was chasing someone she couldn't reach.

The pendant had dragged him backward.

A month ago, in the ruins of the temple, he had dug until his palms bled and his shoulders screamed. Stone shifted like broken teeth. Ash clogged his throat. No body. No blood. Just ruin. And then—half-buried in the blackened rubble near the cliff—Wyatt's pendant. Cold. Soot-streaked. Waiting.

He remembered the weight of it in his hand. Heavier than steel, heavier than bone. Proof of nothing, and everything.

That night, he'd gone to the infirmary. Cam lay in her long stillness, her body locked down by what she had burned through. The walls smelled of herbs and smoke. He had set the pendant on her pillow, close enough that her hand might find it when she woke.

She should have it, he'd thought. Even if it's all that's left.

Her breath had stuttered once, but she hadn't woken. He had adjusted her blanket and walked into the corridor, leaning against the stone opposite her door until dawn. Outside the gates, Sylithra's gold-threaded veins glowed faintly in the dark, her chest rising and falling steady as the fortress's breath. He hadn't moved. He hadn't slept.

And then, the scream.

It tore the fortress apart. Orren hadn't been near her when it broke, but he knew whose voice it was. No one else carried power strong enough to split stone and silence dragons mid-breath. It rattled the marrow in his bones, hollowed the mountain, burned through every wall he'd ever built to keep such sounds out.

He had heard screams before. Hundreds. In alleys slick with rain, in fields black with fire. Mage and unmarked alike—he'd dragged them down for coin, for orders, for the Capital's tally. He'd heard their last breaths claw through the dark. Some defiant. Some begging. Some so broken they hadn't sounded human anymore. He had learned to close his ears, to wall the noise away.

But hers had cut straight through every wall.

Not defiance. Not surrender. Something larger. A sound that didn't just grieve, but split the world open, demanded it bear witness. And for a man who had once thought himself beyond being moved, it had left him shaken—because he knew what loss was, and because he could not forget that once, before the Capital had made him a blade, he had lost someone too. Someone whose silence still hollowed him more than their screams.

A crack of branch snapped him back to the present. Mist clung low, damp against his cheek. He slid behind a birch trunk, peering ahead. A buck moved between the trees, antlers heavy with velvet, hide sleek in the silver wash of moonlight. Its ears flicked, nosing the ground, unaware.

Orren eased the bow from his shoulder. Drew. Breath slowed. The forest narrowed to line, shaft, target.

The arrow flew clean.

The buck staggered, steam curling from its mouth in the cold air, then folded into the ferns with a soft crash. Orren approached, crouching, laying a hand on the still-warm hide. Respect given, always, before taking.

He worked quickly—blade swift, blood sharp in the mist, the forest watching silent. When it was done, he hooked his grip under the antlers and heaved, dragging the weight across his shoulders.

The buck hung heavy—meat, bone, silence. Enough to feed them. Not enough to fill what had been lost.

He started back toward the fortress, boots sinking into moss, mist swallowing his steps.

The kill was simple. It always was.

What lingered was not.

Because silence had taken a shape now—raw, human, unbearable.

Cam's scream had carved it into him, and no blade, no bow, no hunt would ever be enough to bring it down.

Part 2

Afterlight

"Afterlight is not silence—it is the waiting breath. Only in the dark can the hidden path be seen."

Chapter 41: The Day the Sky Went Quiet

The war room filled in waves, the scrape of boots and muted voices dragging silence in with them. It was not noise that struck Corin first, but weight—every arrival pressed the air lower, tighter, as though the stone walls themselves understood what was coming.

Captains set their reports down like offerings to a pyre. Healers carried the smell of herbs and fatigue. Scouts leaned against the walls, their coats still damp with mountain rain, eyes downcast. None asked why they had been summoned; they already knew.

Corin stood at the head of the table and let the room settle. He felt their grief as one body, fractured but bound together by the same absence. For a heartbeat, no one moved. No one breathed loud enough to break it.

Then, from the cliffs beyond the keep, a dragon horn moaned long and low. The sound threaded through the stone and into their bones, mournful, final.

Corin drew breath. His voice followed the horn like an echo, steady though it carved him hollow.

"The search is over. We will begin the rites tomorrow."

The words landed like iron on stone.

He watched the faces break. Ben's jaw locked, shoulders stiff, his silence a dam against a flood. Tessa's fists curled until sparks whispered along her knuckles, her eyes flint-hard. Kaden's head bowed, the hollows under his eyes as deep as the portals he had torn open day after day. Val nodded once, sharp, but her hands trembled against the table before she clasped them tight. Orren said nothing, but his gaze cut like a blade, and his fingers lingered too long on the hilt at his side. Around the room, captains shifted, scouts looked away, healers bowed their heads.

Command is not courage, Corin thought. *It's carving grief into orders. I've buried soldiers before. I've buried kin. And every time, it takes more than it leaves.*

He dismissed them at last. Boots scraped stone, armor rattled, the shuffling of men and women leaving under a silence heavier than any war cry.

As the chamber emptied, Ben lingered. His eyes, hard as steel, caught Corin's as they passed close in the doorway. His voice was low but cutting, edged with grief sharpened into accusation.

"Who will tell her?"

Corin met his stare. He didn't flinch.

"I will. Today. If I end the search, the words must come from me."

Ben's mouth tightened, but he said nothing more. He turned sharply down the corridor, leaving the question hanging like a wound.

Corin's own steps carried him the other way, slower. The halls bled light unevenly, torch and sun and shadow mingling across stone. His hand trailed once along the wall, feeling its cold weight, as if the mountain itself pressed judgment into his palm.

Guilt stalked him as it always did. He had spent years reading fragments, forcing patterns where none existed, mistaking whispers of foresight for full visions. He had acted when he should have listened. He had pushed rebellions before the time, cost lives in fires that never should have been lit. He had believed he was keeper of the prophecy when he had only shards.

I thought I saw the whole design, he told himself. *But I only ever saw splinters. And in my arrogance, I cut the world deeper.*

That arrogance had a price. He had been blind to Caerthalen's snares until it was too late. Blind to Alex's betrayal until the knife was already in their ribs. And now—Wyatt. He could not shake the fear that his obsession with prophecy had left the man vulnerable, had drawn them all too close to the edge without realizing the ground was crumbling beneath.

If I had read clearer. If I had waited longer. If I had listened instead of rushing to shape the world by force of will... would Wyatt still be here?

The thought hollowed him. He stopped outside Cam's door, his breath catching, the weight of his regrets pressing him still. For a moment, he let it strip him bare—raw, human, the side no one ever saw. Then, slowly, deliberately, he drew his mask of command back into place.

He pushed the door open.

The room was dim, a slit window letting in the thin breath of mountain wind. She sat on the bed, spine curved, pendant clenched so tight the chain had cut red grooves into her hand. Down on the cliffs below, Sylithra coiled in silence, her gold-veined scales pulsing faintly like the heartbeat of the mountain. The dragon's hum carried through the stone, low and aching.

Corin stepped closer, then knelt. He had never knelt to soldiers. But this was not a soldier.

"Camomile..." His voice came softer than he meant. "Tomorrow we honor him. It's time."

Her breath caught, ragged. She didn't lift her head, only gripped the pendant harder, the metal creaking under her fingers.

"He's still out there." Her voice trembled but did not break. "I can feel it. I'd know if he was gone."

For a moment, the commander vanished. He wanted to believe her. Wanted to cling to that fragile flame of hope, however irrational. But hope had betrayed him too many times. It had betrayed him when he thought his foresight could save more than fragments, when he thought his choices could force balance into being, when he thought he could keep his sister alive.

"I once thought I'd know too," he whispered, eyes closing for a heartbeat. "When Lira died. But the world doesn't always give us that mercy."

Cam's gaze never left the window; the pendant still clutched like breath itself. He knew she would not come.

He rose slowly. His steps carried him back into the hall, the door shutting soft behind him. The corridor stretched long, lit by torches that guttered against the mountain wind.

Corin paused once at a narrow window, looking out. The sky was paling into dusk, stars already kindling at the edges. Far below, Sylithra shifted, her gold veins pulsing like embers in the dark.

Corin lingered just outside, palm braced against cold stone, throat tight. It was easier to tell soldiers their fight was over than to leave her there—bent under grief he could not lift. Easier to sign death warrants, to bury the dead, to order horns blown and pyres built, than to face the raw refusal in her eyes.

For a moment, he almost went back. Almost.

Instead, he drew in one steady breath, smoothed the lines of his face into command again, and walked on. But the echo of her silence followed him longer than any horn.

◈ ☽⚡☾ ◈

The door clicked shut behind Corin, the sound small but final, and the silence it left behind pressed heavier than his words.

Evening thickened in her chamber, the gold of the sun stretching thin across the stone until it looked more like bruises than light. The fire in the grate had burned low, snapping only once in protest before it sagged into embers.

Cam sat on the edge of her cot, pendant clenched so tight against her chest her heartbeat knocked against it. The chain had carved fine grooves into her skin over the past weeks, red and raw, but she couldn't loosen her grip. Her thumb traced the same groove in the metal again and again until the shape felt like part of her hand.

They think I'm breaking. Maybe I am. The thought shivered through her like glass. *But if this is denial... why does it feel like a pulse under my skin? Why does it feel alive?*

A horn still echoed faintly in the cliffs beyond, low and mournful, its sound stitched into the mountain air like the world itself was grieving.

Sylithra stirred far below, on the lower ledges of the fortress where she roosted. Cam felt it before she heard it: a ripple through the bond, heavy as stone shifting in the earth. The dragon's head lifted, and a rumble rolled outward, soft but endless, carrying up through rock and marrow.

Cam closed her eyes. The sound wasn't comfort—it was resonance. The reminder that her grief was not hers alone but mirrored in scales and flame.

She whispered into the shadows, words she hadn't meant to say aloud.

"If I stand by that pyre... I'll be the one killing him."

Her voice cracked, breaking on the word pyre, and for a moment she pressed the pendant so hard against her chest she thought it might pierce her skin.

The fortress below busied itself with death. She heard it in fragments through the window: voices carrying on the wind, the scrape of timber as they built the pyre, the hollow clang of lowered banners. Each sound was a nail in a coffin she refused to seal.

Not yet.

Her breath came sharp, uneven. If they're ready to let go, if the world says he's gone... then I have to find what they don't see. The missing piece. The temple. The last scroll. The prophecy.

She dug her nails into her palm, holding fast. *If I can find that, maybe I'll understand why this happened. Maybe I'll find a way back to him. Or at least keep him alive—in truth, if not in flesh.*

The thought pulsed under her skin like a second heartbeat. Hope, defiance—she couldn't tell which.

Outside, Sylithra's rumble deepened, brushing against her mind. A thought not words, not entirely:

Little Flame. Threads do not end. They fray. They wait to be rewoven.

Cam's throat tightened. "What if I can't reweave them?"

The dragon's pulse pressed steady against her grief. *Then you carry them. Until you can.*

Tears blurred the gold veins of Sylithra's body, faintly burning against the dark. The light caught in Cam's pendant too, the last sun flashing like a wound across silver.

She leaned her forehead into her palm, breath shaking. *Everyone else has let go. I haven't. And maybe Kaden hasn't either.* Her fingers curled tighter. *And I don't know if that makes us brave... or broken.*

Her body moved before her thoughts. She pushed up from the cot, bare feet cold on stone, and dragged her training leathers from the chest. Her hands shook as she pulled them on, the leather stiff from weeks of disuse, but the motion steadied something jagged inside her.

The pendant stayed looped at her throat, pressing sharp against her collarbone. A tether. A wound. A promise.

She didn't light a lamp. Shadows clung as she slipped into the corridor, the fortress winding her toward the outer steps. The mountain air hit her, sharp with pine and soil, the horizon already bleeding into dusk.

The training ring waited near the tree line—an open circle of stone and packed earth, its posts scarred with grooves from the days practice sessions.

Torches guttered low along the edge, their light wavering against the dark forest beyond.

She stepped inside and didn't hesitate.

Fire came first—violet-black flame leaping to her hand, burning hotter than breath. She struck the nearest post, and the wood screamed, splinters catching the glow.

Then air answered. A rush of wind tore across the ring, scattering ash and snapping banners from their poles. Her next strike carried lightning with it, a crack that split the post's charred surface.

Water followed—called from the night air, droplets coalescing into a spear that shattered on impact. The ground shuddered beneath her as earth surged upward, stones ripping loose in jagged arcs. Shadows flared from the forest's edge, curling around her ankles, stretching like claws. One strike bled too far into the next—flame crashing into shadow—and for a breath the fire burned with a strange gold shimmer at its edges, bright and wrong against the dark. It vanished as quickly as it came, leaving only smoke and the ache in her chest.

Each strike bled into the next, no control, no measure—only grief given form. Fire licked through water. Wind screamed with lightning. Stone broke and shadow mended.

Her body screamed too—muscles trembling, lungs tearing—but she didn't stop. Every strike was a refusal. Every breath, defiance.

Sylithra felt it. The dragon's rumble deepened below, wings shuddering once, echoing her rider's storm. She didn't intervene. Didn't still her. She let the wild grief burn, because sometimes fire had to eat itself out before it left room for anything else.

Cam's legs buckled at last. She dropped to her knees in the ring, chest heaving, flames guttering low around her fists. Sparks hissed in the dirt, earth groaned under her weight, shadows twined around her wrists like shackles unwilling to let go.

She bowed her head and whispered into the smoke:

"I will find you. I don't care what it costs."

The forest answered only with silence. But it wasn't empty.

It was listening.

◈ ☽ ⚡ ☾ ◈

The fortress quieted after the council dispersed, its halls breathing only with torch-smoke and the weight of unspoken things. Orren had meant to turn in—his legs ached from the hunt, his shoulders from the bowstring—but when he reached the stair to his quarters, movement caught him.

Cam.

She slipped from her chamber like a shadow cutting free of stone. No coat, no lantern. Her face was pale, but her eyes—he hadn't seen that look in weeks. Not hollow, not drowned. Fierce. Reckless. Alive with something that was equal parts grief and defiance.

He followed at a distance; footfalls muted against worn stone. She didn't look back, didn't waver. Past the lower corridor, through the arch that opened to the outer yard, she strode straight toward the old training ring at the forest's edge.

The ground there was scarred with grooves, carved deep by years of drills and sparring. The air smelled of pine resin and damp earth. She stepped into the center like a soldier walking to judgment.

Then it began.

Fire licked from her palms, violet tongues spitting sparks into the night. Wind coiled around her shoulders, tugging her hair loose in streaming strands. Water bled from the air itself, droplets hissing as they struck flame. Earth shivered under her boots, hairline cracks spidering outward with each breath. Lightning flickered sharp along her arms. Shadows stretched long, writhing like smoke, then folded back into her skin.

Every element she bore answered her call.

The sound rattled him—it wasn't her voice, not like the scream a month ago. That scream had split the mountain, had torn through marrow and silence alike, raw grief made into a weapon the world itself had to hear. It had unsettled him in ways he still didn't have words for, because it hadn't just been power. It had been loss given sound.

This was different. This was not a breaking. This was a refusal.

She swayed, breath ragged. For an instant he thought she would steady—but her knees struck dirt, shoulders folding in as the last of the elements guttered out, leaving only the echo of power in the ring. His hand twitched toward her, the old instinct to move, to shield. He forced it still.

Not his place.

She stayed there, bent but unbroken, the pendant's silver glint barely visible at her throat.

He didn't tell her he'd watched. He didn't tell anyone at all. Because grief like that wasn't something another hand could steady. It had to burn, had to break, had to carve its own shape in the dark.

So he let her be.

But as he slipped back into the fortress, a thought lingered sharp in his chest.

Part of him respected her for it—respected the way she turned pain into fire instead of silence.

And part of him, though he'd never admit it, envied her.

Because he had only ever learned how to bury grief deep so deep it turned to steel in his hands. He envied her storm—not because it made her strong, but because it made her honest. She let her pain burn in the open. His had only ever been hidden under scars, sharpened into silence, and sold to the Capital as a weapon.

Chapter 42: Ashes for the Living

The lower courtyard of Ember Fortress had been carved into the mountainside long before their time—stone hollowed to hold grief. Today, the air carried it heavy, pressing as thin as the mountain wind.

A single pyre stood at the center. Empty. Waiting.

Banners hung limp, their colors muted to ash in the gray light. Torches lined the walls, their flames struggling against the draft that curled smoke upward like a dark thread unraveling into the sky. Even the air seemed unwilling to stay. The scent of pitch clung thick, acrid in Kaden's throat, and every crack of kindling catching sounded too loud against the silence—as if the mountain itself resented bearing witness.

Corin stepped forward. The weight of command thick on his shoulders. His voice broke the silence, low and resonant, carrying the ancient words of the Dragon Mourning Rite:

"Here we honor the bond severed, though no flame carried him home. Here we light what the world denied that his name not vanish in silence. As dragons return to sky, so do riders return to memory. We keep them not in ash, but in the breath of the living."

When the last phrase fell, Ben stepped forward. His face was carved into stone, but his hand shook once as he touched the torch to the pyre. Flame licked upward, catching dry wood, sparks drifting lonely into the breeze.

Kaden stood among the line of mourners, shoulders straight, throat closed. His eyes fixed on the fire, but it gave him nothing.

Even the flame feels empty. Even the dragons won't cry for him.

He felt the absence sharpest in Sael. The white dragon had not come down from the heights. No keen, no rumble, no shadow across the sky. Only silence, and it pressed colder than the wind.

Near him, Tessa muttered something to Val—sharp, bitter. "She should be here."

Val's reply came soft, strained. "Leave her be."

Kaden caught both. He didn't turn, didn't answer, though the words cut. Tessa's fire was armor, Val's restraint a shield. And between them he stood, silent, holding to the same thread Cam clung to—thin, fragile, but unbroken. If he spoke, he feared they would hear it in his voice: that he carried the same hope, reckless as it was.

Cam's absence pressed just as hard. He didn't need to glance beside him to know. She was nowhere near the pyre. She never would be. Still, he felt her like a ghost at his shoulder, her refusal as present as his own pulse.

When the rite ended, he remained until the last ember faltered, because Corin had asked him to stand. But his heart was already elsewhere—following the pull he knew led skyward.

By the time he climbed the winding steps to the upper roost, the pyre's smoke was only a faint line against the horizon. The wind was sharper here, keening like something wounded.

Tenebrin waited, a shadow coiled against the cliff face. The dragon's eyes opened as Kaden approached, slitted silver catching the thin light. A low rumble rolled through the stone, greeting him not with words but with presence.

Kaden leaned into the warmth of his dragon's shoulder, letting the exhaustion pull at his spine. His chest still felt hollow, scraped out by the rite below. The smoke-scent clung to his hair, his clothes, the back of his tongue—like he had swallowed ash instead of air.

For a moment, he pressed his forehead against Tenebrin's scales, eyes closed. The heat seeping through was steady, grounding. He remembered other warmth—firesides at Haldrin's Keep, laughter that softened stone walls, Wyatt's voice turning sharp nights easy. Now warmth was only dragon-hide under his cheek, and silence that felt like punishment.

"Where is she?" he murmured.

The answer came not in words, but in thought carried on a dark hum that vibrated through their bond:

Flying with the dark one. Chasing wind and cloud.

Kaden's eyes lifted toward the sky. He saw nothing at first—only blue thinned pale with height, the last smoke-thread rising from the fortress below. Then, far above, a shape glinted gold along the edges of vast wings.

His breath left him in a sigh, heavy as stone. "I hope she doesn't do anything reckless."

The dragon's rumble was steady, untroubled, but Kaden felt the echo of doubt in his own chest. Recklessness was all that remained when hope refused to die.

He dragged in one more breath, pushed off Tenebrin's shoulder, and climbed into the saddle.

"Come on," he muttered. "If she's flying blind into storms, we won't let her do it alone."

Tenebrin's wings unfurled, shadows swallowing the cliff. Together, they leapt into the sky—rising toward the glint of gold above the clouds.

Wind roared past, the fortress falling away beneath. Together, they climbed into the sky, angling toward the dark speck rising higher and higher above the pyre smoke.

Toward Cam. Toward Sylithra. Toward the storm they both refused to release.

◈ ☽ ⚡ ☾ ◈

Sylithra's wings carved the sky wide, each span pulling them higher, farther from the smolder of the pyre below. Her flight was not hurried but relentless, each stroke of her wings like the toll of a bell. Gold veins shimmered faintly at the edges of her scales, catching sunlight like threads stitched into shadow.

Cam pressed the pendant hard against her chest, the chain biting into her palm. She refused to look down. She would not give the pyre her eyes. The smoke was for them. The ashes were for them. If she let herself see it, it would be surrender.

Her jaw locked until her teeth ached. *I won't burn with them.*

Sylithra's hum pressed close, a vibration through bond and bone, wrapping her like a second heartbeat.

The fire is for the living, the dragon's thought rumbled, steady as stone. *The sky is ours.*

Cam's throat burned, and her voice came hoarse against the wind. "I can't say goodbye. Not yet... not yet."

The gale tore the words thin, shredding them into mist, but she didn't care. Even torn apart, they were hers.

Cloud closed around them, damp and silver, until all sound seemed swallowed. Then Sylithra broke through—vast wings tearing the veil, sunlight spilling across them in a flood of white-gold. For a single heartbeat, the sky was so endless she almost believed it: that if she reached far enough, she might touch him again—Wyatt, warm, laughing, alive.

And for a breath, she swore she heard it. A laugh carried on the wind, faint as memory, bright as a spark in the dark. So faint she couldn't be sure if it was real, or if her own heart had conjured it from longing.

Her grip on the pendant tightened until her knuckles whitened. The ache in her chest twisted sharper, cutting denial into something harder, fiercer.

There is more to find. The temple. The scroll. The prophecy.

The words flared inside her not like comfort but like fire. Not hope—obsession. Not grief—defiance. A vow beating in time with her heart: she would not stop until she had the truth.

Sylithra's wings tilted, angling them higher, the horizon vanishing beneath them.

And then—movement. A shadow climbing from below, vast wings unfurling dark against the clouds. Tenebrin. Kaden riding close to his dragon's neck, face set hard against the wind.

Cam's chest tightened—not relief, not yet, but something steadier than loneliness. She didn't signal him, didn't break her flight to meet him. She only flew on, pendant pressed against her heart, eyes fixed forward.

If Kaden wanted to follow, let him. Let him keep that thread alive beside hers.

Below, the pyre smoldered unseen, smoke curling thin into the wind and carrying nothing back.

Above, two small specks now—Cam with Sylithra, Kaden with Tenebrin—rising into merciless light, where grief had no weight but the will to keep flying.

◈ ☽ ⚡ ☾ ◈

The fortress stone still held the heat of day when Cam came in from the cliffs, sweat slick on her neck, chest burning with the aftermath of dives that had nearly snapped her spine. She hadn't landed clean once—not yesterday, not the day before, not today—but that wasn't the point. Falling close enough to feel death's teeth was the only thing that made her pulse anymore.

The days since the funeral had blurred, each one stretching into the next like smoke curling off the pyre. By morning she was in the aerial fields with Sylithra, climbing until the air thinned and burned her lungs, diving until her muscles locked and the world spun black at the edges. By afternoon she drilled alone in the ring, sword heavy in her hands, magic bleeding uncontrolled into each strike. By night she lay awake staring at the ceiling until exhaustion dragged her under.

And every time she came back through the fortress halls, she felt Ben's eyes. Not accusation. Not pity. Something sharper—searching, worried, desperate. Once he was in the mess hall doorway when she passed, his hands white-knuckled around a cup. Another time he'd been at the roost steps, watching her dismount with sweat and blood on her palms. He never said a word. Just looked like he was holding something back. She couldn't tell if he watched because he feared she might break—or because he already believed she had.

Until this time.

She almost collided with him in the armory corridor, the smell of oiled leather and steel thick between them. His shadow filled the hall before his voice did.

"You're going to kill yourself like this."

Cam's fingers tightened around the hilt of her sword before she slid it into its sheath. The leather rasped under her hand. "I'm trying to be ready."

Ben stepped closer. His eyes searched hers, sharp and bright, and she saw the cracks in them like lines under ice. "For what?" His voice dropped low. "He's gone, Cam."

Her hand rose of its own accord, clutching the pendant at her throat until the edges dug into her palm. It was warm from her skin, as if it still carried someone else's pulse. The words came out raw, quiet: "I can't grieve him. Not yet. I still feel him."

Ben flinched—not at her words, but at the faith in them. His jaw set, the way stone resists water until it finally cracks. He turned without answering. His footsteps left the corridor hollow, echoing against stone until they vanished.

Cam leaned back against the wall, heart still racing, and whispered to the silver clenched in her hand:

"Why do I hear you?"

The pendant's chain bit into her palm, sharp ridges pressed into skin already tender. The echo of Ben's boots faded down the corridor, leaving only the hush of torchlight and the faint rattle of banners in the draft.

She didn't wait for an answer. She never did. But every day the question pressed harder against her chest. If she stopped searching, he was gone forever. If she kept going, she feared she might burn herself hollow. Obsession had replaced hope, and still she couldn't let it go.

She had already bled herself on the edge of every drill, already carved the question into her skin where the pendant's chain left grooves. She hadn't healed. She had only kept moving—faster, harder, deeper—until she couldn't tell anymore whether she was training or punishing herself.

◈ ☽ ⚡ ☾ ◈

The mountains were too quiet tonight. Even the wind seemed to hold its breath.

Tessa's boots scraped against the worn stone as she crossed the terrace, breath fogging faintly in the chill. The fortress windows burned faintly gold behind her, but out here the air felt sharper—alive in a way warmth never was. Even in spring, the mountain nights could bite if you stayed still too long.

Cam sat on the wall just beyond the torchlight, hair tangled by the wind, the silver pendant at her throat glinting faintly each time she moved. The night made her look carved from the same stone she sat on—still, cold, and unbreakable in all the wrong ways.

Tessa reached out to touch her friend. Cam's skin was like living ice.

"You're freezing," Tessa said quietly.

Cam didn't look up. "I'm... fine. I don't feel it."

Something in that answer made Tessa's chest twist. "You should be inside."

"I can't."

The words came too fast, too certain.

Tessa sat down beside her, ignoring the chill that seeped through the stone. The silence stretched until it hurt. "You really think this is what he'd want?"

Cam's head jerked toward her. "Don't—"

Tessa's voice rose before she could stop it. "You think he'd want to see you like this? You think this—" she gestured at the dust streaking Cam's boots, the raw skin on her hands, the hollow look in her eyes "—is how you honor him?"

Cam's eyes snapped to Tessa's, sharp with something between anger and pain. "You don't get to say his name like that."

"I'm not the one pretending he's still here."

The words came out colder than she meant, and the silence that followed made them worse—the kind of silence that leaves nowhere to stand but inside the wound.

Cam's jaw trembled once before she stilled it. Her voice was low, but it didn't waver. "I feel him, Tess. When I fly. When I breathe. It's not memory. He's still out there."

Tessa exhaled, steam curling in the air. "That's grief, Cam. It tricks you."

Cam's hands fisted in her coat. "You think I don't know what grief feels like?"

"That's not what I said."

"It's what you meant."

The quiet between them cracked wide open. Tessa could feel the cold settle into it—the kind that bites deeper than wind ever could.

She softened, finally. "I don't want to fight you," she said. "I just... I don't want to lose you too."

Cam's breath hitched, the sound small and sharp. She turned away; eyes fixed on the horizon. "You already have."

The words gutted her.

Behind them, footsteps echoed lightly on stone. Val's shadow appeared first, then her voice—soft but edged.

"Tessa."

Tessa turn. "She's going to break," she whispered. "Someone has to stop her before she does."

Val's eyes shifted between them, assessing the wreckage in the air. "Or maybe she's already breaking, and the only thing worse than that is not letting her."

Tessa wanted to argue, but the fight left her with her breath. She stood, coat rustling in the wind. "You both think I'm cruel," she said, voice low. "But at least *I'm* still here."

She left before the tears could rise, boots echoing down the hall until the sound vanished into the fortress hum.

◈ ☽⚡☾ ◈

Cam's throat burned where she'd swallowed too many words. The wind tore at her hair, cool enough to sting, but she let it. She deserved it.

Val lingered a few steps away, the firelight painting gold into her braid. She didn't speak. She just stood there, a quiet kind of warmth in the dark.

Finally, Val said softly, "Whatever you're chasing... don't let it take the part of you we love most."

Cam's breath hitched, too quick to hide. The words landed where her pulse still lived, even under all the numbness. She didn't answer—because if she did, she'd break.

Val stayed a moment longer, then turned and left, her footsteps fading like breath.

Cam sat there until the stars blurred. The cold had finally reached her bones.

But when she closed her eyes, she could still feel the faint, impossible warmth of his hand in hers—like the world refused to let her forget.

The quiet she left behind pressed too tight.

Cam didn't move for a long time. Dew had started to gather along the edge of the wall, catching the torchlight in faint silver glints. She traced them with her fingers, watching them tremble—slow and beautiful and merciless.

The morning sun came gray and thin over the mountains, the kind of light that never quite reached the ground.

Cam hadn't slept. The chill from the night clung to her bones, a weight she couldn't shake no matter how long she stood beneath the rising sun. Every sound in the fortress—the clatter of armor, the murmur of voices—felt distant, like echoes in another life.

By the time the others stirred, she was already gone.

The day passed without shape. She trained until her muscles burned, ate nothing, spoke to no one. The sun climbed, fell, and she barely noticed—only the ache in her body marking the hours she'd lost.

The training ring at the edge of the forest was empty when Cam entered, the last rays of sunlight fading over the trees. Torches guttered low around the circle, their light wavering across grooves carved deep by years of sparring. The air smelled of pine resin and damp earth; above her, the stars pressed sharp through the night, watching.

She drew her sword and began again. Strike, pivot, lunge. Sweat blurred her eyes. Her grip slipped—and a voice brushed her ear, soft, so familiar it almost broke her knees.

Tighter grip on the hilt.

She froze. The words were gone, but her throat answered anyway: "I know."

Silence closed back over her. Only the torches hissed, only the wind rattled banners. Their flicker and snap had begun to feel like omens, torches a fragile hope, banners a brittle loyalty, both straining to hold against the wind.

She swung again, harder, and heard herself whisper: "I miss you."

The answer came like breath on the back of her neck*: I know. But I'm still here.*

Her teeth clenched. "Then show me."

She felt it before she heard it. A pressure at the base of her skull, a thrum in her bones, every instinct screaming at once.

Then a whisper slid across her skin again—urgent, sharp as a spark in the dark:

Duck.

She dropped, knees hitting dirt. An arrow lodged itself in to the post were she had been standing a moment before.

She rolled, dirt and pine needles scraping her palms, eyes snapping up. Five figures stepped out of the shadows around the ring.

Tomas. Edric. Sera. Brann. Niall.

Soldiers she had sparred with. Fought beside. Shared meals with. And every one of them had known Wyatt.

"You should've been at the pyre," Tomas said, voice sharp with accusation. His blade gleamed in the torchlight.

"You dishonored him," Sera spat, her eyes burning. "Hiding while the rest of us said goodbye."

Edric's jaw was tight, his knuckles white on his hilt. "You were supposed to protect him. But you failed."

Cam's grip tightened on her sword. "I didn't fail him."

"Then where is he?" Brann's voice cracked like stone breaking. "Where's Wyatt, Cam?"

The name split her chest like an axe. She couldn't answer. Her silence was enough.

Niall sneered. "Thought so."

They surged as one.

Steel crashed against hers, sparks flying. She staggered Tomas back with a burst of violet fire. Edric lunged from her blind side; she spun low, wind bursting outward, scattering dirt in a gale. Niall slammed into her shoulder, knocking the breath from her lungs.

Her magic snarled, shadows clawing up her arms, lightning itching to burst. She could end this. One strike, one burst, and they would fall. But she didn't.

"Stop!" she shouted, chest heaving.

They didn't.

A blade cut across her side, shallow but hot with pain. Sera's sword clipped her shoulder. Brann's boot slammed into her knee. She hit the dirt hard, sword skidding from her grasp.

They circled her. Five blades, five faces she knew. And each one struck a memory. Brann laughing red-faced when Wyatt had knocked him flat in sparring. Sera stealing bread at dinner and Wyatt covering for her with a grin. Edric once pulling Cam from the mud during drills while Wyatt clapped her on the back, teasing. Each face now turned sharp with blame.

Fire trembled up her arms, violet-black and hungry. Earth cracked under her palms. Shadows coiled at her feet, whispering for release.

I could end them, she thought. *One burst, one call to every element, and they would burn, break, drown, vanish. I could make them pay.*

Sera's voice hissed above her. "You let him die."

Brann's blade hovered at her throat. "Say it. Say you failed him."

The shadows at her wrists flexed like claws. Lightning hissed under her skin, begging to strike. Her heart was a drum in her skull. *Do it,* something darker urged. *Do it.*

Heat seared beneath the leather strap on her wrist, sudden and violent, as if fire had been trapped under her skin. Her mark pulsed there, not seen but felt—a brand tightening with every whisper.

Cam's breath caught. Heat coiled at her wrist; familiar, unwanted, alive. It hadn't stirred in months. Not since Alex's slippery half-truths. Not since Wyatt's fall. She'd almost convinced herself it was gone, that the hunger had burned out with him. But now it woke—sharp, feral, demanding—and every pulse in her body screamed for blood.

Panic surged with it. The shadows bent closer, the power begged release. She was right on the edge, ready to let it tear free. Then—soft, impossible, right at her ear:

Cam... don't.

It was Wyatt's voice. Warm. Laughing. The way he'd sound before a sparring match when he'd tug her braid and whisper duck. For a heartbeat, she swore she smelled smoke and pine, the way it clung to him after training.

Her hands shook. The power trembled at the edge of her teeth—and she swallowed it whole.

"No," she gasped, voice raw. "No!"

The elements flickered, dying back. The shadows faded to smoke. Her body sagged under the weight of the restraint.

Sera snarled. "She's weak."

Brann lifted his blade again—and the shadows of the ring rose like a living thing.

"Enough!"

Kaden stepped into the ring, and the torches bent inward as if dragged by gravity. The shadows had teeth now, curling around the soldiers' boots, pinning them still. His eyes were dark storms, jaw tight enough to crack.

"Tomas. Edric. Sera. Brann. Niall," he said, voice low and lethal. "You have three heartbeats to lower your blades."

No one moved.

The shadows surged higher, slick as oil, lapping at their knees. The ground itself seemed to groan, stone shifting under his will. Sparks of lightning skittered faintly through the dark tide, as if the elements themselves bent toward his fury.

"You don't touch her," he snarled, the restraint fraying in his voice. "Not with your grief. Not with your blades. Not *ever* again."

Sera's lips trembled. "We lost him because of her."

The shadows convulsed, snapping higher—sharp tendrils curling up their legs, hungry to drag. For a breath, it looked as though the ring itself might swallow them whole.

Kaden's hand flicked, and the darkness constricted like a noose. "We lost him because the world is cruel. Because Caerthalen hunts us. Because we're still breathing when he isn't. But if you ever turn your weapons inward again..." His voice dropped to a growl, dangerous as the steel they carried. "...I will cut your shadows out where you stand."

Fear cracked through their defiance. Tomas's sword lowered first. One by one, the others followed, faces taut with shame but eyes still bitter.

As they backed away, Niall muttered under his breath, venom sharp: "Of course Kaden saves her."

The shadows surged at the words—fangs snapping, ready to bite.

"Kaden," Cam rasped.

Her voice caught his name like a rope thrown in a storm. His head turned, shadows pausing mid-snarl. She was still on her knees, hair plastered to her face with sweat and blood, pendant pressed hard against her mouth. Her wide eyes locked on him—not afraid but pleading.

Slowly, with a shuddering breath, Kaden forced the darkness back. Inch by inch the tide withdrew, curling into his skin until the torches straightened and the air stilled.

The soldiers slipped away, boots loud in the silence they left behind.

Kaden crouched beside her then, the fury still in his shoulders, his hands shaking from the violence he'd barely leashed. Not reaching. Not yet.

"You could have killed them," he said, his voice ragged from the shadows' strain.

Cam pressed the pendant harder against her lips, knuckles white. "I know."

"Why didn't you?" His tone was still rough, still sharp with leftover fury.

She dragged in one breath, sharp as broken glass. "I heard his voice. He told me not to. He warned me—I... I swear, Kaden, I heard him."

The anger left him all at once, replaced by something heavier. He exhaled long and heavy, shoulders dropping. "We're both still holding on."

Cam almost laughed, but it tangled into a sob, breaking jagged from her throat. "You're still saving me."

For the first time, he reached out. His hand trembled, but it was steady in intent—not rescuer, not commander, but anchor. "No. I'm standing with you."

Her chest ached. Slowly, she lifted her hand from the pendant and placed it in his.

The ring smelled of smoke and storm, blood and restraint. Overhead, the stars stared down cold and merciless, and somewhere far below, Sylithra rumbled—a low, reverberating sound that sank through stone. A sound that might have been mourning. Or warning. Or both.

◈ ☽ ⚡ ☾ ◈

The library had become her refuge. Her prison. Both.

Days folded into each other until she couldn't tell when one ended and the next began. Morning bled into night, night into morning, and always she found herself at the same table—candles guttering, scrolls sprawled, the Book of Unbinding heavy at the center like a stone she couldn't move.

Her body refused to forget the ambush. The cuts along her side still burned when she twisted wrong, and the bruises across her shoulder hadn't faded as quickly as they should have. Normally her wounds sealed fast—too fast, Ben had once muttered—but now they lingered, sore reminders she carried into every hour she spent hunched over parchment.

By dawn she limped through the library doors, bandages stiff beneath her leathers. By midday, sunlight slanted across her papers, and she was still there, lips moving silently as she matched symbol to symbol. By night, she staggered out hollow-eyed, ink streaked across her fingers, the grooves of the pendant chain still cut into her palm.

Val was the only one who stayed close. She never scolded—never told Cam to rest, never tore the quill from her hand. But sometimes Cam would catch her looking. Not with anger. Not even pity. Something worse: the kind of hurt that came from watching a friend bleed where you couldn't reach.

"You're running yourself raw," Val said once, voice low across the table.

Cam's eyes stayed on the scroll, though her grip on the quill shook. "If I stop, he's gone."

Val didn't answer. The silence that followed wasn't doubt—it was grief agreeing in a language neither of them wanted to name.

Everyone else had their own looks. The captains, the scouts, even the healers who passed her in the halls—eyes that slid away too fast, like she was already half a ghost. Like they'd already buried Wyatt and thought she was losing herself by refusing to.

Except Kaden. He didn't say it aloud, but sometimes, when he crossed the library to set down food she hadn't asked for, Cam thought she saw it: a flicker in his face that said he hadn't let go either. That maybe he believed her. Or maybe he was just as unwilling to stop hoping.

Still, the question pressed harder every day, etched into her chest deeper than any wound:

Why do I still hear you?

One night, when the candles had burned to stubs and the hall beyond was silent, she bent over the scrolls, her voice little more than breath.

"If I can find this last part... if I can fit the pieces together... maybe I can unlock the truth. Maybe I'll know why."

She pressed the pendant against her lips until the edges bit deep. "I have to keep going. For him. For all of us."

The silence that answered wasn't empty. It was listening.

Once—just once in those weeks—she left Ember Fortress. Kaden had gone back to Haldrin's Keep to retrieve more scrolls from the old library, and she had gone with him. The journey was a blur, but the moment her boots struck the familiar stone halls, memory struck harder than any wound. Every corridor carried Wyatt's ghost: his laugh echoing off the training yard walls, his hand brushing hers when they had sparred too close, his scarf around her shoulders that bitter winter morning.

Part of her was glad their circle had moved to Ember Fortress. Here, the stone didn't ache with memory. Here, the ghosts were hers alone, not written into the walls.

Still, her feet betrayed her, carrying her to her old quarters before she realized where she was going. The room smelled faintly of dust and pine sap from the old beams, untouched since the day she left it behind. She gathered what little was hers—spare leathers, a dagger, a few tattered pages. She was halfway through the door when her eyes caught on the small desk tucked in the corner.

Her notebook lay there. Thin, battered, the edges curled from nights of candle-smoke. She flipped it once with her thumb—half-sketched diagrams, messy equations, scattered thoughts about how elements might move together if pushed hard enough. Pages she'd written in sleepless fits, never sure if they were worth keeping.

That's when she saw it.

Wyatt's scarf. Draped across the chair as though he'd only just left, as though he'd return any moment to snatch it up with that half-smile that always dared her to scold him.

Her knees nearly buckled. She lifted it slowly, fingers trembling, and pressed it to her chest. The wool still smelled like him—like smoke and frost, leather and pine sap—even after months.

She closed her eyes and held it tighter, the ache in her chest sharper than any wound her body carried.

For a long moment she stood in that doorway, scarf clutched to her chest, notebook heavy in her other hand, as if she had gathered the last pieces of herself scattered in this place. She almost didn't move. Almost stayed there, where memory still lived.

But the keep was only ghosts, and ghosts couldn't keep her warm.

She carried the scarf all the way back to Ember Fortress. Its scent clung to her hands, to the wool pressed tight against her chest—smoke and frost, leather and pine sap. With her other hand, she gripped the notebook until the leather cover bent under her fingers, as if by holding both she could keep what little of Wyatt she had left.

By the time she reached the courtyard, dusk had spread across the mountain, bruising the sky into shadow and fading gold. The fortress murmured behind her—clatter of armor, the dull echo of voices, doors slamming shut as the keep folded itself into night.

Cam lingered near the far wall, scarf wrapped around one arm, pendant tight in her palm. Her hair stirred in the wind, strands lashing her face. The horizon bled thin, the sun dragging itself low until its light looked more like ash than fire.

At first she thought it was just the torches swaying in the draft. But then—a figure at the edge of the courtyard. Tall. Familiar. Shoulders set just so. The tilt of a head that had leaned toward her a hundred times in laughter.

Her throat closed. Wyatt.

She whirled, heart slamming, pendant flashing silver in the torchlight.

Only empty stone. Only shadows.

The wind shifted. It carried a murmur, low and rough, soft enough to scrape like memory yet sharp enough to pierce her.

Careful.

Her knees trembled. She pressed the pendant so hard against her chest that the chain bit her skin. Her breath shook as she whispered into the hollow air, words tearing her lips apart:

"I'm not ready to say goodbye."

The courtyard gave her nothing. Just stone. Just silence. The ashes had always been for the living—and she was the one left to carry them.

Her hand dragged across her face, rough and unsteady. "If you're gone... I'll feel it. I'll know."

The torches hissed. The banners rattled. And then—thin as a thread, a voice she couldn't tell was memory, madness, or something beyond the world.

You always knew where to find me.

Her breath left her in a broken sound, half sob, half laugh, shattering the stillness. She clutched the scarf tighter, pressed the pendant to her lips until the edges cut. As if by bleeding herself against it, she could make him stay.

But when her eyes opened, the courtyard was empty. Only the wind remained, carrying her grief out into the dark.

Chapter 43: The Hollow World

The Concord Chamber brooded in its half-light. Obsidian-veined walls swallowed the fire from the sconces; the Heartshard on the crescent table breathed a faint pulse, silver crawling through stone like veins remembering a heartbeat. Deyric's hands lay still upon the lacquered armrests. Within that stillness, something older smiled.

The doors opened. Boots scraped. A courier bowed so low his forehead nearly touched the floor.

"The elder twin has fallen," the courier said. The chamber rippled with unease.

Lord Arven Corthal's jaw tightened. "Then one Valehart remains—and we should see the other snuffed out before his shadow grows."

Inside Deyric's quiet, Kaelith savored the irony. Fear could be so beautifully accurate when spoken in ignorance.

Murmurs swelled. Banners along the walls barely stirred, as if even the air was cautious in this room.

Corthal leaned forward, gauntlets clicking against the table. "We end this now: the girl, their strategist Corin Veyr, the girl's father—Benjamin Miles, and the surviving Valehart. Before the outlands mistake grief for a standard."

High Magister Selvara merely traced the obsidian with one long finger, eyes hooded. "Strike the girl and you risk the tether unraveling. The Cradle lies in her blood, not in your prisons." She lifted her gaze to meet Deyric's. "Cut the thread, and you may find the Veil cut you back."

Deyric inclined his head, the measured weight of a statesman. Kaelith tasted the chamber's attention tilt toward him, as it always did when the room desired restraint it could trust.

"No assassin can pass where the Veil does not," Deyric said aloud—voice smooth as wet stone.

Inwardly, Kaelith breathed the thought he did not give them: *Test her again. Break her again.*

Selvara's mouth thinned, but she did not press. Corthal did.

"Your caution is noted, Chancellor," Corthal said, "and overruled by necessity. The Outpost chants her name. Dragons bend their necks. One Valehart already lies cold. Shall we wait for his brother to raise an army of shadows?"

A stir, a hiss like wind under doors. The courier flinched.

Another councilor cleared his throat. "We had already employed a knife. The assassin."

Selvara did not bother to hide her disdain. "Alex Draxen returned with little blood on his hands and excuses."

"Summon him," Corthal snapped.

The far doors opened again. Alex stepped into the circle of light and went to one knee. Sweat gleamed at his hairline; his eyes were bright, too bright.

"Speak," Corthal ordered.

Alex lifted his chin. "No one knows her shadow as I do. Give me one reprieve, and I will end her."

He wore desperation like penance and ambition like perfume. Kaelith watched him without pity. The boy thought his hunger his own. In truth, it was a leash, and Kaelith pulled it taut.

Selvara's rings clicked softly. "You failed."

"I learned," Alex said. The words came quick, obedient to a rhythm not entirely his. "Her patterns. Her protectors. Where she bends and where she breaks. Let me finish what you began—or you will find none willing to dirty their hands as I will."

Corthal's stare was flint. "If you falter again, we will cut you where you kneel."

A captain at the rear spoke, voice clipped. "There is...complication. Orren Hail has deserted his post. He refuses Caerthalen banners."

Silence cracked, then broke into a dozen overlapping denials.

"He cannot—"

"Not the Pale Fang—"

"We carved the mage from him—"

"He was perfected—loyal to the marrow—"

The captain's jaw worked, voice hard as iron. "He was one of our finest—suppressed, refined, molded into obedience. For him to turn is...impossible."

Ah, that knife, Kaelith thought. A blade honed so thin the wielder mistook it for his own will. He had watched the girl at work—how the world leaned, unbidden, toward her. She did not ask for loyalty; the world offered it. Even hunters were not immune. *Especially* hunters.

Alex did not waste the opening. "If she slips again," he said, smooth as oil over water, "then let me turn the knife on him. Orren Hail was your blade once—now he cuts against you. Give me command and I will bring you both their heads."

Selvara's gaze flicked to Deyric. "Chancellor."

Deyric rested two fingers on the table's rim, as if feeling the faint tremor of the Heartshard through stone. The chamber waited. He let the quiet lengthen until even Corthal's breath grew rough with impatience.

Measured words. Longer silences. It took so little to move a room toward the choice it already feared it would make.

At last, Deyric said, "The city does not profit from panic. Nor from paralysis."

Corthal seized it. "Then we act."

Selvara's mouth tightened. "And risk the tether."

"Risk," Corthal said, "is the price of rule."

They called the vote. Hands rose like blades.

Kaelith watched them count, the arithmetic of power clicking into place. How eager they were to believe themselves the arbiters of a world they did not understand. How sweet their certainty tasted when it soured into doom.

"The measure passes," the clerk intoned.

Corthal turned to Alex. "One more chance, assassin. Bring us the girl. Failing that, bring us Orren Hail. There will not be a third."

Alex bowed so low his hair brushed the stone. "You will not regret this," he vowed. Yet the flicker in his smile was triumph, not humility.

When the council relented, something warm and hungry filled Alex's chest—like light poured into a hollow cup. He mistook the heat for anointing. Kaelith curled a thought and watched it settle behind the boy's eyes like a second pupil.

"Go," Corthal said.

Alex rose and backed away, that bright hunger walking out beside him like a shadow that hadn't been there before.

The murmurs resumed—the small sounds of men convincing themselves they had done something necessary rather than something irrevocable.

The Heartshard pulsed, once—silver veins brightening, dimming—as if some far-off tide had tugged at it. Deyric closed his eyes. In that breath of darkness, Kaelith settled deeper into the meat and breath of the man, the better to steer his tongue and temper his pauses.

Even now, months later, Valmira still remembered the scream that had split the sky above Ember Fortress. Villagers swore the birds had fled that day and that storms kept their memory like a bruise. They did not know what had broken the air. Kaelith did. He had heard the girl's grief tear at the edges of the world, and the sound lived in him like a promise.

Let them send their knives.

He had other plans for the woman who could open the world.

Chapter 44: The Sound of Breaking

It had been days since the pyre smoke thinned, but the weight of it still clung to her lungs. Patrols were supposed to be routine—ride the ridge, check the passes, nothing more. She had wanted the silence, a chance to breathe, to let the night carry what she couldn't say.

Instead, she got Orren.

He moved like shadow, deliberate and soundless, his coat whispering against stone. Always watching, always measuring. A man molded to see the threat before anyone else could. Tessa hated that about him—the way he noticed everything and spoke almost nothing.

They were three ridges deep when voices carried through the wind. Steel striking steel. Boots crunching over gravel.

Tessa froze, storm prickling along her skin. Nine men. Six soldiers in the Knighthood's black, and three captains with silver at their shoulders. Too many for a patrol this far from Caerthalen. Too many for coincidence.

Orren caught her arm before she moved. His grip was firm, unyielding, but not cruel. "Nine," he whispered. "Outnumbered. We pull back."

She yanked free, sparks already leaping at her fingertips. "Or we end them."

His jaw tightened. "Reckless will get us both killed."

"Then don't follow me."

"Tessa—" His voice was a sharp whisper. "Don't."

The air tightened, tasting of metal.

The storm broke loose.

She stepped into the open, lightning snapping across her arms, striking two soldiers before their swords cleared their scabbards. They dropped smoking to the dirt. Shouts erupted. Blades gleamed in torchlight.

Behind her, Orren swore low, then moved, bowstring singing as an arrow punched clean through a soldier's throat.

The storm rose hotter in her chest, too much, too fast. She gave it teeth. Bolts split stone, scorched earth. She wanted them to hurt. She wanted someone to pay.

"Idiot girl!" one captain bellowed as she tore through his line.

"Better idiot than coward!" she spat and flung another bolt into his chest.

They closed in tighter. Shields locked, blades gleaming. She pushed harder, lightning biting through the seams.

Her storm surged higher, cracking overhead, thunder rattling the pass. Her control slipped. Bolts spat wild, striking rock, nearly catching Orren as he cut down a soldier at her flank.

"Contain it," he snapped, voice like iron. "You'll bring the mountain down on us."

"I can't—" The word ripped out of her before she could stop it, half panic, half plea.

Images flared, unbidden—Wyatt's laugh, gone in an instant. Alex's hand in hers, his betrayal splitting her open. The weight of both pressed on her chest until she couldn't breathe. The storm roared with it, too big for her to hold.

No, not again—

A memory slammed against her ribs. Her father's voice, rough with smoke and anger, echoing from training yards long past:

'Your power is nothing if you can't cage it. Breathe, Tessa. Lock it down or it'll eat you alive.'

Her fists clenched, nails biting her palms. She dragged one shuddering breath through her lungs, forcing the storm inward until it seared her ribs. The crackling dimmed, not gone—never gone—but caged. Barely.

And that's when a captain struck.

His blade cut low, fast, angling straight for her heart. She saw it too late—the glint of steel, the hiss of air breaking across her chest.

Steel met steel.

Orren slammed into the gap between them, his parry brutal enough to send sparks spitting across the dark. The clang rattled her teeth. For a breath he held the man's strength against his own, shoulders locked, every line of him coiled to strike. Then his dagger flashed upward, quick as a snake, and drove under the captain's ribs.

The man choked, a wet sound tearing loose as blood bubbled on his lips. Orren wrenched the blade free, shoved him down with ruthless efficiency.

Another lunged in before the body hit the ground. Orren pivoted, taking the slash across his shoulder—steel bit deep, crimson spilling hot. He didn't falter. His sword slid in low, angled cruel between armor plates, and gutted the man in one clean motion.

By the time Tessa forced breath back into her lungs, six bodies lay at his feet. Blood slicked his sleeve, bruises darkened his jaw, but his stance hadn't faltered.

He turned, gaze sharp, chest heaving. "On your feet."

Her knees still shook. He offered his hand.

"I don't—"

"You do," he said, no edge in his voice this time. Just truth.

Her pride screamed, but her hand rose anyway. He hauled her upright in one sharp pull.

They walked back to Ember Fortress in silence, the storm still smoldering faint in her chest, her pulse jagged.

The infirmary reeked of herbs and iron. Healers worked in terse silence, binding cuts, stitching wounds, clucking curses at recklessness.

Orren sat like carved stone, his shoulder split open, blood seeping through the bandage as a healer's needle bit. He didn't flinch. Not once.

Tessa hated watching. Alex would've cursed at a scratch; Wyatt would've laughed to hide the pain. Orren gave her nothing—just calm, just silence. It unsettled her more than blood ever could.

She caught the faint scent of rain and steel clinging to him—clean, cold, infuriatingly steady—and for a moment it disarmed her more than his blade ever had. She looked away too quickly, cursing the flicker of awareness before it could take root.

When the healers left, the quiet thickened.

"You nearly burned yourself out," Orren said at last, voice low, still not looking at her.

Her jaw snapped tight. "And you nearly got yourself killed for me."

He shrugged, winced as the stitches pulled. "Better me than you."

His gaze lingered a moment too long, not cold, not condemning. Respect, maybe. Warier than she wanted to admit. And for one dizzying moment she thought he feared her storm as much as he respected it.

The words lodged hard in her chest, heavier than any bandage. No mercy in them, no affection—just flat certainty. But certainty she had not expected.

Her throat scraped dry. "You're not my friend," she said, forcing the words into the air. "But you're not the enemy anymore, either."

Finally, his eyes cut toward her. Not triumph, not gloating. Just quiet acknowledgment, like he'd known all along.

For the first time, his expression shifted—just slightly, but enough. A flicker of something she couldn't name, something she didn't want to.

She looked away before the silence pressed too close. But she didn't recoil. Not anymore.

◈ ☽ ⚡ ☾ ◈

The training yard was slick with rain, stone glinting under the guttering torches. Kaden lingered at the edge of the ring, half-hidden in the shadows, watching her.

Cam's blade struck again and again, each motion slower than the last, her body trembling on the edge of collapse. Sweat clung to her face, strands of hair plastered to her cheek, her breath breaking ragged between swings.

He had seen her push herself before, but never like this. Not even when he first met her, raw and untrained, fire spilling uncontrolled at Haldrin's Keep. Back then her determination had burned bright, but it was tempered with laughter, with wonder. Even her mistakes had carried a spark of life.

Not even in those sleepless nights after the Eldvale temple, when she drifted through Ember Fortress like a shadow. After Alex's betrayal, after Wyatt's fall, she had been little more than a ghost—silent, withdrawn, barely eating, refusing to train or fly. She had vanished into herself, and he had thought that silence would break her.

But this—this was something harsher. Every cut of her sword now felt less like training and more like punishment, as if she believed that if she bled enough, if she broke herself enough, she could drag Wyatt back by sheer defiance.

Everyone else whispered she was consumed by grief, that she was losing herself in the silence he left behind. But Kaden knew better. It wasn't grief that kept her moving—it was the refusal to surrender. She clung to the belief that Wyatt was still alive with a ferocity that terrified him.

And it wasn't only Wyatt he feared losing. If she drove herself too far, if she shattered herself in this obsession, then he would lose her too—and he wasn't sure he could carry both absences.

A part of him wanted to believe it as fiercely as she did. He still woke some mornings certain he would find Wyatt in the training yard, hear his voice cutting through the clamor, feel his shoulder brush against his in passing. Sometimes, when the yard was empty, he swore he heard Wyatt's laugh roll off the stone walls. He never told Cam. If it was only memory, he couldn't take that from her. If it was more... he wasn't sure he could bear the hope.

The three of them had always been a circle—Cam, Wyatt, and him. A tether in the storm. Now one side was gone, and the balance tilted, unsteady. Kaden felt it every time he looked at her, every time he tried to hold both ends of a thread that wasn't meant for one person alone.

Part of him wondered if he should have stopped her sooner. But what right did he have, when he hadn't stopped the one loss that mattered most?

Her sword faltered, the tip dragging against stone. She staggered, chest heaving. That was when Kaden stepped forward, his voice rougher than he meant it to be.

"Cam," he said, low but urgent, "this chasing shadows isn't helping anyone. Not you. Not us."

She froze. The rain ticked softly against stone as her shoulders rose and fell, her grip on the hilt so tight her knuckles blanched. She didn't look at him. Didn't answer.

Kaden swallowed, stepped closer, and let his voice drop to a whisper.

"We've always known when the other was hurting. I'd feel it if he were gone... I think I would. But the world keeps telling me I'm wrong."

The words cracked in his chest, leaving him raw. He hated the silence, hated not knowing which was worse—the emptiness of doubt, or the finality of truth.

"I feel like he's still here somehow," he admitted, the sound barely carrying over the hiss of torches. "And that's the hardest part."

Her shoulders sagged. The blade lowered until its tip kissed the wet stone. The fight drained out of her body all at once, leaving only exhaustion—and something heavier she still refused to name.

◈ ☽ ⚡ ☾ ◈

The rain clung to her lashes, sliding down her cheeks until she couldn't tell what was water and what was tears. Her sword tip scraped stone, but she couldn't bring herself to sheath it. If she let go, even for a breath, the silence would rush in again.

Kaden's words pierced through anyway. *Chasing shadows isn't helping anyone.*

Her chest clenched, the truth of it sharp as a blade. Still, she kept her gaze fixed on the ground. Speaking would make it real and real meant fragile. Real meant someone could try to take it away.

"I don't see him like I used to," she whispered, surprised at the sound of her own voice. It came out cracked, as if unused. "But in the corner of shadows... sometimes I catch a shape. A movement. Like he's just beyond reach."

Her throat burned. She had told no one this. Not Ben, who would try to bury her grief under his silence. Not Val, who would watch her too closely with those wounded eyes. Not Tessa, who would turn pain into fire and force her to admit what she wasn't ready to say. She had kept it caged because once spoken, it could be stolen.

But Kaden—he wouldn't strip it from her. He would just hear it.

"I hear him," she went on, voice breaking on the words, "in my dreams, in the quiet—and sometimes I see him, just out of sight."

Her hand found the pendant at her throat, clutching it so tightly the chain cut into her palm. The bite of pain steadied her, but also made the words come harsher, louder. "The silence isn't empty. It's filled with what I can't hold on to yet."

A faint hum stirred in her mind—Wyatt's voice, gentle, impossible: *Keep moving, Cam.*

Her lips twitched, almost a smile. Almost. She blinked hard until the tears blurred it away. She couldn't let Kaden see her break like that. Not fully.

Kaden's hand settled on her shoulder, warm even through damp fabric. The touch jolted her, and she flinched before forcing herself still. *It's not Wyatt's hand,* her chest ached, *but it's someone. And I need that.*

"Maybe hope is all we have left," Kaden murmured, his voice rough with restraint, "and that might be enough for now."

She nodded faintly, throat tight, but before she could retreat back into herself, he pulled her into his arms. For a heartbeat she resisted, body rigid. But then she felt it—the tremor running through him. He was shaking, trying to hold everything in the way she did.

And then he broke. His breath hitched, and he crumpled against her, the sob clawing raw from his chest.

Cam's own tears came slower, quieter, her storm locked tight behind her ribs. Not because she didn't want to break, but because she couldn't—not yet. Holding Kaden steady felt heavier, more urgent. Her hands trembled as she pressed them to his back, anchoring him as best she could. Every second she kept her grief pressed down felt like fire under her skin, an ache that burned so hot it nearly made her gasp.

But she didn't let it out. She couldn't. If she opened the dam, she feared she'd never stop.

When the storm in him dulled to silence, they turned back toward Ember Fortress together. The pines loomed tall and dark, the air sharp with autumn's first bite. Their footsteps echoed side by side, steady, fragile.

Cam glanced back once. The trees shifted in the wind, and for a breath she swore she heard a second set of steps—familiar, impossible.

Stay with me... please.

And in the pause that followed, thin as thread, came the voice she both longed for and feared:

You know where to find me.

The first night after Kaden's words, she almost believed him. Almost. His hand on her shoulder, the way he had held on even as he broke—it had been enough to quiet the storm for a breath. For that one night, she let herself lean on his strength.

But hope was fragile, a spark smothered too easily.

The second night, the silence pressed in again.

By the third, she couldn't lay still long enough to sleep.

And so the library became her cage.

Nights stretched long, stretching her thin with them. Shelves hunched around her like witnesses while candlelight guttered low, shadows bleeding across the stone floor.

The Book of Unbinding lay open before her, the Veilbind scrolls sprawled in untidy arcs. Her fingers traced faded runes until they ached, joints stiff from hours hunched over parchment. Lips shaped words too old for the tongue, fragments that tasted of ash when she whispered them aloud.

"If I can just fit this together..." she murmured, knuckles smudged with ink, nails bitten raw. "There has to be something I'm missing."

A breath stirred against her ear. *You're so close, Cam.*

Her head snapped up. Candles guttered. Shadows only. No one there.

Her heart slammed so hard it rattled her ribs. The silence pressed in, thick as stone. She shoved the book aside, pages crumpling beneath her hands, and staggered to her feet. She couldn't sit with it—couldn't sit with *him*—not when he was nowhere, everywhere.

The training yard took her next. Steel rang against the night as she cut at invisible foes, strikes wild, breath ragged. She pushed until her muscles screamed, until exhaustion dragged her down like chains around her ankles.

But the whispers returned anyway.

Breath on her neck when no one stood behind her. Shadows twitching in the corners of her sight, darting just beyond reach. She told herself it was memory. But memory didn't follow this closely. Memory didn't answer.

One night, she found herself in the courtyard, sword sheathed, scarf wrapped tight around her shoulders. The torches hissed in the wind, light clawing at the stone walls as if trying to hold the dark at bay.

"I don't know if you're alive," she said aloud, her voice cracking raw. The sound startled her—thin, trembling, almost foreign. "I can't feel you. I can't see you. But I hear you."

The silence seemed to lean in, heavy and watchful.

Then—faint, soft, impossible—Wyatt's voice: *Then don't let go.*

Her chest collapsed inward. Tears blurred her vision until the torches smeared gold across stone. She clutched the pendant at her throat like it could anchor her to the world.

"If you're gone..." she whispered, the words clawing out of her, "...tell me."

Silence answered. Crushing. Suffocating.

Her knees gave, striking stone hard. The pendant cut deep into her palm, leaving ridges that burned. Above her, the night pressed down like a weight, indifferent to her breaking.

The world was quiet. But her heart still beat to a rhythm she could almost hear—*one step, one hope, one thread left unbroken.*

Chapter 45: Flickers and Whispers

The fortress at night was never silent. Torches hissed in the corridors, banners sighed in the drafts that slipped through stone, and somewhere far above, dragons turned in their sleep, their weight shuddering faintly through the walls.

Orren walked them anyway. He always did when his mind refused rest.

He thought of her again. The woman with sparks in her hands and fire in her voice. Tessa Rhalis. He told himself she was a distraction, an irritation that should have burned out after the deadly spar months ago. Yet her words still clung to him—sharp, cutting, and worse, they didn't wound. They stayed.

A memory rose, unbidden: days ago in the training yard. Rain had slicked the stone, torches sputtering low. He had stepped in her path without thinking.

"You watch too much for a man who says so little," she had snapped, her braid plastered damp against her shoulder.

"And you talk too much for someone who hasn't bested me," he had replied, flat but edged.

She'd smirked, wicked. "Not yet. But when I do, I'll make sure you remember it."

Something in her voice had unsettled him—not threat, but certainty. Her green eyes had sparked like a storm brewing, and against his will, he had felt the faintest pull in his chest. Not fear. Not anger. Something worse: anticipation.

He had walked away then, because staying might have meant answering her with something he wasn't ready to name. And now, in the lonely dark, the echo of her voice still prowled the edges of his mind.

He hated how much peace her chaos left behind.

A torch guttered as he passed, light catching against the steel clasp on his arm. He turned a corner—and stopped.

Through the half-open door of the library, a candle still burned. Inside, hunched over a table strewn with scrolls, sat Cam.

Her hair fell loose around her face, shadows pooled beneath her eyes. The Book of Unbinding lay open in front of her, runes scattered like broken teeth across parchment. The air smelled of ink, old parchment, and smoke that clung to stone. It pressed down heavy, oppressive with the hush of words that had waited too long to be read. She spoke low, words he couldn't catch at first—then he realized she was speaking to someone.

His pulse hitched. No one else was there.

"You talk to the pages like they will answer back," Orren said, voice breaking the hush as he stepped inside.

Cam jerked upright, hand snapping to the pendant at her throat as though it could shield her.

"They've given me more answers than most people have," she said, guarded.

He let the door click shut behind him. For a long moment he only watched her, the way exhaustion had carved her thin, every angle of her face sharpened like a blade worn too long. Where Tessa unsettled him with fire and defiance, Cam did it with quiet—an unyielding grief that refused to be hidden, even when she tried. Both made him feel the same gnawing thing he hated: that his own edges were not as solid as he thought.

"I don't know why you saved my life," he said at last. "But I owe you mine."

Her jaw tightened, but her voice was quiet when it came. "Maybe I wasn't ready to watch someone else die."

That struck sharper than he expected. He held her gaze, then forced the words out. "The Capital made me into a weapon. Hollowed me out. I thought that was all I could be." His voice dropped, rougher. "And then you—" He cut himself off, shaking his head. "Something shifted."

She looked back to the parchment, thumb rasping over the chain at her throat. "Don't turn me into your redemption. You'll regret it."

"I had a family once," Orren said, the admission torn out like a splinter. "An older brother. A mother who sang. A little sister, Sarah." The name lodged sharp in his throat. "They're gone. But the hollow they left never closed. I carry it still."

Cam's shoulders stiffened. For the first time, she lifted her eyes and let him see past the walls for a heartbeat. Grief flickered there—recognition, not pity.

He swallowed, softer now. "If you'll let me, I can help. With this." He nodded toward the scrolls. "I can't promise answers. But I can promise I won't leave you alone with them."

Her silence stretched, heavy as stone. Then, at last, she pushed the scroll toward him. Not an invitation, not yet. But not refusal either.

"I don't need saving," she murmured, eyes already back on the text.

"Neither do I," he said, taking the seat beside her.

The torchlight blurred their shadows together across the table as they bent over the pages.

For the first time in years, Orren felt something he couldn't name. Not allegiance. Not command. Something quieter. Belonging, perhaps—or the beginning of it.

Cam shifted, her hand still tight on the pendant. She flinched, as if hearing something he could not, a whisper brushing close enough to steal her breath.

He said nothing. Only turned another scroll beneath the candlelight.

The war room smelled of wax, ink, and dust. Scrolls and maps cluttered the table in uneven stacks; their corners curled from the breath of too many sleepless nights. The candles burned low, their light catching on iron pins that marked passes and provinces like wounds across parchment.

Ben leaned over the table, his shoulders bowed under a weight Corin knew too well. His voice cracked as though dragged over gravel.

"The cradle temple isn't west. I remember it now—north. Isabella and I were there, years ago." His finger traced the frozen coast, knuckles whitening with the force of it. "Gods, Corin, we've been led wrong this whole time. I should tell her."

Corin's eyes lingered on that hand—scarred, trembling—and then on the map itself. The ridges he knew. The coast he had dreamed. His stomach pulled tight with unease. He had seen it, once, in fragments: stone collapsing, shadows spilling, a scream he still heard when the fortress quieted. He had thought it was foresight. But Wyatt had fallen anyway.

He folded his hands on the table, careful, deliberate. "Camomile doesn't need another ghost to chase."

Ben's head snapped up, eyes flaring. "She needs the truth."

Truth. Corin almost laughed, but the sound would have been bitter. Truth had betrayed him before. Truth had let him watch his sister die, let him trust visions that arrived too late to save the boy he had raised like a son.

"Truth without certainty can burn as deep as any lie," he said instead. His tone was calm, flat stone over running water—the voice that stilled soldiers and quieted rooms. "What if your memory falters? What if the temple is nothing but ruin? If we drive her north on half a chance, she will break herself chasing it."

Ben's breath hissed between his teeth. "And if we wait too long?"

Corin felt the question like a blade. Too long was already carved into his bones. He pressed his palm flat to the map, steadying against its tremor. "Then we wait with purpose. Let her decode the scrolls. She has her mother's gift for it—and her own fire besides. When she holds the answer in her hands, then we will move. Not before."

The silence that followed was heavier than any council chamber he had ever stood in. The candles guttered. Far above, the fortress timbers groaned as dragons shifted in their sleep.

Ben's jaw worked, his anger cracked through with something rawer. "I don't like this," he muttered.

"Nor do I," Corin admitted quietly. His voice softened, though the steel beneath remained. "But leadership isn't about what we like. It's about what the world demands."

Ben gathered the map, folding it hard enough to crease the ink, and turned for the door. His boots rang against stone, the sound sharp, hollow, like a retreat in all but name.

Corin did not move. His gaze stayed on the black ink coastlines, the ridges that cut like scars across the page. His fingers hovered above the mark Ben had made, wanting to press down, to claim certainty.

He drew his hand back instead.

Visions lie, he told himself. Or worse—they tell the truth too late.

Sometimes silence was mercy. Sometimes restraint was survival.

And yet, as the last candle sputtered low, guilt gnawed at him, sharp as teeth in the dark.

The library was hushed but not empty. Shadows breathed in the rafters, wax guttered down to the last inch, and smoke curled faintly like ghosts from a dozen burned-out candles. Ben's boots whispered over stone, but even that seemed too loud.

Cam lay slumped at the far table, parchment spread like fallen leaves around her. The Book of Unbinding sat open, its spine groaning under her weight. She had driven herself past the point of exhaustion again, not training her body but hollowing herself in the hunt for answers. That was what frightened him most—that her fire burned inward as much as out.

Her hair fell loose across the pages, strands catching faint gold where the candle still burned. Ink smudged her fingers and cheek, tiny stains that marked just how far she'd gone tonight. He could almost see Isabella in her—the same bowed head over parchment, the same unyielding devotion to truths half the world had forgotten. But there was something harder in Cam's posture. That was his reflection: stubbornness, grit that cut until it bled. The silver glinted faintly at her throat, the chain tight in her fist even in sleep.

Skylith's voice stirred like coals deep in his chest. *She is burning herself hollow, Forgeheart. Will you let her?*

His throat tightened. "What choice do I have?"

He stepped closer, quiet as he could manage, though every board seemed to creak louder under his weight. Skylith stirred faintly at the back of his mind, a low, embered rumble. *You ache because you see her as both child and storm. You cannot hold both forever.*

"I know," he whispered.

Cam shifted in her sleep, breath catching. A murmur slipped from her lips, ragged, so soft he almost missed it. One word. One name.

"Wyatt."

The sound gutted him.

He saw again the boy's easy grin, his reckless devotion, the way Cam's eyes had lit differently when he was near. Now it was only silence. Silence, and her muttering his name like a prayer she couldn't let die.

Ben braced his hands on the table's edge, leaning into the weight of it. He wanted to wake her, to tell her everything—that the temple wasn't west but north, that he had walked there with Isabella, that he would see her safely to its doors himself if that's what it took. He wanted to give her the truth because he had kept too many lies already.

But what if the temple was gone? What if his memory was warped by years of blood and dust, by grief that rewrote the edges of places and faces alike? What if he told her, and she staked her soul on it, only to find ruin? He had seen how obsession already hollowed her—he couldn't be the hand that pushed her deeper.

Corin's words echoed, sharp as steel: *Truth without certainty can burn as deep as any lie.*

He almost spat at that. Corin played strategy like a game of stones; Ben carried scars of every piece lost. But even so, the thought needled him. What if silence this time was protection, not betrayal?

And then, the sharper thought—the one he couldn't shake. He had sworn, once, that there would be no more lies between them. No more secrets. No more silence. He told himself this wasn't a lie. Just a delay. Just waiting for certainty. But silence, he knew too well, could cut as deep as any blade.

He drew a wool blanket from a nearby chair, heavy and smelling faintly of lavender where the healers had stored it. Gently, he draped it across her shoulders. She stirred at the touch, brow furrowing, but did not wake. For a heartbeat, he let his hand linger, brushing a strand of hair back from her temple. A father's reflex.

"I promised you truth," he whispered. His voice snagged on the words, softer than any soldier's vow. "And I keep my promises—just never soon enough."

The words tasted bitter. A half-truth. A delay. The very kind of silence he had sworn he would never use against her. He swore to Cam he'd never be that man again—yet here he was, letting fear weigh his tongue.

Skylith's presence pressed close, sorrow threaded through her flame. *Truth delayed is still a wound.*

Ben drew back, shoulders heavy, and forced himself to turn away. The candle sputtered, throwing shadows over the parchment, over Cam's sleeping face, over the words she had nearly bled herself dry to uncover.

He left her there in the half-light, dreaming of the boy she had lost and the path he hadn't found the courage to give her.

◈ ☽ ⚡ ☾ ◈

The days bled together after that. Ben's silence held, but Cam's nights grew longer, heavier. Sleep gave her no rest—only shadows that sharpened at the edges of the quiet. Silence pressed sharp against her ribs, and the weight of the fortress above her felt like it might collapse into her chest. Rest belonged to others. For her, the dark only made the emptiness louder.

She caught him in the corners first. A flicker at the end of the corridor, a tall shadow crossing the training yard just as she turned her head. Never clear. Never solid. Just enough to hollow her chest.

Each time her breath hitched, her throat tightening around the same word.

"Wyatt?"

No answer. Only the whisper of torches and the ache of her own hope.

In the chambers and narrow stairwells, it was worse. His voice threaded through the hush, too familiar to dismiss—low reassurances, half a joke, sometimes even her name. Sometimes it folded perfectly into memory, a night at the Outpost or a ride through rain. Other times it was nothing she could recall, sharp as an intrusion, like words he might have spoken had he been here.

She pressed her fists to her ears once, whispering back, "Stop." But the silence that followed was worse.

The pendant at her throat became her anchor. Its silver edge bit into her palm when she clutched it too tight, but there were moments it seemed to answer—warming faintly against her skin, as if it remembered more than she did. That terrified her almost as much as it soothed.

"Don't let go of me," she breathed into the chain, the words a plea she didn't dare shape louder.

Now and then, something reached back. A breeze across her hair in a room with closed windows. A brush of warmth against her cheek when no one was near.

Once, when she clutched the pendant too tight, Sylithra stirred faintly in the back of her mind, a low ripple of unease, as if the dragon had felt a thread tighten somewhere she couldn't see. Cam ignored it, told herself it was nothing.

She closed her eyes once, heart hammering, and reached toward it—fingers trembling, desperate. For a breath, warmth brushed her skin, so real she almost gasped. She could almost feel the shape of a hand meeting hers, the weight of someone standing just beyond sight.

Her chest tightened. For that instant, it was comfort. It was him.

And yet—something in the sensation made her flinch, a shiver racing down her spine. Too cold at the edges, too hollow beneath the warmth, like a shadow pretending at flesh.

Then it broke.

Her fingers closed on nothing.

The silence pressed tighter. And then—faint, impossible—the soft rhythm of footsteps, as though someone paced the chamber with her. She held her breath, ears straining, but the sound stopped the moment she tried to follow it.

Frustration cut through her ribs sharper than grief. She wanted to scream, but the sound locked inside her chest.

She sat at her window, forehead pressed to the cold glass, the stars cutting sharp against the black of night. Below, the forest sighed in the wind. Behind her, the fortress slept.

A whisper slid into the quiet, faint as the breath of a dream: *I'm still here. Don't forget me.*

Her hand clenched around the pendant, hard enough the chain burned her skin. Tears stung, but she swallowed them back.

The night gave her no answers, *only echoes*—and still she listened, heart straining toward every whisper.

Chapter 46: Echoes in the Trees

The fortress woke slow in the cold. Dawn bled pale through narrow windows, more shadow than light, and the air carried the bite of autumn. Ember Fortress always felt like it was bracing—stone walls drawn tight against what pressed from outside, the people inside braced against what pressed from within.

Val rose before the others. She always did. Routine was survival. She laced her boots, checked her knives, braided her hair tight, and made her way to the roosts where Virellan waited.

The dragon's scales caught the weak light like storm glass, dark purple veined with silver, her long body coiled but restless. The tether hummed low, tension vibrating under Val's skin.

The air tastes wrong, Virellan murmured, her voice a deep current sliding under Val's thoughts. Storms in the distance. Or something worse.

"Always worse," Val muttered back, pressing her palm against the ridge of Virellan's neck. Her dragon leaned into it, but the unease didn't fade.

She tended her quickly, tightening straps, checking her wings for snags, counting feed portions against what remained of their stores. Small things. Things she could control. Because if she kept moving, kept her hands busy, she didn't have to feel the weight settling over them all.

When she returned to the fortress halls, the weight was everywhere.

Ben stood in the training yard, blade sheathed but shoulders locked tight, as though waiting for a fight that wouldn't come. Kaden sat on the wall's edge, hands idle for once, eyes fixed on something too far away for anyone else to see. Tessa had worn herself out again—sparring until sweat streaked her temples, until her sparks flared unsteady and guttered.

And Cam—

Val's stomach twisted when she passed the library door. A sliver of candlelight slipped into the hall, catching the hunched outline of Cam over a table buried in parchment. Her hair fell loose across her shoulders, her hand clenched around Wyatt's pendant as if it could stop her from unraveling. She didn't even look up as Val moved by, lips forming silent words, a mutter that could have been spell, or memory, or both.

"Still burning herself hollow," Val whispered under her breath.

She chases what cannot be caught, Virellan replied, her voice edged with sorrow. And when she cannot catch it, it will devour her.

The fortress breathed like it was holding its own silence.

It broke when the scouts arrived.

Two of them, wind-bitten and ragged, staggered through the gates and into the war room with news. Rian—sharp-eyed, quick as a kestrel—and Garen, broader, quieter, his beard crusted with frost. Their words carried down the hall, enough to pull Val in their wake.

Inside, Corin and Ben stood bent over the maps. Scrolls lay scattered across the table, corners curled, candles burning low. The scouts shoved parchment aside with hands still shaking from cold.

"Faint magical residue," Rian reported, her voice raw from hours of flight. "Molwyn Forest, near half-buried stonework. Stronger than anything we've felt outside a temple."

"Not natural," Garen added quickly. "We tested it. It clings to the air like rot."

Val felt her shoulders lock. Molwyn. Of all places.

Karethwyn might be vast, older than memory itself, but Molwyn was different. Smaller, yes, but older in another way—its roots wound deeper, its shadows heavier, its secrets sharper. Even the old maps marked it with warnings. There had always been malice in that forest, a place where travelers vanished, where even dragons flew wide.

Her stomach sank, the word sour in her mouth. "Molwyn?" she said, stepping closer to the table. "You're certain?"

Rian nodded, pale beneath her windburn. "I swear it, Valerie. We nearly turned back twice—the air felt... wrong."

"Not just wrong," Garen added. His gaze flicked to Val as if to confirm it. "Watched."

Corin's expression stayed unreadable, but his eyes narrowed, steel catching the candlelight. Ben leaned closer, tapping the jagged line of the forest as though trying to pin it to the page.

Val's unease sharpened. "If there's stonework there, it isn't random. That forest buries what it doesn't want found." She glanced at Corin, then Ben. "And if residue lingers that strong, it means someone—or something—wanted it uncovered."

Virellan stirred uneasily, a ripple of storm through their bond. It smells of endings.

Val's stomach knotted. She didn't answer aloud, only pressed her palm flat against the table, steadying herself.

Ben leaned closer to the map, his own frown cutting deep. "Or traps."

For once, Val didn't disagree. If the first temple had nearly broken them, why did this one feel less like discovery and more like an invitation?

◈ ☽ ⚡ ☾ ◈

The library smelled of ink and fatigue. Candle smoke curled low, heavy in the stale air, clinging to her throat like ash. Scrolls littered the table like bones, fragile and accusing, every line of rune a reminder of how close she was. Too close.

Her vision blurred as she traced the same markings for the hundredth time. The Veilbind scrolls were unraveling under her hands, their meaning slipping into shape like threads knotting into a web—but one strand was missing. One word, one reference, one link in the chain. She felt it in her bones: without that piece, the rest was nothing but air.

She shoved back from the table, chair legs screeching against stone. Her hand dragged down the spines of the shelf until her fingers stopped on the gap where the book should have been. Not there. Her stomach turned cold. She knew she'd seen it, though—the battered leather spine of *The Rune-Lexicon of First Tongues*, set aside in the war room near a scatter of maps.

Her breath hissed out. "Of course."

She turned toward the door.

A whisper brushed her ear. Not memory. Not imagined. Too close, warm enough that the hairs on her neck rose.

Don't go.

Her heart slammed against her ribs. She spun, pendant clutched tight, eyes scanning the library's dim corners. Empty. Only shelves. Only shadows.

Her throat locked, then loosened just enough for a rasp, almost against her will: "I'm not."

The word hung in the hush. She stood there, trembling, waiting for a flicker—warmth, sound, something. For a hand at her shoulder, for the voice to return. Nothing. The silence pressed harder, heavy enough to hurt.

The pendant at her throat pulsed faintly with heat, a single throb against her palm as though it had answered. Hope twisted sharp and cruel through her chest. She swallowed it back, forced her legs to move.

The corridor stretched before her, torchlight dragging long shadows that clung to her heels. She tried not to imagine footsteps following, tried not to glance over her shoulder as she pushed on toward the war room.

The door stood ajar. Inside, Corin, Ben, and Val leaned over the map table with two scouts, their voices clipped and urgent. Candles guttered across parchment crowded with lines of coast and mountain. Words carried sharp and clear into the hall before she slipped in.

"...residue along stone foundations," Rian reported, her voice ragged with cold. "Not fading—pooling, as if drawn there."

Garen's voice added, low and wary: "And near old stonework. Half-swallowed by the earth but still marked."

Cam's pulse jumped.

She murmured quickly, "Looking for a book," and edged past, keeping to the room's borders. Their gazes brushed her once, brief as flint striking stone, then returned to the maps. That suited her. It left her hidden in plain sight.

Her hands sifted through a stack of neglected volumes in the corner until her fingers found it: cracked leather, brittle pages—*The Rune-Lexicon of First Tongues*. She pulled it free and crouched low, flipping it open on her knee, the candlelight crawling across its yellowed vellum.

Columns of runes marched down the page; their meanings scrawled in cramped script. She turned past entries until one caught her breath short.

"Keirash: foundation, cradle, hollow beneath."

Notes scrawled beside it: Marked where residue gathers, unable to pass through. Often near ancient stonework.

Her breath stuck.

Stone foundations. Residue that clung instead of fading. Exactly what the scouts had described. Exactly the gap she had been searching for.

The book slid hot under her fingers as if she'd burned herself on the discovery. The translation was whole now. Complete. She had found it.

A pulse under her wrist, sharp as if someone had pressed a brand against her skin. Heat flared beneath the leather strap, searing through scar and bone alike. Cam's breath hitched, eyes flying shut.

No. Not now.

The mark. The one she'd kept hidden for months, silent as though it had died with Wyatt. It hadn't burned like this since Alex's sly words back at Haldrin's Keep—always there, always waiting, but muted. Quiet. Until now.

Her fingers clawed at the strap as panic coiled in her gut. For a heartbeat she swore she felt it thrum with something outside her—like breath drawn in, like attention turning.

No voice. No words. Just pressure. Watching.

Sylithra stirred in the back of her mind, a ripple of unease pressing against her thoughts.

Little Flame? The dragon's voice edged with concern, as though she had felt the spike too.

Cam swallowed hard, forcing her will down like a lock snapping shut. She shoved the flare deep, sealing it off before Sylithra could press closer.

"I'm fine," she whispered into the bond, quick and sharp. Too quick.

Silence followed, heavy with doubt.

She pressed her palm hard into the pages, grounding herself against the vellum's weight, dragging the flare down, caging it with sheer will. Breath by breath it dulled, but the phantom heat lingered, a brand beneath her skin.

Her throat rasped in a whisper to herself. "It doesn't matter." The words scraped like glass, but she forced them out. "This is it. It has to be."

She looked back at the text, willing her pulse to steady. If she held to this—if Molwyn was the key—then maybe the mark's flare was nothing but nerves. A ghost pain.

But the hollow twisting in her chest said otherwise.

She shut the book quickly, clutching it to her chest as though the others might read the truth in her eyes.

This was it. The missing piece.

◈ ☽⚡☾ ◈

The war room hadn't quieted after the scouts' report. Voices tangled sharp across the table, parchment shifting as Corin moved markers, Ben pacing hard enough that his boots clipped stone. The tension felt alive—less like a council and more like a storm circling its eye.

Corin's tone cut steady through the noise. "We wait. We gather more from the scrolls first. Sending anyone into Molwyn blind is risk without reason."

Ben's reply was harsher, rawer. "Risk is waiting while something festers. You heard them—the residue isn't fading. If there's stonework there, it could already be opening. Do we stand still and let it?"

Val lingered just inside the arc of firelight, Virellan's presence pressing restless at the back of her mind. Every word made her jaw clench tighter. Waiting meant giving Molwyn room to grow teeth. Acting meant walking straight into its mouth. Neither choice sat clean.

The scouts still hovered near the doorway, exchanging nervous glances, as if half-ready to be dismissed and half-afraid to step back into the cold. Ben caught sight of them and snapped, "Find the others. Tessa, Orren—Kaden too. If this turns to planning, I want all of them here."

Rian and Garen nodded quickly and slipped out, boots ringing against the hall stone.

For a few minutes the room breathed in uneasy silence. Corin sorted markers with slow precision, Ben paced like a wolf against the walls, and Val traced every line of the Molwyn forest with her eyes, feeling its weight coil closer. Cam stood apart in the shadows, Lexicon clutched tight to her chest, her gaze fixed on the table as though already translating the debate into an answer.

The scouts returned, ushering in three more figures—Tessa with her braid loose and sparks still twitching along her fingertips, Orren moving with his usual shadowed caution, and Kaden slipping in last, quiet but watchful.

Val's eyes caught on Orren a moment too long. Months ago, she had sworn she would never stomach his presence—mage hunter, weapon of the

Capital, the kind of man whose order had butchered her brother without a thought. The hatred had come easy then. It still burned, but not as clean.

Because over the weeks since Wyatt's death, she had watched. She'd seen him bleed on patrol, hold silence when others snapped, move with a discipline that had nothing to do with cruelty. He wasn't the cold killer she had painted him as, though she couldn't yet bring herself to trust what she saw.

Tessa no longer flinched when he stood near; sparks crackled sharp around everyone but him. Ben and Corin had let him closer into their circles, weighing him not as enemy but as soldier. Even Kaden treated him with a casualness Val couldn't name—wary, but not dismissive.

Orren still felt like a shadow in the room, but not the kind cast by knives. Different. Human, in ways she hadn't expected.

And it stung, because Cam had seen it first.

"What did we miss?" Kaden asked, tone clipped, though his gaze went first to Cam before it flicked to the map.

Corin didn't pause his careful adjustments of the markers. "Molwyn," he said simply. "Scouts found residue. Strong. Along old stonework."

Tessa grimaced. "That forest again." She stepped closer, sparks dying against her skin, and added, "Then let's stop circling it and cut the thing open before it festers worse."

Orren said nothing, but his presence at the table was a shadow all its own—still not trusted, still not dismissed.

Ben folded his arms, voice hard. "Exactly. We can't wait this out. If it's a temple, if it's already stirring, hesitation is the trap."

Corin's eyes flicked to Cam, then back to the map. "And if we walk in blind, that trap will close on us before we know it's there."

The words hung heavy, thick enough that Val could feel Virellan's hum against her skin.

At the edge of the room, Cam's voice cut through. Low, even, but with flint behind it.

"If there's something waiting, we need to see it before it sees us."

The words landed sharp. Corin's gaze flicked toward her, unreadable. Ben exhaled as if he'd been waiting for her to say it.

Val's gut twisted. Cam wasn't reckless for once. She was deliberate. And that was worse. Cam stood rigid in the half-shadow, the Lexicon clutched so tightly against her chest that her knuckles blanched white. Her face was set, but her shoulders betrayed the tension—like she was holding something in, one breath away from breaking silence she didn't dare.

Kaden's eyes hadn't left her. Not once since she'd spoken. He didn't shift, didn't blink, his whole focus narrowed on her as though he could read what she wasn't saying. His silence pressed just as sharp as her words.

Corin broke it first. "A small party, then. No more. We scout, we confirm, and we return."

"Dragons only," Ben added, his tone iron. "We don't risk more than we have to."

The plan began to take shape, piece by piece, every choice sounding heavier than it should.

"Cam and Sylithra lead," Corin said, his eyes still narrowed, as if testing her resolve.

Cam gave a single nod, silent.

"Tessa and Brontheus follow second," Ben said, glancing toward her. His gaze shifted toward Orren. "And he rides with her. If he's to stay among us, let him prove his loyalty where we can see it."

Orren's expression didn't change, but he inclined his head once—silent assent, soldier's acknowledgment.

"Valerie and Virellan," Corin continued. "You take the air. Keep the sky clear, keep eyes where theirs cannot reach."

Val inclined her head. "We'll see everything before they do."

"And Ben," Corin finished. "You and Skylith anchor the rear. The last shield if this turns wrong."

Ben's jaw clenched, but he didn't argue. "It always does," he muttered.

The room held its breath for a beat, the weight of the plan settling like stone.

Val felt the tether hum through her blood as Virellan's voice curled close. *This forest will not welcome you.*

"I know," she answered silently, jaw tightening.

Kaden's gaze still hadn't left Cam since the moment she volunteered. His jaw was tight, his hands flexing once at his sides before stilling. When the others began to disperse, he moved closer to Val, low enough that only she caught his words.

"Keep an eye on her." His voice was low, strained—part warning, part plea.

Val met his gaze, steady. "I will."

But as the council broke apart and she felt Cam's shadow pass toward the roosts, unease coiled tighter in her chest. It was the kind of feeling she hated most—the sense that the forest they hadn't yet entered was already listening.

◈ ☽ ⚡ ☾ ◈

The sun had started to set by the time the dragons left Ember Fortress behind. Their wings carved the sky in steady rhythm, the dragonlink thrumming faint and taut between riders like a living cord of thought.

They curved south over the jagged sweep of the Valthorne range, autumn cliffs blazing red and gold before plunging into shadowed valleys. The mountains broke at last into the darker line of Molwyn. From above, the forest spread green-black and endless, its canopy clenched tight like a fist against the sky. Light barely pierced the boughs. The wind dulled there, swallowed whole by the trees as though the air itself wanted to vanish.

Virellan rumbled, her voice sliding under Val's skin through the bond. *It smells of endings.*

Val pressed her lips thin. "Even the dragons don't want to be here," she murmured aloud, the words nearly stolen by the wind.

Ahead, Cam and Sylithra sliced through the air with merciless intent. Cam leaned into the saddle, body drawn sharp as an arrow, diving into the pathless sky as if daring it to break against her. Her braid snapped behind her like a banner of defiance.

Val's chest tightened. *"She flies like she doesn't care if she falls."*

Or perhaps she hopes she does, Virellan whispered, quiet thunder in her mind.

Val didn't answer.

Behind them, Brontheus held formation, his storm-slick wings beating hard. His growl rolled over the dragonlink, low and warning, every rider feeling it vibrate through their bones. Sparks danced faintly across his shoulders, tethered lightning barely restrained.

Tessa sat tall in the saddle, jaw clenched, her hand brushing Brontheus's neck as though soothing him—though Val saw the sparks twitch across her knuckles. Orren rode pillion, still as a statue. He didn't speak, but his eyes cut ceaselessly below, tracking every shadow and sway of the trees with a soldier's patience. He didn't need a dragon to radiate unease.

Skylith brought up the rear with Ben, the great dragon's flame-colored wings fanning sparks through the tether. Skylith's presence flared warm in the link, steady but taut, her embered breath curling through Ben's steady silence.

The first marks came quick.

Old, jagged stonework jutted from the canopy like the spines of a buried beast, broken bones of some ruin half-swallowed by roots.

Then: claw marks along the trunks, gouges raw and fresh, sap bleeding pale in the light. Mirebat corpses sprawled in the clearings below, wings torn and twisted, their bodies picked apart as though something had hunted them—but not eaten, not clean. Just ruined.

Brontheus growled again, louder this time, his thunder shaking the tether. *Not natural. Not right.*

Val's jaw set. *"Agreed."*

Cam didn't answer, but Val saw her knuckles whiten against Sylithra's harness. The younger dragon's voice curled faintly into the link, molten and sharp*: Something moves below.*

Orren shifted behind Tessa, his shoulders tensing as his head tracked left, then right. At last he spoke, his voice cutting out loud across the wind. "They're circling us. I don't see them, but I can feel it."

Ben's voice followed, grim and clipped. *This forest isn't empty.*

The words rang like iron through the link.

Val's spine prickled. She caught it then—a flicker in the underbrush, too fast, too deliberate to be wind or shadow. Her stomach turned cold. "*It's not just waiting. It's listening.*"

Virellan rumbled, her storm-dark voice pressing close. *Something hears us. Feels us.*

The dragonlink vibrated with tension—Tessa's sparks skittering wild, Ben's silence weighed like a blade half-drawn.

And then—another voice slipped through, unguarded. Not dragon, not deliberate. Cam's. A whisper that bled raw into the tether, so quiet Val almost thought she imagined it.

"This is it. It has to be."

The words clung in the air, startling, too human in the link. Val's breath caught. It wasn't the resonant weight of dragon-thought, broad and steady across the tether. This was smaller. Closer. Like a thought spoken in the dark, almost inside her own skull.

Virellan's low murmur stirred uneasily against her mind. *Something bleeds where it should not.*

Tessa's head jerked, sparks flaring faint at her fingertips. Even Ben glanced forward sharply, as though only now realizing it wasn't his dragon's voice but Cam's own bleeding through.

And Cam didn't even seem to notice. Her gaze was locked on the forest below, jaw set, shoulders braced hard, as if she could force the answer into being.

Below, the forest breathed with them, every branch too still, every shadow too sharp, as though the canopy itself leaned upward to listen.

Then it came—a low, almost imperceptible rumble from deep within Molwyn. Not thunder. The sky above was a perfect, merciless deep violet.

Val's pulse stuttered.

The dragons tightened formation, circling higher above the black canopy. The forest below held its silence like breath, alive. *Listening. Waiting.*

Chapter 47: Thorned and Ancient

The canopy closed over them like a fist. Dusk was falling fast now, the last colors of day bleeding out above the trees. In Molwyn, the shadows seemed to outrun the light.

Light fractured and vanished as Brontheus dipped beneath the green-black tangle, his wings beating slow and careful. The trees here were enormous—trunks wide enough to swallow houses whole, branches vaulted like the pillars of some ancient hall. Even a dragon could vanish in their shadows.

The air grew colder at once, damp enough that mist clung to Tessa's hair, heavy on her shoulders. Every sound dulled—wingbeats swallowed, voices muffled, even her own breath seemed to fall flat against the silence.

She swallowed hard, sparks itching under her skin.

"I thought Karethwyn was old. This place feels older. Like it remembers things it shouldn't."

Brontheus rumbled low, storm-dark in her mind. *Not memory. Hunger.*

Her grip tightened on the reins. *"That wasn't comforting."*

Behind her, Orren sat steady as stone, weight balanced perfectly. She didn't look back, but she felt him there—unmoving, unshaken. Since Wyatt's death, his silence had grated less than it used to. He wasn't the cold mage-hunter she'd hated at first glance. He bled on patrol, kept watch without complaint, and spoke only when there was weight behind it.

She didn't trust him. Not yet. But his presence was grounding in a way she didn't want to name. *Safety from the wrong person.* That disoriented her more than the forest.

Ahead, Sylithra cut through the mist, her scales flashing faint gold veins where shafts of light managed to pierce the canopy. Cam sat rigid in the saddle, braid whipping, her body a line of ruthless focus. She hadn't spoken since they'd left Ember Fortress—not aloud, not over the tether.

Then Tessa caught it. Her lips moved. Whispering. Words torn away by the wind.

Tessa frowned, sparks pricking hotter in her chest. "She's not here. Not fully." The words slipped out, low, meant only for herself.

But Orren heard. His voice broke the silence, low in her ear. "She's somewhere else entirely..."

She glanced back, startled—only to find his eyes weren't on her at all. His gaze was fixed forward, sharp and unblinking, locked on Cam's rigid figure in Sylithra's saddle. And in that look, for just a moment, Tessa caught it—not suspicion, not calculation. Awareness. A predator's stillness before the strike.

It troubled her more than the forest ever did. Mage hunters weren't supposed to care, and yet that focus was sharper than worry—it was vigilance, like he'd already marked a danger none of them could name.

Orren's jaw tightened slightly, and he shifted in the saddle with that same soldier's composure that hid more than it revealed. But the flicker had been there.

Cam hadn't looked at anyone, hadn't broken from her dive.

"She's chasing something none of us can see," Tessa muttered again, this time certain.

The trees pressed low when they descended, branches arching wide enough that even Brontheus's wings could pass but close enough to feel like they scraped the sky. Bark rose in ridges higher than fortress walls, their crowns lost in mist.

Ben's voice broke across the tether, iron-hard. *"Down. All of you. Skylith and I will cover the sky."*

Above, Skylith's flame-bright presence flared through the link, her voice molten and wary. *Caution. The air is not clean here. We'll keep watch.*

Every trunk seemed less like a tree and more like a pillar holding the forest's weight, heavy enough to smother sound itself.

Sylithra banked sharply and came down with Brontheus and Virellan, talons sinking into the root-woven soil. The clearing was tight, mist dragging in low curls. Cam dismounted in silence, one hand still holding Wyatt's pendant. Her face was pale, lips moving faintly—too soft for Tessa to make out, but the sound turned her stomach. Sylithra shifted uneasily behind her, wings twitching once as though haunted by her rider's distraction.

She glanced at Val, then Orren. Neither spoke, but both wore the same expression she felt herself—uneasy, worried. For once, none of them voiced it.

The clearing itself felt like cages where the roots knotted upward. At the center, stone jutted half-buried—slabs carved in spirals, runes faint as old scars. Some had been clawed raw, others burned black, as if someone—or something—had tried to erase them.

Val crouched near one slab, her palm brushing its grooves. "These don't feel like prayers," she murmured. Her eyes narrowed at the jagged spirals. "They're warnings."

Orren had already dropped to one knee beside a gouge in the earth. His fingers hovered over deep, raked marks in the dirt, each groove wider than his hand.

"Recent," he said flatly. His gaze lifted toward the trees, sharp and measuring. "Bigger than a Mirebat."

The air shifted once, a breath of wind that stirred leaves into a faint clatter—then it stilled again, so sudden the silence rang louder than noise. Metallic tang crept into Tessa's nose, sharp like lightning's aftertaste... or blood.

Not a single insect stirred. Not a bird, not a rustle. Nothing.

Brontheus shifted uneasily under her, muscles tight, wings flicking like he wanted the sky between him and this place. Sparks jumped across Tessa's fingers as she tightened her grip on the reins. She stayed mounted, refusing to dismount, every sense alive through the dragon beneath her.

It felt like the forest had shut the door behind them.

Cam spoke then, her voice quiet but audible as her hand tightened around the pendant. "Something feels wrong here."

The words hit the tether like a ripple. Brontheus shuddered under Tessa, wings flexing tight. Virellan's growl bled into the link, storm-dark and warning. Even Sylithra shifted again, talons scraping root and stone as her eyes flashed gold.

A faint crack echoed in the distance, sharp as splintering wood. Too far to see, too deliberate to dismiss. The mist shivered once, then fell still again—like the forest had paused to listen.

Overhead, Skylith's thoughts laced through the tether like a blade of flame. *Eyes open. The forest hunts as we do.*

Val straightened from the slab, her hand brushing dirt from her palm. "I don't like the way this place feels," she said, voice low but carrying.

"I don't either," Tessa muttered at the same time Orren said, flat and certain, "Agreed."

Their eyes met for half a heartbeat—hers sparking with unease, his steady and sharp, like steel braced against the same weight. Something in the look disturbed her more than the carvings had. He wasn't mocking. He wasn't cold. He was watchful, and it showed.

Val turned away, mounting Virellan in one smooth motion, her jaw set. "We keep moving. The sky is safer than this."

Cam mounted Sylithra but fumbled slightly. Tessa had seen Cam mount her dragon thousands of times, and she had never fumbled that badly before. A chill crawled down her spine. Something in her friend was slipping—something Tessa couldn't name. Sylithra's wings twitched again, restless under the weight of it.

The leather creaking under her as she shifted her grip. She felt Orren climb up behind her again, the shift of weight balanced and sure. Too close, too steady, and yet grounding in a way she hated herself for noticing.

Brontheus's wings unfurled, storm-dark against the canopy, and with a single push they were airborne again. His wingbeats were harder now, sharper, like he wanted out as much as she did.

Tessa's hands stayed tight on the reins, her shoulders locked. She muttered under her breath, "Feels like walking into a trap."

Behind her, Orren's voice came steady, low against the rush of air. "Every forest is a trap if you're not the predator."

She almost snapped back, sparks biting at her teeth, but stopped. His tone wasn't mocking, not cold—just matter of fact, the kind of truth he carried like a blade. And damn it, that steadiness almost felt like safety. She shoved the thought down, forcing her eyes forward.

Cam flew ahead on Sylithra, braid whipping, her posture too rigid, too deliberate. Tessa's chest tightened. *She's flying like nothing can touch her. Or like she wants something to.*

That hollow determination cut sharper than grief. Tessa fought pain by throwing herself into movement, training until sparks blistered her palms. But Cam... Cam was chasing something unseen, something that might swallow her whole if she ever caught it.

Shadows shifted below, faint but unmistakable. A branch snapped—a single crack that echoed too loud in the smothered quiet. Brontheus's growl rolled low through his chest, thunder-dark and warning. Ahead, Sylithra tossed her head once, wings faltering as if she'd caught the same scent.

Tessa's chest went tight, sparks threatening to break loose.

She caught Cam glancing down, lips moving—silent words shaped for no one they could see. Tessa's stomach dropped.

She's whispering to someone. And whoever it is, it isn't us.

Behind her, Orren shifted sharply. His posture had been steady as stone until now, but something cut through it—head tilted, shoulders taut, gaze locked on the forest with a precision that made her skin prickle. For a breath, his hand brushed the hilt at his side, though nothing stirred in the shadows below.

"Something's moving with us," he said at last, voice low, certain.

Brontheus's growl deepened a heartbeat later, and Sylithra hissed, wings snapping wide—like even the dragons were only now catching up to what Orren had already known.

Tessa's pulse kicked hard. *How did he feel it before Brontheus?*

The tether thrummed taut between them all. The forest below loomed dark, patient, and listening.

And above it, the dragons circled, their shadows long across the canopy—as if already caught in the gaze of something waiting.

Chapter 48: Wings in the Dark

The last breath of twilight bled out above the canopy. Darkness spread like ink across the branches, bleeding into every gap of light. For one fragile heartbeat, the forest held its silence.

Then it shattered.

Branches split with the sound of bone snapping. Shrieks rose from below, raw and animal, and the canopy erupted. A storm of wings tore upward, black shapes hurling themselves into the air, scattering splinters like knives. The smell hit a moment later—rot and damp iron, the reek of something that should not have been alive.

Brontheus bellowed in her mind, his thunder crashing through the tether. *Above! Mirebats! I will swat them!*

The jolt nearly deafened her. Tessa yanked the reins, Brontheus banking hard beneath her. She felt the shift of his massive body ripple up through her legs, leather creaking, claws ripping bark as he beat for altitude.

The dragonlink flared—too many voices at once, colliding, cutting, drowning each other:

Cam, three o'clock! Val snapped sharp with tension.

Keep tight, don't overextend— Ben barked, but Skylith's roar slammed across the tether, splitting it apart: *Above! Two more—shield her, shield her!*

Sylithra hissed molten and low, words meant only for her rider. *You fly crooked. Hold steady, Little Flame—*

I see it! Val again, too loud, overlapping. *No, left—left!*

Tessa, pull left! Brontheus thundered, his voice rumbling through her bones.

The voices hammered her skull, one crashing into the next, until she could barely hear her own breath.

Sparks crawled across her knuckles as she gritted her teeth. She hated forest fights. No open sky to breathe in. No stars above to measure the danger. Just branches like spears, mist swallowing her sight, and the hard truth that if they fell, there would be no room to rise again.

A gust of hot, fetid air slammed her face. Something big moved below. Brontheus snarled in his chest, wings clipping through falling branches.

"Bron!" she hissed, raising her sword.

Brontheus surged beneath her, wings hammering. Sky! he thundered through her skull, his voice shattering the tether. *All of you—break the line! Fight in the open!*

He banked hard, claws ripping bark, and then they were tearing upward—through branches that clawed at wings and leather, mist dragging like chains. And then, with a single beat, they broke free. The canopy fell away below them, a rolling black sea in moonlight. Shadows followed shrieking, the swarm pouring up into the sky after them. The others burst through the branches a heartbeat later, wings flashing in the starlight.

The air cracked as a Vorrakai exploded upward, jagged wings tearing the canopy wide. Splinters rained like shards of glass. Its scales caught the last threads of dusk like shattered mirrors, reflecting her wide eyes back at her before the dark claimed them both.

◈ ☽⚡☾ ◈

The Vorrakai burst through the canopy first—jagged wings shredding branches, its shriek rattling the air. Mirebats poured up in its wake, a black storm clawing for the open sky.

Virellan surged after Brontheus, wings hammering hard until they broke free of the trees. The canopy dropped away beneath them, a rolling sea of black leaves torn by silver moonlight. Mist clung to their scales as if the forest tried to drag them back down.

Val's breath caught in her throat. They'd gained altitude, but not enough—shadows still clawed upward, dozens of Mirebats swarming to meet them.

I smell blood. Fresh, Virellan growled through the link, her storm-dark voice thrumming with hunger. She twisted her head toward the swarm, eyes flashing silver-white. *Let me dive. Let me tear.*

"Not yet," Val snapped, hauling on the harness. Her muscles burned with the effort of pulling Virellan into line. The dragon snarled, tail whipping, every beat of her wings vibrating with caged fury.

She forced her breathing steady, dragging the chaos into order the way her brother had drilled into her years ago. Tessa held low on Brontheus's left, sparks flashing like fireflies against the dark. Ben and Skylith roared high to the right, flame carving brutal arcs through the swarm. Cam—too far forward, Sylithra weaving erratically, gold-veined wings jerking in and out of the moonlight.

The tether flared—voices colliding like thunder:

"Keep the line!" Val barked, soldier-sharp.

"Cam! Back in formation!" Ben's command cracked like iron.

Sylithra spat molten into the link: *You pull us crooked, Little Flame!*

And then—Cam's voice, soft, human, bleeding wrong into the tether: "*...I hear him...*"

The words hollowed Val's chest.

Sylithra's snarl ripped through the link, vicious and demanding: *...Who?*

Another wave of Mirebats burst free of the canopy, blotting out the stars. Their ragged wings snapped at leather and scales, raining splinters and black feathers.

Left flank! Left! Val shouted, but her command drowned beneath Brontheus's roar, Skylith's bellow, sparks cracking across the tether like fire.

Virellan bucked under her, hunger howling through their bond. *Blood. Blood. Blood.* The word throbbed like a heartbeat, pounding against Val's skull until her vision blurred.

"Hold!" Val yanked the reins, sweat slicking her palms. *"Not yet!"*

Her gut clenched around Cam's whisper, bile rising sharp in her throat. That wasn't the focus of a rider. That was something worse.

◈ ☽ ⚡ ☾ ◈

Flame ripped the sky apart. Skylith roared through the tether, her voice a conflagration that scorched every other thought*: I will crush them all. I will crush anything that dares touch my friends.*

Her fire seared a Mirebat mid-dive, its body spiraling in ash. Ben leaned with her, sword catching another that lunged for Sylithra's tail. Sparks scattered across the twilight-dark canopy, flashing Cam's pale face into view—eyes unfocused, lips shaping words none of them heard.

"Cam," Ben muttered, his chest seizing tight. *We already lost Wyatt. I am not losing my daughter too.*

The tether snarled around him—Val straining to hold Virellan's blood-hunger, Tessa and Brontheus hammering through swarms, Orren's bolts whistling death from behind her. Cam faltering, Sylithra weaving raggedly to keep her alive.

Enough.

Ben's voice cut across the chaos, iron-hard*: Hold formation. Left to Brontheus. Right to Skylith. Virellan—circle high, keep the flank clear. Sylithra, steady. Keep Cam alive.*

The storm of voices bent. Shouts, snarls, panic—forced into order by his tone, by the weight of command no one dared break. The tether snapped taut, tighter, sharper.

Skylith's fire seethed in his bones. *Yes. Pull them into line. Hold them, or they'll scatter and fall.*

Ben carved another Mirebat down, blade dripping black ichor. *"Steady her,"* he ground out to Sylithra, voice flint against the tether. *"Keep her flying. Don't let her drop."*

She falters, Skylith warned, her fury now focused steel. *The Little Flame falters. We protect her or she breaks.*

Ben drove his sword through another shadow, eyes cutting through the swarm. He could not be everywhere. He could not shield them all. But he would damn well try.

And then—movement. Wrong. Sharp.

A glint of metal in the trees, a rider's silhouette where no rider should be. The Vorrakai broke above the swarm, jagged wings slicing moonlight. And on its back—

"Alex," Ben breathed, his gut turning to ice.

His thought speared through the tether, iron and unyielding: *Tessa. Ghost incoming. Vorrakai rider.*

The link shuddered with the force of it. Tessa's fury flared back, sharp and hot as sparks striking steel.

Skylith's growl rumbled low, her fire coiling in his chest. *He dies now.*

Ben's jaw locked, the words catching behind his teeth. For a heartbeat, the fight seemed to fall away—the flames, the shrieks, the storm of wings—all drowned by the sight of that boy's face. Hollow-eyed. Rigid.

Alex.

Alive when he shouldn't be. Riding the Vorrakai like a revenant stitched together by shadow.

Ben's chest clenched, rage and dread tangling until he could barely breathe. If Alex had bent knee to the Capital, if they had his claws in him—then Wyatt's death had only been the beginning.

The tether strained with Skylith's fury, but Ben forced the weight of his vow into it, his voice ringing iron-hard across every mind: *"He betrayed us. He will answer for it—by my hand."*

◈ ☽ ⚡ ☾ ◈

The sky wasn't sky anymore—just a smear of black wings and silver streaks, stars drowned in motion. Her nails dug into Wyatt's pendant until the chain bit flesh, warm blood slicking her palm. Her heartbeat pounded too fast, too loud, like her chest was a drum for someone else's war.

Focus, Little Flame. Sylithra's voice coiled low, steady as a heartbeat, trying to thread through the noise. *Hold with me. Do not slip.*

But there was another. A whisper that didn't belong to dragon or tether. A voice she knew too well.

Cam. Duck.

She obeyed without thought. Sylithra rolled hard, wings snapping wide as a spike tore past, grazing her shoulder. Pain bloomed hot and sharp, soaking through her sleeve. She hissed but didn't stop. Couldn't.

Then the voices hit—an avalanche, all at once:

Val, a whipcrack: "*Cam, focus!*"

Ben, iron-hard: "*Stay with us Cam!*"

Sylithra, molten and furious: *Hold—hold—*

Tessa, breaking raw: "*Cam! What's going on?!*"

Virellan, Brontheus, Skylith—all thundering her name, the storm of it crashing through her skull.

Names, demands, desperation—piling one atop the other until she couldn't tell where she ended and they began. Until it felt like they were tearing her name apart at the seams.

And yet, beneath it, through it—him.

I'm here, Wyatt's voice breathed, closer than breath, steady and certain.

Her chest cracked open. The world blurred. He was here. He wouldn't let her fall.

Her fingers trembled on the reins. Vision doubling—Wyatt's voice twining with Sylithra's, with Brontheus's thunder and Skylith's roar, until she couldn't tell one from the other.

And then, so faint it might have been her own thought, another voice stirred. Cold. Patient.

Let go...

It didn't sound like death. It sounded like rest. Like sinking. Like being held by nothing.

Her grip slackened. For a heartbeat, she felt herself tilt—stars smearing, the tether shredding into static. Sylithra roared in her mind, a wall of fire and fury, but even that was dim beneath the velvet pull.

Let go, the whisper pulsed again, sweet and hollow. *No more pain. No more fight. Just fall.*

Stay. Wyatt's voice cut sharper, fierce as flame. *Stay with me.*

It didn't sound like a plea. It sounded like a command he'd burn himself to give.

Her breath hitched, a sob tearing out of her throat. She clutched the pendant so hard the chain sliced deeper, grounding herself on that single word.

Stay.

Her knuckles whitened, blood running between her fingers. Her eyes blurred. Her body swayed. And still—she almost let go.

One slip. One breath. One choice.

Sylithra's growl burned through her skull, anchoring her with rage: *Little Flame, do not let go.*

Cam dragged air into her lungs like it might drown her. Her grip steadied—just barely. But the truth carved its way through her chest like a blade.

She hadn't held on because of herself.

She had held on because of *him.*

And for a single heartbeat, in the blur of stars and wings, she swore she saw him—Wyatt—shadowed in silver light, hand outstretched, eyes locked to hers.

Then he was gone, ripped from sight like smoke.

Her chest hollowed with the loss, leaving only the ache, only the whisper that refused to fade:

Stay.

◈ ☽ ⚡ ☾ ◈

The canopy broke beneath Brontheus's wings, moonlight fracturing in shards across the scales around him. Orren kept low behind Tessa, crossbow braced, eyes cutting through the chaos with the precision of habit.

The air was a storm—shrieks raking the sky, ragged wings snapping so close he could feel the gust of them against his cheek. The stench of rot and iron clung to every breath, damp and heavy, but he forced it to the edges of his senses. Filter, measure, discard. He'd learned long ago that panic lived in the details if you let it.

The swarm was endless. Mirebats swirled like a black tide, blotting stars with every sweep of their wings. Most men would see a mass. Orren sorted targets. Weighing distance. Angle. Weakness.

Tessa—sparks flashing, riding Brontheus low and hard into the chaos, her voice splitting the tether with every command.

Val—holding the line but fighting Virellan's bloodlust as much as the bats. He could feel the dragon's hunger even from here, a storm barely leashed.

Ben—carving arcs of fire with Skylith, steady but pulled taut between guarding the circle and Cam. Always Cam.

And Cam—spiraling. Sylithra's gold-veined wings jerking uneven, her rider's hands clumsy on the reins. Once, twice, Orren saw her sway, saw her clutch her chest as if she could anchor herself there instead of with her dragon. A fatal mistake.

Brontheus's growl ripped through the sky, thunderous. Tessa's head whipped back, sparks bright against her fists as she shouted over her shoulder:

"Brontheus says he can't hold two if Cam goes down."

Orren's jaw locked. His eyes never left her. "Then keep her steady. If she slips, we won't reach her in time."

Tessa's fire snapped hotter, her voice breaking sharp as a blade. "Then you keep your eyes on her!"

He didn't answer. Didn't need to. His silence was already a vow.

The crossbow sat steady in his hands, bolt notched, every muscle strung taut as wire. He tracked her—every falter, every sway—calculating wind, distance, the drag of the swarm. His hunter's instinct screamed for action, to cut through uncertainty with a clean strike, a choice. But here, in the sky, he wasn't in control. The dragons ruled the air. He had to trust their strength, their bond, their chaos. It chafed.

So he watched. Waited. Preparing.

Not for the kill.

For the breath when everything broke—when Cam slipped, when the others couldn't catch her, when speed and precision would matter more than strength.

That moment would come. Orren was certain. And when it did, it would be his eyes—not his blade—that would decide if she lived.

◈ ☽ ⚡ ☾ ◈

Brontheus dove like a meteor through the shattered dark. The air screamed past her ears, claws of wind tearing through her braid. Below, the Vorrakai burst through the moonlight—its wings like razors, tail thrashing, the rider gleaming silver and shadow.

Alex.

Her stomach turned. For a heartbeat, she forgot to breathe.

The man who'd laughed at midnight watchfires beside Kaden, who'd taught her the quiet kills, the way to move unseen.

Now his face was a stranger's—ashen, empty-eyed, moving like a puppet strung on wire. The Vorrakai didn't answer to him. It dragged him. And still... he smiled.

"Bron—lower!" she shouted.

Hold steady, Brontheus thundered through her skull, his voice a deep quake. *Strike clean, strike true.*

She didn't listen. She rose in the saddle, balance shifting with instinct older than thought—and leapt.

The air tore past in a rush of cold and noise. She hit the Vorrakai's back with a bone-rattling jolt, knees locking to the ridges, sparks snapping from her fingers as she steadied her sword. The beast shrieked beneath her, twisting hard, its scales slick under her boots.

Alex spun toward her, eyes catching what little moonlight remained—flat, silver, inhuman.

"You wouldn't dare," he hissed.

Tessa bared her teeth. Her voice came out low and shaking with fury. "You shouldn't have come back."

He tilted his head, blade glinting. "Orders are orders." His voice came almost distant, as if echoing from somewhere else. "Kill the chosen one. Kill the hunter. Tie up the rest."

He grinned, too sharp. "I should've done it the first time. Thought the Veilborn would finish you all. Should've known better."

A sound built in her chest, half laugh, half snarl. "Then you'll fail again."

Steel collided—sparks bursting, light flashing across their faces. Each strike hammered through her arms, rattling bone and breath. He fought fast, relentless, assassin-trained, every move meant to kill or cripple. But Tessa knew his rhythm. She'd learned it beside him—how he always overreached when he wanted to scare his opponent. How his right guard dropped when he led with rage.

He lunged. She met him blow for blow, her own fury surging hot enough to blind reason.

"You were never a killer," he spat, twisting for her ribs.

She ducked under it, blade sliding across his guard, sparks spraying off their swords.

"Corin's pet," he jeered, pressing the next strike. "Kaden's shadow. The girl who doesn't follow orders but never got her hands dirty."

Her teeth clenched until her jaw ached. "You don't know me anymore."

He barked a short, bitter laugh. "I know enough. You'll never do what has to be done."

She let him push her back—then twisted, using his own momentum to slam her hilt into his jaw. The impact cracked like thunder. Blood sprayed across the Vorrakai's scales, sizzling where it landed.

He staggered, caught himself, grinned—sharp and bleeding. "Still holding back."

"We trusted you, I trusted you! And you betrayed us." Her voice broke open like a wound. "You betrayed me! You sold us out!"

His eyes flickered—human for a fraction of a heartbeat. "You don't understand what they are." Then it was gone, drowned under that hollow smile. "And you still won't kill me. That's why you'll lose."

The Vorrakai bucked, tail slamming against Brontheus's wake. Tessa stumbled, caught her footing, chest heaving, rage burning through her veins like wildfire. The sky spun—dragons and darkness and the flash of steel.

She steadied her stance, meeting his eyes with a cold calm that hurt to hold. "No. It's why I'll win."

He slashed, fast. She feinted left, pivoted low, then drove her sword upward through his side—angled, deep, cruel. The blade sank past leather and muscle, hot blood coating her hands. The sound—wet, awful—ripped through her chest. He froze, breath breaking, shock hollowing his eyes.

"...You...?" he gasped, coughing red.

"You were always better with maps..." Her breath came sharp as she pushed the sword in just a little deeper, meeting his gaze. His hand reached for her, trembling. She pulled the blade free, backing away a step.

Her voice was ice. "And you may be a spy, but I was always better with a sword."

He staggered back, barely catching the saddle ridge. His mouth opened—to curse her, to speak, to beg—but no sound came. His form flickered, blurred.

Not falling. Not fading. Erased.

The air folded, the moonlight bending wrong—and then he was gone.

No shimmer. No wind. No body. Just gone, like the night itself had swallowed him whole.

Tessa stared at the empty space, disbelief and fury crashing into each other until her pulse roared in her ears. "Coward," she hissed, breath shaking. "You run again."

The Vorrakai screamed beneath her, thrashing in agony.

Then Skylith descended—a comet of gold and fire. The dragon slammed down from above, wings cutting flame through the clouds. The Vorrakai's shriek ended in an explosion of light and ash. Fire tore its body apart midair, the blast painting the night red and gold.

Tessa barely had time to react. She pushed off, grabbing a strap on Skylith's harness as the dragon banked hard. The heat seared her face, her fingers blistering as she rolled across scaled hide. Sparks bled from her hair, falling like dying stars as she caught her balance, crouched—and leapt again.

Brontheus swept beneath her, vast wings cutting through smoke. She hit the saddle hard, breath punched from her lungs, vision sparking white.

Orren's voice came low behind her, breathless, darkly amused. "Reckless. But impressive."

She didn't answer. Her hands shook too hard around the hilt. The wind stung her face, salt mixing with sweat and blood. Every muscle trembled with leftover fury—her mind refusing to believe what she'd seen.

Alex's face. That hollow look. That vanishing. That escape.

The tether pulsed through her, dim and echoing—shock, awe, grim pride rippling from the others. The chaos was thinning. Mirebats fell away into the black, scattered by flame and fury.

Brontheus rumbled beneath her, the sound rolling deep through her ribs. *It is done.*

Tessa's grip loosened on her sword. Her pulse slowed. The sky was too still now. Too empty.

Her throat tightened. For a heartbeat, she could hear only her own heartbeat—and the silence that followed.

Then Ben's voice tore through the tether, sharp, panicked, real.

"CAM!!"

Chapter 49: The Illusion of Wyatt

The sky still burned where Skylith's fire had torn it open.

Ash drifted like black snow, glowing faintly before it vanished into the wind.

The air reeked of iron and ozone—charred wings, scorched scales, the ghosts of a hundred dying shrieks.

Cam barely heard the others through the ringing in her ears—Tessa's cry, Val's warning, Ben's command—each voice breaking, bleeding into static.

Her fingers still clutched the reins, but she couldn't feel them.

Couldn't feel anything.

She had watched Tessa strike.

Watched Alex vanish again—like at the temple, like a wound reopening that would never close.

There should have been triumph. Relief. *Something.*

Instead, there was only the hollow thud of her heartbeat echoing too loud inside her skull.

Sylithra beat her wings once, hard, the gust scattering smoke and snow.

The dragon's growl rumbled through the link—low, protective, trembling with barely leashed panic.

Little Flame, stay with me.

But Cam couldn't look away from the space where Alex had been.

From the nothing he left behind.

From the feeling that everything around her was fading—color, sound, breath—all draining out with the last of the firelight.

The silence after battle never lasted. It broke like glass.

A new shriek ripped the sky—lower, guttural, *wrong.*

The sound crawled under her skin before she even turned.

From below, the canopy ruptured.

A Mirebat shot upward trailing ribbons of black smoke—and clinging to its spine came something worse.

Its skin rippled like oil, its limbs long and bent wrong, eyes burning red through the dark.

The air warped around it, cold enough to choke.

Ben's voice cracked across the tether, raw:

"Cam—LOOK OUT!"

But she didn't hear him. Not really.

Her mind was still somewhere else—half in memory, half in that echo of a voice she thought she'd heard before.

Wyatt.

Sylithra felt it first.

The dragon's roar split the air, the tether spiking with heat.

She twisted hard, one massive wing sweeping, claws ripping through the creature as it lunged.

The Veilborn slid off the Mirebat, striking again—its screech high and thin, a sound like tearing metal—as it latched onto Sylithra's neck.

Instinct answered with fire.

Sylithra rolled, a violent, whiplash motion that tore the thing free—but the jolt snapped Cam loose from her trance.

Her body lurched with the motion, the reins burning against her palms, breath caught halfway between a scream and a sob.

Smoke blurred the stars. The battle wasn't over. It was only changing shape.

Wind tore at her hair, cold and sharp as glass.

The world tilted, stars smearing into silver streaks.

And then—a voice.

Soft. Steady. *I'm here... don't let go.*

Her breath caught like it had been ripped from her lungs.

Behind her in the saddle—*Wyatt.*

As if nothing had ever been lost.

The same glint of silver armor catching starlight. The same tilt of his head when he smiled—gentle, infuriating, so achingly *alive*. The same calm that used to anchor her when the world burned.

It wasn't possible. It wasn't real.

But gods—it *felt* real.

Her throat closed around his name. "Wyatt?" she whispered, the sound cracking like glass.

He looked at her, eyes bright and unbroken, full of the quiet certainty she had dreamed of every night since he died.

Hold on, Cam, he said, voice warm as breath. *I've got you.*

For one impossible heartbeat, the world stilled.

Everything else—dragons, fire, blood, terror—bled away.

The link dimmed to a whisper beneath it all.

Only him. Only that voice. Only the impossible peace of hearing it again.

And she *believed him.*

Gods help her, she believed.

A tear broke free, lost to the wind.

If this was madness, she would live in it forever.

Sylithra's snarl shattered the illusion like lightning cleaving stone.

Cam!

The dragon twisted violently, claws raking through air. Her wing struck the Veilborn full-force, tearing it free—but the jolt ripped the reins from Cam's hands.

The world dropped.

For one breathless, beautiful instant, she was weightless—and Wyatt was there.

Right there.

Hand outstretched, close enough that she could almost feel the heat of his palm against hers. The last time she fell, he caught her.

This time, he wasn't real enough to try.

"Wyatt—"

Her stomach dropped; the world flipped inside out. Wind tore her scream to shreds before she could hear it.

Then *the sky broke.*

Air twisted around her like shattering glass.

Light fractured, violet-black and gold, bleeding together until the stars themselves screamed.

The tether erupted in her mind—Sylithra's voice lost to the storm, every bond snapping, pain lancing white through her skull.

"WYATT!" she tried again, but the name tore apart halfway through, swallowed by the wind.

A seam split open beneath her—not summoned, not called.

Born from the raw, unbearable grief that had nowhere else to go.

The Veil answered her.

The world itself tearing open like a wound to catch her fall.

She plunged through it—into shadow that glowed like dying embers, into light that throbbed like a heartbeat too slow to save her.

Sylithra's roar chased her down, a sound too wild, too broken to be anything but love.

And then—

Silence.

◈ ☽ ⚡ ☾ ◈

The sky broke—and then went still.

Smoke drifted upward in thin gray threads, curling through the torn air where Cam had been. The rift shimmered once, edges glowing violet-gold, and then dimmed—closing like a wound that didn't want to heal.

No one spoke. Not at first.

Ben's breath hitched, a sound too soft to be a word. "Cam..."

The name fractured on his tongue, half prayer, half denial.

Tessa sat frozen in Brontheus's saddle, sword still clutched in her shaking hand, eyes fixed on the place where the light had vanished. Her mouth opened—nothing came out. Only the hollow rasp of breath.

Val's hands trembled against Virellan's harness. "She—she's gone," she whispered, as if saying it could undo the silence pressing around them.

But the tether said otherwise—quiet, ruptured, one voice missing where it had always been.

Orren's jaw locked. He scanned the air, the forest, the ash drifting through the smoke-streaked sky. His knuckles blanched around the crossbow still loaded in his grip. He had seen people vanish before, but never like this. Never into nothing.

The dragons circled low, restless, wings cutting through smoke and shadow.

Only Sylithra's cry broke the stillness—ragged, unending, the sound of something ancient mourning what it could not reach.

Her grief poured through the link, wildfire and winter all at once. It struck them each in turn—Ben's chest seizing, Tessa bowing her head, Val covering her mouth, Orren flinching as if struck.

And then—something else.

A flicker.

A faint thrum beneath the noise, so soft it might have been imagined.

Ben felt it first.

A pulse in the bond—not sound, not voice, just warmth—like a heartbeat pressed against the edge of silence.

He caught his breath. *"Sylithra...?"*

The dragon's wings faltered mid-beat. Her eyes flared gold through the smoke. *I feel it too.*

For one heartbeat, the world seemed to breathe again.

Then the pulse faded—gone as quickly as it had come, leaving only the wind and the scent of ash.

No one else noticed. Only Ben and Sylithra.

But in that flicker, that impossible breath in the dark—they knew.

Cam was not gone.

Not yet.

Chapter 50: If There is a Way Back

Snow had come early this year.

It fell in thin, restless spirals over the outer wall, dusting the black stone white. The air smelled of iron and frost, and each breath burned cold on the way down. Ember Fortress hadn't been silent—not even in winter—but now it felt like the world itself was holding its breath.

No drills in the yard.

No laughter in the hall.

Even the dragons had gone quiet.

A week and a half had crawled by since that night, each dawn colder than the last, each day emptier without her.

Kaden leaned against the parapet; fingers pressed into the frost-coated stone until they ached. The cold helped. It kept the thoughts from clawing too deep.

He should have been there.

He should have gone.

If he'd insisted—if he'd flown with them—maybe Cam would be here. Maybe she wouldn't have fallen.

But it had been his turn to run the outer patrols, to check the wards with Corin, to go over the reports.

Duty first, always.

And duty had kept him grounded while the people he loved burned in the sky.

The thought struck so hard he almost laughed—soft, breathless, wrong.

He had done everything right. Every order followed, every rule kept. And still, it wasn't enough to save her.

What good was discipline if the world fell apart anyway? His hands clenched, nails biting through his gloves until the sting steadied him again.

His jaw tightened, breath coming sharp. Below, the snow swallowed sound as it fell. He could almost pretend the silence was peace, but it wasn't. It was waiting.

He'd never realized how loud waiting could be.

Every creak in the fortress, every echo of wind down the stone corridors sounded like her voice about to answer—and then didn't.

Even the shadows seemed to listen, stretching long across the snow like they were waiting for her too.

Tenebrin stirred in the back of his mind, a ripple of storm-shadow through his thoughts. *You're thinking in circles again.*

"Maybe if I'd gone, there wouldn't be circles," Kaden muttered.

The dragon didn't answer at first. Only a low pulse of wind and whisper pressed faintly against the edge of his awareness—the mental equivalent of a steady gaze. Then: *Her bond still hums. Faint, but alive.*

Kaden shut his eyes. "You don't know that."

Sylithra knows. She would feel it if death had taken her. And she has not mourned her completely.

The words dug deep, but they didn't stop the memory that hit like a blow.

The storm had broken hours ago. Dawn was just bleeding over the horizon when he saw them coming—Brontheus, Skylith, Virellan, Sylithra—dragons scorched and bleeding, riders half-frozen, their silhouettes rimmed in pale gold light.

But not all of them.

He'd felt the tug hours earlier, in the middle of the night—like something in his chest tearing sideways. It had jolted him upright, breath strangled, the room still dark. He'd tried to shake it off, to lie back down, but the pull wouldn't stop.

It sat in him like a weight behind his ribs, a low hum that refused to quiet.

His shadows had stirred then, curling around his wrists like smoke, flickering through his vision like a second heartbeat he couldn't silence. For a moment, the darkness had whispered to act, to find, to tear the sky open if he had to.

He'd shoved it down. He always did. Because every time he let it rise, it felt too much like the thing he feared he might become.

So he'd forced the shadows back, pressed cold water to his face, and waited for dawn to come.

When it did, the feeling hadn't left. It had only grown sharper—right until he saw the dragons.

They'd descended in silence. And before they even touched ground, he knew.

He'd run before they dismounted.

"Where is Cam?" he'd shouted, the words echoing off the walls.

Ben's eyes had been hollow. Tessa's hands still trembled around her sword. Val wouldn't meet his gaze. Orren only said it straight: "She fell."

"Fell?!" he'd repeated, as if saying it might make it make sense.

Val's voice cracked. "There was a light. Violet-black and white gold. And then—she was gone."

Gone. Not dead. Not buried. Just gone.

That word had kept him awake every night since.

Now, on the wall, the memory still burned. His shadows twined faintly around his boots, restless, alive in the cold. He forced them still with a sharp exhale, though his pulse raced harder for it. They wanted to move—to reach. And sometimes, when the silence grew too long, he almost wanted to let them.

Because what if the shadows weren't danger this time? What if they were trying to lead him to her? The thought scared him more than losing her ever could.

It would be so easy to let go. To stop fighting it. The shadows always promised strength—but they wanted more than strength.

They wanted surrender. And that was what scared him most.

A tremor caught in his throat. The ache rose too fast to swallow. He braced his palms against the stone, bowing his head until his hair brushed the frost. He'd cried for his parents. For Wyatt. For every loss that carved another hollow in him. This was different. This was the breaking that came when you ran out of places to hide the pain.

But now, for the first time in years, he felt it breaking through—the grief that refused to stay buried.

"I can't lose her too," he whispered, so low the wind nearly stole it away. "Not her."

Tenebrin's silence was heavy—then, finally: *You will not. Not while I still draw breath.*

It should have steadied him. It almost did.

He could still feel the pull. The faint hum of something across the bond he couldn't name. Not strong enough to trust, not weak enough to ignore.

"She could be anywhere," he whispered, his breath misting in the air.

Tenebrin's reply was shadowlike without sound. *Then we'll find her.*

Kaden opened his eyes to the falling snow. The flakes clung to his gloves, to his lashes, to the faint wisp of shadow curling at his feet.

He didn't know if the warmth in his chest was hope or denial.

"She's alive," he said, the words soft but iron in his mouth. "We'll find her. I swear it."

The wind took his breath, scattering it into the frozen air.

But the vow stayed—anchored, quiet, unshakable.

A pulse sparked faintly across his chest. Not magic. Not light.

Something older—something that hummed on the same thread that had once bound him to Wyatt.

He remembered that night—the twin flicker that had told him his brother still breathed, even when the world said he didn't.

And now that same pull stirred again, low and stubborn.

He didn't know where Cam was. Didn't know how far she'd fallen.

But like with Wyatt—he felt it. The echo that refused to die.

He looked to the horizon, to where dawn broke pale and thin over the snow.

"She's alive," he whispered again.

And this time, he almost believed it. Almost.

A gust swept the wall, scattering snow from his boots. He didn't move. Couldn't.

For the first time he let the shadows rise—not in anger, not in fear, but in reach.

A single thread curled upward from his palm, soft and dark, catching the dawn light before fading back into him.

He stared at the space it had been, breath steadying.

Maybe the darkness wasn't only ruin.

Maybe it could be a way back, too.

◈ ☽ ⚡ ☾ ◈

Snow still clung to the windowsills, dulling the morning light to gray.

The library smelled of old vellum and smoke; the hearth fire had burned low hours ago, leaving only a faint orange heartbeat among the shadows.

Val had barely left this room since the night Cam fell.

Days had blurred together—ink stains, candle smoke, the rustle of brittle parchment.

Every surface bore some trace of her search: The Book of Unbinding propped open by a half-empty mug, Veilbind scrolls unrolled across the floor, maps pinned and repined to the same stretch of wall until the tacks wore grooves in the stone.

If she stopped reading, she started shaking. If she stopped looking, she started remembering.

So she kept moving. Kept turning pages. Kept hoping that somewhere in these lines Cam had left an answer she could still reach.

The library had become her vigil.

And every rune she traced, every half-deciphered symbol, felt like another chance not to fail her again.

Val sat at the long reading table surrounded by the wreckage of Cam's work—

scrolls half-unrolled, ink bottles gone dry, maps curling at the edges where candle heat had warped them.

The Book of Unbinding lay open before her, its runes faintly pulsing, like it resented being awake.

She had read the same paragraph three times without absorbing a word.

Her fingertips traced the glowing script anyway. *The balance is shifting.*

The phrase appeared again and again in the margins, Cam's handwriting sharp, hurried, desperate to catch meaning before it slipped away.

Val swallowed hard. "You were onto something," she whispered. "And I should have listened."

Her voice broke on the last word.

She had told herself Cam's obsession with the scrolls was just exhaustion, just pressure, just one more sleepless night.

But the truth was simpler, crueler: she hadn't wanted to believe her friend was right. Because if Cam was right, then the world really was unraveling—and Val couldn't bear another impossible fight.

She closed her eyes, pressing her palms flat against the parchment. "I should've been there," she said quietly. "I should've tried harder."

Her fingers tightened on the edge of the table until her knuckles whitened.

Cam's laugh still echoed in the corners of this room—that low, unguarded sound she made when the impossible finally started to make sense.

Val could almost see her again, bent over the maps, ink staining her fingertips, eyes bright with some discovery no one else could quite see yet.

She'd burned herself to keep everyone else warm, and Val had called it recklessness.

But it wasn't recklessness. It was faith.

And Val had been too afraid to follow it.

"You believed in everything," she whispered, voice cracking. "Even me. And I still let you stand alone."

The silence pressed closer.

Only the faint crack of frost outside the windows answered her.

She forced herself to breathe and turned back to the notes.

Cam's field book from Haldrin's Keep lay half-buried under other pages, the spine cracked, the corners still smeared with dirt and ash.

Val opened it carefully, scanning Cam's familiar shorthand—the small loops and slashes of someone writing faster than their thoughts.

Two northern temples. Half-finished coordinates. Questions instead of answers.

She turned another sheet.

Keirash: foundation, cradle, hollow beneath. Below it, in smaller letters—*Molwyn? Or north by the Veilrend Sea?*

In the corner, a symbol circled three times: the same mark etched into the third Veilbind scroll.

Her pulse quickened.

She skimmed the rest—notations about elemental convergence, fragments of energy, sketches that blurred together into spirals of light. She didn't understand all of it, but one line stood out, bold beneath the rest:

Fourth scroll—proof of the Cradle. Beyond the mountains.

Val sat back, the chair creaking softly. It wasn't madness. Cam hadn't been losing herself.

She'd been chasing something real—something old enough that even Corin's records barely whispered of it.

The realization hurt more than relief ever could. She'd doubted her friend when she needed belief most.

The fire guttered, throwing a shimmer across the open maps. In the wavering light, the inked lines almost looked alive, the northern coast glowing faintly where Cam's notes had layered one on top of another.

Val gathered the papers with careful hands. Her throat ached, but her movements were steady. "You left us a trail," she whispered. "I'll follow it this time."

The words lingered, half vow, half apology.

She stared at the map again, at the faint ink trail leading north.

The words Cam had written came back to her—the violet-black light, the white-gold shimmer.

Teleportation. It sounded absurd, but... Cam had never done anything by halves.

And Val had seen Kaden open portals before. The color was different. Wilder. But Cam was *different*.

Maybe the Veil had answered her call. Maybe that light wasn't an ending at all, but a door. A terrible, reckless, beautiful door.

Her heartbeat picked up.

"It's possible," she murmured. "Gods, it's actually possible."

The thought rooted deep, solid enough to stand on.

She wasn't certain. But it was a place to start. And what else did they have, if not that?

Val let herself imagine Cam's voice—not as memory, but as echo. The sound of laughter in the hall. The weight of her hand on her shoulder.

It hurt, but it steadied her.

For the first time since that night, the ache in her chest shifted—still sharp, but steady now.

Not the kind of pain that begged to be quieted. The kind that demanded to be answered.

She closed the Book of Unbinding, its last rune dimming to silence, and stood.

Outside, the fortress bells marked the shift to midmorning.

Somewhere down the hall she could hear Ben's voice—low, steady, trying too hard to sound composed—and Corin's answering tone like frost against stone.

She tightened her grip on the stack of journals and headed for the war room. When the door opened, blue ward-fire washed over her face.

The two men looked up from the map table as she crossed the threshold.

"I found something," she said.

Ben's eyes lifted to hers, weary but alive again, just for a breath. Corin's fingers hovered over the parchment, tracing the faded ink.

"What kind of something?" he asked quietly.

Val drew in a long breath. Setting the maps and notes down in the war table. "Cam's notes. They point north. A temple. And maybe the missing scroll."

The war room went still.

For a heartbeat, no one moved.

Then Ben and Corin exchanged a look—quiet, brief, but heavy enough that Val felt it all the way down to her ribs.

Her eyes narrowed. "What was that?"

Corin straightened, the motion too slow, too careful. "Nothing you need to worry about yet."

"Don't do that," she said, her voice cutting through the cold air sharper than she meant it to. "Don't lie to me. Not after this."

Ben exhaled, running a hand over his face, eyes flicking toward the frost-fogged window. "It's not a lie," he said quietly. "It's something we thought we didn't say for good reason."

Val's pulse picked up. "The north?"

Corin's silence was answer enough.

She stared between them, disbelief turning sharp. "You knew."

Ben's jaw worked, guilt threading through his tone. "We knew it existed. Not what she'd find if she went looking."

The words hit harder than she expected.

Val folded her arms. "Well," Val snapped. "Looks like she found it anyway. And you can stop pretending you're protecting us. Because if there's even a chance she's alive out there, I'm not sitting here waiting for another ghost."

Corin's gaze dropped to the map again, tracing the northern mountains where Cam's ink had marked the Cradle's edge.

Ben didn't look away from the window.

The silence that followed was jagged as ice—and for the first time since Cam fell, Val felt something close to purpose again.

◈ ☽ ⚡ ☾ ◈

The war room burned cold.

Blue ward-fire crackled low in the hearth, its light bending through the frost-glazed air. Shadows crawled along the stone walls as if listening, stretching long over the maps that covered the table. Each breath came out white. The wards were supposed to keep the warmth in. Lately, they only reminded him what it felt like to freeze.

Corin stood across from him, shoulders squared but drawn tight. His eyes followed the map spread between them—north to the Veilrend Sea, south to Molwyn's black forests, west to the Eldvale mountains, east to Caerthalen's coast. His hand hovered over the Cradle Temple, tracing the faint ink where Cam's notes had bled into Val's additions.

She'd marked it with a circle. Just like Isabella used to.

Val stood at the table, arms folded, the faint tremor in her hands betrayed only by the light glinting off the journals she'd brought. Corin hovered beside her, gaze fixed on the northern maps. His breath fogged faintly in the cold air; the wards always drew the warmth away.

Ben leaned against one of the pillars near the wall, his shoulder pressed into the chill. He'd stood like that for a while, silent, letting Corin's muttering fill the room.

He could still feel Val's glare from earlier—sharp enough to cut through stone. Every time he looked up, he caught the edge of it, that silent accusation that said *You knew. You let her go anyway*. He didn't blame her. He couldn't. Because she was right.

He kept his eyes on the maps instead, pretending to study the ink. It was easier than meeting the anger he deserved. Easier than seeing Cam's handwriting and remembering the moment he chose silence over trust.

The sound of quills scratching down the hall had faded hours ago. Only the crackle of blue fire answered them.

"She's not on any thread," Corin murmured. His voice was too low, almost drowned by the whispering fire. "The foresight is blind. The scrying—blank. Even the Book's gone quiet."

Ben folded his arms tight across his chest. "Then say it plain."

Corin's eyes lifted. "If she's alive... the Veil is holding her. And it's not ready to let go."

The words landed heavy in the silence. They'd been talking like this for a week and a half—in fragments, half-belief and half-denial.

Ben's chest felt hollow. His heartbeat hadn't slowed since the night she fell.

He glanced toward the table again. Cam's handwriting cut through the parchment—sharp strokes, impatient circles, arrows leading to nowhere and everywhere at once. He should've told her.

Gods, they both should have.

They had sat in this very room months ago, when the first fragments of the prophecy surfaced. Corin's voice had been steady then: The northern temples are too dangerous. Let her focus on what's within reach.

And Ben, still trying to keep her safe, had agreed.

Now that silence had a body. A cost.

If they'd told her about the Cradle, she wouldn't have chased Molwyn. She wouldn't have been there when the sky tore open.

He closed his eyes, forcing down the burn in his throat.

The words sat heavy between them like another ghost they didn't have room for.

Ben's throat ached at the thought, but he kept his voice steady. "Then we find where it's holding her."

Corin didn't look up. "I've already sent for them," he said quietly.

"Who?"

"Kaden, Orren, Tessa." Corin paused. "They should be here any minute."

As if on cue, the war room doors groaned open against the wind.

Snow swept in around three dark shapes—Kaden first, his coat edged in frost; Orren a step behind, pale and unreadable; Tessa striding last, her braid undone, her eyes sharp despite the sleeplessness that clung to all of them. They looked like ghosts who hadn't realized they were still alive.

"Tell me we found something," Tessa said, her voice cutting through the cold. "Anything."

Corin nodded once. "Val found something."

Val stepped forward, setting her hand on the scattered maps. "Cam's notes," she said. "They were all over the library—half of them burned, half illegible. But this one..." She pointed to a smaller map spread near the edge of the table. "She wrote over it herself."

Orren came closer, studying the faded ink. "What kind of notes?"

Val's finger moved to the northern coast. "Two locations. Both temple ruins. One marked with a symbol next to this bay—up here, near the edge of Valmira, to the north Veilrend Sea. The other just says: Where the Hollow was first born."

Kaden leaned in closely at the end of the table, his eyes narrowing. "'West is wrong I know that now,'" he murmured aloud Cam's notes. He looked up at Val. "The Hollow's origins were never in Eldvale."

"That's what she thought too," Val said. "She wrote that in the margins—questioned it. But it fits what she was researching before she fell."

Ben watched them, his heart heavy but unwilling to hope too loudly. "You think she tried to reach one of them."

Kaden crossed to Val on the other side of the table, gaze flicking between her and Ben. "You think she teleported."

Val nodded once. "The light we saw—the violet-black, and white gold—none of us could explain it. But Kaden's right, she could've opened something. I've seen Kaden open portals before, but this was... different. Wilder. It could have been her. The color was different, but it was a portal. Or something close."

Kaden's mouth tightened. "Teleporting somewhere you've never seen is reckless. Even I can't anchor a jump like that without risk." His voice dropped. "She could've aimed for one temple and ended up near the other—or somewhere else entirely."

"Or the Veil itself," Corin said quietly.

Val nodded grimly. "She wasn't coherent after the attack. Between Alex, the Vorrakai, the Mirebats—she was half bleeding, half spent. Her magic was unraveling before she even fell. She may have been thinking of the north when she fell or something else."

Ben's stomach turned. The idea had haunted him for days, and still it didn't feel real. "If she tore a gate by accident..." He trailed off, unable to finish.

"Then she's somewhere beyond the mountains," Val said. "Near the Cradle. I think she was aiming for it."

Silence settled thick around them. The kind that hummed with too many unsaid things.

Orren's voice broke it. "Then we can't leave either site unsearched. Not if she's trapped. Or dying."

Corin exhaled slowly. His eyes lingered on the northern mountains—the Cradle's edge glowing faintly under the wardlight. "Those temples were abandoned for a reason. There's Veilborn activity near both."

Kaden's tone snapped cold. "So is the cost of doing nothing." His voice cut through the air like a blade, quiet but sure. "You can't protect us from this one, uncle."

The older man's gaze met Kaden's—steady, unflinching. "I'm not trying to protect you. I'm trying to make sure we don't lose anyone else."

Ben's gaze swept the table—the faces illuminated by blue flame and fading maps. Tessa's jaw clenched. Val's fingers twitched near the edge of the parchment. Kaden's eyes burned with quiet fury. Orren said nothing, but his knuckles whitened around the knife hilt at his hip.

Every one of them was waiting for him to choose. To say something that would make the world make sense again.

But it wouldn't. It couldn't.

He looked to Corin. The older man's expression was unreadable—all iron restraint and quiet regret.

They didn't need words. Both of them knew what they'd done.

"If we'd told her," Ben said softly, "she might not have gone south."

The words burned in his chest before he even knew he'd spoken them.

Corin's eyes closed briefly. "I know."

"She trusted us," Ben went on, voice low and raw. "And we made her fight blind."

Corin didn't answer. He didn't have to.

Ben drew a breath, forcing himself upright. He stared down at the map, at the inked ridges cutting through Karethwyn's north like scars.

"Then we fix it."

He looked around the table—their faces drawn, eyes hollowed by grief but still burning with that same stubborn spark. "She'd do the same for any of us. We're not leaving her out there."

Val's head lifted. "How?"

Ben straightened, the decision falling into place even as his heart rebelled against it. "We split. Two teams. Fast and light. One to northern mountains, one north to the bay by the Veilrend sea. We cover both."

Corin hesitated. "It'll stretch us thin."

"So will losing her for good."

The words came out like steel, quiet but final.

Corin studied him for a long moment, then nodded. "I'll handle the deployments. We move at dawn."

The group stilled—the air itself holding its breath.

For the first time since she fell, something flickered among them. Not certainty. Not peace.

Just the thin, defiant spark of hope.

Ben looked down at Cam's handwriting one last time, her inked circles glowing faintly in the firelight. His throat tightened, but he managed a whisper meant only for her.

"Hold on, kid. We're coming."

The ward-fire answered with a soft crack, blue light flaring across the map like dawn breaking over snow—or a promise trying to be born.

⟐ ☽ ⚡ ☾ ⟐

Snow drifted slow and soundless over the fortress wall.

The wind had died sometime after dusk, leaving only the faint hiss of flakes against stone. The world beyond was little more than white and shadow, sky and earth blurring until they were the same color of cold.

Kaden stood alone at the parapet, hands braced on the frost-slick edge, watching the night fade toward gray. The war room's firelight still burned behind his eyes—maps, voices, Ben's vow echoing like a heartbeat that wouldn't quiet.

They had a plan now. It should have been enough to steady him.

It wasn't.

Tenebrin's voice unfurled through his mind, smooth as smoke, dark as the space between stars. *We shall find her, Shadowborn.*

The words hit like breath after drowning.

He pressed a hand to the parapet, feeling the stone bite into his palm, grounding himself. Below, the courtyard lay still—tracks half-buried in snow, torches guttering low. The fortress slept uneasy, but not silent; dragons stirred in their roosts, wings shifting against the wind, sensing the same unease that kept him upright.

"You sound certain," he murmured.

I am.

A faint pulse stirred in the bond—shadow meeting shadow, a whisper of heat where there should have been none. The contact steadied him, but only barely. Because certainty was dangerous. Hope was dangerous.

He looked out toward the mountains, where the horizon blurred into stormlight. The snow slipped through the cracks in the stone, melting against his gloves before freezing again. Hope felt like that—thin, fragile, melting as soon as it touched him.

And still he held it.

His shadows stirred at his feet, faint tendrils curling through the snow before dissolving in the wind. For once, he didn't force them still. Let them breathe, he thought. Let them reach.

And for a heartbeat—just one—something reached back.

A pulse that wasn't his. A tremor of fire, cold, and grief tangled into one.

The air around him shivered. His breath caught.

Tenebrin's eyes flared faintly in his mind. *You felt that too.*

Kaden didn't answer. Couldn't. The sensation faded as quickly as it came—like the echo of a scream carried from miles away. But it left a hollow ache beneath his ribs, raw and familiar.

"She's fighting," he whispered.

Yes.

Snow fell harder, the world vanishing into white. He didn't know if the heat in his chest was hope or pain—but it was real, and that was enough.

He closed his eyes, leaned into the wind, and let the words slip free.

"Hold on, Cam."

The wind carried them into the dark, toward whatever thread still tied them.

Chapter 51: The World Had Not Finished With Her Yet

A week and a half ago. The same night the sky split.

At first there was nothing.

No ground. No sky. Just black—thick, star-pierced silence stretching forever.

She floated there, weightless, breath shallow and slow, her body an afterthought. The stars pulsed like heartbeats in the dark, distant and small. Every sound came warped—as though she were listening from beneath water.

She thought she should be cold. She wasn't.

She thought she should be afraid. She couldn't remember how.

Something brushed her cheek. A whisper of warmth—rough skin, calloused thumb.

Wyatt.

Her mind seized on the name like a thread of light. A figure leaned over her—his outline flickering at the edges, bending through darkness. His touch lingered, half-fire, half-memory.

"You're so close, Cam..."

The words were soft, blurred, echoing. They shouldn't have reached her here, yet they did—stretching across distance like prayer. She tried to turn toward him, to find his face.

"Wyatt...?"

The light fractured. Pain bloomed through her chest—sharp, absolute.

The world vanished.

Then there was firelight.

Gentle, orange, alive.

A stone cottage breathed around her—cedar smoke, wool, the faint hum of rain on the roof. The air smelled of warmth and ash. Her body felt whole again. She could feel the weight of her hands, the curve of the blanket under her palms.

She didn't know this place.

And yet some small, impossible part of her did.

Wyatt sat by the window. Firelight traced his jaw, his shoulders, the soft rise and fall of breath. He turned as if he'd been waiting all along.

When he smiled, something in her chest ached so violently she almost couldn't breathe.

He reached for her. Fingers brushed hers—warm, steady, real. The kind of touch that anchored, that promised home.

No words. None needed.

Only the hush between heartbeats.

Outside, the wind began to rise. Rain lashed the shutters, a rhythm that sounded like wings. She wanted to stay in that sound, in that warmth—but the air was too still. Too perfect.

It wasn't real.

This isn't real, she thought. Not yet.

She tried to speak, to ask where they were, but the words shattered before they formed. The dream fractured with them, the cottage falling apart in a rush of sparks and cold air. Wyatt's hand slipped from hers. The fire went out.

And memory rushed in.

The sky. The screech of the Mirebat. The Veilborn.

Sylithra banking hard, scales flashing red through lightning. The spike that tore across Cam's shoulder.

The smell of burnt air, the roar, Waytt, the fall and the sky splitting open.

Then the pull—wind and light folding over her—falling, falling, until everything went black.

Cold. Sharp and painful.

It hit like a blow. Her lungs convulsed. Wet leaves plastered her face, the ground soft and sucking beneath her palms.

Cam gasped once—no air. The next breath stuttered, sharp and broken, her chest burning.

She dragged air in like a drowning woman. It hurt. Each inhale scraped.

Her throat felt raw. Her heartbeat pounded in her ears. For a moment she couldn't move—her body wouldn't listen. Only the trembling in her hands proved she was still alive.

When she tried to lift her head, the world spun. Her vision blurred, edges bleeding. A sob tore loose before she could stop it—small, startled, human.

It was then she realized what was wrong.

The silence.

No echo in her mind. No pulse of another presence.

She reached inward, instinctively—searching for Sylithra's tether, the heat and thunder of her dragon's bond.

Nothing.

Only static, thin and distant, like a heartbeat heard through walls.

The bond was still there—but dulled. Faint. Too far.

Her breath caught again. A different kind of pain this time—not the physical kind, but the hollow ache of absence.

She swallowed hard, forced her shaking arms under her. Her muscles screamed. It took three tries to roll onto her side, mud slick beneath her.

She saw the blood on her sleeve—dark, half-dried from the spike wound, reopened by the fall. Cuts scored her hands and knees, shallow but stinging.

Too fast. Too wrong. Silver veins crawled along her shoulder—proof she was healing faster than her body could bear.

The forest loomed around her—trees hunched like watchers, roots curling over stone. The air was dense, wet, alive. When she blinked, the path in front of her seemed to change; shapes shifted at the edges of vision.

Karethwyn.

She knew these trees.

But they didn't know her.

She tried to rise again. Her legs gave way. Her breath came out ragged, too loud in the silence. The forest didn't answer. The world felt endless.

A gust stirred the branches, showering her with rain that was cold as ice. The sound of it filled the space where her dragon's voice should have been.

Find them, she told herself. *Find him.*

But the compass in her chest spun wild. Even thinking his name hurt. Saying it might shatter her.

Her arms trembled, elbows sinking into the cold mud. The sky above blurred silver through rain.

"Survive... first," she breathed, the words barely more than air.

Her arms folded. She stayed where she fell, cheek pressed to the earth.

Feel it later, her mind whispered. *When it's safe. When it won't break you.*

Rain continued—soft at first, then steady, drumming against the leaves. It soaked through her hair, down her spine, into the soil.

She stayed there, bent and breathing, until the forest blurred to gray.

Cam closed her eyes and let sleep take her.

No movement. No sound but the storm.

And somewhere in that rhythm, low and far away, thunder rolled—slow, patient, almost kind.

Like a heartbeat.

Like a promise that the world had not finished with her yet.

Chapter 52: Breaking Point

Dawn broke cold over Ember Fortress.

Snow dusted the courtyard stones, turning every breath to steam and every step to sound. The air carried that brittle stillness that came before storms—too sharp, too clean, like the world had been scrubbed of warmth. Even the sky looked unfinished, pale light leaking through cracks in the clouds.

Skylith crouched low near the gate, wings furled tight, her scales catching the light like embers frozen under glass. Brontheus loomed beside her, restless, smoke coiling from his nostrils as if the cold itself were an insult. Their breath mingled in the air—fire and storm, heat and thunder—an echo of everything the world had taken from them.

We will find your daughter, Forgeheart, Skylith murmured, her voice a low, rippling heat in his mind.

Ben didn't answer. Words felt useless now. He checked the straps on his pack a second time, then his sword, then the small bundle lashed to the saddle behind him. His hands moved with mechanical precision, but the edges of his gloves trembled—something he pretended was just the cold.

The courtyard smelled of iron and smoke. Beneath it lingered something older—ashes that no snow could bury.

Across the yard, Val stood with her arms folded, hood drawn up against the wind. The frost in her hair caught the weak light, and for a heartbeat she looked far older than she was. When she saw him looking, she gave a single, steady nod—no words, no demands. Just the kind of understanding that lived between people who had already lost too much.

Ben's chest tightened. He turned away before she could see it. There were too many things she deserved to say to him, and none he was ready to hear.

Tessa swung onto Brontheus with practiced ease, her braid whipping in the wind. Orren climbed up behind her, silent as always, his eyes already scanning the horizon. They looked like figures carved from the same winter—grim, ready, unyielding.

Ben rested one gloved hand against Skylith's neck. The dragon's pulse thrummed beneath her scales, steady and alive, a heartbeat against his palm.

Wyatt.

The thought struck like flint. The world still felt wrong without him—off-balance, one beat behind. And now Cam...

A dozen memories clawed for the surface—her laugh, her impossible fire, the way she faced the world like it owed her an answer—but he shoved them back before they could take form. He couldn't see her like that. Not yet. Not when she might already be gone.

You've buried too many ghosts to start building new ones, Skylith's voice flickered, a whisper between flame and smoke.

He didn't respond. He only tightened his grip; jaw locked against the cold.

"Not this time," he muttered, voice barely sound.

Skylith crouched lower, wings unfolding with a rush of heat that seared the frost from the stones. Snow spiraled upward as she leapt, the courtyard falling away beneath them in a blur of gray stone and blue wardlight.

The fortress shrank to a speck below, a single flame in an ocean of white.

The sky widened—gray, endless, waiting.

High above them, the clouds were already moving wrong—wind curling east when it should have blown north. The air smelled faintly of ozone, of something old and waking.

None of them noticed.

Not yet.

◈ ☽ ⚡ ☾ ◈

Snow fell slow and silent over the northern ridges.

It whirled around Tenebrin's wings in pale spirals, melting to steam where it touched the dragon's dark-gray scales. Each beat of his wings pushed them higher into the morning sky until Ember Fortress was only a smear of smoke and stone far below.

They flew north—into the cold, into the silence, into the unknown.

Virellan flew beside them, Val's silhouette small against the dragon's wide purple-gray wings.

Above them, Sylithra cut through the haze like a shadow of starlight, her gold-veined scales catching what little sun there was. The great dragon made no sound, but her presence pressed against the bond like a heartbeat, constant and watchful. She didn't need to speak for them to understand why she came. She hadn't asked to join the flight. She had simply looked at them, and no one had dared tell her no.

Below, the world stretched white and endless. The Karethwyn forests rolled toward the Veilrend Sea, every tree rimed in frost, every river frozen to silence. Somewhere beyond that expanse was the place the map ended—and the last trace of Camomile Layton.

Val's voice slipped through the dragonlink, quiet and uncertain.

"Do you really think she's still alive?"

Kaden's answer came fast, sharper than he meant.

"I'll know if she isn't."

The wind stole the edge from his tone, but not the truth behind it.

He could still feel her—faint as an ember under ash, but there. The bond between them had always been more than friendship, more than prophecy. It was the unspoken understanding of two people who'd carried too much too young. Losing her would mean losing the last thread tying him back to what was left of Wyatt.

Tenebrin's voice rolled through him, low and resonant. *She burns still, Shadowborn. The flame flickers, but it has not gone out.*

Kaden's throat tightened. He looked out over the endless sweep of snow, where the world blurred into cloud and sea. The cold bit at his eyes until they watered, but he didn't blink.

"I couldn't save my brother," he whispered into the wind. "I won't fail her too."

Val glanced over from Virellan's saddle, her expression unreadable, but he caught the small, steady nod she gave him through the storm.

Tenebrin rumbled beneath him, gathering strength in his wings.

Then we fly until we find her.

Kaden leaned forward, the wind cutting through his hair.

"Hold on, Cam," he said, barely more than breath. "We're coming."

The dragons banked north, three shadows against the gray sky, their wingbeats fading into the rising storm.

◈ ☽ ⚡ ☾ ◈

The wind bit hard enough to sting. Frost gathered along her lashes as Brontheus climbed through the cloudbank, each wingbeat punching a hollow rhythm into the morning sky. Ice crusted along the edges of Brontheus's wings, splintering and falling away with every beat. Snow tangled in Tessa's braid and stung her cheeks, the air so cold it cut like glass when she breathed. The world below blurred to white and gray—fortress, forest, river—everything swallowed by distance.

We fly toward the cold, Brontheus rumbled, voice like rolling thunder across her bones. *Toward the wound in the world.*

"Yeah," she said quietly, breath catching in the wind. "I know."

The dragon's scales thrummed with power beneath her palms, faint arcs of lightning tracing between them before fading. His storms were close to the surface today. Restless. Waiting.

They had split at dawn—two paths into the unknown.

Kaden, Val, and their dragons, Tenebrin, Virellan, and Sylithra, had headed toward the north Veilrend Sea, chasing the coordinates scrawled in Cam's notes.

Ben, Orren, and Tessa had taken the other route northeast up toward the Valthorne Range, where the air already tasted of snow and static.

Ahead, Skylith cut a molten path through the gray, Ben a dark shape against her back. Even at this height, Tessa could see the set of his shoulders—rigid, locked, carrying too much. He hadn't spoken since the courtyard. None of them had.

The silence between them was the kind that pressed against bone.

We used to laugh on these flights, she thought. *Race the sunrise. Shout until the dragons told us to shut up.*

Now even the air seemed to mourn with them—thin, cold, unwilling to carry sound.

She glanced over her shoulder. Orren sat behind her, steady despite the updrafts, his eyes sweeping the horizon with the focus of someone who saw danger in everything—and usually wasn't wrong. His calm always carried an edge, like he was built from quiet knives.

"You're staring," he said flatly, voice just loud enough to reach her through the wind.

"I'm thinking," she shot back.

"Same thing, sometimes."

She exhaled through her nose, half a laugh, half frustration. "You always this talkative before dawn?"

"Only when the company insists."

Their eyes met for a heartbeat, the wind between them snapping like a live wire. Then he looked away first, scanning the horizon again.

She rolled her shoulders and turned back forward.

Brontheus rumbled beneath her, lightning crawling faintly along his wings. His power was always close to breaking loose; she felt it like static in her teeth.

Your heart beats too fast, Stormsinger, he murmured. *Storm inside. Let it breathe.*

Tessa patted his neck, grounding herself on the warmth of scale and pulse. "If I let it breathe, we'll both end up burning something down."

Then let the ashes fall where they must.

That earned a small, dry laugh. "You sound like her."

The fire-born?

"Cam," she said softly. "Yeah."

Perhaps she learned it from me, Brontheus rumbled, voice dipping low, fond in a way dragons rarely were.

The ache that followed the words was sudden and sharp. Wyatt gone. Cam missing. The circle splintered piece by piece. And still they flew—because stopping would mean admitting how empty the sky had become.

They flew as long as they could that first day.

The sky had burned a brittle blue at noon and bled gray by dusk, light draining until even the dragons' fire felt muted. When the winds turned erratic, they set down in a hollow of rock and frost, just long enough for the dragons to rest their wings. No one spoke while they ate. The stars above them looked close enough to shatter if she breathed too hard.

By the second morning, they rose before dawn. The cold had deepened into something alive—biting at their hands, turning every exhale to crystal.

The storm that had stalked them since Ember Fortress finally broke over the peaks, a white roar tearing across the ridges. Snow flew in every direction, spinning so thick it erased the horizon and sky alike.

Far ahead, the clouds thickened—dark veins threading through pale light. A bruise on the horizon.

"Stormfront," she murmured, though the word carried more weight than weather.

Brontheus's growl vibrated through her spine. *Not a storm I know.*

Behind her, Orren leaned slightly forward. "Hold course north," he said, voice low but cutting clean through the wind. "If we divert now, we lose the current."

She twisted enough to glance back at him. "You sure about that? You don't feel that pressure?"

He met her gaze evenly. "I feel it. Doesn't mean we flinch."

A wry smile tugged at her mouth. "You sound like a dragon rider."

Orren's brow twitched, just a fraction. "Don't insult me."

"Not an insult." She turned forward again, wind pulling the words thin. "Just means you're finally starting to sound like one of us."

Lightning flickered under Brontheus's wings, echoing her pulse. "You know," she muttered, turning back toward the clouds, "one of these days, that calm of yours is going to get us both killed."

"Or keep us alive," he said.

Her mouth twitched. "Guess we'll find out."

The wind rose. The clouds swallowed the sun whole. For a moment, everything was shadow and motion—their formation stretching thin across the pale morning sky.

Below them, the peaks of the Valthorne Range unrolled like a frozen sea; above, the light dimmed to a thin, trembling coin behind the haze.

For a while there was only wind—the steady thunder of wings, the pulse of heartbeats shared through the dragonlink. Even the air felt watchful.

Threads of shadow drifted at the edge of sight, moving against the wind.

No one spoke of it. But every rider felt it—the weight in the air before something breaks.

And still they flew.

The peaks stretched below in a blur of white and shadow. The wind tore across her face, sharp enough to sting, but she didn't mind it. The cold meant she could still feel something.

Brontheus cut through the storm like a blade, his wings carving great arcs of silver through the clouds. Each wingbeat thudded through her spine—a rhythm she'd flown to since she was sixteen. It should have been comforting. It wasn't.

The silence pressed too close.

Not peace. Not calm. Just waiting.

Ahead, Skylith was a faint ember through the haze—Ben's shape outlined against her molten glow. Even at this distance, she could tell from the way he sat that he was locked in his head again. The whole sky seemed to carry the weight of it.

She shifted her grip on the reins, feeling the ache in her shoulders. Two days of flight. Two days of holding the cold at bay. Of pretending not to hear the whisper of the storm chasing them north.

Orren moved behind her, steady as ever, his balance perfect even through the crosswinds. The man was infuriatingly composed—like the world would have to break in half before he even blinked.

"Getting colder," he said, his voice almost lost to the wind.

"Yeah. It's biting."

He leaned a little, scanning the horizon. "Still better than waiting around to freeze at the fortress."

Tessa's mouth twitched. "Didn't know you were capable of optimism."

"Don't tell anyone."

For a moment—just one—the exchange almost felt normal. The kind of banter she hadn't had since before everything fell apart. Then Brontheus's low growl rolled through her bones, deep enough to cut through the wind.

Something stirs below, he warned.

Her pulse stumbled. She leaned forward in the saddle, peering through the haze. The forest blurred beneath them—frozen, endless, eerily still.

Then—movement. A ripple in the white.

"Bron?!"

The dragon's muscles bunched beneath her. *Hold tight.*

For a heartbeat, everything stopped—the wind, the clouds, even the sound of her own breath. The world seemed to hold itself still.

The air screamed.

A sudden screech split the clouds as Mirebat erupted from the tree line—black wings slicing through the snow, hundreds of them, shrieking as they climbed toward the light.

Orren swore behind her. "Gods—"

Seconds later, the Wraithcalls joined them—hollow, human, wrong. The sound tore through the dragonlink like glass through silk.

"Left flank! Keep formation!"

Watch the—

The voices cut out. Static. Then silence.

"Ben?" she called, but the word vanished into the wind.

Brontheus roared, the sound deep enough to rattle her ribs. Lightning arced across his scales, tearing through the nearest Mirebat mid-flight. The creature exploded into ash and snow, wings disintegrating before they hit the ground.

Another dove from above—she saw it too late. Claws scraped across her shoulder, ripping leather. Brontheus twisted hard, and the world tilted.

Orren's arm snapped around her waist before she could slide off the saddle. The movement was instinct—sharp, strong, no hesitation. His other hand clamped onto the harness strap just as Brontheus righted himself with a violent jolt.

"Try not to fall," she gasped, breath catching in the freezing air.

"Working on it," he muttered, voice rough against her ear.

For a heartbeat, everything was too close—his grip, the heat of him against her back, the smell of steel and frost. Then another shriek split the air, and they both moved in the same instant.

Tessa raised her short blade, slashing upward as a Mirebat dove low across Brontheus's flank. Orren twisted behind her, throwing a knife that struck true through another's throat. The creature shrieked once and fell, its body trailing black smoke into the snow below.

Brontheus roared again, lightning rippling along his wings. *Too many,* his voice thundered through their bond. *The storm hides them.*

"I see that," Tessa hissed, wiping blood from her cheek.

Orren's voice came steady despite the chaos. "We have to climb—get above them!"

She nodded once. "Bron—up!"

The dragon surged skyward, muscles coiling with raw power. Snow and shadow blurred around them, Mirebat scattering in their wake.

But the storm wasn't letting go.

The wind screamed, white swallowing everything—the horizon, the mountains, even Skylith's fire below. For a moment Tessa thought she saw her, golden flame cutting through the blizzard—then it vanished, snuffed out in a breath.

"Skylith!" she shouted. No answer.

The silence hit her like a blow. The dragonlink was gone—cut off, empty. She reached inward instinctively, searching for Ben's voice, Skylith's fire, anything. Nothing. Only the roar of wind.

We're alone, she realized.

Brontheus banked hard to avoid a diving shadow, his wingtip clipping a Mirebat mid-strike. The impact spun them sideways again. Orren's grip tightened; Tessa felt the tremor in his hand even as his tone stayed calm.

"Still with me?"

"Barely," she gritted out.

Brontheus growled, fury building. Hold fast, Stormsinger. The wind hunts with us still.

"Then let it hunt," she muttered, raising her blade as lightning sparked along Brontheus's wings. "Because I'm done running."

The dragon's roar shook the storm. Lightning split the sky.

And the storm answered back.

◈ ☽ ⚡ ☾ ◈

Silence hit harder than the storm.

The wind still screamed, snow still tore past in violent sheets, and beneath it—nothing. No firelight ahead. No Skylith. No echo of Ben's voice through the storm. Just white and distance swallowing everything.

Brontheus's wings beat heavy against the wind, the great dragon straining to hold altitude. Tessa's shoulders were tight; her hands locked on the reins. She hadn't said a word since the last strike. Her braid whipped across his arm, damp and half-frozen, and still she didn't look back.

Orren's hands ached from gripping the harness. He glanced down once—the forest below was a smear of shadow and broken ice. Whatever waited down there, it was waiting for the living to fall.

When Brontheus dropped low to avoid a ridge, Orren was thrown sideways, almost clear of the saddle. He caught himself at the last instant—hand closing around Tessa's waist once more. She jolted, breath catching, but didn't pull away.

"Still alive," he muttered.

"Barely," she answered, voice ragged from cold.

Her tone held that same edge he'd heard mid-fight—a spark she'd never bother to hide. He wasn't sure if it was anger or adrenaline that kept her steady, but it worked.

The blizzard swallowed them whole again. No horizon. No sky. Only motion.

Then the noise changed.

The storm didn't quiet—it *bent*. Like the air itself was listening.

He stilled.

Every sense sharpened until the world was a blade. The hiss of snow against leather, the pulse in his ears, the faint hum of energy beneath the ice. Too much. Too alive. He'd been feeling it since Ember Fortress—sounds that shouldn't carry this far, colors too bright, shadows that moved when he wasn't looking.

And now, something else.

A pulse beneath it all—low, violet, and strange. It crawled under his skin like heat that wasn't heat, like someone—or something—had just noticed him.

It wasn't threat. It wasn't human.

And it wasn't hers.

Still, it felt like recognition.

He forced a breath through his teeth, shaking it off. "Not now," he muttered.

Tessa leaned forward against the wind. "What?"

"Nothing," he lied, eyes narrowing against the white. "Keep flying."

Brontheus's growl rolled through the storm like thunder answering thunder. The dragon climbed, snow swirling in its wake, and the pulse beneath Orren's skin faded—but didn't vanish.

He gripped the hilt at his belt, jaw tight.

Whatever that was, it would come for him again.

And when it did, he'd be ready.

◈ ☽ ⚡ ☾ ◈

Karethwyn did not end.

It only repeated itself—tree after tree, shadow after shadow, the same pattern of frost and root until her eyes blurred. The air was heavy enough to breathe like water. No birds. No tracks. No sound but the dull crush of her boots against snow.

She didn't know how long she'd been walking.

The days bled together until time stopped meaning anything. One sunrise blurred into the next—if it was sunrise at all. The light never truly changed, just dimmed from gray to silver to gray again, a color that didn't belong to sky or snow or breath.

The first night she tried to build a camp. She stacked branches too brittle to burn, tore bark with bleeding hands, whispered every spark spell she knew. The magic sputtered once, twice, then faded into smoke that died before it rose. By morning, her fingers had split from the cold. She wrapped them in torn cloth and kept walking, her skin stiff with frost and blood.

The second day came with wind. It screamed through the trees, tearing needles from the pines and hurling them like glass. She leaned into it until her muscles locked, until her face went numb, until even pain felt far away. Her lips cracked from the cold, and when she licked them she tasted iron.

At midday she found a stream sealed under glass-clear ice. She knelt, cracked it open with the hilt of her knife, and drank what she could before her lips turned blue. The water burned all the way down, sharp and metallic. She laughed once—too loud, too wild—because even that hurt felt like proof she was still here.

The second night she dreamt standing up. She thought she saw movement in the trees—a pale shape, maybe a deer, maybe something else—but when she blinked it was gone. The world rearranged itself every time she looked away, like the forest was shifting around her instead of letting her pass.

By dawn her boots were soaked through. Frost stiffened her coat; her braid had frozen solid against her neck. Her breath came out in ragged bursts, white ghosts that vanished too quickly. She began talking to the silence just to keep her voice working. She asked the trees for directions. She apologized to ghosts she couldn't name.

Once, she thought she saw smoke in the distance—a faint gray thread winding through the air. She stumbled toward it, half-running, heart stuttering with sudden hope. When she reached the clearing, there was nothing. Only her own footprints and the echo of her breathing.

By noon she was shaking. Her stomach ached, her legs heavy and slow. She thought of Ben's lessons—dig beneath roots for the pale knots, scrape the frost from berries, chew pine needles if you have to. She obeyed them all. The berries were bitter, the roots soft and tasteless, but they were something.

The sky stayed fixed in that same colorless light. Snow fell in fine threads that clung to her lashes and hair, softening everything until even her shadow blurred. Every tree looked the same. Every path ended where it began.

When she tripped over a root, she didn't get up right away. She stayed there, cheek pressed to the snow, breath fogging in small bursts. The cold felt easier than the motion. Safer. The forest smelled of ice and old earth. She could almost imagine lying there until it covered her completely—until she was just another frozen shape among the roots.

But the pull in her chest refused to let her stop. That low, steady hum—like heartbeat, like command—dragged her upright again. She hated it. Hated that even now, when everything else was gone, it still told her where to go.

On the morning of the third day, the world was a mirror. Every step sank a little deeper into snow, every breath burned like smoke. Her hands shook too badly to hold anything anymore. Somewhere above the canopy, a crow cried once and fell silent, the sound folding in on itself like it had never happened.

She kept moving anyway.

The cold had become part of her—inside her lungs, under her skin. When she breathed, it burned like glass. She could feel herself thinning, unraveling with every step.

She told herself she'd stop once she found a clearing, a sign, anything familiar. But every direction led her back to the same narrow paths, the same haunted silence. The forest didn't want her to leave.

And she didn't dare stop long enough to think about why.

When the light finally dimmed, she found a hollow beneath a fallen pine, dry enough to keep a spark. She gathered what twigs she could with numb fingers and coaxed a small fire to life. The flame wavered like it didn't trust her. She couldn't blame it.

She sat with her knees pulled tight to her chest, chewing on a few bitter berries she'd found hours before. They burst like frost in her mouth—cold, tasteless.

Smoke drifted up through the branches, vanishing into the gray. The fire painted her fingers gold, but the warmth never reached her bones.

"I bet you'd say I'm doing it wrong," she sighed murmuring into the dark, voice hoarse from silence.

Wyatt would've laughed—low, quiet, the sound that always found her no matter how far she ran.

And then—for a breath, she heard it.

A soft exhale, a shift in the air behind her.

She froze. The fire cracked, throwing light across the trees.

He stood just beyond the glow—hood up, head bowed, one hand resting on the hilt of his blade. The edges of him wavered, like heat through glass.

"Wyatt?" Her voice splintered.

He didn't move. Didn't speak. The wind carried no breath, no heartbeat. Just silence.

Then the light flickered, and he was gone.

The forest swallowed the space he'd filled.

Her chest hollowed. "You're not real," she whispered, but her voice shook. "You never are."

She pressed both hands to her eyes, fighting the sting there. The fire popped, scattering sparks into the dark.

"I don't need you," she said, but it came out a plea.

The only answer was the slow hiss of snow melting into flame.

She stared until the embers dimmed to coals, her reflection fading with them. When the last spark went out, the cold rushed back in.

She lay down beside the ashes; arm curled over her face. The earth felt unyielding beneath her, too solid to dream on.

Her last thought before sleep was the echo of his voice—*You're so close, Cam...*—and the way the words always lingered long after the visions ended.

By morning, the fire was gone. Only a thin curl of smoke and the smell of burnt pine remained.

She rose, brushed frost from her hair, and started walking again.

She didn't dare remember.

The forest was gray, the light thin and cold as breath. Each step sank a little deeper into snow. Somewhere above the canopy, a crow cried once and fell silent, the sound folding in on itself like it had never happened.

She tried south again. She lit a spark against a tree to mark her path, a trembling thread of violet-gold flame that hissed and died.

Hours later, she found the same mark still smoking.

Her hands started to shake. "No..."

She spun, tried another path. Then another. Every turn brought her back to the same stretch of trees, the same patch of frost.

Her voice cracked when she spoke. "No matter where I go—it's north. Always north!"

The words fell flat in the stillness. Nothing answered.

She turned in a slow circle, searching the trees as if they might rearrange themselves into a door. Her breath came fast and shallow, misting the air in quick bursts that vanished before she saw them fade. Even her heartbeat felt wrong—too slow, too loud, echoing through her ribs like something trapped inside.

She thought she'd gotten used to silence by now, but this one was different.

It listened.

She pressed her hands over her face, breathing hard, willing the sound of her heartbeat to drown everything out.

The cold cut through her coat now, clean as a blade. It crawled down her neck and into her chest until every breath stung. The forest waited, ancient and still, like it knew what she was about to do and pitied her for it.

You're fine. Just keep moving.

Wyatt's voice whispered in the memory, warm, patient, steady as stone.

Her throat seized. She opened her eyes and saw him standing in the ghost-light of her mind—mud-streaked hair, soft grin, the way his shoulders relaxed when he saw her coming.

The image hit too fast, too sharp. She bit it back until it hurt.

"Don't," she whispered. "Don't do that. Not now."

The wind stirred through the branches—gentle, almost kind—and that broke her.

Her knees hit the frozen ground.

The sound of it—bone on ice—echoed through the trees like a small, final thing.

She stayed like that, breathing through her teeth, her breath coming out in white bursts that hung before fading. Her palms pressed into the earth until they ached. It was the only thing that still felt real.

"I don't know where I'm going anymore!"

It ripped out of her throat raw. Too loud for the stillness.

Nothing came back.

No answer. No echo.

Just her.

Her body started to shake. First her hands, then her shoulders. She wasn't cold anymore. She was burning under her skin, caught between a sob and a scream she couldn't free.

She struck the ground again, her fist colliding with ice. Pain flared up her arm. She hit it again. Again. Until blood welled between her fingers.

"Why—why does it keep taking everything?"

Her voice broke. "Why can't you just stop!"

The scream that followed didn't sound human. It was animal, torn from the deepest part of her.

And the world answered.

Magic surged outward, no longer restrained, no longer sane.

Fire erupted first—violent, uncontrolled, searing a ring into the frost.

Ice leapt to meet it, crawling up tree trunks, cracking bark to crystal.

Wind spiraled through the clearing, lifting her hair, tearing leaves and ash into a whirling storm.

Shadow pulsed at her feet, swallowing what little light was left.

She was at the center of it—all of it.

And she didn't stop it.

"Fine!" she shouted into the storm, throat raw. "Then take me too!"

The fire answered in kind, rushing outward, feeding on her grief until it painted the forest in red.

Her vision blurred with heat and tears. She tasted salt and smoke and iron.

"Please," she gasped. "Please, I can't—"

She doubled over, hands clawing at the dirt as if she could bury the power, bury herself. But the magic kept coming, drawn by the thing she could no longer hide: she missed him.

Not in a quiet way.

Not in a way the world could soothe.

She missed him like breath. Like heartbeat. Like home.

Her voice cracked around his name. "Wyatt—"

That single word broke the storm's rhythm. It made everything worse.

Flames arched higher. Ice screamed as it froze them midair. Shadows lashed out, devouring the edges of her light.

She could still see him—faint, flickering, the way he'd looked before he fell. The way his hand had slipped from hers.

Her chest seized. "You said you'd come back," she whispered. "You promised. You promised me."

The promise tasted like ashes.

She screamed again, until her throat tore. The magic shattered outward in waves. Trees split, the ground cracked, snow lifted in a violent spiral. It was as if the world itself couldn't hold her grief anymore.

Then, finally, everything fell silent.

The fire guttered. The wind died. The shadows thinned to smoke.

Cam fell with it.

She hit the ground hard, mud streaking her face, her palms raw and shaking. For a long moment she didn't breathe. Then, slowly, the air came back—thin, unsteady.

The forest around her steamed. The earth still glowed faintly where her magic had burned through. She could smell scorched pine, hear melting ice dripping like rain.

Her tears hadn't stopped. They just kept coming.

She pressed her hands over her mouth, trying to hold them in, but the sobs broke through anyway—harsh, ugly sounds pulled from the hollow in her chest where his name used to live.

"I can't let you go," she whispered between breaths. "I can't—I can't—"

Her body shook until there was nothing left in her.

All the anger, the guilt, the terror—all of it melted into one unbearable ache.

When the tears finally slowed, she was still on her knees, the world around her a ruin. The air smelled like endings.

Her voice was a whisper when it came again, almost lost to the cold.

"I don't want to move on."

The wind passed through the clearing, soft as breath.

She bowed her head and closed her eyes; her forehead pressed to the blackened earth. For a long time, she didn't move. She couldn't.

Snow began to fall again—gentle this time. It melted against her cheeks like small mercies.

When she finally looked up, the world had gone quiet.

Smoke drifted through the pale light, curling around her fingers.

Her breath shuddered out. "I'm still here," she said, hoarse, broken.

It wasn't a victory. It was a confession. The wind didn't answer. The words didn't sound like defiance this time. They sounded like beginning.

But something in the forest exhaled—a sound so faint she might've imagined it.

Cam closed her eyes and let the silence settle.

The grief didn't leave her. It never would. But for the first time in months, she didn't fight it.

She just let it live.

For a moment, in the hush between breaths, she almost thought she heard him again—quiet as snow, steady as before. Not a voice calling her back this time. Just a warmth that said, *stay alive.*

Chapter 53: First Signs

Dawn came thin and colorless.

Light filtered through the forest like breath through glass—soft, fractured, trembling against the frost. The trees glistened where snow had frozen in the night, and the ground beneath her was a patchwork of white and ash, the scars of what she'd burned through before collapsing.

Cam stirred under the roots of a fallen pine. The hollow had sheltered her from the storm, but the cold had settled in her bones. Every muscle ached. Her ribs felt bruised with every breath, and a dull, slow pain pulsed near her side where a jagged wound had half healed and split again. She touched it gently; her fingers came away red. Her magic flickered weakly at the contact—just a glow, a whisper of heat—but it sputtered out before it could mend anything. The faint scent of smoke lingered on her skin, like the memory of fire refusing to leave her. The light inside her was quieter now, working slow and small, like it was learning how to exist without burning her alive.

When she finally sat up, the forest turned with her. Frost drifted from the branches, slow as falling dust. The air tasted of iron and pine sap, sharp enough to sting the back of her throat. She could still remember the tumble from the ridge last night—the way the ground had vanished under her feet, her body slamming into rock and root, the rush of pain that stole her breath before everything went dark. She had tried to heal herself then, lying there in the dark, whispering broken words through chattering teeth. Nothing had worked. Her power had felt far away, unreachable, like it was watching her instead of answering.

Maybe it was mercy that she'd passed out.

She stayed there for a while, breathing. Listening. The forest wasn't silent anymore—not the way it had been. She could hear faint things now: the creak of ice in the boughs, the whisper of something moving far off, the heartbeat of snow falling from a high branch. The world was softer, slower. As if everything, even the air, was giving her time.

When she stood, her knees almost buckled. But she caught herself on a tree trunk, hand pressed against the rough bark, grounding in the rhythm of it—the pulse of something living and ancient running beneath her palm. The forest was cold, but not cruel. Not anymore.

She looked south. The way she'd been trying to go for days. Every instinct said home lay that way. But when she tried to move, the trees themselves seemed to close ranks—branches leaning toward one another until the path narrowed, shadows deepening until even the air thickened. The pull she'd been fighting for days hummed faintly in her chest, steady and patient. It didn't force her. It just waited.

"Fine," she murmured, voice rough. "North, then. If that's where you want me to go."

The wind shifted, brushing against her cheek like an answer.

So she went.

The snow crunched beneath her boots, every step releasing a small sigh of air. Her legs shook, but she kept walking. She didn't fight the pull this time; she let it guide her—whatever it was. It wasn't dragging her north. It was drawing her through herself, like a current she had stopped resisting. The more she let go, the more she felt him—not close, not clear, but somewhere just beyond reach. Still there, like a pulse behind the world.

After a while, she realized she was no longer cold. Or maybe she just couldn't feel it the same way. Her breath came steady, her thoughts quiet. There was no plan anymore, no direction, only movement. The rhythm of her footsteps matched something deep in her body, an echo she couldn't name—one she'd once shared with someone else. The ache in her chest pulsed with it, steady and low, as if the world itself refused to let her forget.

Branches stirred above her. A shape shifted in the underbrush—a shadow low to the ground, moving wrong, too fluid for any creature she knew. She didn't reach for her weapon. Didn't flinch.

"Don't follow me," she said quietly.

Magic rippled out from her like breath, invisible but heavy. The forest seemed to inhale, then exhale with her. The shadow hesitated, edges rippling as if it understood. It sank back into itself, gone as quickly as it had come. The space it left behind felt aware, but not threatening—like the world had chosen to leave her path open.

She kept walking.

The air grew warmer by degrees. Dawn slid between the trees in fractured golds, the light bending strangely as it fell—sigils flickering where the sun struck bark, faint runes curling through the mist. They were not symbols she recognized, but they felt familiar, like something she used to know before she learned to name it. Each one shimmered and faded as she passed, whispering along the edges of her vision—reminders that the Veil was nearer now, that she was walking a border the living rarely touched.

The pull inside her deepened. It was not a command. It was invitation.

Her hand brushed the nearest tree; the bark thrummed faintly beneath her fingertips, answering her touch. A whisper rode the wind then, low and fragmented, syllables half-formed.

"Cam..."

Her head snapped up.

The sound came again—soft, close, impossible.

She froze, heart pounding, every breath catching like glass in her lungs.

Nothing moved. Only the wind, threading between the branches.

She let out a shaky laugh, more breath than sound. "The forest's alive," she whispered. "Or I'm losing my mind."

Neither possibility scared her. Maybe both were true.

Her boots slid over a rise in the path. And then she saw him.

Wyatt.

He stood just ahead, turned slightly toward her, the light catching the edge of his coat. His shoulders were bare of snow, his hair dark against the pale air. He looked as he had before the fall—alive, whole, steady. For an instant, the world remembered how it used to be.

Her breath hitched.

She blinked once.

Gone.

Only sunlight filtered through the branches, shifting with the wind.

Her heart stumbled. Her knees almost did too. "You're not real," she whispered, but it came out soft, trembling. "You never are."

The forest didn't answer, but the wind moved through her hair like a hand.

Keep going, it seemed to say.

Her lips pressed together until they hurt. "I hate when you do that," she murmured, but she stepped forward anyway.

Smoke lingered faint in the air—pine tar, ash, memory. She caught herself whispering his name, just to hear it in her own voice. "Wyatt."

It sounded small. Not pleading, not broken—just human. The sound of someone learning how to live beside the ghost she still cared for.

The pull inside her steadied, not outward but inward, as though it were threading her back together one breath at a time. The more she followed, the lighter she felt—not in her body, but in the space around her ribs where grief had lived too long. It didn't fade. It shifted—like light through smoke, reshaping what it touched.

For a long moment she only breathed, listening to the quiet hum beneath her ribs.

She wasn't numb. She wasn't healed. But something had changed. The ache was still there—it just didn't hollow her out anymore. It filled her instead, shaping her from the inside, leaving room for breath.

The forest around her brightened, snow glittering on every branch. Shadows still moved at the edges of her vision, but none came close. They watched her pass. Respectful. Recognizing. Like they, too, remembered what it meant to keep walking after loss.

Her legs shook. Her palms were raw. She didn't cry. She didn't need to.

She walked.

Each step felt deliberate, a quiet vow.

Not to survive. Not even to escape. Just to be. Just to keep the promise of stillness she'd once made to the man who told her that home wasn't a place—it was a heartbeat.

The path wound through frost and fog until even the air shimmered. She felt it then—the Veil—close enough to taste on the back of her tongue, humming like a heartbeat older than her own. It was the same rhythm that had carried her through the fall, the same pulse she felt when she said his name. Still there. Still answering.

She stopped once, looking over her shoulder.

The forest had shifted behind her—branches leaning to seal the path she'd taken, as if to keep her from ever turning back.

"Guess that's settled," she said softly. Her breath rose white and vanished.

When she faced north again, the light seemed to part for her.

She walked toward it, slow and certain, her grief moving with her instead of against her. She hadn't let go. Not yet. Maybe not ever.

But she wasn't breaking anymore. For the first time since the world had burned, she didn't feel lost.

Not found either. But not lost.

And far ahead, somewhere deep beyond the tree line, something vast and unseen stirred—an old magic waking to the sound of her steps.

The Veil was waiting.

Chapter 54: Threads to the North

The storm hit like a living thing.

Wind clawed at Kaden's face, sharp as knives, tearing the breath from his lungs. Tenebrin surged through the gray, wings heaving against the gale's unrelenting drag. Snow slashed sideways in white sheets, so thick it blurred the horizon into nothingness. The world had become wind, cold, and the burn of breath.

Hold your course, Tenebrin rumbled through the bond, his voice deep and even despite the strain. Frost clung to his scales, but his eyes still gleamed pale silver in the stormlight.

Kaden leaned low, pressing close to the warmth of the dragon's neck. "Trying," he hissed through chattering teeth. Every movement was a fight—the wind wanted him gone, peeled from the saddle and lost to the sky.

Tenebrin bucked suddenly, a guttural snarl vibrating through his chest. The air itself felt wrong—dense, folding back on itself, dragging rather than pushing. The dragon's wings caught an eddy that shouldn't have existed, flinging them sideways before he forced them level again with a furious beat.

Somewhere ahead, Sylithra's dark silhouette cut through the clouds—massive, sure, gold-veined wings shimmering even in the gray. The only thing more constant than her presence was her voice, low and measured across the dragonlink.

We're way off course.

The words slipped like a blade through static.

Kaden blinked against the wind, shaking sleet from his lashes. *"Off course how?"*

Not weather, Sylithra answered, her tone like stone under pressure. *Something beneath the current pulls east. Not storm—something older.*

Tenebrin's growl rumbled low through his bones. *I feel it too. Not sky wind. Earth wind. Wrong direction.*

Kaden's stomach turned. "Great," he muttered under his breath, tightening his grip on the reins. "Because that's exactly what we need—a haunted storm."

Val's voice broke faintly through the link, distant but steady. *"Kaden—Virellan's fighting the updraft"*

He turned, squinting through the swirl of snow until he caught a glimpse of them—Virellan's wide gray-purple wings struggling just below, Val crouched low against the dragon's spine, hair torn wild by the wind. Even through the storm's chaos, her focus was razor-sharp, her jaw set.

"Stay high," he sent across the bond. *"We'll break through the worst of it together."*

The reply came as static, then her voice, soft but certain. *"Just don't let go."*

He almost smiled. *"Wouldn't dream of it."*

The storm rose in one sudden, violent surge—a wall of air that threw them both higher. Tenebrin roared, wings locking, body cutting through the clouds like a blade. Then the wind broke—sliced clean—and they burst through the upper veil.

Light exploded across the sky.

For a heartbeat, even the storm forgot how to breathe.

Below them, the world opened in silence.

◈ ☽ ⚡ ☾ ◈

The air cleared just long enough to steal her breath.

Virellan leveled out with a pained grunt, wings trembling against the crosswinds. The cold was still vicious, but it wasn't what made Val's stomach drop.

Below—where forest should have stretched unbroken—was ruin.

A wide scar cut through the snow, black and gray, ash swirling in lazy spirals between broken chimneys and splintered beams. The rivers were frozen mid-run, locked in place like veins turned to glass. Smoke drifted faintly in the air, though there was nothing left to burn.

Ash swirled in slow circles, rising instead of falling, as if gravity itself refused to touch this place.

It wasn't just destruction. It was absence.

A silence too heavy for mere ruin.

She stared, unable to breathe. "Gods..."

Her voice disappeared into the wind.

The snow didn't fall right here. It drifted in spirals, rising instead of settling. Each flake dimmed to gray before it touched the ground, as if the air refused to cleanse this place.

Sylithra's shadow coiled wide above them, her wings folding and unfolding in slow, uneasy rhythm. *The Veil... is thick here,* the dragon murmured, her tone almost reverent.

Val shivered—not from the cold, but from what pressed through the air. The wind wasn't just weather anymore. It hummed with a pattern, subtle but insistent, like a low voice speaking through snow. Beneath it, her magic stirred—water, illusion, the whisper of currents answering something unseen.

Her fingers twitched. She wasn't calling it. It was calling her.

"Kaden?" she sent across the link.

His reply came slow, heavy. *"I see it."*

Tenebrin flew level beside her now, massive wings cleaving the gray. Kaden's face was half-hidden by his hood, but even through the distance she saw the change—the recognition, the quiet dread.

She felt it too, through the bond. Guilt. Memory. The same ache she'd sensed in him since Wyatt fell, sharper now, buried under layers of command and silence.

His silence was deafening. She could feel the edge of it through the link—the kind that came from guilt, not distance. So she pushed warmth through, just a thought, a pulse of steady calm. *"You're not alone."*

His answer came like a sigh, thin and almost breaking. *"I know."*

Snow whipped between them, glittering like shards of glass.

Below, the ashes shifted. For a heartbeat, they formed patterns—curving lines, sigils half-buried by frost. She blinked, and they twisted into something else—a shape so familiar, letters strung together.

A name.

Gone before she could read it.

Her heart stuttered. *"Did you— "*

"I saw it," Kaden cut in, his tone tight.

Virellan let out a hiss, her voice coiling low in Val's chest. *This place remembers.*

Sylithra's wings flexed above them, each movement sending ripples of gold light through the storm. *We are seen,* she rumbled softly.

Val's breath fogged. She couldn't tear her eyes from the devastation below—the twisted frames, the pale outlines in snow where walls once stood. There was a shape to it, a story half-told in ash and ice.

"What happened here?" she whispered, though she already knew the answer.

No one spoke.

Tenebrin's growl rose from below, rolling like thunder under their hearts. The world screams beneath the ice.

Kaden's hand tightened on the reins. His gaze stayed on the ruins long after they passed overhead, his silence saying more than words ever could. The look in his eyes wasn't shock. It was recognition.

He knew this place. He just couldn't bear to name it.

Val turned her focus forward. The clouds were closing again, swallowing light and sound, but something deeper than storm still hummed in her blood. The Veil was near. The pull was stronger here.

And as the wind dropped to a low, rhythmic whisper, she realized it wasn't weather at all.

It was breathing.

Each gust drew the frost in and out like lungs beneath the ice.

The storm did not follow them.

It led.

Chapter 55: Blood in the Snow

Snow lashed across Skylith's wings, hissing like knives against her scales.

The wind burned Ben's cheeks raw, his breath freezing as soon as it left him. Skylith's dull orange glow pulsed beneath the pewter sky, her light fractured by the storm, each wingbeat slower, heavier. The air had grown thick enough to taste—iron, smoke, and the faint sting of ozone.

They'd lost the others hours ago.

The storm had split them apart near the ridge—one violent downdraft, a flash of white, and then nothing but static across the dragonlink. Tessa, Orren, and Brontheus had vanished into the clouds before Ben could even call their names.

Skylith had wanted to turn back.

He hadn't.

The sun was sinking fast behind the stormfront, its light a dull smear of gold bleeding through the clouds. Night would fall soon—too soon—and once darkness took the range, even Skylith's fire wouldn't be enough to see by. But he kept going anyway.

"Too long. It's been too long."

He shifted in the saddle, jaw locked, his shoulders rigid with exhaustion and refusal. Every gust felt like punishment. Every mile of endless white below looked the same—no sign of her, no trace, only the hollow ache of distance.

Skylith rumbled low, the sound deep enough to tremble through his bones. *We've searched half the range,* she murmured, her voice ember-warm even through the cold.

"I know." His voice came out rough, cracked by wind and worry. "But she's here. She has to be."

If she is we will find her, Forgeheart, Skylith said, the title a reminder of who he was before the guilt set in. *And we will find her alive.*

Ben exhaled, a plume of white mist tearing loose from his mouth. "I want to believe that, Sky."

Then do.

The dragon's tone softened to smoke and silence.

Below, the forest began to change.

The treetops bent in unnatural directions, their needles singed black, branches brittle as bones. The snow between them was streaked with red—thin veins at first, then long drags that gleamed faintly even through the storm's dim light.

Skylith's head twitched, nostrils flaring. *Blood.*

"I see it."

He guided her lower. The clearing unfolded beneath them like a wound—trees split, snow churned dark, the air itself trembling with heat that shouldn't exist in winter.

Bodies lay scattered across the drifts: deer, wolves, something that might've been a bear—all torn open, some burned to ash, others clawed apart by something that had no business being in the Valthorne Range.

Skylith's growl rippled through him, low and dangerous. *This is wrong.*

The ground bore the proof: claw marks deep enough to gouge the frozen earth, grooves melted smooth where fire and ice had collided. The snow hissed faintly where it touched the wounds, steaming like it couldn't bear to stay.

Ben stared. The world had gone utterly still—not peaceful, but *vacant*, as if the air itself had been scraped clean of life.

Even Skylith's wingbeats sounded wrong, muffled, like the sky was swallowing the noise.

It felt like flying inside a held breath.

"This isn't wild magic," he said, voice low. "It's something else."

The Veil stirs here.

He frowned, pulse tightening. "You think this is her doing?"

Skylith's pupils narrowed to thin slits. *No. This feels older. Hungrier.*

They glided low over the trees, branches snapping beneath the downdraft. The silence grew heavier, folding in around them until even the rhythm of his own heartbeat felt intrusive.

"Cam..." His voice cracked, barely sound. "If you don't come back soon..."

The wind took the rest. Tore it apart like the words were never meant to survive.

Grief pressed sharp under his ribs, but beneath it, something colder coiled tight—a deeper instinct that whispered not where is she, but what else is listening.

Above, the clouds began to twist.

Gray spiraled into gray, drawn toward an unseen center. The air trembled. Light flared faintly inside the storm—not lightning, but something older, slower, deliberate.

It pulsed once.

And Ben swore it was looking back.

For the first time since Isabella's death, he felt hunted.

Skylith's wings jerked. Her head snapped to the east, eyes molten with sudden focus.

"What do you see?"

Not see, she answered, her tone sharp as steel drawn from flame. *Feel.*

He turned. The clouds shifted.

Something moved inside them—tall, skeletal, and *wrong*, bending the light around its shape before vanishing as if the air itself closed over it.

Then—silence.

Not absence, but *pressure*.

Like the world was holding its breath, waiting for him to remember something he'd tried not to touch.

Memory found him anyway.

And he did.

Karethwyn.

Before Haldrin's Keep. Before she knew who he really was. Before the word *father* had weight between them.

Cam—nineteen, too thin, too angry, still learning what it meant to trust anyone. She stood in a clearing ankle-deep in mud, dragging his sword through the dirt.

"It's too heavy," she'd snapped, breath fogging in the chill morning air, fingers white around the hilt.

"Then lift it anyway," he'd said, crossing his arms. "You don't get stronger waiting for someone to make it easier."

She'd glared at him like she might throw it at his head just to make a point.

And then—jaw set, shoulders shaking—she'd lifted it again.

He'd almost smiled then. Almost.

And when she finally held it steady, breathless and disbelieving, she'd laughed—a short, bright sound that cracked the frost in the air.

She hadn't known who he was yet.

To her, he was just a soldier with too many scars and not enough patience. A teacher she didn't ask for but refused to give up on.

But gods, he'd known. He'd seen Isabella's fire in her, the same stubborn light. And in that laugh—he'd heard home.

He blinked—and it was gone.

The memory tore away like a page burned mid-sentence.

Only the storm remained.

Skylith's body went taut beneath him, her tail curling inward, claws cutting through the wind. *We should not be here,* she hissed. *The ground remembers blood.*

Ben pressed a hand to the back of her neck, grounding himself in her heat. "I know."

Something bleeds that is not prey.

The words turned his blood cold.

A streak of red cut through the snow below—fresh, steaming, too bright against the pale.

Whatever it came from was still alive.

Ben's fingers found his sword hilt by reflex. He knew it would be useless if this was a Veilborn trace, but it was something to hold.

Movement flickered in the corner of his vision—too fast, too silent.

The trees swayed once, snow cascading in a soft veil, then stilled.

He swallowed hard. "You'd have hated this, kid..."

The name lodged in his throat. *Cam.*

Skylith's wings trembled once, unease rolling through their bond. *We must move.*

"Not yet," he said, scanning the horizon. "Not until I know what did this."

Then be ready, she warned, voice dropping to a growl. *Because it's still here.*

The sky groaned. The pressure deepened. The scent of iron filled the air.

Ben tightened his grip on the reins, heart hammering in rhythm with Skylith's.

He opened his mind through the dragonlink, voice sharp and clear as a blade drawn through the cold:

"Tessa. Brontheus. You hearing this?"

Nothing. Only static.

He tried again, louder, pulse thrumming. *"We're not alone out here."*

His eyes swept the storm, narrowing as light began to fracture across the clouds. *"And whatever's coming... it's not looking for mercy."*

The air split with a flash of colorless light.

It was not thunder that followed, but a sound older—like stone remembering fire.

Every sound vanished.

Even Skylith's heartbeat paused beneath him.

And then—the world exhaled.

Chapter 56: Hunter's Vigil

Night draped itself over the Valthorne like a shroud.

Mist coiled through the skeletal treetops, pale and restless beneath Brontheus's wings. Each slow, deliberate beat sent tremors through the air, scattering frost and silence alike. The dragon's glow was faint—lightning caught deep beneath scales of green and black, too subdued for comfort.

Orren sat behind Tessa, the leather of the saddle creaking beneath his gloves. Below, the forest shifted and breathed, every shadow feeling too alive, every glint between the branches an accusation. He scanned the dark with the precision of a hunter, but tonight the dark seemed to stare back.

The wind carried howls—thin, distorted things. Not wolves. Not anything mortal.

Clawed tracks tore through the snow below, weaving like scars through the brush. A nest of bones lay shattered at the base of an oak, slick with frost and old blood.

"They're getting bolder," Tessa murmured, her voice barely carrying over the wind. Unease flickered across her features, a flash of lightning through a cloudbank.

Orren didn't answer. His gloved hand tightened on the edge of the saddle. In the rare lull between gusts, something pressed at the edge of his awareness—distant, cold, insistent. From the northeast.

That pull again.

He'd felt it for days now—always tugging him the wrong way, against the direction they searched. Like a breath drawn somewhere far ahead—waiting for him to exhale. At first, he'd blamed fatigue. Then madness. But it persisted, patient as breath, a thread winding through his blood. Sometimes it felt like a heartbeat that wasn't his own. Sometimes it whispered her name.

He exhaled sharply, mist curling past his lips.

It started as a whisper—then memory answered.

You should follow it, Cam had told him once, when he had mentioned it to her weeks ago.

The memory rose, unbidden and unmerciful. Two weeks ago, dawn still half a rumor. The training ring had been slick with frost, breath and steam rising in equal measure. She'd been there before sunrise—again—sweat and dust streaked down her neck, hair tangled, eyes too bright. He'd watched her burn through every form he knew, pushing until her magic crackled uncontrolled around her fingers.

He'd stepped in without thinking, catching her wrist before she could draw another sigil.

"You're pushing yourself too hard, Cam."

She'd looked up, jaw set, breath ragged. "I have to."

"For what?"

No answer. Just silence—and her hand tightening around the pendant at her throat. Wyatt's. The movement had been small, but something in it made him still. He'd been trained to see weakness, to exploit it. But what he saw in her wasn't weakness—it was will. Fear and fire and something he didn't have a name for.

He remembered how it felt to touch her shoulder—awkward, unfamiliar, his hand hovering like he'd forgotten what comfort even was. He hadn't meant to stay there, but she hadn't pulled away.

He'd lived a decade without touch that wasn't violent. Without voices that didn't order or curse.

Cam had never asked for anything from him—not loyalty, not penance, not even trust. She'd saved his life once, and that was enough. For someone like him, it was everything.

He'd forgotten what it was like to *care* until she'd looked at him.

That was the last time he saw her before she fell.

The memory settled heavy as armor. He blinked hard against the burn behind his eyes.

"We need to find her soon," he said, voice rougher than he meant.

Tessa's shoulders stiffened. "You're not the only one who cares if she's dead."

The words hit like a blade slipping past old scar tissue. Orren's jaw flexed. "She's alive," he said simply.

Tessa glanced back, hair catching in the wind. "We'll find her," she said he voice softer than he'd ever heard from her, but doubt threaded the words like static.

He didn't respond. He couldn't. He hadn't slept since the night she vanished—since the world had folded in on itself and swallowed her whole. The hunter haunted by the one mark he couldn't track.

Brontheus rumbled beneath them, low and restless, wings shifting through the cold.

Fresh tracks glimmered in a patch of moonlit snow ahead—too clean, too deliberate. They vanished into a bank of rolling fog, faintly lit from within.

Tessa leaned forward. "Up ahead. Do you see that?"

A flicker—blue-tinged, distant, pulsing—flared and died.

Orren's breath caught. Every instinct screamed contradiction: danger and recognition, hunger and warning. He leaned forward, voice barely a rasp.

"This doesn't feel right."

The fog stirred as if breathing—and for a heartbeat, he thought he heard her voice. It wasn't a word, just the shape of one. Enough to make him forget the cold.

Chapter 57: Alone

Snow swallowed the world in white.

The storm had long since passed, but its ghost lingered—wind curling through the ravines, whispering against the ridges like breath through a wound. Ben leaned into Skylith's neck as they descended, her scales dulled to ember-gray beneath a veil of frost. The cold bit through his coat and gloves, finding every seam it could.

Her talons struck the drifts with a deep, muffled crunch, snow bursting around them in pale clouds. The shock ran up his legs as he dismounted. For a moment he just stood there, steadying his breath, gloved fingers pressed to the warm seam between her scales.

The cold here was sharper. Older. It didn't simply sting—it searched, as though testing whether he belonged.

Silence.

No wind. No creak of branches. No life.

The world held itself perfectly still.

It was the kind of stillness that didn't last. The kind that waited to see who would move first.

He had learned to listen to silence. It told him when something waited. When something remembered.

Now, in that brittle quiet, something pulled at him—low, coiling, foreign.

It began low in his chest, a pressure between heartbeats—subtle at first, then insistent, like a thread tightening through bone. Not north. Not south. Not any direction he knew.

He frowned and reached absently for the pendant at his throat, the old one he'd never taken off. It burned faintly cold against his skin.

"Stay close," he murmured.

Skylith's answering growl rumbled through the snow, low and uneasy. Her wings shifted restlessly, scattering frost from the joints. *Even she felt it.*

He began to walk. Each step sank deep into the snow, crunch muffled and swallowed by the stillness. His breath came harsh, white plumes fading quick in the dark. He brushed the trunks as he passed—pines heavy with frost, bark cold enough to burn through the glove.

Every instinct in him whispered *wrong place, wrong time*, but the pull didn't care. It wound tighter, like a string drawn through his ribs, tugging him forward into the mist.

"Cam," he muttered before he could stop himself. Her name cracked the silence like a fault line.

For a heartbeat, he thought he felt her—an echo of warmth, faint and impossible.

He followed it.

Through the misted pines, the shape took form: a shadow against white.

The ruins rose slowly from the snow, emerging piece by piece—a pillar, an arch, the hint of a roofline fractured against the sky.

A temple.

Half-buried in ice, its jagged edges jutted like broken teeth gnawing at the clouds. Sound changed here—each breath came back to him a half-beat late, as if the air itself were remembering it. The carvings along its stone ribs were too worn to read, but power still clung to them like dust on bone. The air thickened, metallic with old wards and something darker beneath.

Ben stopped. His gut twisted.

The cold here wasn't just cold—it *watched.*

He could almost feel eyes tracing him from the shadows of the pillars. Skylith's low hiss carried through the trees, scales flickering with dull firelight that couldn't seem to take hold.

"This isn't right," he whispered. Frost curled from his breath, drifting upward and vanishing.

He took one step closer. Another. The ground creaked beneath his boots—ice shifting, settling, sighing.

Then the wind died altogether. The silence deepened until even the pulse in his ears faded.

And from somewhere within the ruin—deep, resonant, ancient—the air drew a breath and something stirred to answer it.

Chapter 58: Ghosts in the Woods

The forest had forgotten color.

Frost glazed every branch, every root, every breath. The air was so cold it cut instead of cooled; each inhale scraped her throat raw, tasting of iron and pine. Cam's boots crunched through the undergrowth, the sound dull and heavy beneath the snow's weight. The cold had crawled past her clothes hours ago—it lived in her bones now.

The pull hummed in her chest—soft, steady, unrelenting—the only compass she had left. It wasn't loud anymore, just constant. A heartbeat that didn't belong to her.

Her breath ghosted through the air, scattering into gray. It felt borrowed, like the world was lending her air until she remembered how to take her own. Every exhale felt like it carried a little more of her away.

She didn't know how long she'd been walking. Time bled strange in this place. Light dimmed and flared without reason—one moment silver, the next bruised blue—like the forest itself was breathing around her. Frost-laced branches leaned inward, heavy with snow, as if listening for her next step. Even the wind seemed to hesitate, waiting to see whether she would keep going.

Then the mist stirred.

A figure took shape between the black pines—slow, deliberate.

Wyatt.

He emerged as if the fog had been holding him all along. His edges wavered like smoke, but his eyes—soft blue and warm—were exactly as she remembered.

Her heart stuttered. "Wyatt?"

He didn't answer. Just fell into step beside her, silent as snowfall.

The rhythm of his stride matched hers perfectly, every crunch of snow in unison. Each time she glanced sideways, his outline shimmered—there, gone, there again—like light glancing off moving water.

Cam swallowed hard, voice raw from cold and silence.

"I'm trying," she whispered. "I don't... I don't know what you want from me."

No answer. He never answered.

His gaze stayed fixed on her, steady and unreadable. It felt like both forgiveness and accusation, and she couldn't tell which hurt more.

A memory cracked through the cold—his hands over hers on the hilt of her blade, heat and steadiness guiding her stance.

You'll never hold it wrong if you trust your breath.

The echo was so clear she almost looked down, expecting to see their fingers together again. But when she looked back, he was only mist and shadow.

"Say something," she murmured. "Please..."

Still nothing. Only the whisper of their steps and the hum in her chest that refused to quiet.

The world dimmed as evening bled into night. Her legs trembled, the numbness in her feet crawling upward. When she stumbled, she caught herself against a twisted, frost-scarred tree and sank down, bark biting through her gloves. The cold leached the strength from her muscles until even breathing felt borrowed.

Wyatt knelt in front of her—or the echo of him did.

His edges flickered, fading and reforming with each breath she took. The air between them thinned, rippling with faint gold light, warmth pulsing beneath her ribs. It beat in time with her heart—too perfect to be coincidence, too impossible to accept.

He reached out, tentative, fingers trembling with light.

She lifted her own hand, desperate to bridge the distance.

For a breath—just one—warmth answered.

Not touch, not fully. A pressure like remembered skin. Like hands aligned the way they had been a hundred times before, training yard dust and steel between them, his grip steady over hers.

Her breath hitched. Hope flared sharp and dangerous.

She leaned into it.

Her fingertips slid through nothing but cold air.

The warmth vanished. The pressure collapsed. The space where his hand should have been went hollow all at once, like something torn free instead of simply gone.

The emptiness hit harder than the cold.

Her voice broke against it, a hoarse whisper scraped raw by grief and frost.

"Don't leave me."

For a heartbeat, everything stilled—the forest, the wind, the world itself.

Then his voice brushed the air beside her ear, quiet and certain.

"I won't. I'm here."

The sound vibrated through her bones, low as thunder beneath stone. When it faded, the silence felt wrong for being empty again.

Where he had been, the mist shimmered faintly, a thread of gold twisting upward before vanishing into the dark. Cam pressed her hands to her chest, trembling. She could still feel the echo of his pulse inside her ribs—faint, persistent, alive.

Her own heartbeat followed it, uneven at first, then steadying—two rhythms learning each other again.

And for the first time the silence didn't feel entirely alone. It felt like waiting.

Chapter 59: Eldvale's Ghosts

The wind screamed through the Eldvale peaks, thin and sharp enough to cut. Fine shards of ice stung Kaden's face, clinging to his lashes and the fur lining of his hood. The air here had weight—brittle, listening, alive in a way the southern winds never were. His breath froze the moment it left him.

Tenebrin's wings beat a steady rhythm beneath him, each downstroke rolling through the dark like thunder muffled by snow. Even the dragon's scales, black shot with violet sheen, shivered under the cold.

The pull in Kaden's chest refused to fade. It sat there—heavy, insistent—like a hand pressing him forward. Each step tugged a thread he couldn't see but couldn't bear to cut. Not pain exactly, but not guidance either. A pressure that felt half-remembered, as though the mountain itself expected him.

The peaks narrowed ahead, ridges rising like serrated stone. Nothing moved but the snow. Yet the silence between gusts made his skin crawl. The mountains weren't just cold or empty. They were *listening.*

Tenebrin's thought brushed his mind, low and taut.

This place remembers blood.

He didn't argue. He could feel it too.

They crested the final ridge. Below them the valley opened, gray and hollow, and the temple came into view—hunched beneath its shroud of snow. Half-buried spires jutted like broken teeth. Black ice clung to the walls, gleaming faintly whenever the light shifted.

He knew this place.

Here, the Veilborn had found them.

Here, Alex had turned on them.

Here, Wyatt had fallen.

Tenebrin angled his wings, dropping lower until the downdraft tore the snow into spirals. His talons struck the drifts with a heavy thud, sending a tremor through the frozen ground. Kaden's breath hitched as they landed—his pulse quickened with memory he hadn't meant to call back.

He swung down from the saddle. His boots sank deep into the snow, and for a moment, the world blurred—half present, half ten years gone.

Memory rose like breath in the cold—uninvited, unmerciful.

They had been eleven—barely tall enough to see over the table in Haldrin's library, scrolls piled high around them. The air smelled of wax and dust and the faint sweetness of old parchment. Kaden had been practicing glyphs and runes for hours, tracing circles in chalk across the stone floor, trying to master a simple teleportation mark.

Wyatt had watched, chin propped on his fist, pretending to study but mostly smirking.

"You're overthinking it," he'd said. "You always do."

Kaden scowled, then drew the circle again—faster, sharper—and the world twitched. Shadows rippled outward from his fingers like spilled ink, crawling across the floor.

The chalk snapped in his hand. The air went cold.

"What did I—?"

He stumbled back, heart hammering. He'd read about this. Shadows like that weren't supposed to appear—not with Air magic. Not unless something deeper was inside it.

Wyatt was already on his feet. He kicked through the mark until it broke, the shadows evaporating in a hiss of smoke.

"Kaden," he said quietly, eyes wide but steady, "you're not Veilborn."

"You saw it."

"I did. And you're still not."

Kaden swallowed. "How do you know?"

Wyatt hesitated, then looked down at the mark, voice lowering like a secret. "Because I've seen them too. In dreams. There is a difference, Kade."

Kaden blinked. "Dreams?"

Wyatt nodded. "Yeah. They feel real. There's a man there—shadows everywhere—and I can't wake up until he looks at me. But I think... I think it's showing me something. Like we're supposed to see it."

Kaden shook his head. "You shouldn't want to see it."

"I don't," Wyatt said softly. "But whatever it is, we'll face it together. If either of us ever goes too far..."

"The other pulls him back," Kaden finished, voice small.

Wyatt smiled—crooked, certain. "You promise?"

Kaden nodded. "I promise."

The wind tore him back to the present. The memory shattered like glass. For a moment, he could almost hear Wyatt's laugh in the storm—then even that was gone.

Tenebrin's tail brushed against him, the scales cold as obsidian, the touch grounding. The dragon's mind pressed close, warm against the cold ache in Kaden's chest.

You still carry him.

"Yeah," Kaden whispered. "I know."

Overhead, Sylithra circled once, her golden-veined wings scattering faint light across the snow. She landed beside Tenebrin, snow bursting around her talons. Through the dragonlink her voice slid into his mind, low and uneasy.

The Veil clings to this place. Something old... awake.

Kaden exhaled, a plume of frost curling through the air. "You're not wrong."

Val and Virellan remained in the sky—silent sentinels against the gray.

The air around the ruin prickled with Veil magic. Faint, but insidious. Like static before lightning. It crawled over his skin, seeking seams in his coat and wards. Tenebrin's pupils narrowed to slits, wings twitching in restrained agitation.

In the ruin's shadow, the snow had been disturbed—drag marks, clawed impressions, shallow but fresh. The shapes were wrong: too long, too thin, not animal.

He swallowed hard, scanning the tree line. The storm-muted forest gave no answer, yet the sense of being watched pressed colder and closer, sliding like ice along his spine.

"Stay sharp," he murmured, though the wind stole the words away.

He approached the nearest wall. The stone was slick with frost and soot, veined with black ice that pulsed faintly in the half-light. He brushed the surface with his glove. Frost flaked away, revealing a mark beneath.

A circle—carved deep, hollow at its center.

The sigil throbbed once, faint as a dying heartbeat.

Kaden froze, heartbeat racing. Recognition struck hard. He knew that sigil.

The mark of the Prince—cut deep, waiting, as if it had been carved for him.

Chapter 60: Threads of Letting Go

The northern ridges tore at her boots, jagged and slick with ice.

Wind needled through the seams of her coat, biting hard enough to make her bones ache. Each breath scorched her throat before freezing in the air. Every step was a battle between body and will.

Still she climbed.

The pulse in her chest—steady, insistent—guided her through the cold. It wasn't loud anymore, just constant, a rhythm folding itself into her own heartbeat. Sometimes it felt like a memory of warmth trapped beneath her ribs.

Snow crusted her lashes. The world had narrowed to white and stone, to the rasp of her breath and the echo of that pulse. It carried her forward when thought faltered, when pain blurred into motion.

Then—movement at her side.

A shimmer where the air bent.

Wyatt walked there again.

Silent as mist, edges hazed by frost-light. He didn't speak, didn't guide. He simply matched her stride, the echo of boots over ice keeping time with her own.

She didn't look at him right away. She was afraid he'd vanish if she did. But the pull between them steadied her pace, a tether humming just out of reach.

At last she whispered, voice cracked from cold and distance,

"I know... I'm coming."

The sound fell into the snow and didn't return. Yet something in the wind shifted—gentler now, almost listening.

Frost spidered over the nearby pines, spreading like veins of glass. Mist coiled around her ankles, trailing behind her in faint silver threads that glowed before fading. Each one marked a piece of her she'd shed: fear, resistance, the endless need to look back.

She thought of what she'd left behind—the ruins, the shouting, the faces she couldn't save. The south was grief and fire and unanswered questions. Ahead was only silence. But silence didn't always mean loss. Sometimes it meant space enough to breathe.

"Wyatt," she murmured, unsure why she said it. The name just felt right in the silence, like the pull wanted her to speak it aloud.

The figure beside her tilted his head, faint as an afterimage. For a heartbeat she felt warmth brush her hand—air, nothing more—and still it steadied her.

Her legs shook, but her pace didn't falter. The forest's slope eased, the path curling upward through sheets of ice that gleamed like mirrors. In one reflection she caught a glimpse of herself beside the ghost of him—two shapes moving as one blur of light and shadow.

Each step forward felt lighter. Not because the climb grew easier, but because she had stopped fighting the pull. She had stopped fighting herself.

The wind softened. The hum in her chest answered with a slower beat, calm and sure. The ridge opened before her—a sweep of frozen valley and distant peaks lost in cloud. Below, the world stretched endless and waiting, its silence vast enough to hold everything she hadn't yet said.

She closed her eyes. For the first time since the fall, she let her shoulders drop, her breath settle, her heart unclench. She felt the faint pulse again—two rhythms overlapping, steady, alive.

She exhaled, letting go of the south, of resistance, of every brittle piece still clinging to grief.

When she opened her eyes, the ghost beside her had faded, but the warmth remained.

She moved with intent—north, toward whatever waited in the heart of the wilds.

Chapter 61: Ember Fortress in Fall

Snow fell in soft veils over Ember Fortress, cloaking the black stone in white. The air smelled of iron and smoke, of a city trying to forget that winter had teeth. Corin stood on the battlements, gloved hands resting on the rimed stone, watching flakes melt against the heat of his breath.

Below, the courtyards glowed faintly with torchlight. The guards moved like shadows—tight lines, curt orders. Something restless had crept into their rhythm tonight. Even the dragons in the lower roosts stirred more than usual, their scales rasping against the stone as if they too felt the air change.

Flickers of light danced along the outer walls—flashes from the watchtowers, signaling movement in the snowfields. The pattern came too often to be routine.

He pressed a hand to the parapet, feeling the cold bite through the glove. The stone beneath his palm thrummed faintly, as if remembering old battles. The fortress had withstood three sieges in his lifetime; it had outlasted kings, generals, and the lies of peace. But tonight the silence was different. Too deep. Too deliberate.

He exhaled slowly, the breath turning to mist that blurred the world below.

The ache behind his eyes sharpened—a warning hum that had become too familiar. He pressed two fingers to his temple, as if the gesture could hold the visions back. They never came cleanly now. Only fragments. The shimmer of fire through snow. A woman's scream torn from memory and prophecy alike.

Lira's laughter echoed faintly in the wind, carried from another winter entirely.

It had sounded like defiance once. Like hope.

And then the crack of fire when she fell.

He closed his eyes, jaw tightening. He had told himself for years that time dulled everything. But time, he'd learned, only thinned the veil—it never sealed it.

When he looked north, the horizon pulsed faintly with light—white fading to bruised gold, the color of warning. He could feel the threads of bloodlines and prophecy pull taut inside his chest, each one whispering its own name, its own cost.

Somewhere beyond that horizon, the Hollow stirred. He could feel it. A presence both near and impossibly far, slipping between breaths. The shape that haunted every vision, waiting for its door to open.

"The Hollow Prince is coming," he murmured, the words carried off by the wind.

He watched the snow drift down, quiet and steady. Beneath it, the world seemed to hold its breath.

"The Hollow doesn't wait," he whispered, a vow more than an observation. "It follows."

◈ ☽⚡☾ ◈

Far below the battlements, another watcher listened to the same silence and found it full of memory. Snow spiraled through the upper roosts, soft against the heat of his scales. Sael stood motionless, wings half-furled, his breath curling in slow ribbons of steam. The fortress lights pulsed against the dark like tiny hearts.

Sylithra, Tenebrin, and Brontheus had flown north—threads of fire vanishing into the storm. Their absence hummed through the fortress, an unfinished chord that shivered the air. He could still taste the echo of Sylithra's warmth where their minds had touched last: gold fire threaded with night-blue calm. Her farewell had not been words, only a pulse of faith—*Hold the line, love.*

He had answered in kind. *Fly safe, my heart.*

That pulse still lingered inside him, bright and steady beneath the cold.

Tenebrin's parting had been different. Younger. Fierce. The wind in his voice had carried that restless confidence only youth could make sound brave. *You'll see us soon, elder. She'll bring her flame home.*

Sael had rumbled low in answer, pride and worry tangled in the same breath.

Do not let your light outrun your shadow, little brother.

Now only silence filled the roosts. Silence and snow.

He was meant to follow them. Every wing in him ached for flight, to chase their glow through the clouds. But something older than instinct had anchored him here.

The bond had not broken.

It had only gone quiet.

He could still feel it—faint as a whisper through ash—in the hollow between wingbeats, in the still moments before dawn when the fortress dreamed. A rhythm that matched his own. A pulse that refused to die.

Alive.

He turned his gaze north. The wind brought no sound of wings, only the scent of old magic rising from the stone below. Not from sky or storm—but from beneath. The call came from the deep heart of Ember Fortress, where wards met the bones of the mountain. The place where the Hollow once stirred.

He knew the taste of that darkness. He had felt its breath across centuries. But woven through it now was something else—something warm, familiar, stubborn.

His rider's echo.

He closed his eyes and exhaled. The heat from his lungs melted the snow at his feet, steam rising like ghosts.

The others searched the world for her flame. He would keep vigil for the ember that still burned below. The ember that was his.

From the battlements above, Corin's mind flickered—quiet fire wrapped in iron control. The human's foresight trembled with warning, threads of fear too loud to ignore. Yet even in that noise, Sael sensed the same truth pressing in from every horizon.

The Hollow Prince was stirring.

Sael opened his eyes. Snow gathered along his horns, glittering like frost-fire. He spread his wings once, testing the air, but didn't rise.

The Hollow does not wait, he thought. *It follows.*

And somewhere beyond the storm, a heartbeat answered; steady, defiant, human.

Chapter 62: Mirror in the Ice

Brontheus's claws scraped over the narrow ridge, sparks of ice skittering down the slope. The wind sliced through Tessa's leathers like knives, stinging the skin beneath. Every breath she took burned and froze all at once.

Icy gusts howled between the pines, tossing plumes of snow into the air until the world blurred into shifting white. The sky and ground had become the same color—gray, hollow, endless.

Ahead, Orren moved like a shadow—shoulders hunched, crossbow raised, eyes cutting through the veil of snow. Tessa matched his steps, though unease tugged low in her stomach. It wasn't fear exactly. It was that other sense—the one she'd tried to smother for years—the *pull* of the storm inside her warning something was wrong.

A glint caught her eye.

Half-buried in snow, a sheet of frozen water shimmered faintly between the roots of a pine.

She slowed.

The wind dropped away, leaving only the crackle of snow as she crouched and brushed the ice clear with one gloved hand.

Her reflection should have stared back—proof of warmth, of breath—but the ice held only stillness.

No reflection met her gaze.

Not hers.

Not Orren's.

The surface rippled instead—distorting the light until a silhouette bled through.

Tall. Hollow.

A shape she almost knew.

A shudder ran through her chest, sharp and uninvited. For a breath, she swore she saw *him*—steel gray eyes behind the frost, the edge of a familiar jaw, the faintest hint of a smile.

Alex.

The name struck her harder than the wind. Her throat closed. *No. He's gone. He's gone.*

But the figure didn't fade. It leaned closer, its form warping as if trying to step through.

Brontheus's growl thundered behind her—a sound that wasn't warning so much as command. The vibration hit her through the soles of her boots, echoing up into her ribs.

Her pulse raced, but she forced herself to move. *Trust the storm*, she reminded herself. *Trust what it tells you.* She had ignored that voice once before, and it had nearly killed her.

Her voice cracked against the wind.

"Orren... we need to move. Now."

◈ ☽ ⚡ ☾ ◈

Orren froze mid-step, scanning the snow-laden trees.

Nothing moved.

But the cold *watched*.

The air here carried memory—iron and ash and something older. It was the same cold that had crept into his bones years ago on another hunt, one that ended with his squad scattered across a frozen valley. He still dreamed of their faces, the frost blooming on their armor, the way silence swallowed the dying before he could reach them.

This was that same silence.

The weight between his shoulders tightened. Every instinct he had screamed the same word: *hunted*.

He turned, crossbow steady, eyes sweeping the tree line. The storm hissed through the branches, but beneath it ran a different current—deeper, rhythmic.

A pulse.

A *pull*.

That violet shadow again. It flickered at the edge of his sight, threading through the mist like smoke, tugging him toward the east. Toward *something* that wasn't supposed to exist. The same pull he'd felt the night Cam fell.

It thrummed in his chest, wrong and familiar all at once—like remembering someone's breath after they'd already stopped breathing.

He forced his voice steady.

"Keep moving," he said, but the words were for himself as much as her.

His fingers tightened around the crossbow grip, the thought rising cold and certain:

Whatever this is... it's following us.

◈ ☽ ⚡ ☾ ◈

Snow crunched beneath Kaden's boots as he stalked through the outer ruins of Eldvale. The world here was bone and wind—columns jutting like ribs, frost clinging to every stone. The sky had that strange brightness that came before twilight, pale and endless.

Val and Virellan descended from the clouds in a rush of snow.

"All clear," Val said, brushing frost from her braid. "No movement beyond the ridge."

Kaden nodded, though unease crawled through him. The air felt *thick* here, like breathing through glass. "Stay close," he said quietly. "The Veil's heavy tonight."

They moved between the pillars, their footsteps whispering over the ice. The ruins pulsed faintly beneath the snow, old runes flickering to life where his boots touched.

Then the ground tilted.

The wind vanished.

Light twisted.

A rush of vertigo swallowed him whole—and suddenly the ruins were gone. He blinked and found himself standing inside a stone chamber he didn't recognize. Gold light shimmered along the walls, alive and moving.

At the center, an altar.

And before it—Cam.

She was barely standing. Dirt streaked her cheeks; dried blood crusted at her temple. Her hair hung in snarled ropes around her face, matted with leaves and ash. Her coat was torn, one sleeve ripped at the shoulder, dark with something that wasn't all mud.

Her eyes—those fierce blue-gray eyes flecked with silver—looked sunken, rimmed red with exhaustion, but still burning with that relentless spark that refused to die.

The air shimmered around her—not light, not magic, but heat rising from overuse, from everything she'd given and kept giving. Gold flickered across her skin where it met shadow, as though the world couldn't decide whether to claim her or save her.

Her lips moved, shaping a name—soft, broken.

And for one heartbeat, the sound echoed through him like his own pulse answering.

He gasped—and the world shattered.

The ruins snapped back into place. Wind. Cold. Snow.

Val was beside him instantly, eyes wide. "Kaden! What happened?"

He braced a hand against a broken pillar, trying to steady his breathing. "I—I saw her."

Val frowned. "Cam?"

He nodded, swallowing hard. "Yeah. But it wasn't a dream."

The words hung between them. The air felt charged, alive. He didn't understand it, not fully, but he knew it wasn't his imagination.

"I think she's in trouble," he whispered.

Val's gaze hardened. "Then we go."

Kaden nodded, the pulse in his chest answering like an echo from miles away. He didn't know what it meant—but it beat in perfect time with another heart.

Chapter 63: The Last Threshold

The ridge broke open before her in a sweep of gray light.

Snow drifted down in slow spirals, soft as ash, soundless. Dawn pressed faint silver into the horizon; the sky had begun to pale—the color of steel just before it catches flame.

Cam dragged herself over the final rise, boots sinking deep into the crusted snow. Every muscle ached from what felt like weeks of walking, the ache so constant it felt like another heartbeat. Wind scoured her coat, sharp with the sting of salt.

She stopped.

Salt.

The word tasted like childhood. For one reckless second she almost turned to say, *dad, do you smell it?*—a habit that hadn't had a listener in years. The echo hurt; she swallowed it like cold.

It struck her like memory. Clean, cold, unmistakable. The scent of home—the Veilrend tides breaking against eastern cliffs, the taste of brine that had always lived in the morning wind. She hadn't realized how much she missed it until now.

She could almost hear the gulls, the crash of waves she'd once sworn she'd escape — and for a moment, the horizon sounded like forgiveness.

Beyond the ridge, the world widened into a frozen bay. Ice drifted on dark water, and past it the North Veilrend Sea stretched endless and alive.

And there—at the edge of the cliffs—stood a temple.

The Cradle Temple. Its spires jutted from the rock like the bones of some ancient beast, half-buried in snow, half-remembered by the world. She'd read about it in Corin's notes, traced its name in the Book of Unbinding until the letters blurred. This was the place she'd been seeking since the night Wyatt fell.

Her knees gave way.

She sank into the snow at the basin's edge, breath shaking, tears cutting cold trails through the dirt and dried blood on her face.

The air shifted.

Something moved through the silence—not wind, not memory, but the sound of her own name caught between worlds.

When she looked up, he was there again.

Wyatt stood beside her—solid enough for the light to catch on the edges of his coat, the shadow of his jaw. Not flesh, not entirely spirit, but something in between. The sight of him ached like hope and hurt all at once.

Love pressed up under her ribs, the old, bright kind—and with it the reflex to step back before it could burn her. She didn't. Not this time. But the urge lived in her bones.

The pull in her chest thrummed low, deep, steady—not toward the temple anymore but slightly towards the west, like a buried heartbeat calling from under stone. She didn't understand it. She only knew she couldn't turn away from either call: his, or her own.

Her voice broke against the wind.

"I can't follow you everywhere," she whispered. "I'm not leaving you behind—I just... I need something that isn't borrowed from grief."

Wyatt didn't answer. He never did. But something in his expression softened—as if he understood.

The shimmer of him wavered, light thinning into the air.

"Stay," she whispered, desperate, but the word dissolved before it reached him.

When he faded, the emptiness bit deep—but it didn't hollow her the way it once had. Beneath the ache, something steadier stirred. Not release. Not peace. Resolve. The kind that builds slow—like dawn behind cloud, unseen until it touches everything.

Keeping people at arm's length had kept her standing; it had also kept her starving.

She drew a slow breath; the salt wind burned her throat clean. The horizon brightened, gray turning to the faintest gold.

Cam rose, her body trembling but sure. The temple loomed ahead, its gates lost to snow and mist.

She almost said, *Come with me*, the way she never said it to anyone. The words reached her tongue and stopped—old training, old thorns. She went anyway.

She stepped forward, careful, deliberate.

The forest didn't answer.

But it didn't resist either.

She didn't know what waited beyond that threshold—truth, death, or something in between.

But she knew this: she was done standing still.

She wasn't letting go of him.

She was learning how to keep him and still keep herself.

And with that, she walked toward the light rising over the bay—not away from loss, but toward the life that waited beyond it.

Chapter 64: Breath of the Cradle

The forest broke away without warning.

Cam stepped from the trees into a hollow of white and silence. Her boots sank into snow that glittered faintly in the midday, each crunch swallowed almost immediately by the stillness. Even her breath seemed to hush itself, turning to light instead of sound. A stone basin spread before her, vast and circular—like the hollow of the world.

No wind stirred. No birds called. Even the air felt suspended, as though the land itself was holding its breath.

Her hand found Wyatt's pendant at her throat. The metal was cold against her skin.

"If I'm wrong," she whispered to the emptiness, her voice cracking, "let this be the end of it."

Nothing answered. Only the sound of her breathing, slow and uneven.

A narrow path wound ahead, half-swallowed by snow and ice. The afternoon light had turned gold now, threading through the canopy in fractured shafts that struck the broken dome ahead. The temple rose from the basin like a ghost—jagged, half-collapsed, and ancient beyond memory.

Each step forward pulled her more by instinct than choice.

The cracked stone doors hung open, tilted and heavy with frost, as if waiting for her. Inside, the air pressed close and cold, heavy with age. Dust glittered faintly in the shafts of light that cut through the cracks in the ceiling.

Faint runes spiraled along the walls and floor—worn smooth by centuries yet still pulsing with dim light. They brightened as she passed, matching the rhythm of her heartbeat.

Cam slowed, fingers brushing a line of old sigils. They were warm beneath her fingers.

"You've been waiting too, haven't you?" she murmured.

The temple didn't answer, but the air seemed to thrum in quiet recognition.

At the center of the chamber, the altar rose—ancient, cracked, veined with faint traces of gold beneath the stone. She stopped before it, knees trembling, exhaustion crashing over her in waves.

Her fingers curled around Wyatt's pendant again. The metal chain creaked softly under her grip.

"I made it, Wyatt," she whispered.

The pendant flashed once—brief but brilliant—and the altar answered with a low hum, a sound felt more than heard.

Light spilled through the cracks in the stone, crawling up the walls like living veins. Glyphs ignited in golden fire, weaving together across the dome in patterns older than language.

The ground shuddered beneath her boots. From deep within the altar came a grinding groan, and a stone panel shifted aside.

A recess lay beneath—a sealed cylinder of smooth, pale stone, faintly glowing from within. No markings. No symbols. Just light, quiet and steady, pulsing like breath.

Cam didn't touch it. Her hand hovered over the surface, trembling. She wasn't ready. Not yet.

The air thickened.

Then, from somewhere unseen—through the walls, through the air, through the spaces between—came a voice. Not hers. Not human.

Not power, but healing.

Not force, but wholeness.

Her breath caught. She'd heard it before. In her dreams. In her fire. In the moments between waking and sleep when the Veil whispered through her blood.

The words did not strike like command. They settled—like something inside her recognizing its own name.

She had always reached for flame first. For force. For the heat that ended a threat before it could end someone she loved. She had burned and called it strength.

But this...

This felt like being asked to open her hands.

Her knees gave out. She sank before the altar, the cold stone biting through her tattered coat.

Outside, light gathered on the snow—gray giving way to gold.

For the first time in months, the weight she carried—the grief, the guilt, the fear—didn't crush. It loosened. Just enough to breathe.

Cam bowed her head, eyes burning, and exhaled.

"I hear you," she whispered. The words trembled into the silence, soft as prayer.

Then, quieter still—

"Finally."

The temple held its stillness.

At the altar's heart, the cylinder glowed steadily, ancient magic pulsing like a heartbeat—waiting, patient as dawn, for the one who would choose to unseal it.

Chapter 65: Light of the Prophecy

Dawn broke through the fractures of the dome.

Pale gold spilled through the cracks in the ceiling, painting the ancient stone in threads of light and shadow. The air shimmered faintly with dust and warmth, like breath trapped between worlds, slow and dreamlike, catching in the quiet.

The temple breathed with her.

Each exhale clouded faintly in the chill, soft as prayer.

Cam remained where she'd fallen—on her knees before the altar, the stone cold beneath her palms. The hum in the walls had faded to a low pulse now, steady and patient, as if the place itself waited for her next move.

Her fingers found the edge of the hollow again. Inside, a faint light glimmered.

She drew the cylinder free.

The stone was smooth and cool, carved with faint grooves that caught the light. The seal released with a soft sigh, and a wisp of old air drifted out—smelling of ash, ink, and time.

Beneath the dragonhide wrapping lay two scrolls.

Cam's breath caught.

She lifted the first—the fourth Veilbind scroll—its surface brittle but unbroken. Faint symbols shimmered across the hide, shifting as though resisting being read. They pulsed faintly under her touch—alive, unwilling, like words that remembered being spoken once before.

She laid it carefully on the altar, pressing her hand to its edge. The hum deepened, resonant, familiar.

When the words came, they weren't read—they were remembered.

"The flame and the mirror will meet, and in that meeting, the world will split.

What was sealed will tremble.

What was hidden will burn.

Only one can hold the gate.

Only one can close it.

If the flame bearer falters, the Hollow shall drink deep.

The wound will widen—too vast for healing, too loud for silence.

The balance will break, and with it, the breath of the world.

He shall not die.

He shall become."

Flame and mirror.

Fire and reflection.

Him and her.

Life, and the echo left behind.

Cam's hands trembled. Heat bloomed in her chest, rising through her lungs, bright and heavy. There was more but Cam couldn't translate it, not here.

The scroll pulsed beneath her fingers—once, like acknowledgment.

Light flared in the runes beneath her knees, rippling outward.

Her gaze shifted to the second scroll, wrapped more tightly, the material darker and lined with gold thread. The moment she touched it, the air shifted. The hum rose from pulse to song.

She unrolled it slowly. The script shimmered in the light—lines curling and merging like smoke caught in wind.

The floor around her lit in response, runes spiraling outward in concentric rings. The chamber filled with Veil-light—radiant, alive, breathing in rhythm with her heartbeat.

The scroll lifted slightly from the altar as words formed in the air above it, gleaming like molten glass:

"One shall awaken who was never meant to sleep.

Born of hollow purpose and endless night,

he will carry what was left behind—

a crown of ash, a name unspoken.

The flame and the mirror will meet,

and in that meeting, the world will split.

What was sealed will tremble.

What was hidden will burn.

Only one can hold the gate.

Only one can close it.

When sky and stone remember, and the dragons speak as one,
the chosen flame must choose again.
Not between power and peace,
but between—"

Her chest tightened. She stared, unable to look away as the glow rippled through the dome. The words shimmered, then sank back into the air like they had always been part of it.

At the bottom written in the corner was a note, '*Four parts, three truths—one hidden.*'

"One hidden..." she murmured.

A third truth. One she hadn't seen yet. But the hidden part made no sense to her.

Her hands shook. The meaning pressed deep, sharp and sure, carving its way beneath her ribs.

The truth didn't strike—it unfolded, slow and merciless, until it filled the space inside her where fear used to live.

Her breath hitched. Tears welled, blurring the gold light.

"Bu it's... it's always been me."

The pendant around her neck pulsed once—soft, steady—its rhythm echoing through the stone, through her bones, through the very air.

A single heartbeat of magic.

Not command. Not call. Just recognition.

The temple quieted again.

The light dimmed to a warm, steady glow.

And then—

A tug. Familiar. Low. Deep in her chest.

The same pull that had guided her north all this time, stronger now—twisting her toward a shadowed doorway behind the altar, half-hidden in the rock. The air there shimmered faintly, like heat rising from snow.

She turned toward it, heart racing.

Then—

A sound.

Soft. Definite.

A footstep—behind her.

Cam froze, breath sharp, every muscle going still.

The light seemed to hesitate, trembling in the corners of the room.

Silence folded around her again—thick, waiting.

Cam didn't move. The air around her held its breath.

The light on the altar flickered once, then went out.

For an instant, the silence glowed—then even that breath of light was gone.

Chapter 66: The Figure in the Light

Snow muffled every sound.

The storm's echo lingered in the mountain passes, a whisper that wound through the ravines like breath through stone. Skylith's talons cracked through a crust of ice. Steam rose from her nostrils in twin plumes, vanishing into the wind. The world smelled of iron and storm-worn stone—the kind of air that held its breath before saying a name.

Ben slid from the saddle, boots sinking deep into the drift. The world was motionless—no wind, no cry of distant wings. Even the air felt thin, stripped of life.

The temple loomed ahead, half-buried in the snow, its ribs of stone jutting from the slope like the bones of some ancient leviathan. At first glance it looked right—the sigils, the spiral archways, the same worn geometry as the ones in Corin's sketches. But something about it was wrong. The wrong orientation. The wrong silence.

He adjusted his grip on the torch and crossed the threshold. The flame's light scattered across the stone, gold bleeding into gray. The floor was slick with frost. His breath clouded in the dark.

"Cam?" he called softly. His voice vanished before it touched the walls.

He moved deeper, methodical, the old soldier in him counting steps, checking corners, reading the walls like terrain. Nothing. Just echo. Dust. Silence that watched back.

Outside, through the dragonlink, Skylith's voice slid into his mind—low, taut.

Something is wrong.

Ben paused. The pressure in his chest tightened until he could feel his heartbeat against his ribs. "Stay close," he murmured, though he knew she already was.

A gust surged through the entrance, sudden and sharp. The torch guttered.

Another breath—and the flame died.

Darkness swallowed the corridor.

He drew his blade. The sound of steel against leather was swallowed almost instantly by the cold. He stood still, listening.

The chill that wrapped around him wasn't the weather. It was heavier—old and aware, like a hand closing over the air itself.

His pulse pounded in his ears.

"Cam?" he whispered again. Silence.

Then—a sound behind him.

A single, deliberate footstep on stone.

Skylith's growl rumbled faintly through the link, distant and warning.

Ben turned, muscles coiled.

A gust swept through the ruin, carrying the acrid scent of smoke and charred pine—like a battlefield long dead. His breath caught in his throat.

A voice, familiar yet cold, came from the dark.

"You're late."

Something in him stopped; not heart, not breath, but the part that still believed in what was gone.

The wind howled once, hard enough to rattle the stones—then everything went still.

The torch on the ground flickered, flared once—and went out.

◈ ☽ ⚡ ☾ ◈

Mist choked the cliffs of the Valthorne range.

Snow hissed through the pines, seething off the enormous branches in ghostly veils. Below, the ravine stretched wide and black, the last traces of battle rotting in its hollow—mirebat corpses stiff in the frost, wings torn and glistening with decay.

Brontheus glided low through the smoke-tinged air, his talons slicing through shallow streams gone ink-dark with ash. The dragon's light pulsed faintly beneath his scales, a dim heartbeat in the gray.

Tessa leaned forward in the saddle, eyes burning from wind and sleeplessness. Every shape between the trees looked like her.

"She's here," she murmured. "She has to be."

Orren moved below the ridge, silent through the underbrush, crossbow slung but ready. His eyes swept the forest—every broken branch, every hollow echo.

He shook his head once. His voice, when it came, was barely sound.

"She's not here, Tessa."

For a moment she didn't breathe. Her fingers tightened into a fist on Brontheus's scales until her knuckles blanched white.

"I can't lose her too."

Orren looked past the ravine toward the distant line of the Karethwyn forest, its dark trees spearing the pale horizon. The wind tugged at his coat, carrying the faint scent of salt from the north.

His gaze lingered—a silent implication.

Northeast.

◈ ☽ ⚡ ☾ ◈

Lanternlight wavered against the walls of the hidden chamber beneath Ember Fortress.

Maps lay unfurled across the table, their edges curled and scorched, ink blotted by melted wax.

Corin stood over them, shadows carving deep lines into his face. The air smelled of parchment and fatigue.

His hand traced the same fragment for the hundredth time, lips moving around the words:

"The Hollow Prince cannot be slain by blade or fire."

"Only Flame and Mercy may unmake him."

"If shadow touches the flame-bearer, he rises forever."

A cough rose low in his chest.

He froze.

It had begun like this before.

Ash drifting across blackened fields.

Warnings carved into stone posts at the border.

Do not breathe the bloom.

Anthony had laughed. Corin had not.

The second cough settled more than the first.

He pressed his knuckles lightly against his sternum until the tightness settled. Years ago, the healers had told him the same thing they told

Anthony: it would sleep if tended. It would wake if neglected. And one day, it would not sleep again.

He had chosen his work anyway.

"We're running out of time."

One by one, he crossed out fallen fortresses—Haldrin, Valthorne, the Keep at Rellis—until only one remained circled in fading ink: Ember Cradle.

The memory tried to surface again—white-grey pollen floating in still air, beautiful as snowfall.

He shut it down.

He gathered Cam's scattered notes, aligning them with the fragments of the Veilbind scrolls. Beneath his fingers, the inked words blurred briefly before sharpening once more.

Not power, but healing. Not force, but wholeness.

Heat crept under his collar. Subtle. Familiar.

He ignored that too.

He sealed the copied translation into an envelope, wax bleeding red over the emblem of balance. No name marked the front—only a sigil for a messenger yet to be chosen.

Around him, the fortress groaned in the wind, weary stone shifting like an old soldier's breath. The rebellion was unraveling to threads.

Their fate rested on a woman haunted by grief... and a missing flame-bearer.

Anthony had come back changed.

So had he.

Corin stared into the lanternlight.

"Is this salvation," he murmured, voice steady despite the quiet ache beneath it, "or the start of the end?"

◈ ☽ ⚡ ☾ ◈

Light bled gold through the cracked dome, soft and reverent.

The air in the chamber trembled faintly, as though the world itself was listening. The scrolls on the altar still pulsed with slow light, their glow casting faint shadows across her face.

Cam stood in the center of it all, breath shallow, exhaustion ghosting through every limb. The pendant at her throat warmed softly, pulsing in rhythm with the runes.

Then the light shifted.

It dimmed—not fading, but bending, drawn toward the grand doorway of the temple. The air shifted with it, warm and sharp, the scent of smoke threading through snow.

She turned.

A figure stood framed in the pale morning beyond, blocking the spill of light. Tall. Still. Cloaked in shadow.

For a heartbeat, the chamber forgot to breathe.

The silhouette took a step forward into the threshold where gold met gray. The light caught along the edge of a familiar shape—shoulders she knew, posture she'd memorized in another life.

Her breath caught.

The scrolls' hum faltered, light flickering in response to her pulse.

The figure's voice broke the silence—quiet, steady, cutting straight through the air:

"Happy birthday, Cam."

The world tilted sideways.

Cam's heart slammed against her ribs. The sound of it filled her ears, drowned everything else.

"No," she whispered, shaking her head. "You're not—"

Her throat closed. Tears blurred the light until it fractured.

"You're not real—"

But the light behind him did not fade. It grew.

Epilogue

Caerthalen. Dawn on the fall equinox.

Sunlight pooled through the lattice windows of Deyric's high chamber, washing over marble and gold. The air shimmered faintly—fractured, wrong.

Above the city, the Veil split open like broken crystal, its shards invisible to every eye but his.

Deyric rose from his knees. His shadow stretched across the floor—and within it, something moved.

The air convulsed. A figure stepped from the rift.

Kaelith.

No longer echo, no longer myth—but flesh woven of shadow and silver flame, hollow light burning through stolen skin. Deyric's.

Frost veined outward from his feet, crawling through the stone. His breath turned the air to ice.

He lifted his head. When he spoke, the voice wasn't only his own.

"The thread has broken. Now... we begin."

Outside, the first snow of a false winter began to fall, spiraling through sunlight that had turned too pale.

From far above, the view widened—the world itself dimming under clouds not born of weather.

Only one golden thread of light remained on the horizon.

It flickered once—and went out.

Darkness.

No sound. No breath. No world—only pressure.

He floated weightless, caught between pulse and silence.

A heartbeat thudded somewhere close, not entirely his own.

Cold crawled inward through his chest, threading its way toward the center of him until even thought began to frost. The dark shifted around him like water, heavy and slow, pressing him down.

A muffled roar passed over—wind, or maybe waves. It was hard to tell the difference anymore.

Something metallic touched his tongue. Blood, or memory.

He couldn't tell.

Images flickered like cracks in the dark—

Starlight tangled in snow.

A laugh, bright and too close.

A hand reaching, always reaching.

He reached back.

Fingers brushed warmth—then slipped through light that wasn't there.

The cold answered instead.

Fear flared, small and human, before exhaustion took it.

Only ache remained. Only the need to keep hold of what was already leaving.

Somewhere beneath the weight of the dark, a spark moved.

Tiny. Defiant. Refusing to die.

It remembered warmth, and a name spoken like a promise.

It pulsed once, then again, as if remembering how to beat.

Light flickered through the void—not bright but living. A pale gold shimmer rippled across unseen space, and for a heartbeat he wasn't alone.

The vibration came first—low, thrumming, steady. Not sound, not sight. Presence.

It trembled through the dark like wings folding against wind.

He couldn't name it, but it knew him.

The world around him seemed to draw a breath.

The black pressed inward, curious, listening.

Something ancient recognized him—something that had expected him to stay gone.

But he didn't. The warmth slipped away, the silence waited to claim him—and still, that spark refused to die.

He sank deeper, but not quietly. The dark rippled around him, startled.

The thread had not broken after all.

Acknowledgement

To my mom—thank you for encouraging me, even in the moments I doubted everything. Your belief carried me further than you'll ever know.

To my sister—who listened to every tangled thought, every rambling dream, and never once made me feel like I was too much. The threads of this story are woven with your quiet strength.

To my children—you are my light and my anchor. You remind me what it means to keep going, to create from truth, and to stay grounded in love. This book is yours as much as it is mine.

And to the version of me who didn't think she could finish this:

You did.

You made it.

And now you're free.

Author's note

When I began writing *Inheritance*, I thought it would be a story about destiny—about uncovering lost prophecies, decoding ancient truths, and facing the consequences of power.

And it is.

But as the story deepened, I realized it was also about something quieter: the *price* of holding on, and the courage it takes to let go.

If *Heritage* was about what we're given, *Inheritance* is about what we *keep*.

Cam inherits more than bloodlines and prophecy—she inherits grief, memory, and the burden of hope. Wyatt inherits silence and survival; Kaden inherits truth he can't unsee; Tessa, Val, and Orren inherit a world already fractured, and must decide which pieces are still worth saving.

Even the dragons inherit their riders' wounds, carrying the echoes of every choice made in fire and fear.

But inheritance isn't just what's passed down. It's what we *become* when the past refuses to let go.

This book asks a different question than the first:

If heritage is the story written for us—then inheritance is what we choose to write in its margins.

For Cam, Wyatt, Kaden, and all those standing at the edge of the unknown, this isn't an ending.

It's the moment the past starts to burn, and the future begins to breathe.

If this story found you in some small way—if it left a spark you can't quite name—carry it forward. Share it. Speak it. Whisper it to someone who still believes in dragons and light.

The next chapter of this world begins in Threads,

where the story of flame and shadow continues to unravel—and the bond between heart and prophecy will be tested in ways none of them could have foreseen.

Thank you for walking beside them, and me.

Your belief keeps the fire alive.

— Alysabeth Vale

Follow future updates, behind-the-scenes lore, and exclusive previews on my substack @Alysabethvale or on Instagram, Facebook, or TikTok @Alysabeth_vale.

Sneak peek at book three: Threads

Ghost of Flame

There was no sky.

No ground either—no up or down, no edge to measure against. Only a cold, endless dark that pulsed like a slow heartbeat, each thud reverberating through nothing.

Wyatt existed inside it.

Not floating. Not falling. Simply *there*, suspended in a space that refused to name itself.

Pain came first—not sharp, not sudden, but distant, like an echo of something that had already happened. His chest felt hollow, as if breath had been taken from him and forgotten. He tried to inhale and felt nothing move.

Instinctively, his body braced for the burn in his lungs.

It never came.

I'm dead, he thought dimly.

The idea didn't frighten him the way it should have. It arrived heavy and dull, like a truth he had known long before this moment—one he had been circling for years without admitting it.

Then something tugged.

Not his body—he wasn't sure he still had one—but something deeper. A pull behind his ribs, threaded through his spine, tight and aching, like a hand closing around his heart.

Cam.

The thought of her cut through the void like heat through ice. The tether flared—faint, wounded, but unmistakable. Not gone. Never gone.

Strained.

The word settled into him with quiet dread. He had felt strained bonds before—frayed by fear, stretched thin by distance—but this was different. This felt raw. Exposed. As if something essential had been torn open and left unguarded.

Wyatt tried to reach for it. The effort felt like pressing his hands against glass that refused to shatter—solid, unyielding, cruel in its stillness.

A ripple moved through the dark.

Voices followed.

They did not come from any one direction. They seemed to exist everywhere at once, woven into the fabric of the nothing around him.

"She was too close," one said—low, resonant, threaded with something like regret.

"We tried to reach her," said another. This voice was sharper, more brittle, as if it had been worn thin by time. "But the rift shifted."

A pause.

"Pulled him instead."

Wyatt's awareness snapped sharply into focus at the word *him*.

Me.

The tug on his chest intensified, the bond flaring painfully bright before dimming again, like a flame starved of air. Images bled through him in fragments—Cam's face twisted in determination; her jaw set the way it always was when she'd already made up her mind. Her hand tightening on the hilt of her sword. Light tearing the air apart.

A portal.

A choice.

Not his.

Not hers.

Someone else's.

Don't miss out!

Visit the website below and you can sign up to receive emails whenever Alysabeth Vale publishes a new book. There's no charge and no obligation.

https://books2read.com/r/B-A-DKVFF-SNOAJ

BOOKS 2 READ

Connecting independent readers to independent writers.

www.ingramcontent.com/pod-product-compliance
Lightning Source LLC
LaVergne TN
LVHW100500110826
845146LV00002B/465

* 9 7 9 8 9 9 4 5 2 8 4 7 1 *